The Love Bond

"If it were up to me," I said, "I would tie her up and drop her down the nearest cistern. And drop that bag in after her. On her head."

"I take it that means yes," Cullin said mildly.

I glared at Kerri, who glared back at me as she vaulted into the mare's saddle.

"And one more thing," she said, her voice harsh. "If you ever try to kiss me again, or even touch me, I'll carve out your liver and feed it to you for breakfast. Is that clear?"

I raised both hands in surrender. "I'd sooner kiss the mare," I said. "Or the sword. It'd be warmer . . ."

———

Books by Ann Marston

The Rune Blade Trilogy

Kingmaker's Sword
The Western King*
The Broken Blade*

*coming soon from HarperPrism

First Book of the Rune Blade Trilogy

KINGMAKER'S SWORD

Ann Marston

HarperPrism
An Imprint of HarperPaperbacks

HarperPaperbacks   *A Division of* HarperCollins*Publishers*
10 East 53rd Street, New York, N.Y. 10022

Cover illustration by Yvonne Gilbert
Map by Barbara Galler-Smith

First printing: August 1996

Printed in the United States of America

HarperPrism is an imprint of HarperPaperbacks.
HarperPaperbacks, HarperPrism, and colophon are trademarks of HarperCollins*Publishers*

❖ 10 9 8 7 6 5 4 3 2 1

Notes

The year is divided into eight seasons:

Late Winter	Imbolc to Vernal Equinox (February 1 to March 21)
Early Spring	Vernal Equinox to Beltane (March 21 to May 1)
Late Spring	Beltane to Midsummer Solstice (May 1 to June 21)
Early Summer	Midsummer Solstice to Lammas (June 21 to August 1)
Late Summer	Lammas to Autumnal Equinox (August 1 to September 21)
Early Autumn	Autumnal Equinox to Samhain (September 21 to October 31)
Late Autumn	Samhain to Midwinter Solstice (October 31 to December 21)
Early Winter	Midwinter Solstice to Imbolc (December 21 to February 1)

The four sun feasts are Midwinter Solstice, Vernal Equinox, Midsummer Solstice, and Autumnal Equinox.

The four fire feasts are Imbolc, Beltane, Lammas, and Samhain.

Pronunciation Guide

The "C" in Celi is the hard Celtic "C", so Celi is pronounced "Kay-lee."

The "dd" is the Welsh "th" sound, as in *then,* thus Jorddyn is pronounced "Jorthun."

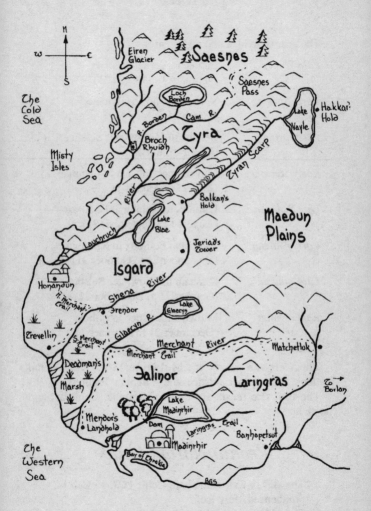

Prologue

He dreamed again of the Swordmaster. He leapt, kicked, and spun, the long, gleaming blade slicing arcs through the air around the ethereal figure opposite him. The twilight, neither dawn nor dusk, cloaked the Swordmaster's face in shadow. The boy saw only the glitter of brilliant, intense blue eyes in the indistinct face as he danced with the sword. Left hand to right hand, then in both hands, the boy's sword sprang back and forth in answer to the Swordmaster's flowing motions. The boy moved like a living flame, thrusting, parrying, attacking, and defending. The sword felt like an extension of his arm, a living part of him just as surely as his hand and his arm were part of him.

Around and around in the strange light they danced. The boy heard the Swordmaster's voice, patient, quiet, calm, instructing—always instructing. Guiding him, directing him, focusing him.

The Swordmaster allowed no mistake to go ignored or overlooked. Each error brought the dance to a halt, and the clumsy or incorrectly performed maneuver repeated until it was flawless.

"You must flow like water with the blade," the Swordmaster said. "You must swirl like leaves in a wind. You must never be still. Give your enemy no opening, for if you do, surely his steel will cleave your body. You must seek out your enemy and learn his weaknesses before he finds you and exploits your own weaknesses."

So the boy danced until the sheer exhilaration of the contest swept him away. His body moved, lithe and precise, with the needs of each exercise. His movements, stylized and distinct, flowed together easily, and he knew the satisfaction of winning another step toward perfection.

When the contest was over, the Swordmaster vanished.

Instead of waking as he usually did, the boy found himself still in the dream landscape.

He stood at the foot of an almost-symmetrical hill in that mystic, transitional time between sunset and dusk, when the sky to the west was still streaked with light and color. Bands of red and orange flamed behind the hill, illuminating the triple ring of standing stones that circled the summit of the hill like a diadem. Imposing menhirs arranged in an outer ring stood starkly black against the luminescent sky, crowned in pairs by massive lintels. The middle ring of stones bulked slightly smaller, gracefully joined all around by capstones, polished like jet to reflect the incandescent glow of the sky. The inner ring, standing alone without lintels, was not a ring at all, but a horseshoe enclosing a low altar stone.

Behind him loomed the vast, cone-shaped bulk of a mountain, taller than any of the other mountains in the soaring, crenellated ridge beyond it. He did not have to look at it to know it was there. In the dream, this place was familiar to him, known and welcoming. He knew all the rivers that gathered the waters of those mountains and drew them down to the distant eastern sea hundreds of leagues away.

He waited at the bottom of the mound, conscious of the weight of the longsword on his back. The air was warm yet, and the fresh scent of crushed grass beneath his feet rose strongly around him. A breeze stirred gently and ruffled his hair, which glowed redly in the fading light of sunset. Casually, he lifted an unhurried hand to brush away a lock of hair that fell into his eyes.

A man appeared in the opening in the foot of the horseshoe, dwarfed by the giant stone Dance. He came forward slowly to look down at the boy watching at the bottom of the hill. The boy could not see the man's face, but knew he was not smiling. Giving the impression of great age and wisdom, the man stood quietly, erect as one of the menhirs, unmoving, watching the boy there at the foot of the mound, and the boy found himself transfixed by that piercing, distant gaze.

The man on the hill spoke. In spite of the great distance between them, the boy heard him clearly.

"So," he said, his voice soft and welcoming, "you are mastering the sword I sent you."

"A welcome gift, Swordmaster."

"It was always for you. I am glad you have awakened at last."

The boy smiled. "No," he replied, speaking as quietly as the man. "I am here only in a dream."

"Of course," the man said. "But in dreaming, you awaken." He raised one hand. "The time will come when you will know."

"Yes," the boy said. "It will come."

The last of the light faded, leaving the mound and the stone circle starkly silhouetted against the pale glimmer of the sky. As the boy turned to walk toward the black bulk of the cone-shaped mountain, the landscape began to disintegrate and disappear around him.

PART

1

The Mouse

1

Mouse awoke in the dark, shivering in the crisp, damp chill that came only an hour or so before dawn along the coast of Falinor. Fragments of his dream drifted like mist through his head but, as always, he could remember nothing of the shape and substance of it.

He held himself still through habit, listening carefully. It was too dark. Too quiet. He heard none of the familiar night sounds of other sleeping bodies close by, and a cold hook of apprehension clutched at his belly. Something was wrong.

The chamber where he lay smelled damp and musty, with an overlying stench of decay. Cautiously, he rolled onto his side. Pain struck his whole body at once, and he cried out with it. The bruises on his face and arms throbbed, and his left eye had swollen shut. The open cuts on his back left by the lash burned like the fury of Hellas. He fell back, gasping, to the cold stone floor. Nausea churned in his empty belly. He gagged and retched, then spit out a mouthful of bitter bile.

He shuddered as he remembered why he was there, naked and alone in the dark. He remembered what would happen to him when morning came. Tears stung his eyes. Impatiently, angry with himself, he lifted one hand to scrub them away. This was no time for tears. He was almost sixteen, and a man, and tears were not for a man.

He shivered again. Almost a man. After they finished with him in the morning, if he still lived, he would be no man at all, and no chance ever to become one.

And Rossah? Rossah, who had been meant as a gift to Lord Mendor's son Drakon to mark his coming of age . . .

Sudden visions flashed through his mind. The gleeful intensity in the faces of the houseguards as they beat him . . . The hideous rapture on Drakon's face as he bent over Rossah with the dagger in his hand . . . Bright blood splashing on pale straw . . .

Mouse bit his lip to suppress the cry that rose in his throat, and he lurched to his knees. Agony scythed through his chest as the broken ends of a rib grated against each other.

He knelt there on the cold stones, chin on his chest, breathing in shallow gasps as he waited for the pain to subside. The urgent need for revenge formed under his heart. Anger grew in his belly, a hard knot of fury that pushed the pain and grief to one side.

He huddled into himself, concentrated on the cuts on his back, on the swollen bruises on his face, his chest, his thighs. There was a trick, or a gift, he had discovered by sheerest accident when he was a child. If he withdrew into a far corner of himself and focused on visualizing his hurts as whole and healthy again, the pain vanished and the injury healed itself. But the trick was not without cost. When it worked, it left him limp and drained and exhausted for a day or two, barely able to drag himself around to attend to his duties.

With relief, he found it worked this time. The stinging agony in his back and shoulders eased, the ache of the bruises faded. The swelling around his eye subsided, and he was able to open it. The stabbing pain of the broken rib abated.

Then, even as the exhaustion of the effort began to creep through him, out of sheer desperation, he tried something he had never done before. He concentrated on the muscles of his body—arms, shoulders, chest, back, legs—willing them to a strength beyond that of a sixteen-year-old boy, seeing them as hard and tough and useful as those of a fully trained warrior in the peak of condition.

Mouse got to his feet. All his life, they had beaten him. They called him disobedient, obdurate, rebellious, obstinate. He could add mulish and bullheaded to that list. They had not been able to beat it out of him. They had never broken him as they had broken the other slaves. He wouldn't let them do it to him now.

Foxmouse they called him—or just Mouse—because his hair was as red as the pelt of the little rodent. But he had seen the tiny rodent successfully fend off cats that threatened its young. If his namesake could defy enemies so much bigger and stronger than it, he could try to do no less.

The tiny cell contained one unglazed window. It showed as a pale oblong in the dark stone of the wall. Two iron bars transversed it vertically. Even without the bars, it was too narrow for a grown man to climb through. But Mouse was not a grown man—not yet.

Mouse went to the window and put his hands to the bars. Taking a deep breath, he began to pull. He strained until the muscles and sinews of his arms popped and stretched with the effort. But the bars remained stubbornly and firmly straight in their mortar bed.

Gasping for breath, he let go. He thought about the house-guards who would come for him with the dawn and drag him to the pens where they castrated sheep, where they used the same filthy pincers on troublesome slaves. He thought of them laughing as they left him to bleed to death or recover as best he could after the *gentling*.

"No," he whispered. "No! By all the gods, I won't let them do that to me."

And he had to avenge Rossah . . .

Cold rage flooded his belly, seeping through his body like oil into a wick. His muscles tightened, shivering with the intensity of his anger. He clenched his fists until his fingernails dug painfully into his palms.

Mouse turned his back to the window and reached up above his shoulders to grasp the bars firmly. He used the entire weight of his body, the full strength of his anger and grief, the leverage of his hips against the stone. The effort caused bright sparks and whorls to dance before his eyes, and the blood roared in his ears. The rough stone ground cruelly into the naked flesh of his hips. Every muscle distended and strained, and began to tear. He gritted his teeth hard enough to crack his jaw, and pulled harder.

The bars gave way so suddenly, he staggered forward and sprawled full-length onto his belly, cracking his forehead painfully on the opposite wall. Bright flashes exploded behind his eyelids. He shook his head, trying to clear it. It was a few moments until he could find the strength to sit up. He still held the two iron bars in his hands.

It was the mortar, he realized fuzzily. It must have been old and rotten, weakened by years of exposure to the damp, salt air.

He got to his feet, then had to reach out to steady himself with one hand against the cold stone of the wall as another wave of dizziness and nausea washed over him. When he finally trusted his balance again, he went back to the window.

Dawn was coming quickly. Already, a pale glimmer of light showed above the eastern wall of the landholding. Mouse dropped one of the iron bars to the floor and tossed the second out the window. It took him only seconds to scramble up to the broken sill. He took a deep breath, then expelled it to make himself as small as possible as he squeezed into the narrow opening. The rock frame scraped his skin raw and he felt warm blood trickle down his back and chest. He bit his lip against the pain and strained harder.

He popped through suddenly, and tumbled to the packed earth below the window, knocking all the wind from his body. He lay there gasping for a moment, then groped around until he found the iron bar, and scrambled to his feet.

To his left, the back wall of the holding rose two man-heights. Beyond that wall lay the river, a sheer, dizzying drop to the deceptively smooth water below. To his right lay the main gates, guarded day and night by Lord Mendor's most trusted houseguards. Ahead of him, across an expanse of open courtyard, stood the stables—and a hiding place.

Limping, Mouse ran to the back wall. Roughly built of raw stone, it provided enough chinks to serve as hand- and footholds. Tucking the iron bar under his arm, he swarmed quickly up the wall. At the top, he paused to look down at the dark, glimmering river and the swirling whirlpools that were plainly visible in the first light of dawn.

No, not that way. Die one day he undoubtedly would, but not now. Not that way, and not before he made a determined effort to avenge Rossah. He had no wish to drown in that turgid, yellow water.

He turned away. Balancing carefully, he made his way along the narrow wall toward the stables. He was nearly to the stable roof when the reaction from the healing hit him. He stumbled, then caught himself barely in time to avoid tumbling off the wall into the river. He went awkwardly to his hands and knees. The sharp rocks dug cruelly into his flesh, drawing more blood. Cold sweat broke out on his forehead and chest, stinging in the raw abrasions. His body trembled with fatigue. He closed his eyes and clung desperately to the wall, fighting off dizziness.

Finally, he crawled unsteadily the rest of the way to the stable, gripping the edge of the wall with a strength born of terror. Using very nearly the last of his stamina, he slithered under the eave of the thatched roof and fell heavily to the floor of the loft. Below, one of the horses snorted, startled.

Mouse had spent most of his life in the stable. He knew it better than anyone else knew it, even the Stablemaster. As a child, he had found secure places to hide from the Stablemaster's wrath. One of those places was right there in the Stablemaster's own stable, a small cleft in the thatching of the roof, barely large enough to conceal a full-grown man, but roomy and comfortable for the boy Mouse had been. He still fitted into the small hollow, but the fit was tighter now.

Even in the thick gloom shrouding the loft, Mouse had no trouble finding the hiding place. He crawled up into it and wrapped himself in the old horse blanket he had stolen so many years ago. Trembling and shivering with exhaustion, he closed his eyes. Only sleep could replenish the strength and energy healing himself had cost. Once he was strong again, he would find a way to exact his revenge.

His last conscious thought was of the dogs. But they would track him to the wall and think he had gone over into the river. Perhaps they would think him dead and not bother hunting any farther.

It was dark when Mouse awoke. He lay huddled in the old horse blanket, the iron bar cradled in his arms. He woke slowly, not moving, and listened intently without opening his eyes.

A quiet murmur of voices came from the stable below. Mouse could not quite make out the words, but he recognized the voices of the other two stable slaves. The soft, unmistakable sounds of hay being tossed into feeder troughs and the quiet snuffles and snorts of feeding horses told him it was not long after the dinner hour. It would be at least four more hours until midnight, when the Stablemaster would retire, sending the two stable slaves to their beds before him. Mouse thought it might be safe to leave the stable an hour after that.

Every muscle of his body screamed in protest as he snuggled deeper into the blanket. Hunger gnawed at his belly, and thirst raged in his throat. But he was used to that and could ignore it for a while longer. He closed his eyes and tried to think of a way to accomplish the revenge he needed more desperately than he needed to ease the hunger and thirst.

A sudden shout from the stable yard startled him and he froze, hardly daring to breathe. A troop of horses clattered into the stable, their iron-shod hooves clashing loud on the polished stones of the floor. One of the dogs growled, then yelped as a hard hand cuffed it.

"Hela, Gredad," the Stablemaster cried. "Any sign of the lad?"

Gredad swore. "None," he said. "We took the dogs along both banks of the river as far as the estuary. He's gone to the sea, is what. Drowned and dead. Good riddance, is what I say."

Mouse clutched the iron bar. His fingers tingled as the strength of his grip forced the blood out of his hands. They wouldn't be looking for him within the Holding. He had time for his revenge.

Gredad grunted. "Lord Mendor wanted to see his balls roasted and fed to the pigs. 'Twould barely appease young Lord Drakon, though. He wanted the lass, but unsullied. He's mad enough to spit."

"Let him spit," the Stablemaster muttered. "Serve the little bastard right."

Gredad chuckled. "You'd be well to guard your tongue, my friend," he said. "That young whelp never forgets an insult and never lets one go without retaliation."

"Well, I can't say as I blame him about the lass. She was a choice morsel."

"Oh, very choice indeed." Gredad's laugh seethed with lewd pleasure.

Mouse squeezed his eyes shut against the pain of grief stronger and sharper than the pain of his abused muscles. Nothing would ever erase the stark images of the brutal use Gredad and the houseguards made of Rossah. Nor would Mouse ever forget the appalling expression of ecstasy on Drakon's face as he watched. Or how Drakon looked when the men were finished with Rossah, and he stepped forward, his dagger drawn . . . And when he was finished, he casually told the guards to throw Rossah's body onto the dung heap behind the stables. He discarded her as if she were nothing but trash.

Mouse set his teeth into his lip to bite back the moan of pain. Nothing but trash . . .

Lying in bed with Rossah two nights ago, Mouse had told her he would die if it might prevent her having to go to Drakon's bed. She had placed gentle fingers over his lips and shaken her head.

"I will go as I must," she whispered. "Nothing can prevent it, and I would not have you die for me. It's only your love that makes all this bearable."

"Like you have?"

"Yes. It's real. You can't wish away reality."

"We could go to Isgard, where nobody knows we're slaves."

"And how would we live?" Again, she put her fingertip to his lips. "No," she said. "Come, kiss me again. We haven't much longer. Don't waste the time talking of impossible dreams."

"I hate him," Mouse whispered fiercely against the softness of her hair. "I hate Drakon."

Below, the Stablemaster set the slaves to caring for the guards' horses. Mouse fell asleep again, his eyes stinging with unshed tears.

There was no sound but for the quiet breathing of the horses when he awoke. Carefully, he lowered himself down to the loft floor and crept to the ladder. He held the iron bar firmly tucked under his arm as he made his way down to the aisle between the box stalls. One of the horses, still awake, turned lazily to watch him as he stole past, but made no sound.

Mouse paused at the stable door, peering out into the paddock. The full moon turned the yard into a place of pale washed silver and hard black shadows. Nothing moved. He heard nothing but the soft soughing of a gentle wind in the boughs of the fruit trees. No lights showed in the windows of the main house, which bulked large against the star-splashed sky.

He started across the yard toward the shelter of the laundry and ran full tilt into a man who stepped out of one of the privies next to the stables. The man grunted in pain and cried out as Mouse caromed off him to his knees in the packed dirt.

Gredad! Oh, gods, it was Gredad.

The guard captain recovered quickly from the winding Mouse had given him. "You!" he cried, staggering to his feet.

Even as Gredad opened his mouth to shout for the guard, Mouse swung the iron bar. It caught Gredad on the side of the head. The sound it made was like dropping an overripe melon onto a stone floor. Mouse's belly contracted into a knot of revulsion as Gredad collapsed like an empty sack.

Mouse caught Gredad by the heels, dragged him back to the privy, and shoved him inside. He dropped the bloody iron bar on top of the body and closed the door, then stood leaning against the unplaned wood, panting and listening hard. But nothing disturbed the silence. Nobody had heard Gredad's startled exclamation.

Mouse darted across the yard to the laundry house. He needed something to cover his nakedness. Garments and bedding hung, some dry, some still damp, from lines strung across the back of the shed. Identifying articles only by touch, he found a shirt, a tunic, a pair of breeks, and a thick, warm woolen cloak. Drakon's, by the luxurious feel of the fabric. There was even a pair of boots, sent for cleaning and polishing, that fitted reasonably well.

Pleased, he dressed quickly. The clothing was loose in the waist and a little short in the arms and legs, but it would do. A short length of line wrapped twice around his waist served as a belt to keep the breeks from falling around his ankles.

Fumbling in the dark along the shelf next to the huge washtubs, Mouse found flint, steel, and tinder and shoved them into his shirt. He nearly knocked over a lamp as he groped farther along the shelf, but snatched it up in time to prevent spilling the oil.

He ran across the yard to the barracks, his belly quivering in excitement and rage. The muscles of his legs and back ached and burned at the exertion, but he did not stop running until he came to the wall of the barracks. Except for the two guards at the front gate, and the few who stood guard within the main house, all the guards would now be asleep in the barracks. Mouse dropped to one knee and pulled the flint and steel from his shirt.

The barracks was a long, low building, built of timber rather than stone. Within, rows of bunks lined the walls, providing little privacy for the guards, but far more comfort than afforded by the slave quarters only a short distance away. The roof was thatch, and dry after a long, hot summer.

Mouse's hands shook so badly, he could not strike a spark from the flint. He sat back on his heels, rubbed his hands against his thighs, and clenched them into fists for a moment. Coldly, deliberately, he closed his eyes and thought about Rossah lying on the dunghill, discarded like a broken ewer. He thought about how her warm, silken flesh had taught him the glory of all the ways a man and a woman fitted so delightfully together. She had given him the only love he had ever known, and in return, he had eagerly and joyously given her all of his. He thought about how she had screamed and screamed and screamed at the brutal use the guards had made of her body before Drakon released her to death.

It was enough. Calm and steady, he struck flame to the tinder and lit the lamp. He waited with patience until the wick caught fully and burned well. Then he stepped back and tossed the lamp up into the thatch.

The thatch caught immediately. At first, only a small flame flickered in the straw and reeds, but as the oil spilled out of the lamp, the fire spread, slowly at first, then more quickly as it grew. The slight breeze fanned it as it fed on the dry thatch. Mouse heard a loud *whuf*, and suddenly the whole roof exploded in one huge, bright burst of flame. Seconds later, the ancient, dry timber caught, and flame engulfed the whole building.

Mouse ran back and ducked behind the laundry shed. The door of the barracks burst open and two or three half-naked guards stumbled out as the first screams rose into the stillness of the night. Moments later, a man staggered out into the yard, his clothing burning like a torch. His bubbling screams rang loud even over the roar of the flames as he fell and rolled feebly in the dirt.

Mouse watched in grim satisfaction. "Burn, you louse-infested sons of whores and vermin," he muttered. "Burn and die in agony, and may maggots feast in your charred flesh. Hellas take your black souls."

The roar of the fire and the shrieks of the dying guards roused the house servants and the slaves. Pandemonium erupted in the yard as men began running out to see what was wrong. Lights appeared in the windows of the manse. Lord Mendor leaned out of an upper window, shouting orders at the running figures in the yard.

"Come down," Mouse whispered fiercely, the strength of his need knotting his fists. "Come down so I can kill you. You and that slimy maggot you call a son."

But Mendor remained at the window, shouting orders. He did not come down.

Mouse recognized the two guards from the front gates trying to organize a bucket brigade to douse the blazing barracks.

For the first time since he had pulled the bars from their mooring in the holding cell, it occurred to him that he had a real chance of escaping. With all the panic and rushing around in the yard, there was a possibility he could steal a horse and make a break for the gates. Dressed as he was in Drakon's clothing, there was even the likelihood that he might not be recognized. In the dark, no one might notice the color of his hair, which uniquely identified him.

He saw the half-dressed Stablemaster running with a bucket from the watering trough. That was all he needed. He turned and sprinted for the stable.

The first box stall contained Lord Mendor's blooded stallion, the one called Strongheart, and the swiftest horse in the stable. Mouse opened the door to the stall, led Strongheart out, and guided him to the door of the tack room.

Mouse found a torch, the end wrapped in pitch-soaked rags, and fumbled with the flint and steel. The torch sputtered and smoked, but gave enough light so that he could find what he needed in the black interior of the tack room.

Strongheart snorted and tossed his head as Mouse slipped the bridle over his ears. Mouse held the horse firmly, gently scratched the long, aristocratic nose as he murmured soothing words. Strongheart submitted without further fuss and stood obediently docile while Mouse finished saddling him.

Mouse grabbed the torch and turned for the door. As he led the horse out into the stable yard, Strongheart shied violently and laid his ears back at the sight and smell of the burning building. Men burned, too. The stench of roasting, charred meat blowing about on the wind knotted Mouse's belly with nausea, and unexpectedly, made his mouth water.

A sudden shout made Mouse spin around. Drakon and one of the stable slaves ran across the open ground toward the stable. Drakon shouted again, drawing the dagger from his belt, and leaped at Mouse. Mouse used the only weapon he had. He swung the torch with a strength born of anger and desperation. The pitch-soaked flaming end slammed into the side of Drakon's head. Drakon's hair burst into flame and he fell while the young stable slave gaped openmouthed in frozen shock. Mouse left Drakon there, screaming in pain and clawing at his head, and pulled Strongheart into the open.

He pointed the horse in the direction of the gates, which the guards had left wide-open in their rush to see what was causing all the noise. Seeking safety from the fire, the horse was already moving when Mouse vaulted up into the saddle and clung like a cocklebur as the horse's stride lengthened to a full gallop.

A figure appeared out of the gloom ahead of Mouse. Heart beating wildly in his chest, Mouse leaned closer to Strongheart's neck, determined to run down both horse and rider if he had to. But at the last moment, the stranger pulled his horse to the side of the track, allowing Mouse to pass unimpeded. Mouse had just time to get an impression of a big man wrapped in a brightly colored cloak, astride a big, dark horse, and a glimpse of hair turned to flame red by the reflected glow of the fire behind him. As Mouse swept past, he thought he heard the echo of laughter behind him.

Mouse did not look back as Strongheart found the road and turned north toward Isgard.

Six days later, a cold, autumnal downpour found Mouse only a league or two from the border between Falinor and Isgard. He had sold the horse and saddle once he was clear of Mendor's Landholding, where they would not be recognized. The coin he got for them not only procured a much less memorable horse, but gave him enough left over to buy a little food. Mouse's time in the stables was not ill spent. The horse was thin and bony, its coat unkempt and scruffy, but it had a good breadth and depth of chest, which spoke of stamina and strength, if not blinding speed. Mouse liked the look in its eye. It stood its ground, wary but calm, as Mouse ran his hands over its rough coat, then carefully opened its mouth to look at its teeth. A sound-winded and willing horse, even if not a handsome one, it was an inconspicuous mount, but Mouse thought it would prove reliable.

The fine clothes Mouse had stolen might have made him conspicuous even on the sorrel, but the days of road dust and being slept in soon reduced them to the same scruffiness as the big gelding. Although Mouse had little doubt Mendor knew who burned the guard barracks and stole the horse, he hoped he would not be recognized without Strongheart.

The inn was small and cheap, an inn where men with little to spend on luxury might find shelter on a wet, stormy night against the misery of the cold rain. The sign over the door, depicting a bell and hammer, hung askew on its rusting pins, the paint cracked and faded. The tables in the common room were deeply scarred and crusted with spilled food. A thick miasma of stale drink, old cooking odors, and rotting vegetation from the too-long-unchanged rushes on the dirt floor mingled with the stench of a midden heap far too close to the kitchen. Mouse's nose wrinkled at the smell, but the light that gleamed though the open door was welcoming, and it looked warm and reasonably dry inside.

For a copper coin, the innkeeper, who smelled nearly as bad as his common room, allowed Mouse to stable the sorrel and throw it a handful of oats and an armful of hay. Two more coppers bought him a corner near the littered hearth where he could sleep wrapped in his cloak beneath the low, soot-blackened beams of the ceiling. Another copper brought him a heel of dark bread, a wedge of cheese, and a flagon of sour ale served by a ragged and dirty child of indeterminate gender. It was not much, but it was enough to ease the ache of hunger in his belly, and the ale returned the warmth the rain had stolen from his body.

Mouse finished the sketchy meal quickly. The rain stopped while he ate, but the air blowing through the unglazed windows was still heavy with damp. The second horn of ale went down quickly. Between the ale and the heat of the fire, Mouse let himself relax. Wrapped in the unaccustomed comfort, he leaned his elbows on the table and drank more slowly.

So, he was a little drunk and hardly noticed when the bounty hunter walked in. The man stood at the door of the common room and looked around. He was not tall, but he was solidly built and powerful-looking, and he wore a longsword on a silver-studded baldric at his left hip, two daggers arranged in leather sheaths at his belt. His lank black hair and black eyes marked him as a Maedun. His presence silenced what little conversation there had been in the common room. The Maedun were known for their willingness to kill and the pleasure they took from it. Mouse tried to shrink down into invisibility within his cloak, berating himself for allowing himself to become a little drunk and a lot careless. The bounty hunter's gaze came to rest on him, and he began walking across the room toward him. The Maedun towered over Mouse as the boy huddled on the bench.

"You've had a good run, boy," he said sourly. "Almost worth the reward Mendor will pay me for you." He drew the sword and held it lightly in his right hand as he stood grinning ferally down at Mouse. "Stand up. We're starting back to the Landholding right now."

Despair turned to scalding anger. Mouse came off the

bench like an arrow from a bowstring. Too late, the Maedun
brought up the sword to slice at the boy's head. Mouse ducked
under the arm and his shoulder sank deeply into the bounty
hunter's unprotected belly. The breath left the man's body in
an explosive grunt. The sword clattered to the earthen floor as
Mouse's weight bore the Maedun back toward the stone
hearth. The man went down heavily on the flagstones, and
Mouse rolled free. He bounced to his feet, spun, and snatched
up the fallen sword.

The Maedun had already pulled one of the daggers and
come to his knee when Mouse whirled back to face him. But
even as the bounty hunter drew back to throw the dagger,
Mouse lunged forward and sank the blade of the sword into
the man's belly. The bounty hunter slumped back, wild astonishment on his face, and groped for the steel buried deep in his
flesh. Then his face went blank and empty, and he sagged back
onto the blackened flagstones.

Mouse yanked the sword free, bent to snatch up both the
dagger in the bounty hunter's limp hand and the one still at his
belt. No sound came from the small cluster of men at a table in
the corner. None of them moved as Mouse straightened up.
They watched him for a brief moment, then all of them deliberately turned their backs, unwilling to involve themselves in a
quarrel that was none of their making. There was no sign of
the innkeeper or the urchin who had served the meal and the
ale. Mouse thought they might be crouched behind the serving
bar. He thrust both the daggers into his belt and, still holding
the sword, ran for the door. He flung it open and ran out into
the muddy courtyard.

And slammed right into the waiting arms of Dergus
Keepmaster, head steward to Lord Mendor.

The Keepmaster grabbed Mouse's arms, spun him around,
and shoved him backward into two Falian border guards. The
sword fell into the soaked weeds with a muffled splat. Mouse
sagged in the grip of the guards, sickened by the knowledge
that Dergus had, after all, a little magic. He must have used it
to track him. Mouse still smelled the stench of it on him, and
revulsion knotted tight in his belly, raising every hair on the

back of his neck as his skin prickled and shivered. Magic. He hated magic. It made his skin crawl.

Dergus Keepmaster carefully wiped his hands on a silken handkerchief. He hated to soil his own hands by actually touching a slave, even to kill him for Lord Mendor. Hence, the bounty hunter, Mouse reasoned, still dizzy from the reek of magic.

"Bind him," Dergus ordered distastefully. "And chain his legs."

"Now what's the lad done to make you so upset with him?" a new voice asked.

Mouse shook the hair out of his eyes and saw a man framed in the light of the doorway behind Dergus. The newcomer was tall and broad, and seemed to fill the doorway. His face was in deep shadow, and Mouse saw nothing of his expression, but there was laughter in the voice. Mouse frowned. He had seen the man before. He was certain of it, but he could not remember where.

"Seems to me to be a shocking waste of manpower," the man continued, amusement lilting through the words. His Falian was slightly accented but fluent and correct. He stepped out into the courtyard. The light behind gleamed on hair turned to a blaze like flame in the dark. "Three men just to hold one scrawny boy?"

Dergus straightened his tunic. "The boy is an escaped slave," he said coldly. "He burned half my lord's manse and killed several guards in his escape. He also badly wounded my lord's son, and for that, Mendor will have his head."

The hint of a smile curled at the corner of the wide mouth. "A fractious and vexatious lot, these slaves," the newcomer murmured. He glanced over his shoulder back into the inn. "And he's just polished off a nasty-looking specimen of a bounty hunter, too," he remarked. "Mayhaps you're right. He's more dangerous than he looks, that one."

"He's going back for hanging," Dergus said. "You would be well-advised to stay out of affairs that do not concern you."

"Just out of curiosity, how much was he worth to the bounty hunter?"

"Three silver."

"Three silver?" The man glanced at Mouse and grinned. "A lot for a lad his size." He turned back to Dergus. "How much is he worth to his lord?"

Dergus spit into the mud at the man's feet. "About that much," he said. "He also despoiled a girl the lord was saving for his son."

The other man nodded gravely. "A *very* dangerous boy, then," he agreed. He reached for the purse at his belt. "He might be worth something to me, if you want to sell him and save your lord the trouble of killing him quickly. I'm in need of a slave to work the galley, and he looks strong enough to last a year or two before the work kills him. What do you say to three silver?"

"Seven silver," Dergus said quickly.

The stranger laughed, and again, Mouse had the feeling he had heard that laughter before. "Seven silver? Even you're not worth seven silver, my friend. Four, then?"

Mouse sank his teeth into his lower lip, watching the stranger closely. If he had known Dergus all his life, the stranger could not have chosen a better way to persuade him. Mouse saw only Dergus's profile, but he read the avarice there, saw the swift calculation and the smile when Dergus came to the conclusion that four silver for Mendor with one left over for himself would satisfy Mendor's thirst for Mouse's neck, especially when Mendor heard of the fate awaiting the runaway slave in a galley—a slow, lingering death for most men.

"Five and he's yours," Dergus said.

"Five it is," the stranger said, smiling. "And he might even be worth it."

"I'll have the guards shackle him for you," Dergus said. "Give me the silver."

The stranger dropped five silver pieces into Dergus's greedily outstretched hand. From the expression on Dergus's face as he heard the healthy jingle of the purse when the stranger closed it again, he was wishing he had pushed the price up a little higher.

"Don't bother shackling him," the stranger said. A hand like an iron collar gripped Mouse's arm. "He'll not be running out on me." He bent and scooped up the sword Mouse had dropped when Dergus grabbed him. "I believe the boy had a horse. I'll be taking that, too."

"For another silver," Dergus said quickly.

The stranger laughed. Mouse wondered how a laugh could be so full of mirth and, at the same time, sound so dangerous. He watched the stranger with renewed interest.

"Don't get greedy, little man," the man said softly. "That horse might be worth two coppers, but certainly no more. You can afford to be generous after what I paid you."

Dergus turned sourly away, beckoning the guards to follow. They mounted and rode off into the wet night while Mouse stood helplessly with the stranger's hand gripping his arm. When they were gone, the stranger turned and dragged Mouse to the stable. Once they were inside, he let go of the boy's arm. Mouse got his first good look at his new master in the guttering light of a torch that gave off more smoke than light.

The man was his early thirties. He was a big man, tall and heavy boned, the webs of muscles laid neat and flat across his frame. He was dressed as a Tyran clansman in a kilt of a green-and-blue tartan, a white wide-sleeved shirt, and a draped plaid of the same tartan, secured at his left shoulder by a large, round brooch embossed with a clan badge. His tall boots were of good, soft leather, and the baldric holding the sword across his back was studded with silver interspersed with red stones. His shoulder-length copper red hair, streaked liberally with gold, was worn loose but for a single thick braid plaited with a leather thong by his left temple. It was longer than the rest of his hair, as if he never cut the hair that went into it. Mouse had heard of that. A clansman's braid was his strength, both in battle and in love. He gave it up only in death. The Tyr's eyes were a soft, clear green above a beard of copper gold. A large emerald on a short length of delicate gold chain swung from his left earlobe. Mouse had never seen a Tyran clansman before, but there were more than enough tales spun by bards of their fighting abilities.

The clansman carefully placed the dead bounty hunter's sword onto the straw, then put his hand to Mouse's chin and turned his face to the light. "Let me look at you, boy," he said. "I bought and paid for you. I want to see what kind of a bargain I got." He laughed as Mouse tensed to make a break for the door. "Don't try it, lad. I'll snap your neck for you if you move." He studied the boy for a moment, then nodded. "Small and scrawny," he commented. "But you'll grow a fair bit before you're finished. And you'll fill out into a man's shape when you've stopped growing. How old are you?"

The clansman's grip on Mouse's chin made it difficult to speak. "I don't know," he said. "Almost sixteen, I think."

"Then you've a lot of growing time left."

"I'll die of overwork on that galley before I grow much taller," Mouse said hoarsely.

"What galley?" the Tyr asked, grinning widely. "I'm a dreadful liar, boy. I own no galley."

"Then why—?"

"Did I buy you? Hellas knows. But now that I've got you, what am I to do with you?"

Mouse had no answer for him.

The Tyr grinned. "I could sell you again," he said. He paused. "Or I could even free you."

Mouse looked up at him, his mouth gone suddenly dry, unable to breathe for a moment as his heart kicked painfully against his ribs.

"How much is your freedom worth, boy?"

"Everything," Mouse said softly, hardly daring to hope.

"You cost me five silver," the Tyr said. He reached out with his free hand and took the two daggers from Mouse's belt. He held them up to the dim light and frowned as he studied them. They were a fine matching pair, the hilts inlaid with silver and gold wire in an intricate design. He nodded. "A fair exchange," he murmured. "A pair of daggers for five silver, and I make a profit on the transaction. Fair enough?"

Mouse's knees gave way and he sagged in the Tyr's grip. "Fair enough," he whispered, hardly daring to trust him.

The Tyr let go of Mouse's chin, eased him down into a

heap of straw, and sat on his heels in front of the boy. His expression softened and he smiled. "There are no slaves in Tyra, boy," he said, "and I'm a man who hates slavery. It's against the laws of all the gods, and against the laws of nature. Men were made to live with no chains binding them. You're free to go where you choose."

"Do you mean that?"

"Trust me," the Tyr said, and suddenly, irrationally, Mouse did. Completely and without question.

The Tyr laughed again, and Mouse knew where he had heard that laugh before. "You were at Mendor's Landholding when I escaped," he said, startled.

"Aye, I was. I had business with him." He grinned widely. "You created quite a kerfuffle that night."

Mouse frowned and clenched his fist. "I wish I'd killed Mendor."

"Aye, well, you didn't do his son a whole lot of good, if that's any compensation." The Tyr drew a dagger from a boot sheath and replaced it with one of the silver-chased daggers. "You might want this," he said to Mouse, handing him the slender weapon. Hesitantly, Mouse took it and slipped it into the top of his boot.

"Where will you go?" the man asked, more gently.

Faced suddenly with real freedom rather than mere headlong flight, Mouse stared blankly at him. "I have no idea."

"I have need of men to work with me, if you're interested," the Tyr said. "I have a band of merchant train guards. We need good men for this coming season. It pays your keep, ten silver per trip and a bonus for any fighting. Interested?"

Unable to speak, Mouse nodded. Then he cleared his throat and said, "But I don't know how to use a sword or bow . . ."

The Tyr grinned. "You're scrawny now, but you managed that bounty hunter well enough," he said. "You'll learn, I think. Men with red hair like ours learn as well as they want to. Stubborn, we are. Very stubborn."

"Stubborn is one of the least offensive things they called me." Mouse smiled for the first time. "Then, yes. I'm interested."

The Tyr stood up and extended his hand to help Mouse to

his feet. "I'm Cullin dav Medroch dav Kian," he said. "And you?"

"They call me Foxmouse. Or just Mouse."

One red-gold eyebrow rose in surprise. Or amusement. "Mouse?" he repeated. "What kind of a name is that?"

Mouse shrugged. "A slave name," he said bitterly.

"Well, it surely is no name for a free man and one of Cullin dav Medroch's merchant train guards. I'll give you my grandfather's name. He's not needing it anymore."

He picked up the bounty hunter's sword with his left hand and tossed it to Mouse. Mouse reached up automatically and grabbed the hilt before it hit him in the face. For the first time, he saw that it was truly a wondrous sword. The blade shone with a silvery gleam in the dim light of the torch. Runes he could not quite read spilled down the center of the blade, glittering like facets of a hundred gems. When he tried to look closely at them, they blurred and ran together, as if seen through a thin curtain of moving water. The plain, leather-bound hilt was long enough to be used two-handed. An echo of his dreams reverberated faintly through him as he hefted the sword and found it balanced perfectly in his left hand. When he switched to an experimental two-handed grip, the balance shifted subtly so that, again, it was perfect.

"From now on, you're Kian," Cullin dav Medroch said. "You'll have to earn a last name. But Kian's a good name. A name with pride on it." He smiled grimly. "And don't you ever forget that."

Kian straightened his shoulders and shed the slave name like a man shrugging off an ill-fitting cloak. "I won't," he said fervently. "By all the gods, I won't."

Cullin grinned. "Then get your horse, Kian, and come wi' me. What we both need is a good night's sleep in a decent inn. We'll talk again in the morning over our fast-breaking."

PART

2

Kian

3

I cannot look back, now, on that time before I met Cullin dav Medroch dav Kian, without feeling that it all happened to someone else. That boy named Mouse was someone I knew, perhaps, but I cannot feel that he was really me. His time is as blurred in my memory as the first seven or eight years of his life were blurred in his. What I have become—who I have become—since then has turned Mouse into a faded painting on a crumbling wall. I can feel nothing of the pain he endured, only pity for him and admiration that he survived. There is an odd detachment in my mind when I try to think of him, a separation as sharp, as keen as the blade of a dagger. Sometimes, it is strange to think that nearly ten years of my life were spent as someone else, but it is something I do not allow myself to dwell on. There is enough in my life now to compensate. I am content to let Mouse be who he was, and let me be myself.

I hardly remember the long, hard ride to the inn across the Isgardian border. Exhaustion, reaction, and relief combined to send me into a daze, where moving was like wading through a pond of thick pitch. I nearly tumbled from the sorrel when we finally stopped. I think it must have been sometime near dawn. Cullin used more of the silvers from his purse to buy a small room on the second level of the inn. I was hardly aware of anything but the clean smell of the bed the innkeeper led me to. I was asleep almost before I toppled into it.

The late morning sun streaming though the window like warm honey finally woke me. I lay naked in a soft bed, covered by a quilt of such fine quality it felt like silk against my skin. Confused and disoriented, I sat up abruptly, spilling the bedclothes over the edge of the bed onto the floor. The clothes I had worn lay across a chair near the bed, neatly folded, cleaned, and brushed, the boots, polished to a glowing sheen, tucked under the chair. A longsword lay across the folded cloak, catching the sun like burnished silver. I stared at it blankly and tried to sort out where I was, how I got there, and why I was there.

Someone knocked softly. I snatched the quilt off the floor and pulled it up over my hips as the door opened and a serving girl entered carrying a tray laden with food. She was followed by a man with hair almost as red as my own who moved with the grace of a mountain cat. The memory of the previous evening rushed back, and I relaxed. The slave called Foxmouse was a thing of the past. In his place stood a man named Kian, a free man, a man who would prepare to be a merchant train guard. I fell back on my elbows and wanted to laugh out of sheer exultation.

Cullin dav Medroch smiled. *"Rhoch'te ne vhair, ti'rhonai?"* he asked.

Still stunned from the deep and profound slumber, I smiled back. *"Vhair chinde,"* I replied, then gaped at him as I realized I had no idea what he had said, and even less what I had replied. A chill of apprehension shivered down my spine. Was it some kind of magic? "What language was that?" I demanded.

Cullin dav Medroch laughed and closed the door behind him. "One you obviously recognize," he said cheerfully. "Awake now, are you? I expect you slept well."

Not trusting my voice, I nodded.

The girl set the tray onto the bed by my knee. It held a jug of milk, fresh bread and cheese, and a bowl of dried fruit. She gave me a shy smile. "If you wish anything more, let me know," she said. "I'll be happy to serve you." She bobbed a small curtsy to me and slipped out of the room. I stared after her, startled. Nobody had ever shown deference to me in my life. I wasn't sure how to react.

"Hungry?" Cullin asked.

I looked at the food. There was more of it on the tray than all three of Mendor's stable slaves saw in one day. "Starving," I admitted.

Cullin grinned again. "Aye, you look it," he said. "Well, get yourself outside of that lot, and we'll have a good start at putting some meat on those bones. You'll need it if you're going to swing that sword."

I wasn't sure any one person could eat that much food, but when I finally reached the point where my stomach felt stretched tight, there wasn't a lot left on the tray. I pushed it away and reached for my clothing.

"First a bath, I think," Cullin said. "You're still wearing quite a lot of Falinor. I'll have the innkeeper send up a tub and hot water to wash it off. When you're finished, I'll be downstairs."

I had never in my life experienced anything as wonderfully luxurious as that bath. I reveled in that huge vat of steaming hot water, blissfully aware that even paradise offered nothing finer. The cake of soap the innkeeper provided smelled faintly of fresh herbs, and it made a wondrous lather on my body and in my hair. When I finally climbed reluctantly out of the cooling water in the tub, my fingers looked as wizened as raisins. Drakon's stolen clothing felt sensuously and lavishly fine against my damp, glowing skin. It wasn't until I was dressed and on my way down to the common room that I began to wonder why Cullin dav Medroch was doing this for me. Cullin owed me nothing. If anything, I owed him even more than my life.

Cullin was waiting at a table near the door, his plaid flung back over his shoulders to reveal the long, two-handed sword slung across his back in an ornate scabbard. Even relaxed, he looked dangerous and deadly. Not a man one wanted as an enemy.

"Why are you doing this?" I asked. Something wasn't right. Everything he had done so far—rescuing me, freeing me, bringing me along with him. He had to have a reason. Not knowing what it was bothered me.

He grinned and ignored the question. "You almost look as if you belong in those clothes now," he said. "Are you ready to leave?"

I didn't move. "Why are you doing this?" I repeated.

"We'll talk as we ride," he said, rising from his chair with fluid grace. "I have to be in Honandun very soon, and the day's half-gone already."

Still, I didn't move. "What language was that?" I asked. "When you came into the bedroom, you said something." My voice rose. "What language was that?"

"We'll talk on the road," Cullin said again. He turned on his heel and strode out the door. I stood unmoving for a moment, then followed him quickly. I didn't have much choice.

For the first hour, we rode hard along the packed surface of the road leading north and west from the border. There was little chance for conversation. The sorrel, much livelier for good feed and expert care the stableboys at the inn had given it, was still no match for the bay stallion Cullin rode, but it struggled gamely to keep the pace Cullin set. When he finally drew off the road and dismounted by a small stream surrounded by trees and lush grass, I was more than ready for a rest, and so was the sorrel.

We let the horses drink a little. Cullin tossed me a cloth to rub down the sorrel. He looked at me across the withers of the stallion as he attended to it.

"Tell me about your parents," he said. "Do you remember them?"

The question surprised me. I had never thought about who my parents might have been. No one had ever spoken to me about them. I shook my head. "I never knew them," I replied. "My mother either died when I was very young, or she was sold away."

"And your father?"

I gave a bitter grunt of laughter. "Who knows? It might have been Lord Mendor for all I know. Nobody ever bothered to tell me. A slave's parentage isn't important."

"You weren't born into slavery," Cullin said quietly.

I looked up at him, startled. Cullin stood with his forearms resting across his saddle, regarding me gravely. His eyes were brilliantly green. There was an expression in them I couldn't quite read. I began to protest that I had never known anything else but slavery, but Cullin shook his head.

"No," he said. "You don't have that air about you. No man born to slavery would be as fiercely independent as you. No born slave could have killed that bounty hunter."

"I remember nothing else but being a slave," I muttered, ducking my head and paying meticulous attention to the task of rubbing down the sorrel. But his words had touched close to one of my persistent childhood fantasies—that I had been kidnapped as a child and forced into slavery. In my daydreaming, my father—usually a nobleman, sometimes even a prince— came to rescue me. I outgrew those hopeless fantasies quickly under the harsh reality of the lash of the Stablemaster's tongue, and the very real sting of the short whip he used to discipline his slaves. I looked up to see Cullin regarding me with a curious expression on his face. Somewhere between speculation and hope. Even though he had not changed his stance, I thought I detected an overtone of tenseness, almost expectation. But even as I watched, it was gone, as if it had never been, and I wondered if I had really seen anything.

"What is your earliest memory?" he asked, his tone casual again.

It was a strange question. I frowned and studied the now-glowing hide of the sorrel. Finally, I looked up at him. "Standing beside a horse, very much like this, with a curry-comb," I said. "I was almost as tall as the horse's withers. I might have been seven." I raised my hand to rub the long-healed ridge of scar tissue behind my ear, hidden beneath my hair. "And headaches. Blinding headaches. Sometimes so bad I couldn't see because my vision was so blurred."

"Do you still get headaches?"

I shook my head. "No. I learned how to ignore the pain." That wasn't exactly the truth. It was during the worst of one of those headaches with my temples throbbing and nausea coiling in my belly when I had found that quiet place inside myself where I could reach out and stop the pain, to correct and repair the damage.

"You remember nothing before you were seven?"

I shook my head. "No."

"Very odd," he said quietly. "Most people remember quite a

lot from when they were very young." He grinned. "I remember falling from my father's horse when I was hardly big enough to walk. And I remember my father laughing as he plucked me out of the mud. I was annoyed with myself for falling off, and even more annoyed with my father because he laughed at me, but he picked me up and set me back on the horse, mud and all. Made a terrible mess of the saddle. He made me clean it off by myself later." He swung up into the saddle. "Time to go. The horses are rested enough now, I think."

We progressed at a less tumultuous pace, keeping the horses to a brisk walk, only occasionally allowing them to break into a canter. Cullin rode easily, back straight, one hand on his hip. I watched him in mixed curiosity and puzzlement. The stories I had heard about Tyran clansmen did not lead me to believe they went around rescuing runaway slaves simply because they hated the idea of slavery. He was clearly in a hurry to get to Honandun on the coast of Isgard, but he had taken the time out from his journey to let me rest and recover a little from the exhaustion of running. I wondered why he bothered to bring me along with him, particularly why he offered me employment. I had no skill with a sword or a bow. In order to be of any use to him, someone was going to expend a lot of time and trouble to train me. He had to have a reason.

"You still haven't told me why you rescued me," I said, pulling the sorrel up closer to his stallion. "Or what language that was."

"Tyran," he said absently, scanning the low hills around us. "I was testing out a theory."

"A theory?"

He turned and flashed a grin at me. "Your hair," he said. "I thought you might very well be Tyran. I wondered if your mother was Tyran and taught it to you, or if you remembered it if she did."

I stared at him for a moment. Finally, I said: "And I answered you." I shook my head. "But I don't know what you said, or what I said, either."

He grinned again. "I asked if you'd slept well, and you said you had."

He suddenly pulled his stallion to a halt and dismounted.
He dropped to one knee to examine the dust of the road carefully, then rose and looked off toward the low hills in the east.

"Trouble," he said quietly.

"Trouble?" I repeated.

"We've been following a troop of riders for the last league
or so," he said. "They met someone else here. Look at this."

I got down beside him and looked at the marks on the road.
It was obvious, even to me, that a scuffle had taken place here,
and not that long ago, either. I bent and brushed my fingers
across a dark stain in the dust of the track. Blood. Thick
splashes of it were still sticky in the grass along the side of the
road. But whoever shed the blood either rode off with the
mounted troop and their captives, or was carried away,
because there was no sign of any bodies.

Cullin stood on the side of the road, looking first at the
blood, then in the direction the tracks led. East. Not west
toward Honandun and his business there. The sun glinted off
the copper gleam of his hair and limned his beard with flame.
His hand went to the hilt of the sword at his back in an auto-
matic gesture, loosening the blade in its scabbard. One of his
eyebrows quirked in speculative consideration.

"What is it?" I asked.

"Maedun mercenaries, I think. They took three people
here." He caught the reins of his stallion and swung into the
saddle. "Those Maedun are becoming entirely too arrogant, I
think," he said softly. "It might be time someone taught them a
few manners."

Maedun mercenaries, employed by the Royal House of
Falinor, had made several visits to Lord Mendor's
Landholding. I watched them strut insolently around the yard,
demanding and getting the best from the kitchens and wine
cellars, and the best-looking of the slave women to warm their
beds at night. Some of them preferred boys, and got them, too.
In any large company of them, there was always one who
stank of magic, a warlock whose job it was to ensure nobody
dared attack them. I made myself as invisible as possible
whenever they came. Just the thought of them made me shiver.

I wanted nothing whatsoever to do with their kind of magic. With *any* kind of magic. Then or now.

"You're going after them?" I asked. "Won't it be dangerous?"

He laughed. "Aye, well, Tyra and Maedun have been uneasy neighbors for centuries," he said. "We've learned a thing or two about them in that time. A few tricks here and there."

In spite of myself, I grinned. "A fractious and vexatious lot, those Maedun," I said.

He laughed again. "A true clansman's attitude, that," he said. He gestured toward the bloodstains and scuffed ground. "This wasn't that long ago. Not much more than an hour or two. We should catch up to them by dusk."

"What about your business in Honandun?"

"It can wait one day more if necessary."

4

We lay well hidden behind a low outcropping of rocks on the top of the hill and looked down at the encampment. We had left the horses back in a small copse of alders so they wouldn't disturb the horses in the camp and betray our presence. Sunset was a little over half an hour gone. The moon would not rise for several hours, and the darkness was almost complete. The faint glow of a campfire led us to this ridge overlooking the stream.

Eight men sat around the fire in the shelter of a wide bend in the little burn, their backs to the steep embankment. There were more men we couldn't see outside the circle of light cast by the small fire, perhaps four or five more, judging by the tracks Cullin and I had followed.

"You were right," I said softly, mindful of the still air and quiet night, and the propensity of sound to travel. "Maedun mercenaries."

"Aye," Cullin replied. "Such a tedious lot, these Maedun. Now, the question is, do they have a warlock with them?"

"I could tell you if I could get closer," I said.

He glanced at me in the dusk. "Could you now?" he murmured.

I felt myself blush. "Aye, I could," I said, unconsciously mimicking him. "Magic like theirs leaves a stench on a man."

The look he gave me was decidedly brimming with thoughtful appraisal. "It does, does it?" he said. "Aye, well, I suppose it might at that. D'ye think you can get close enough to find out without them noticing you?"

I had spent all of my life practicing the art of invisibility. Surely creeping up on a camp would be little different from avoiding the quick and brutal hands of the Stablemaster or the guards at Lord Mendor's Landholding. "Yes," I said positively.

Cullin nodded. "Then give it a try, lad. But in a moment. We need to take a good look first."

The troop was camped in a hollow formed by the wide bend of the stream. Low bushes of willow, alder, and silverleaf grew thickly against the rocky outcropping behind them. The hillside below us was bare but for the coarse, dry, brown grass and the occasional thornbush. The air was thick with the smell of water, and the sharp, resinous scent of burning thornwood.

The Maedun had not picked the best place to settle for the night. Although the steep embankment offered shelter from the winds that swept down from the mountains of the west and north, it turned the camp into a trap in the event of an attack. But it was typical of what I had heard of the Maedun in high country. These hills were not mountains, but they were considerably higher than the coastal plain. The Maedun disliked mountainous regions. Some say it's because their own country is so featurelessly flat; others say it's because the magic of their warlocks and wizards is weakened by the high country.

I moved slightly to ease myself away from a sharp rock that dug into my hip. Cullin pointed to something barely out of the circle of firelight. Following his pointing finger, I saw the prisoners. Two men and what looked like a young boy. They lay bound ankle to wrist, wrist to ankle, without struggling, still and quiet in the shadows.

"Isgardians, do you think?" I asked.

Cullin shook his head. "I don't know. I can't see well enough. Well, whatever they are, they deserve better than ending up as Maedun slaves."

"Nobody deserves slavery," I muttered, moving toward the camp. "I'll be back."

Cullin caught my arm. "Be careful."

I grinned. "I will. I was thinking if there was no warlock with them, someone might slip down there and set up a small amount of tumult and confusion among the horses. Then it would be a simple matter for someone else to skulk through the shadows and cut the bonds on those prisoners."

Cullin's answering grin was quick. "Aye," he agreed. "You think well for someone who says he was always a slave." He reached over his shoulder and made sure the sword on his back moved easily in its scabbard. "Someone might even consider giving those Maedun a lesson in good manners." He pointed to a low mound of thornbush a few yards short of the stream. "I'll wait there. Can you signal if it's clear?"

"I do a fair imitation of a nightjar," I said.

"Good. When you give the signal, we'll move. I'll meet you back where we left the horses. Be careful." Without further word, he touched my shoulder and melted into the shadows, moving to the left toward the horses. I made sure of my dagger in its boot sheath, then moved off to the right.

There wasn't a lot of cover on the side of the hill, but I had the advantage of a moonless night. The men below were sitting around a fire and their eyes would not adjust quickly enough to see something moving in the dark beyond the firelight. But if they did have a warlock with them, he might be able to find me if I got too close.

The sound of their laughter became clear as I crept through the coarse grass. The ground beneath the grass was rocky and hard. I had to move slowly and cautiously so not to disturb the loose stones. I'd heard not so much as a rustle in the grass as Cullin slipped away.

When I reached the bank of the stream, I was less than a dozen yards from the nearest mercenary. I was downwind. I could smell the strong ale they were drinking, and the scent of cooking meat coming from the pot on the fire. But there was no stench of magic. No warlock. Nothing to prickle my skin or raise the hairs along the back of my neck or my arms. I lay absolutely still for a long time, watching the mercenaries. Perhaps this band wasn't large enough to warrant having a warlock assigned to it. This was only a small band. The troops who had come to Lord Mendor's Landholding usually numbered more than thirty. And with thirty, there was only the one who raised the hackles on my neck.

Finally convinced there was no warlock with them, I cupped my hands around my mouth and gave the harsh, grating cry of a nightjar. Moments later, it was answered from somewhere downstream.

I began to move slowly. I had to stand up to leap across the narrow stream, but I made it in one jump. A burst of laughter from the men around the fire covered any sound I might have made on the loose gravel. My heart thudded in my chest hard enough to tear it free it from its moorings, and I realized I was holding my breath. I forced myself to breathe normally, then dropped to my belly again and crept forward.

The three prisoners lay huddled together near the embankment. Only a yard or two from them, I sank down onto the gravel strand and unsheathed my dagger, then settled down to wait for Cullin to set up his diversion.

I didn't have long to wait. The high, yodeling shriek of a clan war cry split the night. At the same instant, a dozen or more terrified horses burst away from the picket lines and galloped directly at the campfire. One of them sailed over the flames and went flying past the prisoners, narrowly missing one of them. It passed me running flat out, ears laid back, tail raised like a flag. I rolled quickly out of its way, barely in time to miss getting trampled. The other horses, confused by the fire, bewildered by the terrifying howling behind them, milled around among the startled mercenaries for a second or two, then veered sharply and thundered off downstream. I caught a glimpse of Cullin, plaid billowing behind him, leaping onto one of the horses and wheeling after the fleeing animals.

The reaction of the Maedun was all I had wished for. They dived for their weapons, shouting orders to each other, and ran downstream after the horses. I scrambled forward and put my hand gently over the mouth of one of the prisoners.

"Don't cry out," I said softly as the man gave a hard start of shock. "I'm here to help."

The man rolled over and stared at me, his eyes showing only as dark pools in his pale face. He nodded, and I cut the bonds on his wrists and ankles. The blood rushing back into feet and hands after being bound so tightly must have been painful, but he made no sound. Seconds later, all three were free, but the youngest, the one who lay between the two men, didn't move.

"My daughter is badly hurt," the first man said.

"Not dead?" the other man asked quickly.

The first man put a hand to the young girl's throat, then shook his head. "She's alive . . . "

"Can you carry her?" I asked. "We don't have much time before those Maedun come back to make sure you're still here."

"I can carry her," the first man said. He scooped the girl up into his arms, cradling her gently against his chest, then nodded. "Where to?" he asked.

"This way," I said. We didn't bother with stealth as we splashed through the stream and scrambled up the bank on the other side. I could still hear the Maedun shouting to one another as they tried to round up the panicked horses, but Cullin no longer warbled that strange war cry. I don't know how far he chased the horses, but there was a lot of noise downstream. With luck, it would be a while before the Maedun returned to check on their prisoners. We would be long gone by then.

The man rose straight up out of the ground itself just ahead of me, roaring in a language I didn't know. The naked blade in his hand whistled as he swung it at my neck.

I leaped back and nearly stumbled on the uneven ground of the hillside. The wind of the sword's passing ruffled my hair as I went to one knee.

"Run," I shouted to the others, then the hilt of my own sword was in my hands, the blade raised in defense.

The Maedun crouched in front of me. He flexed his wrists, his sword describing purposeful little circles in the air as he sized up my stance. He leaped at me. His blade met mine with force enough to knock me to the ground, and he staggered past me. The sword in my hands seemed to quiver with eagerness as I lurched to my feet. The Maedun swung his sword again and somehow, my blade was there to meet it. Steel rang on tempered steel, then the Maedun stepped back and swept his sword in a vicious stroke for my legs. I thrust my blade down and across and caught the other squarely. My follow-through snap of the wrist ran my blade slithering upward along his until it caught against the cross guard. It jerked the Maedun off-balance and he stumbled. I lunged forward, the sword held balanced in both hands. The point of the blade thrust home in the Maedun's belly, just above his hipbone. His weight nearly pulled me down with him as he fell.

The breath rasped in my throat as I tugged to free the blade. As it came loose, the Maedun's body rolled down the hill. It finally came to rest, bent forward around a rock, and didn't move.

I scrambled up the hill, still panting, and stood for a moment to sheathe my sword. The others waited for me there. "This way," I gasped, and began to run.

Cullin was already at the alder copse when we came stumbling up. He was mounted on his stallion and held the reins of three other horses. Seeing one of the men carrying the girl, Cullin bent forward and held out his arms.

"Give the child to me," he said quickly. "Then mount up."

The girl's father handed her up to Cullin without protest. Cullin tossed him the reins of one of the horses, and he swung up into the saddle quickly.

"Will they follow us?" he asked.

"I don't know," Cullin replied, shifting the girl to a more secure position across his saddle and against his chest. "Perhaps not. It depends on how badly they want you."

"Not that badly, I hope," the second man muttered.

"In any event, it's not a good idea to wait around for them," Cullin said. "Let's go." He wheeled the stallion and set off toward the road.

We moved as quickly as we could. Running the horses in the dark was dangerous. We needed to put as much distance as possible between us and the Maedun, but none of us needed to break a neck if one of the horses stumbled.

The moon rose presently, and we made better time on the road. An hour later, we came to a small village. It was little more than a huddled cluster of rudely built stone cottages, but it boasted of an inn to accommodate travelers. Even then, it looked like nothing more than a rough sheepherder's bothy, but it was dry and warm inside. A good fire blazed cheerfully in the hearth, and the common room was cleaner and more comfortable than we expected.

The innkeeper's wife, a short, roundly built woman with cheeks as red as mountain ash berries, made concerned noises over the unconscious girl Cullin still carried, and led us immediately to a sleeping room in the back of the inn. There was only one bed in the room, but it was wide enough to hold several people. The innkeeper's wife made Cullin put the girl down on it, then bustled off to find hot water, clean cloths, and her bundle of herbs.

The girl's father sat on the edge of the bed and soothed the golden hair back from the girl's pale forehead. She was very young, not much more than thirteen or fourteen. Even unconscious and pallid as ashes, she was very pretty, her features delicately molded in her oval face. She looked fragile as porcelain.

Her father looked at Cullin. "I wish to thank you," he said quietly. "We tried to fight them when they caught us on the road. Rhegenn managed to wound two of them, but one of them hit Kerridwen on the head with the flat of his sword. She hasn't regained consciousness since."

The man called Rhegenn put his hand to the other's shoulder. "She'll be all right, Jorddyn," he said. He turned to us. "I'm Rhegenn ap Sendor. This is Jorddyn ap Tiernyn. We're emissaries from my lord Jorddyn's kinsman, Kyffen, Prince of Skai, in Celi."

Cullin's eyebrows rose fractionally, and a glint of interest sparked in his green eyes. "You're a long way from home," he said.

"Yes, we are," Rhegenn said. "We were on our way back from Madinrhir in Falinor when the Maedun caught us."

The innkeeper's wife came back into the room carrying a steaming basin of water and a pile of clean cloths. She shooed Jorddyn ap Tiernyn away and leaned over the girl. We watched her in silence as she worked. Finally, she stepped back, shaking her head slightly.

"What can you do for her?" Jorddyn asked.

"Not much, I'm afraid," the woman said quietly. "The child's taken a bad blow there. I fear her head's broke. I can't help."

Jorddyn sat beside his daughter again. "Have you no Healer in the village?" he asked the woman.

She shook her head. "None but me, and I've naught but my herbs, I fear, sir."

"A Healer?" I asked. A half-formed ghost of an idea glimmered in my mind. I took an involuntary step closer to the bed.

Jorddyn looked up at me. He was as blond as his daughter, his eyes a clear hazel brown, flecked with green near the pupil. "In my country, we have men and women who can Heal by touch," he said. "I've not seen anything like it here on the continent, though."

I looked down at the unconscious girl. She breathed in short, painful gasps through half-parted lips. The delicate skin beneath her closed eyes was darkened, almost bruised. Before I realized what I was doing, I had stepped forward and sat on the edge of the bed, my hands reaching out to cup her temples between them. I wasn't aware of Jorddyn moving quickly to give me room on the edge of the bed. I was completely focused on the dark smudges of the girl's eyes.

I had been able to do nothing to save Rossah. Perhaps I could make it up in some small way by helping this girl-child—if this gift, or talent, or whatever it was, would work with others as it worked with me. All I could do was try. I owed it to Rossah, and I owed it to me. Perhaps I owed it to this girl, too.

Carefully, hesitantly, I reached for that quiet place deep within myself. I don't remember what I was thinking as I pressed the palms of my hands against the unnaturally cool skin of the girl's head, but I do remember that her hair felt like finest silk under my fingers.

It happened in an unexpected rush. Suddenly, I was swirling deep in pain that wasn't mine. Images that weren't my own flashed through my head, too fast to comprehend any of them. Mountains, tall and snowcapped even in the heat of summer. Placid blue lakes. White, boiling rivers. Gentle clear brooks. The sea breaking against the sheer faces of cliffs, throwing salt spume high into the air. Faces of people I didn't know. Pictures of rooms I didn't recognize. Voices singing songs I had never heard. Jumbled, tangled images, all tumbled together without order, without sequence. And through it all, a sense of rightness, of belonging, of fittingness. Whatever this wild fusion was, it was something completely and utterly right.

Carefully, I pulled back slightly from the jumble of confused images and concentrated on the pain. I located its center and focused on it, fixing my attention on the pain, and only that. Slowly, a picture formed, showing me what the injury had to look like when healed. I pulled at the pain, drawing it away from the girl and into me. Slowly, gradually, I imposed my picture of the healed place on top of the injury. At first, I was afraid it would not work, that I would fail and the girl would die beneath my hands.

Behind me, I heard a man cry out as the girl began to thrash on the bed. Someone whimpered, but I don't know if it was I or the girl. Her eyes opened, pupils wide and staring, leaving only a thin ring of glorious golden hazel around them. Her blind gaze fixed on mine and the link between us strengthened and solidified.

It began to work. I *felt* the injured place on the back of her head draw together, the bruising and swelling begin to disappear. I thought I could see the wound lose its angry, distended appearance and take on the healthy glow of normal tissue.

The staring expression left the girl's eyes and they looked into mine calmly and serenely. A gentle tranquillity settled over her features as pink spread under her skin again. She closed her eyes. A deep sigh raised the thin chest before her breathing settled into the quiet rhythm of profound and natural slumber.

I could do no more. I hoped it would be enough. I staggered back from the bed, stumbled to my knees.

"She'll be all right, I think," I gasped, my own head throbbing with what might have been the memory of her pain, or my own from simple reaction to the exertion of Healing. Cullin caught me as I began to slip to the floor. I was very near unconsciousness myself as he picked me up as easily as he might pick up a child of five.

From a long distance away, I heard Rhegenn's voice say, "A Healer, but untrained . . ."

Then Jorddyn said, "You must be proud of your son."

"Yes," Cullin replied. "I am."

As he carried me from the room, the warm, soft darkness swept down to enfold me. Fuzzily, I mumbled, "Son? No, they're confused because we both have red hair . . ."

"*Vhair ne, ti'rhonai*," Cullin said, his voice fading into the dark pressing closer about me.

I think I heard myself say, "*L'on sahir, ti'vati*," before the world winked out on me.

5

I awoke in the wide bed where the girl had lain. I was alone. There was no sign of the girl, nor of Jorddyn and Rhegenn. Or of Cullin, either. I had no idea how long I'd been sleeping, but the day outside the narrow window was bright and clear. No trace of a headache fogged my mind as I sat up, and nothing remained of the weariness and exhaustion. Obviously, I had slept for a long time.

The innkeeper's wife was in the common room, supervising a small boy who turned a spit by the hearth. The smell of roasting meat filled the air, and my mouth watered. The woman looked up, saw me, and smiled.

"Ah, awake, are ye?" she said. "There's bread and cheese to break your fast, and nice fresh apples. Picked 'em myself this morning." She led me to a table and fussed over me while I ate.

"Where is everybody?" I asked between bites as I wolfed down the bread and cheese. I was ravenously hungry, and the bread was still warm from the oven, and the cheese golden yellow and well aged.

"The girl and her father left with the other man two days ago," the woman replied.

I looked up at her. "Two days? I slept for two days?"

"Closer to three," she replied.

"And the others left already?"

She nodded. "Aye. In the morning, right after they awoke. Your friend was still asleep, too. Two days ago. Ye've been sleeping a long time, laddie. Ye must have been nigh exhausted."

"I suppose I was," I said. "I've never done that before. Healed someone, I mean. I didn't realize I could do it."

"Well, the child was still sleeping, too, when they took her with them. For the coast, her father said. They had to meet a ship."

I finished the last of the bread and cheese, then picked up an apple and bit into it. The taste of the juice, tart and sweet, filled my mouth like a burst of sunshine. "Where's Cullin? My friend? He didn't leave, too, did he?"

She laughed. "Leave you here by yourself?" she asked. "He's not likely to do that, is he?"

"I don't know," I said. "Where is he?"

She made a motion with her head toward the door. "Out there, behind the stable. He left word for you to join him when you were able."

Picking up a second apple, I thanked her and went outside. I found Cullin right where the innkeeper's wife said he would be, behind the stable on an open patch of short grass, practicing with his sword. He had stripped off his plaid and his shirt. His bare chest gleamed with the sweat of exertion, but his face was calm and relaxed, showing no sign at all of the effort his body put forth. He stepped lightly on the balls of his feet, lithe and flexible as a dancer. He moved with sinuous grace through the last form of the sequence, then spun to face me.

"Pick that up," he said, pointing to the sword I had taken from the bounty hunter. It lay atop Cullin's neatly folded shirt and plaid at the edge of the small lawn. "You say you're untrained. We're about to change that."

I finished the last of my apple and went to pick up the sword. The hilt fitted my hand easily and naturally, the balance of the blade felt perfect as I hefted it. Before I could turn, I heard Cullin shout, "Guard yourself!"

I whirled around to see him coming at me, his sword describing a glittering and deadly arc through the air as it swung toward my head. Without thinking, acting on pure instinct alone, I flung up my arm, met the slashing blade with my own. My weight balanced on the balls of my feet, I bent and swung my blade down as he stepped back and swept his sword backhand in a wicked slice aimed at my legs. Somehow, my sword was there, and his slithered harmlessly off the blade I thrust down to catch it. Three more times, Cullin attacked and three times I parried successfully. Finally, he lowered his sword and stood there, watching me with that disturbing mixture of appraisal and speculation in his eyes.

"Enough," he said quietly

I lowered my sword, suddenly angry and confused. I was out of breath and sweating freely in the mild autumn air. "You deliberately tried to kill me," I cried. I had trusted him. Trusted him, damn him, and he attacked me as if I were an enemy. I should have known better. I should have known that friendship and trust were not for the likes of an ex-slave who could not even name his own parents.

A hint of a smile twitched at the corner of the wide mouth. "Aye," he admitted. "So I did at that. Now it's your turn to try to kill me."

I watched him closely for a moment, wondering how he possibly expected me to do any damage to him. But I was angry, and the anger made me reckless. It almost felt as if the sword itself initiated the movement as I raised it again. I sprang forward, taut with tension and purpose, moving automatically in a sequence as familiar and as practiced as walking. Cullin leaped nimbly back. His sword came up to parry the vicious swing I aimed at his chest. I spun and cut at his legs, and, as he swept his sword down to deflect mine, reversed the swing to thrust for his shoulder. In amazement, I saw sweat bead on his forehead. We danced around that small patch of short grass for a long time, thrust and parry, sweep and repulse. He adroitly eluded every attack I launched at him, but I avoided his proficiently enough. Finally, he merely stepped back, leaned away from one of my swings, and lowered his sword.

"Enough," he said again.

It took me a moment to realize he was no longer fighting. I caught myself in mid-lunge at him and stumbled, then stood panting and staring at him for a moment. My shirt was soaked with sweat, the waistband of my breeks sodden. Chest heaving from the exertion, I flung the sword down angrily. "Why?" I demanded. "Why were you trying to kill me?"

"Pick up the sword, Kian," he said quietly. "Never insult a good blade like that. He deserves better treatment."

I stood staring sullenly at him for a moment without moving.

"Pick it up," he said again, an edge of steel in his voice.

I bent to snatch up the fallen sword, wiping the edge against my breeks to clean off a few shreds of grass. "You tried to kill me," I said again.

"Are you dead?" he asked mildly.

"Of course not," I said hotly. "But certainly through no fault of yours."

He retrieved his scabbard from the grass by his plaid, then saluted me with the sword before he rammed it home into the scabbard. "Kian, you told me you were untrained."

"I am."

He raised an eyebrow. "Then pray explain how an untrained boy could parry each thrust made by an expert swordsman. And how could that same untrained boy make me work like a demon to fend him off?"

I stared, first at him, then at the sword in my hands. Echoes of a dream drifted through my mind, but I remembered no shape or substance. Only fragments, like images seen through smoke.

"I don't know," I said at last.

Cullin bent lithely to pick up his shirt and plaid. He slipped into the shirt and spent a moment carefully fastening the laces at wrists and throat. Finally, he looked at me and said, "I think I know."

I looked at him blankly.

"Come wi' me, Kian," he said quietly. "We're due a talk." He walked across the yard and sat on the low stone wall that separated the stable yard from the orchard. He motioned me to sit beside him. "You've been asking a lot of questions since we left Falinor. I suppose it's time I answered as many as I can."

I hesitated, then went to join him. Apprehension settled in a hard lump in my belly as I hoisted myself up onto the wall beside him. I sat there, my fists twisted into a knot on my knees. Unable to speak, held frozen by emotions I dared not even try to identify, I waited for him to begin. He sat quietly, collecting his thoughts, his gaze fixed on a starling teetering precariously on a branch of the nearest apple tree.

"You asked why I bothered to bring you along with me," he said.

I nodded dully. "Aye," I said. "It seemed a lot of trouble."

"Well, it might seem so at first," he agreed. "But it isna so much trouble when you realize you're a Tyr, a clansman true-born for all your eyes are brown and not green or gray."

"But I—"

He held up a hand to stop me. "Hear me out," he said. "Twice I've spoken to you in Tyran, and twice ye've answered me in kind. Part of you remembers. And then there's the sword work today. Every Tyran clansman by the time he's seven has spent three, sometimes four, years with a swordmaster." The corners of his mouth curled up briefly. "You've just proved that, even if your head forgot how to handle a sword, your body certainly didn't."

Again, fragments of a half-remembered dream swirled through my head, and were gone before I could make sense of them. The slight breeze began to dry the shirt on my back, and I shivered with the chill of it. I clenched my teeth against the cold and stared at the starling in the apple tree. It cocked an impudent eye at me, then casually flew to another branch deeper in the tree.

"Tell me something," he said quietly. "How do you feel the name Kian fits you?"

It was an odd question and I had to think about it for a moment. "I—I don't know," I said at last.

"You answered to it well from the start."

I bit my lip, frowning. "Well, I like the name better than Mouse."

He laughed. "Aye, I can see how you might."

"Still," I said, "I don't see why I'm worth all the trouble—"

"Kian, most of these last nine years, I've spent tracking down rumors of redheaded slave boys. I've been from Maedun and Saesnes in the north down to Laringras in the south, from the coast of Isgard to as far east as the Great Salt Sea. Nine years. I've seen a lot of redheaded slaves in that time. Some I bought and set free. I've told you how I feel about slavery. Most of them I left with their masters because they didna have the spark to thrive on their own. And most of them were either too young or too old to be the boy I was seeking anyway." He shifted his position and reached up casually to scratch the hollow above his collarbone. "In nine years, I'd just about lost hope that the boy I sought still lived. Nine years is a long time to go on hope alone."

"Who are you looking for?" My voice came out tight and strained through the knot of apprehension gripping my chest. A muscle jumped near the corner of my jaw.

He laughed. "Slaves with red hair," he said. "Like yours."

"Why were you looking?"

He smiled. A rueful gesture, not one of amusement. "I had to," he replied. "Then I heard a story about a redheaded slave boy on a landholding in Falinor near the mouth of the Glaecyn River."

"Mendor's Landholding," I said.

"Aye, so it would seem," he said. "I almost decided to let it go. I've a merchant train waiting for me in Honandun, and I've not a lot of time. But I couldna afford to take the chance that this time, it might be the right boy. That this time, my search would be successful. That's why I was there the night you escaped. I followed the Keepmaster and the bounty hunter to that dreadful inn."

I couldn't look at him. Instead, I studied the whitened knuckles of my fists. "Was it?" I whispered. "Successful, I mean?"

He shrugged. "I think so," he said at last. "I wasna sure when I first saw you, but after today, after watching you use that sword . . . Aye, I'm fairly certain it was successful."

"Cullin . . ."

He looked down at me.

"Is Kian really my name?"

Again, he said, "I think so."

"Jorddyn thought you were my father," I said. I glanced up at him. Even in the strong sunlight, he didn't appear to be much over thirty. Far too young to be father to someone my age. I had not even realized the hope had sprouted until I felt it wilt in me. "Are you?"

Amusement gleamed in his eyes but didn't touch his
mouth. "No, I'm not your father," he said quietly.

"I thought not," I said. I couldn't tell if I was bitterly disappointed or vastly relieved. I had never belonged with anyone,
and wasn't sure if I wanted to. I didn't know how to belong
with anyone, to be part of a family.

"Jorddyn was wrong," Cullin said. He shook his head and
the sun glinted in the copper red of his hair. "I'm not your
father, but I truly believe now I'm your uncle."

The colors around me suddenly seemed preternaturally bright
and glaring—the green of the grass, the blue and green of
Cullin's plaid lying neatly folded out not far from my feet, the
swiftly browning white flesh, still rimmed with red, of the
apple core I had dropped on the other side of the patch of
grass. For a long moment, I forgot to breathe. My heart
seemed to be making a creditable effort to leap right out of my
chest. When I finally found my voice, it sounded rusty and
creaky.

"You think you're my uncle," I repeated. "Does that mean
you're not certain?"

He sighed, then smiled. "I'm certain," he replied. "After
that demonstration with the sword, I'm more than certain.
Besides, you favor your father somewhat, and your eyes are
the same color as your mother's were."

"My mother's . . ." I said faintly.

He looked at me sideways. "Ye look a little like I walloped
you over the ear with the flat of my sword," he said. That
earned him a grimace of exasperation, and he grinned. "Aye,
well, I suppose it's a lot to be taking in at once," he conceded.

"Just a little," I agreed.

Cullin sat a little straighter. "You were born in the
Clanhold of Clan Broche Rhuidh in the western highlands of
Tyra," he said quietly. "Within sight of the sea. Your father
was my older brother Leydon. Your mother was his wife
Twyla. She wasna a Tyr. She never spoke of her home, only
that she had run from something or someone and Leydon had

rescued her. There was never a doubt but that she was well-born. I always thought she might have been Saesnesi with perhaps a little Maedun blood—her dark eyes, ye ken."

I asked the first question to pop into my head, inconsequential as it was. "Was she pretty?"

He smiled. "Pretty?" He tilted his head to one side as he thought for a moment. "That's odd. I don't know. She was kind and she was gentle and she had a beautiful smile. But pretty? I don't know. There was no mistaking it was a love match with her and Leydon. You just had to look at the pair of them to know it. Our father was upset about the marriage for a while. My eldest brother Rhodri had married the daughter of a neighboring laird, and our father had picked out the daughter of another for Leydon. He was annoyed to see the chance of an alliance dwindle."

"What happened?"

Cullin chuckled. "Ah, well. He got over being annoyed. He married me to the laird's youngest daughter."

I looked up at him, startled. "You?"

"Aye, lad. Me." He shrugged eloquently. "We don't get along all that well. Not that it matters. I spend most of my time away from the Clanhold anyway. Gwynna's a good woman, and she's borne me two fine daughters." He smiled, and his pride in his daughters lit his eyes like a beacon as he spoke. "But Gwynna's no a comforting woman to be around for long, ye ken. Ye might say we agreed to disagree."

I nodded. "I see," I said, but I didn't. I looked up at him again. "What of my father?"

"Leydon?" He closed his eyes for a moment, then opened them and stared off into the distance. "Leydon was my favorite brother. He was eight years older than I, and I idolized him. He was tall and strong, quick as a mountain cat. He always had time for me when I was a wee lad. He never minded me trailing along after him. You favor him a little, as I've said, but his eyes were gray as smoke, not brown. I was ten when he left the Clanhold. He said he wanted to see something of the world before he settled into the position of Master of the Sword for the clan. When he came home three years later, he had Twyla with him. You were born three months after they came home. Leydon called you Kian after our grandfather." He laughed with the memory. "You were a lusty wee bairn. Good lungs you had. Healthy and robust as a young stallion. I used to carry you around on my shoulders when you were two and three. You ran me ragged trying to keep up with you. By the time you were four, you showed a lot of promise with both a sword and a bow. Sturdy as an ash tree, with a good eye. Quick and graceful as your father with the sword."

I watched him, fascinated. It was a captivating story, but it was a story about people I didn't know, people I had no recollection of. Cullin reached out and put a hand to my head. His fingers found the ridge of scar tissue behind my ear.

"You have no idea at all who I'm talking about, do you, Kian?" he said gently.

I shook my head. "No," I said softly.

"Because of this, I think," he said, and traced the scar with his blunt finger. "Do you know how you got it?"

Again, I shook my head.

He frowned and his eyes clouded. "You were almost seven. Twyla had been very quiet for more than a fortnight, then one day, about a season before your name day, she told Leydon they had to take you to her father. To tell him he had a grandson. She said something about how you had to be presented in the shrine, and she owed at least that much to her father. So she and Leydon started out for Honandun. I went with them, along with a half dozen guards." His voice trailed off, and an expression of pain turned down the corners of his mouth.

"What happened?" I asked.

"We were attacked as we came out of the mountains," he said quietly. "Bandits. They came so quickly, we hadna much chance to defend ourselves. It was almost dark, and we were just beginning to set up camp. I remember seeing one of them knock you down, then something bashed me in the head."

His eyes were curiously glazed and blank as he paused for a moment. He wasn't seeing me, nor was he seeing the orchard and the stable yard at the little inn. I merely waited in silence for him to continue.

Finally, he shook himself like a dog shedding water. He glanced down at me. "When I woke up, the bandits were gone, and so were you. Almost everyone else was dead." His fists clenched in his lap and he grimaced. "I found your mother. She was dead. I wept for her, Kian. It hadna been an easy death for her."

I remembered Rossah and shuddered, grateful he gave no details. I knew well enough what happened to a woman used by men little better than beasts.

"And my father?" I asked quietly. "Your brother?"

"I found Leydon still alive, but dying. Ah, Kian, he had taken so many wounds . . . But he sold his life dearly, for all that. He took five or six bandits with him." Cullin shook his head. "He told me he saw them take you away, and he made me swear I'd find you and either take you back to the Clanhold, or see you home."

"See me home?" I repeated, unfamiliar with the expression. From the way he used it, it meant something different from what the words suggested.

"A clan thing," he said softly. "I promised him. And when he died shortly after that, I saw him home, too."

I sat quietly for a moment, trying to assimilate all he had said. It was too much. It made my head whirl. I reached up unconsciously and touched the scar hidden by my hair. "I don't remember at all," I whispered.

"Aye, well," he said. "I've heard of a blow to the head doing that. Sometimes memory comes back, sometimes it doesn't. It may be that you sealed it off when you discovered the way of Healing." He looked at me, speculation and consideration sharp in his eyes. "Twyla had it, too, ye ken. The Healing. That's where you got it from, along with the eyes. And she could sense magic, too."

I took a deep breath, held it for a long time, then finally let it out. "I—see," I said slowly. I looked up at him again. "And *ti'rhonai*. That means nephew?"

"Aye, and foster son, too. There's no much difference."

"I called you *ti'vati* once, I remember. Uncle?"

He nodded.

"Or foster father."

Again, he nodded. He laughed. "You might say I inherited you," he said. "Rhodri's three sons of his own. I've two daughters, but no son. You were my responsibility from the time I swore to Leydon I'd bring you home."

Emotions I couldn't identify jumbled together into one huge, tangled knot in my belly. I'd been no one's responsibility but my own for as long as I could remember. Suddenly finding myself with not only an uncle, but aunts, cousins, and a grandfather as well, left me feeling hollow and empty as a blown egg.

Cullin put his hand on my shoulder. "It's no so bad, Kian," he said with a smile. "It'll be at least three seasons before we go back to the Clanhold. Ye'll have time to get used to me by then, and I'll tell you all ye need to know about the others.

6

We left the small inn early the next morning and reached Honandun a sevenday before Samhain. The merchant train he had contracted to guard was ready the next morning, and we left before I had a chance to explore the first city I had ever seen. A fortnight past Midwinter saw us in Thrakia in Laringras, on the coast of the Great Salt Sea, where Cullin introduced me to some of the more bewitching delights a city offered. I subsequently discovered what wine sickness could do to a man's will to live the morning after.

There was another merchant train, this one carrying silks, spices, and exotic fragrances, eager to contract for Cullin's services for the trip back to Honandun. We arrived a fortnight after Vernal Equinox and Cullin announced we were leaving for Tyra the next morning.

It was still a fortnight before Beltane—the hills and mountains showed a faint bloom of soft green and the lochs reflected the gentle blue of the sky—when we left Isgard and entered Tyra.

Cullin was right. In the three seasons since I'd met him, I had grown used to him, although it still gave me an odd sensation somewhere under my breastbone when I thought too hard about the fact that he was my uncle.

During the long journey south, then back north, Cullin spent the evenings with me, practicing with the sword or bow. He was patient with me, but implacable about mistakes. He let me get away with nothing clumsy or poorly executed. I sweated freely, practicing sequences over and over until they met with his approval, which was never grudgingly withheld, but difficult to obtain. For three seasons, as we traveled, he told me about his home and his family, so when we finally left the lowlands and began winding our way through the passes and glens of Tyra, the land looked almost familiar to me.

Cullin pointed out towering crags to me as we rode, naming them, and I thought I should recognize them.

It was a rugged country, all rocky, snow-covered peaks, wide valleys, and narrow gorges. In the glens, we rode past small herds of black cattle with wicked, curving horns and flocks of small sheep whose fleece looked faintly blue. Tiny villages, some no more than five or six stone-built houses, nestled into the flanks of the valleys, but none of them too small or too poor to offer a traveler welcome with a meal and a pallet by the hearth for the night. The men, like Cullin, wore kilts and plaids, and the women wore gowns with a plaid of finer fabric draped over their shoulders. I saw a lot of different tartans as we rode, varying from predominantly red, through brown, yellow, black, and green. Eventually, the tartans the people wore began to show predominantly blues and greens, much like Cullin's tartan, and Cullin announced we were now on Broche Rhuidh land.

It was still nearly a sevenday before we reached Glenborden, where the Clanhold stood. I got my first view of it as we topped a small rise in the glen and stood looking down the vast sweep of the broad, green valley. I reined the sorrel to a sudden stop and simply sat there and stared, my mind gone suddenly blank.

I had been expecting a manor house similar to Mendor's Landholding in Falinor, I suppose, large and solid but not overly imposing. The Clanhold of Broche Rhuidh was large and solid, but there the resemblance to Mendor's house stopped. Broche Rhuidh was stone-built, rising gracefully from the top of a small shoulder of the mountain. Behind it, the sheer face of the granite crag towered high enough to scrape the belly of the clear sky. The living rock of the cliff itself formed the back wall of the Clanhold. Crenellated towers stood at each corner behind battlements fashioned of the same rock, but the massive gates stood flung wide in the warm late morning sunshine. Behind the walls, the Clanhold itself stood huge and graceful, solidly rooted in the mountain.

I looked at Cullin, aware that my mouth hung open. "You didn't tell me Broche Rhuidh was a palace," I said faintly.

Cullin looked at the Clanhold judiciously, then at me. "Aye, well, I suppose it's big enough," he said. "And it's comfortable. Cold in winter, though." He urged the stallion forward, leaving me still gaping on the brow of the hill.

I kicked the sorrel into a canter to catch up. "Cullin?"

He turned, grinning at me over his shoulder.

"Cullin, is your father a king?" I pulled the sorrel up even with the bay stallion and reached out to touch Cullin's arm.

Cullin laughed. "A king?" he repeated. "Hellas, no. But I must have mentioned he was Clan Laird."

"Aye, you did," I said, looking at the awe-inspiring structure ahead of us. "But you didn't tell me what it meant."

He grinned. "In Isgard, the title would be prince, I think," he said. "There are no kings in Tyra."

"A prince," I repeated faintly. "That makes me—"

"A young lord," he said matter-of-factly. "Merely the son of a younger son. If we hurry, we'll be in time for the noon meal."

I followed him, still slightly stunned, remembering those fantasies of my childhood. In my imagination, the father who came to rescue me was always nobly born, sometimes even a prince. But those were daydreams. At least, I thought they were mere daydreams. "A young lord," I muttered to myself. "Hellas-birthing. A young lord . . . "

They came out to the courtyard to meet us as we rode in. I recognized them from Cullin's descriptions as they stood on the wide, stone steps leading up to the broad, carved doors. The tall, straight man with red hair fading to gray was Medroch, Cullin's father, the Clan Laird. Beside him stood another man, his hair the color of polished oak. Cullin's brother Rhodri was not quite as tall as their father, but he had a good expanse of shoulder narrowing to lean, muscular hips. The woman at his side, slightly plump and smiling, was Rhodri's wife Linnet. Three boys, ranging in age from twelve to sixteen, stood on the step behind her—Rhodri's sons, Brychan, Landen, and Tavis.

Slightly apart from them was another woman, tall, slender, and beautiful, her hair the gold of a wheat field in the autumn sun. She held a young girl of about three by the hand, her other hand on the shoulder of another girl of about six, who stood in front of her. She had to be Cullin's wife Gwynna. The children were Elin and Wynn. Both the girls had hair like freshly minted copper coins, and stood gravely regarding their father as he dismounted in the courtyard, the youngest with a finger in her mouth.

Medroch stepped forward to meet us as we mounted the steps. He held out his hands, and Cullin put both of his into them, bowing slightly from the waist.

"Well come home, Cullin," Medroch said, his voice deep and mellow. His eyes, gray as smoke, clear as water, turned to me. "Leydon's son?" he asked.

"Aye," Cullin said. "I've brought him home."

The sharp, gray gaze searched me up and down in frank appraisal. "Ye favor your father," he told me. "But you've your mother's eyes. Be welcome here, Kian dav Leydon. This is your home." He held out his hands to me.

Following Cullin's example, I placed my hands in his and bowed. "Thank you," I said, and my voice sounded rusty and hoarse.

Cullin greeted his brother warmly, placed a kiss on Linnet's upturned cheek, then presented me to them. In a daze, I acknowledged the introductions and stood in a stupor as Linnet kissed me and bade me welcome. When I turned again to Cullin, I found him standing with his arms around Gwynna, kissing her with a fervency and enthusiasm that belied his wry phrase, "agreeing to disagree." He finally stepped away from her, bent to scoop up both children into his arms, and brought them over to present them to me. They were shy, but both gave me smiles.

"There's a meal waiting," Linnet said at last. "Cullin, take Kian to the bathhouse and both of you get cleaned up. We'll serve the meal when you're finished."

Cullin and Gwynna retired to their suite for three days, appearing only occasionally for meals. Again, it didn't quite fit with Cullin's ironic description of their marriage. When I commented on their absence the first evening Cullin and Gwynna failed to appear for dinner, Rhodri threw some light on it for me.

"It's a strange relationship, ye ken," he said, smiling. "For the first while, they canna keep their hands off each other. Ye couldna get a sheet of parchment between them." He laughed. "You wait. By the end of the fortnight, they'll still be standing close, but it'll be nose-to-nose and toe-to-toe, arguing about everything from the way Cullin trims his beard to the way Gwynna mends the girls' smocks. They won't admit it, but they love each other with a grand passion. They just canna live with the other for long."

I made a noncommittal reply and returned to my meal. But I smiled.

Sympathetically aware of my sense of strangeness, everybody left me alone for the next few days, letting me adjust at my own speed. I wandered the Clanhold, exploring the rooms and corridors, studying the rows of portraits hanging in the Great Hall. I paused before one of them, a painting of a young man, red-headed, gray-eyed, with a smile very much like Cullin's, but clean-shaven. He wore a bonnet with a sprig of rowan tucked behind the clan badge, the plaid secured at his shoulder by an ornate brooch fashioned to look like a leaping stag with a large, yellow stone glittering between its great rack of antlers.

"My son, Leydon," Medroch said at my shoulder, startling me. "Your father. That was done just before he left the Clanhold, about three years before you were born."

"Is there one of my mother?" I asked, still looking at the portrait. Even though I could see the likeness to myself in him, Leydon dav Medroch was a stranger. I could not remember him at all.

"We have no portrait of Twyla," Medroch said quietly. "She never wanted one done."

I nodded, and he left me to continue my exploring.

The language came back first. I don't know when it was I suddenly realized that I not only understood everything being said around me, but I was as fluent with Tyran as they. Cullin had used the language with me during our journey south, but I had stumbled and stuttered when I tried to speak it. Here at the Clanhold, it came naturally and easily, and I pondered that development in silence.

Then one day about a sevenday after we arrived, I wandered out of the house and found my way to a high cliff overlooking the sea. On some instinct, I followed a narrow little track until I came to an enclave tucked into a tumble of rocks. A thicket of silverleaf maple, salt-bitten and twisted, clung tenaciously to the stony soil among the rocks. I found a moss-covered stone in the sun and sat, watching the breakers crash against the cliff wall on the opposite side of the small bay, sending spume purling high into the air.

I looked up as a shadow fell across me. Cullin stood there, dressed only in kilt and shirt. "I used to come here and watch the sea," I said quietly. "And I gathered eggs on that wall over there."

"Aye," he said. "Ye did. This was one of your favorite places as a child. Is it coming back then, Kian?"

"Some things," I said. "Only a little."

"Well, it might never all come back to ye," he said. "But ye ken that you're home."

"I'm home here," I said. "In this spot. But not in the house yet."

"Ye can stay here, if ye wish," he said. "Or ye can come wi' me when I leave again."

I looked up at him. "I'll come wi' you," I said. "I canna feel I belong here. It's too grand for the likes of me."

He laughed. "Aye," he agreed. "I've always felt that way myself." He stood for a moment, watching the seabirds circle endlessly over the water, searching for fish. Then: "I'd be pleased to have you with me, Kian," he said quietly. "I've grown fond of ye these last seasons."

The feeling of relief that swept through me caught me by surprise. Pleased by his words, I grinned up at him. "Was I worth the five silver?" I asked.

He considered that. "Aye," he said gravely. "I expect so." He touched one of the silver-chased hilts at his belt and smiled. "In any case, the daggers certainly were."

A fortnight later, we left Broche Rhuidh for Honandun and another merchant train. That began a pattern we were to follow for the next seven years—traversing back and forth across the continent with merchant trains, and once every year or so going back to Broche Rhuidh to see Cullin's family. We seldom stayed more than a season at the longest, and most visits were only a few days longer than a fortnight. It was a rhythm of life that suited us both. Cullin's small band of guards was much in demand, and we never had to seek contracts actively. The merchants came to us.

Cullin had an easy manner with both the guards and the merchants. He possessed the ability to fit himself deftly into the company of nobles and soldiers, merchants and farmers. When the occasion demanded, he could outlord the haughtiest of noblemen and the next minute, be down on the floor of a tavern, drinking ale and throwing dice with a troop of soldiers. He had the happy faculty of blending seamlessly into his surroundings. He spoke at least six languages, not counting Tyran. When he undertook to teach me, I discovered I, too, had a flair for languages, and he informed me that was something else I had inherited through my father from my grandfather.

He also undertook to teach me manners. All I remembered was living as a slave. Under Cullin's tutelage, taking my cues from him, I learned how to comport myself in any company and found out I also had a good flair for acting.

Cullin had been right about my growing. Over the next seven years, I stretched up to within a thumblength of his height, but fell short of his weight by nearly two stone. The active life spent mostly outdoors and the work with the sword gave me a man's shape to match my height. In a kilt, shirt, and plaid, and a golden topaz on a fine chain in my left ear by the braid in my hair, I looked as much the Tyran clansman as Cullin. We made a good pair. When I was eighteen, Cullin formally adopted me and we slipped into the relationship of foster father and foster son. It was comfortable for both of us.

They were busy years, and happy ones for me. I was content for the pattern to continue.

7

The road, little more than a narrow track, wound through the towering cedars and firs at the base of the cliffs. It followed the course of the river through the spur of mountains thrusting north from Laringras to curve around the east border of Falinor and Isgard. Overhead, thick gray clouds obscured the tops of the peaks in every direction, and filled the chilly air with a fine, wet mist that was trying to make up its mind to become drizzle.

Southern mountains in early spring, I thought in disgust as I rode nearly a furlong ahead of the straggling merchant train. I hated southern mountains in early spring. I hated drizzle and mist. I hated rain forests. And I especially hated mountains in early spring when they stood shoulder deep in drizzly mist and choked by rain forest. Too cursed many places for bandits to lie in ambush, waiting for an unwary merchant train. Too much chance we might have to earn every silver the merchants paid us for the whole trip in the half season it took just to get through these passes.

It was less than a sevenday to Vernal Equinox, the beginning of early spring. We had spent the season between Midwinter and Imbolc traversing the Ghadi Desert. Deserts are tricky, but they're mostly dry and hot, and the air doesn't threaten to choke a man with fog and drizzle, or trickle cold into him to turn blood and bone to ice. A fortnight past Imbolc saw us into the dry eastern slopes of the mountains. Now, we were over the Divide and into the wet rain forest of the western slopes, and coming to the last stage of the journey. With any luck, we would be in Honandun a few days after Equinox.

If we don't drown first, I thought morosely. *Hellas.* I had forgotten how wet spring could be here.

It was my turn to ride front guard and I was feeling sorry for myself as I tried to huddle deeper into my plaid to keep the damp chill from seeping right down into my bones. "This is no place for man or beast," I complained bitterly to Rhuidh, who merely flicked his ears once, then ignored me.

A quick flash of movement among the giant cedars caught my eye. Just a glimpse of something the wrong shape. No leaf shivering under the glancing blow of a drop of moisture, nor animal dodging behind a massive trunk.

Still hunched within my plaid, I scanned the area around us carefully. "You being the beast, and me being the man," I said to Rhuidh, "you'd think together we'd have a lot more sense than this. Horse sense is a myth, sure as Hellas." Again, the horse stolidly ignored the remark.

There. Another flash of movement. This time, I was certain it was a man-shape hiding in the trees. As unobtrusively as possible, I made sure the sword on my back was loose and ready. If I had spotted two bandits, that meant there had to be eight or ten more I couldn't see.

At least a dozen of them. Eight of us, not counting the merchants, of course, who were next to useless in a fight anyway. Not exactly fair odds. Cullin was probably worth half a dozen bandits all by himself, and I was almost his equal after nearly eight years of training. In those eight years, we had never lost so much as one pack animal to bandits in these passes. But I wasn't about to let myself get complacent about it. There was always a first time, and carelessness was not good for business.

I slowed Rhuidh and glanced back over my shoulder like a man expecting his relief to come trotting up the track behind him. Sure enough, I saw Cullin approaching. Negligently, he lifted a hand to scratch his nose, his big hand hiding the anticipatory grin he wore. He had seen the bandits. I rubbed my ear to tell him I had seen them, too. He merely grinned again and motioned me back toward the main body of the merchant train.

The bandits sprang their trap two furlongs farther along the track, where the pass narrowed as the river plunged through a cataract between the high walls. Even as I spurred Rhuidh to meet the first rush of the attack, I saw I had guessed wrong. There were more than a dozen of them. Perhaps fifteen.

The merchants were already gathering the pack animals into a tight, easily defensible bunch as my raised sword clashed against the swinging blade of one of the bandits. I kneed Rhuidh sideways, and his shoulder slammed into the flank of the bandit's horse, knocking him off-balance. The bandit grabbed for his saddle horn, and I relieved him of his head, then whirled to meet the next bandit. Out of the corner of my eye, I saw Cullin wheel his stallion, his blade flashing about his head, to take on two bandits at once.

I ducked as the bandit, a man with the dark hair and eyes of a Maedun, swung his sword. His lips drew back over his teeth in a snarl and he twisted in the saddle to avoid my counterthrust, then ducked and slashed his sword at my belly. I barely got out of the way in time by hauling Rhuidh around and sliding sideways in the saddle. I turned back to the bandit to find his blade slicing toward my neck. I ducked and managed to get my sword up to parry his.

Then a strange thing happened. His eyes widened and his mouth fell open in shock. He yanked his horse back a step or two. I hesitated, surprised at his reaction, and saw he was staring at my sword. He muttered a word that sounded like "Celae," and began to wheel his horse away from me. He didn't get very far. An arrow from the bow of one of the archers caught him through the throat, and he pitched forward into the mud of the track.

The battle was over. When I looked around, I could see four or five bandits enthusiastically demonstrating how quickly their horses could take them away. Cullin stood near the huddled pack animals, wrapping a scarf around a wound on his left arm. He pulled the knot tight with his teeth as I dismounted beside him.

"Let me see it," I said, reaching for his arm.

He pulled it away and shook his head. "Just a scratch," he said. "It'll heal well by itself. Are you all right?"

"Aye, not even scratched," I said. I looked over my shoulder. There was no sign of the retreating bandits now. A few of them lay in the mud, groaning over their wounds. More lay still in death. We had given a good accounting of ourselves.

"They'll not be bothering us again, I think," Cullin said. "We'll have earned our bonus again this trip."

"Aye," I agreed. "And tomorrow, we'll be out of these accursed mountains."

"Not like Tyra, is it?" he asked.

I laughed, thinking of the heather-clad hills and mountains around the Clanhold of Broche Rhuidh, the Red Tower. "No verra much," I said. In this season, the glens would be touched with soft green and the water of the lochs would ripple quietly under the gentle blue of the sky. "Not much like Tyra at all."

Cullin laughed and turned away to gather in the guards and take stock. We had taken a few minor wounds, but had lost none of the men. We had not been so lucky the last time we were in these mountains. One of our men had taken a spear through the lungs, and even as I tried to Heal him, I felt the dark, spreading numbness of a mortal wound in him. The force of his life flow ebbed under my hands and evaporated like water on hot stones. Helplessly, I watched him slip away, unable to do anything for him but ease his pain as he died. It wasn't something I wanted to experience again.

Within half an hour, we had the merchant train moving again.

We were out of the mountains the next day, out into the gently rolling hills of Isgard. Six days later, we descended onto the wide coastal plain only a league or two from the outskirts of Honandun. We encountered no more trouble.

The merchants were quick to pay Cullin's fee and were generous with the bonuses. Cullin paid the men. Most of them had wives or sweethearts in the city, and scattered with their full purses. Left to ourselves, Cullin and I set off to find a tavern.

The Isgardian soldier came at me, sword clutched in both hands, teeth bared in a snarl, and murder in his eye. To begin with, the man was drunk. But off-duty Isgardian troopers, like any other soldier, often were. Still, he should have known better than to gibe a Tyran clansman about his kilts, and he certainly should have known better than to draw a dagger. Cullin took exception to the insult, and exploded into outraged indignation in the face of the weapon.

Originally, I'd had no intention of becoming embroiled in the fray. The day has not yet dawned when one Tyran clansman could not handle at least five Isgardian troopers in a tavern brawl. If Cullin had need of my assistance, he would call for it. So I had snatched my ale mug and the full flask out of danger, and hopped up to sit on the bar. I tucked my feet under me, sitting tailor-fashion, content to watch the entertainment.

Cullin dav Medroch was an impressive sight when annoyed. Grace and economy of motion in action, and worthy of admiration. I was enjoying myself immensely until I suddenly caught a whiff of a distinctive stench in the air, sharp and unmistakable as the scent of impending lightning and thunder before a storm. I straightened and glanced around, frowning.

Magic. I *hate* magic. It set the hair on my arms and the back of my neck prickling erect, a deep chill knotting in my belly.

Hackles rising like a wolf, I looked quickly for the source, and found a young Maedun hedge wizard, little more than a boy, unsure and hesitant, yet eager to prove himself. Young and untried he might be, but he was fully capable of weaving magic enough to put paid to Cullin's fighting ability. The boy hurriedly fashioned his spell even as I watched. Swearing, I carefully set down the mug and flask, and slid off the bar top with reluctant resignation. Cullin would doubtless be upset with me if I let a half-grown Maedun spell weaver deprive him of a good brawl. I picked up a convenient stool and broke it across the young hedge wizard's back. It discouraged his enthusiasm for joining in on the excitement. That was when the Isgardian trooper chose to try to decapitate me. So much for my resolve to let Cullin have the pleasure of redressing his own insults.

I ducked under the Isgardian's arm as his sword swung in a wide arc that surely would have removed my head had it landed. But swords are notoriously unhandy weapons for close fighting, and the trooper was off-balance and not seeing too clearly, being awash in sour ale.

"Kian! Your back!" Cullin's voice sounded clearly over the uproar in the tavern.

I grabbed the Isgardian's wrist as he stumbled by me and swung him around. As he lurched past, I caught him by the neck of his jerkin and the seat of his breeks, and tossed him into the Maedun mercenary who had launched himself at my back. The Isgardian met the Maedun in mid-leap, and both of them went sprawling to the hard-packed dirt floor in a tangle of arms and legs.

Kilts flying, Cullin leaped over the two spraddled bodies and sailed past me to bury his shoulder in the pit of the belly of another Isgardian soldier. The soldier made a strangled sound as all the air exploded out of his lungs, and he crashed back onto the only unsmashed table in the tavern. The table, like the others, did not weather the collision well. It collapsed under the combined weight of Cullin and the soldier. I winced and put a hand to my own belly in sympathy. I wouldn't want sixteen stone of joyously irate clansman barreling into me like that. It was likely extremely uncomfortable. Mayhaps even a trifle painful.

Cullin extracted himself from the resultant kindling, climbed to his feet, and meticulously straightened his kilt and plaid. Except for the tavern keeper and the barmaid, we appeared to be the only two people in the tavern still standing. The dismayed tavern keeper, huddled safe with the barmaid behind the bar, looked to be near apoplexy as he surveyed the ruin of his tavern.

I snapped the hair out of my eyes and grinned at Cullin. "You'd be getting old I expect, *ti'vati*," I said. "Five years ago, you could have handled twice as many all by yourself."

Affronted, Cullin assumed a pained expression. He drew himself up to the full of his considerable height. Even disheveled and disarrayed as he was, Cullin dav Medroch was impressive. Any Tyran clansman looks imposing in kilts, full-sleeved shirt, and knee-length soft boots, his plaid pinned at his right shoulder by a clan badge, but Cullin looked fiercer than most. His bright red hair falling loose to his shoulders except for the single braid at his left temple, the light of battle still illuminating his face, he looked magnificent. The emerald dangling from his left ear glittered the same color as his eyes in the dim, smoky light. He breathed only a little deeper than usual.

"Were I not drunk," he said with great dignity, "I should not have needed any intervention on my behalf from a mere lad like yourself."

"Mere lad," I said in disgust. I was nearly as big as he. Certainly no mere lad.

"It was, after all, my kilt he scoffed at," he said. "It was my fight."

"Aye. It was. Until that hatchling wizard decided to addle what wits you still retain."

He considered that information gravely, then dismissed it. He shrugged. "He failed."

"Only because he found my argument persuasive."

"Aye. Or mayhaps powerfully distractive."

"Aye. Mayhaps." I straightened my own kilt and settled the plaid aright on my shoulder, then grinned at him. I stooped to pluck an unbroken ale mug from the debris, filled it from the rescued flask, and handed it to him. "What do you intend to do about this mess?"

He nudged a limp Isgardian with the toe of his boot. The man made a snoring sound, and Cullin grinned. "They will no doubt in good time be collected by someone whose appointed station in life is to take care of such disagreeable tasks," he said. "Leave them. They look comfortable enough, do they no?" He drained the mug and let it fall to the floor.

"Oy!" the tavern keeper cried as we turned to leave. "What about this damage to me place? It'll cost me twenty silver to fix it."

Cullin crossed the room to lean negligently on the bar. He grinned and, in the face of that vast display of white teeth, the tavern keeper shrank back among the casks of ale and wine stacked behind the bar.

"Little man," Cullin said softly, "for twenty silver, I could buy this palatial establishment *and*, no doubt, your toothsome daughter there." He jerked his chin at the barmaid. The girl took a startled step backward, turning first white at the threat, then pink at the compliment.

Not to be diverted when the subject was chiming silver, the tavern keeper bared his own teeth in an ingratiating grin. "Sir, your pardon I beg of you. But this poor tavern be all I have to support a wife and eight squalling young'uns."

I bent and relieved two of the inert bodies of their slender purses, and tossed them to Cullin. He plucked them out of the air with one big hand, hardly bothering to look, and spilled their contents on the scarred and stained planking of the bar. He frowned at them, stirring them thoughtfully with a blunt forefinger, then took two silver from his own purse and added them to the pile of coppers and silvers.

"That should be enough," he said. "I'm loath to think I be the cause of a man's brats crying hungry."

The tavern keeper's hands were but a blur of motion as he scooped the coins from the bar and stashed them safely. "I thank ye, kind sir," he said with another obsequious smile. His teeth were bad and showed black gaps. "Be sure I'll tell of the generosity of Tyran clansmen."

"Ye'll no see verra many of us if ye dinna stop selling that horrid sour ale," Cullin said. He pushed himself away from the bar and grinned at me. "A decent inn, I think, Kian," he said. "With good food and excellent wine. What say you to that?"

"I'd be agreeable," I said.

He flung his arm about my neck and laughed as we stepped over the clutter of broken tables, shattered stools, and sprawling bodies to the door. "And a woman or two," he said. "A couple of soft, tender, sweet-smelling women." He laughed again. "That'll do for me, then. Ye'll have to find your own."

We found a good inn. It was expensive, as were all good inns in any seaport, and Honandun was no exception. But we were heavy with silver paid by the merchants for delivering the goods train safely to the city. It had been a long trip from Volda, and a hectic one. I bore a new scar on my ribs from a bandit's arrow, and Cullin's hardened leather left wrist guard was ruined by a lucky knife thrust. The bonus in gold had been well and truly earned this trip.

We had just finished a well-prepared meal with a fine Borlani wine when I heard Cullin make an appreciative soft whistling sound. I turned toward the door in time to see a woman enter the common room. The man who accompanied her was as nondescript as the woman was memorable.

Oddly enough, I had seen her before. Only that morning, as we escorted the goods train to the waiting ship. Tall and richly dressed, she had been disembarking from a newly arrived ship as Cullin and I rode past behind the string of pack animals. What struck me about the woman was not her beauty, for beautiful she was not. Her features, even though regular and well-defined, were far too strong for beauty. Handsome, mayhaps. Certainly striking. She carried herself with an ease and a competence more common in a man than a woman. She was tall for a woman, as graceful and purposeful when she moved as the wing of a seagull.

As I guided my horse through the throng, she looked up and our eyes met. A shock of startled recognition quivered through me. Those eyes were the same color as my own, a deep, golden brown, as uncommon in these parts as blue pearls. But her hair was a rich, dark honey gold with no trace of the rust red of mine in it. She wore it braided and drawn severely back from the bold planes of her face, caught up in a netting of woven gold thread.

She did not smile, nor did she drop her gaze like a modest Isgardian woman would. Neither did she look away. Instead, her gaze held mine for a long moment. I felt a sense of challenge in her. I was the one who finally broke the contact. When I looked back moments later, she had vanished into the crowd.

Cullin's chuckle brought me out of my reverie with a start. I realized I was still staring at the woman, who had been escorted to a table by her companion. She looked up, caught me watching her. Her expression didn't change as she looked away without haste, obviously dismissing me as a negligible annoyance.

"Not that one, lad," Cullin said with quiet amusement. "That one's too like my lovely wife. You'd abrade yourself on her inflexible will if you tried holding that one on your lap."

Cullin had left Gwynna at the Clanhold six seasons ago with a passionate embrace, but more than happy enough to leave her to go on about his own affairs. Gwynna, he often remarked, had the face and body of a goddess, and the disposition of a mountain cat. "A pity," he said. "But she throws beautiful fillies . . . "

He raised his hand casually. One of the serving girls darted over to refill his cup with the pale, crisp wine. Her pert and saucy mouth curved upward as she bent closer to him than was strictly necessary. Before she straightened, she flipped back her profusion of dark curls and whispered something I didn't catch into Cullin's ear. He smiled and shook his head. She stepped back, pouting prettily, and he picked up a half-silver and flipped it to her. She caught it, laughing, and walked away, her hips swinging outrageously.

Presently, he stood up and stretched. "Bed for me, I think," he said. "Are you coming?"

"In a moment," I replied.

The serving girl hurried across the room to intercept him as he headed for the stairs to the sleeping rooms. She caught his arm, smiling impudently at him. He laughed, then turned her around and gave her a gentle swat on the bottom. She walked back to the serving counter, pouting, and Cullin climbed the stairs, still laughing.

I had another flask of wine, watching the serving girls. They were all pretty, but I decided I was too fuzzy around the edges to trust my judgment. I might not be able to pick a woman who would not try to leave with my silver in the small hours, so I simply made my way up to the room, pausing only briefly on my way up the stairs to glance again at the woman with the strange eyes. She did not look back.

The room was clean and comfortable, the bed linen freshly changed. I ordered a bath to rinse away the dust of three seasons' travel from Laringras with the merchant train, then slipped naked between the sheets of the bed. Before I became too comfortable, out of habit, I made sure my sword and dagger were within easy reach of my hand, then closed my eyes and let sleep take me.

8

For the first time in many years, I dreamed again of a gently *symmetrical hill, lush with grass, rising against a sky streaked with the brilliant colors of sunset. At the top, settled like a crown on the brow of the hill, stood a Dance of stones. Tall, blunt menhirs, crowned in pairs by massive capstones, rose starkly silhouetted against the vivid sky. Within the outer circle of the Dance stood a second one, the stones shorter, but crowned all around. And within the second circle, an inner horseshoe shape of taller, narrow stones, enfolding within it a polished black altar stone, like a jewel cradled safely in cupped hands.*

The scent of fresh, growing things rose around me like a haze—the crushed grass I stood upon, the perfume of moving water nearby, the fragrance of wildflowers. I breathed the air deeply into my lungs, drawing strength and life from it.

Power radiated from the Dance. Power that flowed into my bones, into my flesh, into my sinews like music. There was magic here, but it was a gentle magic, a magic that sang in my blood. It reached into me and tapped the same centered well I could reach when I needed Healing power to visualize my hurts as whole again. It resonated with that inner energy like flute and harp combine to form harmony. Surrounded and wrapped by peace and contentment, I watched the sky fade to dusk behind the circle.

As the last light faded, for the first time, I noticed the man by the altar. He stood with his back to me, paying me no attention at all, giving no sign he realized I was there. He held his body loosely and easily, yet straight as one of the menhirs. His hands hung at his sides, relaxed and comfortable. He gave no outward signs of either patience or impatience, but I knew he was waiting, and had waited a long time there by the altar. He simply stood in communion with the power of the circle and waited.

A soft footfall sounded in the grass behind me. Expecting to see the Swordmaster, I turned slowly and raised my sword to meet the challenge. The dark figure of a man stood silhouetted against the timeless glow of the sky. A brief jolt of surprise shot through my chest. Not the Swordmaster, this figure stood bathed in an aura of menace. The sword in his hand radiated darkness, spilling it like water around the man.

"So I have found you at last," my opponent said, his voice flat and uninflected.

I drew in a deep breath, the fresh-scented air filling my lungs. The smile that pulled my lips back from my teeth had nothing to do with amusement. I felt light and ready, anticipation an airy evanescence in my blood. Something long outstanding was about to be resolved, something important.

"Perhaps I have found you instead," I told the dark figure.

"Perhaps, indeed," he replied. "We shall see how well the sword fights for you."

I flexed my hands on the plain, leather-bound hilt. "Or I fight for it?" I asked evenly.

"As you say." He leaped forward forcefully, and I found myself fighting for my life.

Time had no meaning in this strange dreamscape. Tirelessly, back and forth across the flower-strewn green velvet of the grass, the dark stranger and I battled each other. At first, we seemed evenly matched, our skill equal, neither of us able to find a weakness in the other and exploit it. Then gradually, I became aware that it was I who gave ground more often, that it was I on the defensive more often than on the offensive. Desperately, I sought the reserves of strength and stamina the years of training with Cullin had given me. But they were not there.

A strange combination of helpless despair and desperate, fatalistic determination filled me. I lunged forward aggressively, my blade thrusting recklessly at the stranger. The tip of the blade caught against the crosspiece of the hilt of his sword. The follow-through snap of my wrist wrested the sword from his hand. It glittered as it spun away, high into the air, then suddenly vanished as if swallowed up by its own darkness.

The stranger stepped back and saluted me ironically with his empty sword hand. "This round to you," he said softly. He turned abruptly and faded into the darkness.

I looked up at the Dance at the crown of the hill behind me. The Watcher on the Hill stood as motionless as the menhirs around him. Then, slowly, he turned to drift silently toward the altar in the center of the Dance.

Even as I began to move my foot in a first stride up the hill, the dream faded.

Something was making a Hellas of a racket in the street below my window. It woke me up. Getting roused suddenly and noisily out of a sound sleep is not my favorite way of beginning a day. Cullin tells me that I tend to become cranky and difficult to get along with when awakened too abruptly after a night in the tavern. My response has always been that it is a character flaw I learned from him.

This particular morning was no exception. I rolled off the bed and staggered to the window, cursing under my breath as I buckled my kilt around my hips. I leaned out to see what was causing the din.

The commotion appeared to center around a knot of men directly beneath my window. The sun flashed on drawn blades as four people circled warily in the middle of a cluster of avidly shouting spectators.

Hellas. A fight. And a completely lopsided fight at that.

I stared blearily down at the seething mob of humanity below and tried to sort it out. It seemed to be three Maedun mercenaries against one slender, fair-haired youth who wielded a hefty longsword with a skill sharpened by sheer desperation. I watched for a moment or two. No one in the crowd of eager spectators was inclined to step in and even the odds on the patently inequitable contest, and some were obviously laying bets on the outcome. At the edge of the crowd stood a small group of Honandun city guards. They, too, gave no indication of putting a stop to the entertainment. But then, city guards don't care much who gets slaughtered in the

streets as long as it isn't a Honandun citizen or any other
Isgardian.

It offended my sense of fairness, or aroused my foolhardy
notions of justice. Or something. Or maybe I was merely irritated because the noise had wakened me. I sometimes don't
think with clarity and precise logic when I'm only half-awake,
and perhaps still suffering from just a titch of wine fever.

I grabbed my sword and took the quickest route to the
street, which happened to be out the window and straight
down.

My sudden arrival, half-naked and obviously annoyed, in
the middle of the fray caused a momentary flurry of consterna-
tion among the three Maedun mercenaries currently attempting
to add a blond head to their collection. Faced suddenly with a
two-front battle, the Maedun hesitated. The young swordsman
used the opportunity to take a large collop out of the sword
arm of one mercenary. One of the others turned obligingly into
my blade. The last melted quickly into the crowd, dragging his
wounded comrade with him.

The young swordsman swung around, presumably to thank
me for saving his golden locks. Then I discovered I was wrong
on all counts. Swordsman—no. Swordswoman. Young, lithe,
skilled, and obviously deadly, but definitely not male. Not
grateful, either. Golden brown eyes blazing in a paradox of
burning rage and icy scorn glared at me. Lips I might have
considered kissing under different circumstances drew back
from perfect teeth in a snarl, and the greatsword in the strong,
brown hands swung up to challenge me.

"They were mine, you witless savage," she hissed. "I need
no help from a half-naked barbarian to deal with scum like
that."

It was her eyes that triggered the realization I had seen her
before. It was the same woman I had seen by the docks, the
woman who had come to the inn last night for the evening
meal. The clothing fooled me for the moment. Gone was the
opulent gown, the rich gold ornamentation in the hair. She
wore trews and boots crossbound to the knees, and a full-
sleeved shirt under a short tunic. An engraved leather baldric

crossed the tunic, supporting a scabbard for the sword across her back. I recognized neither the style and cut of the clothes she wore, nor the cadence of her speech. Not Isgardian or Falian. But woman she was, Outlander or no, and she gave every indication of wanting to skewer me like a rabbit spitted over a fire. It seemed like a good time to test Cullin's theory of distraction.

I reached out quickly, snaked an arm around her neck, and pulled her against me. I bent and kissed her astonished mouth, and for an instant or two, the air around us fizzed gently. The reaction startled me almost as much as it startled her. I let her go quickly before shocked immobility could turn to anger and action.

"Thank you, my lady," I said with ironic courtesy in my best High Isgardian. "Your gratitude quite overwhelms me."

She hissed and spit like a Tyran mountain cat, using a language I didn't know. The tone needed no translation. It was obviously a colorful and fanciful recitation of my parentage and lineage. I touched my forehead in a polite salute, then turned to go back to my comfortable and expensive bed in the inn.

I sensed rather than saw the movement behind me, and spun around, crouched low, my sword held in both hands and raised to deflect the wicked and deadly arc her blade described in the air as it swung toward my head. Just before her blade met mine with a ringing clash and metallic slither, she pivoted it in her hand so that, had the blow landed, the flat of the sword would have merely bounced off the back of my head. Painful, mayhaps, but less so than having my height reduced a handspan or two by the cutting edge. Even as I realized she did not mean to kill me and checked my counterstroke, a strange thrumming like the sound of thousands of bees quivered through the steel of my blade and up my arms. It set my teeth on edge, raised every hair on my arms and the back of my neck, and knotted the pit of my belly.

Hellas-birthing. Magic! Again! I could feel it, and I could smell its characteristic stench in the air.

Gods, I really *hate* magic.

I almost dropped the sword as I tried to yank it back, out of contact with the other blade. Once I had it free, the strange thrumming stopped. The magic-aversion reaction faded. I raised the sword again, for defense, and stepped back to give myself room. But there was no need. The woman stood with her own blade held limply in both hands, wide eyes staring at me in shock. Eyes the same color as good Tyran whiskey, the same color as my own.

"Where did you get that blade?" she whispered.

She no longer looked as if her dearest heart's desire was to raise a considerable and substantial knot on the back of my skull. I lowered my sword. "I stole it," I snarled, and turned away.

She caught up to me before I had taken three steps. With surprising strength, her hand on my arm swung me around to face her again. "Where did you get that sword?" she demanded, her voice harsh with urgency. "That's a Celae Rune Blade."

It was all I could do to remember to close my mouth. I tried not to stare back. In the eight years I'd had the sword, she was the only other person besides me to see the runes etched deeply into the blade. Runes I had no idea how to read.

"I told you," I said. "I stole it."

She shook her head. "No," she said firmly. "A Rune Blade can't be stolen."

I pulled my arm away. "I stole this one," I said. "I took it away from the man who was trying to kill me with it, then I used it to kill him, and kept it."

Wordlessly, she held up her own sword. The light flashed off the shining blade, the runes spilling along it sparking like the facets of gems.

"Like calls to like," she said quietly. "Can you see them?"

"The runes? Yes."

She swore. I don't know what she said, but it sounded like a potent oath. Then she glared at me. "How does an uncouth barbarian like you have the right to carry a Celae Rune Blade?"

I decided I'd had quite enough of standing in the dusty

street, dressed only in my kilt, talking to a woman who had a tongue like a fistful of rusty fishhooks. I turned my back on her, mustered as much dignity as a half-naked man could, and strode back into the inn.

Cullin was waiting in my room, fully dressed and looking indecently fresh and alert. He grinned at me as I stomped in and tossed the sword on the bed.

"I leave you by yourself for one night, and you find a fracas to leap into," he said. "And you not even dressed decent."

I scowled at him as I pulled on my shirt. "I hate this city," I said. "It's hip deep in magic."

He shrugged. "We meet with Moigar today. Another pack train. Tomorrow morning, maybe."

"It can't be too soon for me, *ti'vati*."

But Moigar didn't keep his appointment with us. We waited in the tavern for two hours past the arranged meeting time. It was annoying, but not too serious. There were plenty of other brokers in the city to deal with, and all of them knew our reputation. In the eight years I'd been with Cullin, we had never lost a pack animal to bandits. Cullin could name his price to any of the brokers, and they would be more than happy to pay it.

The woman entered the tavern and paused at the door to let her eyes become adjusted to the poor light. She wore her trews and tunic, the hilt of the greatsword rising above her left shoulder. I saw her before Cullin, and swore softly. I pushed my stool farther back into the shadows, hoping she wouldn't see me. I didn't need another round of sparring with her tongue. Cullin grinned at me, then moved his stool so that his shadow fell across me, too, hiding me more efficiently.

"'Tis a sad day when I see you hide from a woman, *ti'rhonai*," he said.

"You said it yourself," I said sourly. "Abrasive was the right word."

The woman stood by the door, looking around as if seeking someone specific. A half-drunk Honandun seaman approached her, swaggering with self-assurance. He said something to her, his hand reaching for her arm in a confident gesture. She gave him a look one might normally use on an unidentified and highly offensive object sticking to the sole of one's boot, then plucked his hand from her arm like it was a repugnant insect. When he insisted on pressing his suit, her left hand made a swift, knife-edge movement. The seaman yelped and his eyes grew wide with pain and shock. Clutching at his groin, he stumbled backward, unable to get away from her fast enough.

"Not a woman to take lightly," Cullin murmured, amusement glinting in his green eyes.

"Her tongue is more lethal than her hands," I muttered, reaching for the ale jug. Cullin laughed softly.

The woman looked around again, then moved purposefully across the room. She stepped up to our table and stood there, looking down at Cullin. Me, she spared no glance for, although I knew she was aware of my presence in the shadows. I hoped she could not make out my face in the dimness of the poorly lit tavern.

"You be Cullin dav Medroch?" she asked in the Isgardian common tongue.

Cullin gave her his best smile and leaned back in his chair. "I be."

"I was told you be the man who can help me." Her words were lightly accented, her voice low but clear.

"That would depend on what help you require," Cullin said, still smiling.

"I have come from Celi to seek a man," she said. "It be urgent I find him. I have gold to pay for your services."

"A long journey from Celi," Cullin said. "I trust you had a pleasant sea crossing."

Her golden brows drew together in a frown of impatience. She obviously had no time for pleasantries. "My business be important," she said. "Do you want my gold or no? There be others I might hire."

Cullin studied her carefully. His smile didn't waver, but his eyes became shrewd and penetrating as he watched her. He said something to her. It sounded a little like Tyran, but the vowel sounds were strangely twisted and the consonants softened. I came tantalizingly close to understanding it, but the meaning escaped me. It didn't escape the woman, though. She took a step backward, eyes wide in surprise.

"So," Cullin said. "Not Celae after all. Tyadda, then."

"How do you know the old tongue?" she demanded.

Cullin held up both hands, palms up. "Look at me," he said.

I saw the change in her face as she looked at him carefully. She saw past the outward signs of a mere merchant train guard, and saw the man few people outside Tyra, except possibly me, ever saw. She recognized the tartan in the plaid he wore, then she saw the fine golden yellow stripe through the blues and greens in it that marked his as belonging to the house of the Clan Laird. The gold stripe Cullin wore was narrow, indicating a younger son, but still not something to be scoffed at.

"I see," she said softly. She may have seen what he meant, but I failed to. I said nothing, though. She already had a low enough opinion of my intelligence and astuteness.

"Might I sit down?" She had switched to Tyran, again accented lightly, but clearly understandable.

Cullin reached out, snagged an empty chair with the toe of his boot, and drew it across the rough plank floor to our table. The woman placed it more conveniently and sat. "I come from Skai," she said. "It's said the yrSkai and the Tyr were once one people centuries ago. Perhaps we are kin."

Cullin smiled lazily. "Mayhaps," he agreed. "Whom do you seek?"

"A man of my country," she said. "Kin to the Prince of Skai."

"His name?"

She shook her head. "I don't know. All I know is his mother was Ytwydda, daughter of Prince Kyffen. She disappeared on the eve of her marriage to the oldest son of the Duke of Dorian, some twenty-seven years ago. We have learned she had a son."

Cullin raised one eyebrow. "Tyadda Seer?" he asked.

He had startled her again, but she nodded. "Yes. The son would be twenty-six or twenty-seven now."

"But you have no idea what he looks like?"

She shook her head.

"A difficult assignment," Cullin said, pouring another mug of ale and offering it to her. "You don't know his name, you don't know what he looks like. How do you propose to recognize him when you find him, provided, of course, you do find him in the first place."

"I'll know him," she said with conviction. She frowned. "There was a young man this morning. A clansman like yourself. He carried a Celae Rune Blade . . . He might know something. I'd like to know where he got that sword."

Cullin laughed. "You mean my son, Kian?"

She sat up straight. "Your *son*?"

I had been sitting back in the shadows, watching the woman as she spoke. Gradually, I became aware of a tingling on the back of my neck. I put my hand up to rub the uncomfortable itch, but it wouldn't go away. There was something about the woman that made me uneasy, something besides the unpleasant prickle of magic I had felt when our swords crossed this morning, but I couldn't put my finger on it.

"Who sent you to me?" Cullin asked.

"My father," she said. "He said you had helped him once before. His name is Jorddyn ap Tiernyn—"

"Oh, gods," I said. "And you're Kerridwen al Jorddyn."

She turned to stare at me. "How do you know my name?"

I leaned forward into the light, the prickle on the back of my neck intensifying. "You've changed a lot since you were thirteen," I said. "I trust your headache has disappeared."

9

Kerridwen al Jorddyn leaped to her feet and stared at me. "*You?*" she cried. "It was you who Healed me back then?"

I sat up straighter. "Yes," I said.

I knew better by now than to expect gratitude, but even then, her reaction surprised me. She slapped her hand down on the table hard enough to make the ale in the mugs slosh over onto the scarred planking, placed both hands on the table and leaned forward intensely, glaring at me. "You idiot," she said softly. "You stupid, ignorant, barbaric imbecile. Do you know what you've done?"

I stared at her. "What I've done?" I repeated blankly.

"You dim-witted fool!" She leaned farther forward, her eyes flashing sparks. "How could you be so bloody stupid?"

I stood and placed my own hands on the table, leaning forward to glare back at her. "Now wait just a moment," I said, confused and angry.

"No, you wait just a moment," she cried. "And to make everything worse, you had to go and kiss me, too. You idiot! You cretin!"

"Now, look—"

She raised her fist and shook it in my face. "You look," she said shrilly. "Didn't you feel it when you crossed swords with me?"

"What, the magic?" I shook my head. What was the woman trying to get at? "Yes, I felt it, and I hated it."

"How could you be so incredibly stupid?"

"Me, stupid?" I blinked, then jabbed my finger at her. "You were the one who tried to take my head off!"

"Don't you know anything?" She kept her voice low, but the intensity in it had the same effect as a shout. "By all the seven gods and goddesses, don't you know anything at all, you cretin? Do you know what you've done?"

"How could I know what I've done when I'm just a stupid barbarian?" I demanded. "Suppose you try explaining it to me. Words of one syllable or less. I'm only an idiotic cretin, remember."

She made a disgusted noise with teeth and tongue and slammed one fist down onto the table. Again, the ale sloshed.

Cullin remained sitting back comfortably in his chair, looking back and forth between the two of us, highly entertained. "Your turn, I believe, my lady," he said to her, smiling pleasantly, obviously amused.

Kerridwen directed her glare at him for a moment, then drew a deep breath, struggling for control. "When you Healed me all those years ago," she said, "it began a bonding. And when you kissed me, then crossed swords with me, the swords completed it. We're bonded, you imbecile." Her voice rose. I've never heard anyone scream so quietly before. "Bonded, damn you. It was never supposed to happen with anyone but—" She broke off and put both hands to her face for a moment, scrubbing them across her eyes and cheeks. When she dropped them, she seemed calmer. "Do you know what that means?"

"No," I replied, a little calmer myself now, too. But I couldn't help remembering the flood of images that swept through my mind all those years ago when I had cupped the delicate temples of a thirteen-year-old child between my hands. Was that a bonding? Or was it simply part of the Healing? And that impression of the air around us fizzing when I kissed her, and the thrumming sensation as our swords crossed this morning had been unlike any reaction to magic I'd ever had before. Surely not a bonding.

She groped for the chair behind her and pulled it back to the table so she could sit on it. Without speaking, Cullin handed her a mug of ale. She took a long swallow, then looked at me, her expression bleak. "If it was a proper bond, it means our lives are woven together," she said more quietly. "One life, two bodies, if it was proper." She shook her head. "But you're not Celae. I can hope it wasn't a proper bond. Perhaps it's not permanent."

The thought of being bonded to a woman like her was a bit

overwhelming. She was most emphatically not what I visualized when I thought of a life mate. I wanted no more of it than she appeared to want. "I certainly don't feel bonded," I said firmly.

She slanted an oblique glance up at me, but she said nothing.

"Are you two through shouting at each other?" Cullin asked mildly, still amused.

"I wasn't shouting," Kerridwen al Jorddyn said with cold dignity. She looked at me again. "How do you come by a Celae Rune Blade?" she asked. "Let me see it again."

I sat back and folded my arms on my chest. "You make a lot of demands, my lady," I said coldly. "Do they not teach common politeness in Skai or in Celi?"

Her lips tightened. "Please," she said as if it hurt her mouth.

I drew the sword from its scabbard on my back and laid it on the table. "I told you this morning," I said acerbically. "I stole it."

"Rune Blade?" Cullin reached out one blunt finger and ran it down the blade across the runes. "I've never seen runes on the blade," he said. He glanced quizzically at the woman, then at me. "You never mentioned runes, Kian."

I shrugged. "I thought it unimportant," I said. "I can't read them."

The woman shook her head. "But you can't *steal* a Celae Rune Blade," she said. "It's not possible—"

Cullin grinned. "He stole that one," he said. "Or mayhaps he inherited it, the owner no longer being in need of a sword. He took it away from a bounty hunter, and killed the man with it. He was unarmed at the time. I was there. I saw it."

The woman was about to say something else when Moigar came running into the tavern. Moigar never runs. His bulk made walking quickly a tedious chore. He looked around, spotted Cullin, and hurried over to the table.

"I've come to warn you, Cullin," Moigar said breathlessly. "The city guard be out searching for you."

Cullin's brows rose in inquiry. "Whyever for?"

Moigar collapsed onto a stool and fanned his sweating face with one hand. "One of those Isgardian troopers you encountered last night was apparently the cousin of the Ephir. You damaged him rather severely, I'm told. He be after your blood."

I reached for the ale jug. "I knew this would happen sooner or later," I said. "So why not today? The rest of the day has been perfectly delightful, too."

Cullin cocked an eyebrow at me. "How long did they stay annoyed with us last time?" he asked.

I shrugged. "Three or four seasons?" I said. "I'm not sure. But that time it was only the captain of the city guard we tossed out of the tavern. For the cousin of the Ephir, it might take a little longer."

"He be nursing a broken nose," Moigar said, a smug upturn at the corners of his mouth. "He be a vain man, be Tergal. He don't take kindly to anything might spoil his attraction for the ladies."

"Perhaps half a year, then," Cullin said. "Or even a year."

"Trevellin near the Falinor border is pleasant this time of year, I'm told," I said. "And they have need of merchant train guards."

Cullin finished his mug of ale before he stood. "Aye," he said. "Mayhaps it's best if we take ourselves out of the way of trouble for a while. It willna take long to get the horses."

"I'll find your men, Cullin," Moigar said. "And send them on to Trevellin to meet you."

We walked out into the street, right into a knot of seven Honandun city guards.

Cullin stopped dead in the street and stared at the Isgardian troopers. He swore loudly, and an expression of acute dismay spread across his face. The Isgardians saw it and began to grin in anticipation of chopping us into stewing chunks.

"Seven of them," Cullin said in disgust.

"Aye," I said, knowing my part. "And only two of us."

"Outnumbered," Cullin said.

"Indeed."

Cullin watched the troopers draw their swords and slowly drew his own. "This is an insult," he said. "Only seven for two of us."

I drew my own sword and moved to his left side. "It isna fair," I agreed. "But then, mayhaps they dinna know better, *ti'vati*."

Cullin tested the balance of his sword and grinned. "Only three each and we'll have to share the last."

I heard the hissing susurration of drawn steel. Out of the corner of my eye, I saw the woman, Kerridwen al Jorddyn, step up to Cullin's right side.

"Two each, and we can flip for the one left over," she said firmly. "Crowns, he's mine. Falcons, you can share him."

The grins on the faces of the Isgardian troopers faded. The leader eyed us warily and motioned his men to spread out in a bid to surround us. I swung around to cover Cullin's back, saw the woman had already done so, then moved so that each of us had a full one-third arc of a circle to cover.

The good citizens of Honandun, never ones to become involved in another man's quarrel, had scattered. The street in front of the tavern was deserted except for us and the troopers. That was good. I hate tripping over noncombatants in a fight. It can spoil your timing.

Cullin faced the troop leader, the grin widening on his face, the light of battle in his eyes. His earring glittered and swung as he snapped the long braid back over his shoulder out of his way. "They gather their courage, *ti'rhonai*," he said. "I told you before that you should cover that face with a beard. It almost frightens me, too."

I flexed my fingers on the hilt of my sword, feeling it settle against my palms, perfectly balanced. "No, it's your teeth, *ti'vati*. I would—"

The troop leader sprang forward, his sword slicing down at Cullin's belly. Cullin stepped back and shook his head in disappointment and well-feigned pity. "Did they no teach you anything about proper handling of swords, man?" he asked sadly, then whirled into action.

As the troop leader swung his sword, two of the troopers came at me, and I lost track of what Cullin was doing as I spun to meet them. I had spent eight years under the tutelage of the best swordmaster ever to come out of Tyra, a land renowned for its swordmasters. I was not the equal of Cullin dav Medroch, but I was more than a match for the two Honandun guards. They were slow and clumsy. I ran my blade through the thigh of the first even before he had his sword fully raised to strike. The second, wary now, leaped back, then attacked more cautiously.

I was at least a handspan taller than he, and my sword was longer. I had a lot of reach on him. He couldn't get close enough to do any damage. In the end, tired of playing with him, I feinted a blow to his head, then lowered the sword and tangled it in his feet. He went down like a fallen tree and his sword went spinning out of his hand. I brought the flat of my blade down on the side of his head to discourage any thoughts he might have had about trying to retrieve the blade.

When I turned back, Cullin was standing with his foot across the throat of the troop leader, leaning on his sword, watching Kerridwen, the grin still in place. She had left one guard sitting in the dust of the street, moaning over a bleeding sword arm. The one guard still remaining fought desperately as she beat him inexorably across the street, her blade flashing almost too quickly to be seen.

"She moves well," Cullin said calmly. "A bonny fighter, yon wee lassie. D'ye think she needs our help?"

"She disdains help from barbarians and savages," I said. "Or so she told me this morning."

"Ah." He grinned again. "You could get the horses ready, I think. I'll stay for a moment and discourage this fellow down here"—he gestured toward the guard leader, who lay completely still, his throat under the sole of Cullin's boot—"from trying to stop us. She should be finished playing with that wee mannie fairly soon, now."

"I suppose we'll have to take her with us now," I said.

"I suppose so. They're going to be severely vexed with her after this, I fancy."

I nodded, then sighed. "I was afraid of that."

He laughed. "We owe it to her to get her away from here, at any rate. I'll meet you at the stable in a few minutes."

I sheathed my sword and left him still admiring the way

Kerridwen handled her blade. The inn was only two streets away. I remembered Kerridwen had stayed at the inn as well, and flipped a copper to the stableboy.

"The Lady Kerridwen's horse," I told him. "She's in need of it in a hurry. Saddle it quickly and bring it here."

He snatched the coin deftly out of the air and flashed me a wide grin. "Aye, sir," he cried, and darted to a box stall in the back of the stable.

By the time I had Cullin's bay and my sorrel saddled, the boy had led a black mare out into the courtyard. I flipped him another coin and was rewarded by another grin. A moment later, Cullin and Kerridwen came dashing around the corner.

"We're going that way," I said, pointing south.

"I'm going with you," she said. "I'm not letting you or that Rune Blade out of my sight until I sort out what's going on." She snatched the mare's reins out of my hand, then turned and slapped a heavy leather pouch into Cullin's hand. "That should cover your fee for the next season or two."

Cullin weighed the pouch judiciously, bouncing it gently on his palm. "What say, Kian?" he asked me, the corners of his mouth twitching. "Do we take her along?"

"If it were up to me, I'd tie her up and drop her down the nearest cistern," I said. "And drop that bag in after her. Onto her head."

"I take it that means yes," Cullin said mildly.

I glanced at Kerri, who glared back. "Tcha-a-a-a," I said, and mounted Rhuidh. "If we're going, we'd best go before the whole of the Honandun guard comes boiling around that corner."

Kerri vaulted into the mare's saddle and crowded the horse close against the sorrel so that her knee pressed hard into mine. "And one more thing," she said, her voice harsh. "If you ever try to kiss me again, or even touch me, I'll carve out your liver for roasting, and feed it to you for breakfast. Is that quite clear?"

I pulled Rhuidh back a step and raised both hands, palms out in surrender. "I'd sooner kiss the mare," I declared positively. "Or the sword. It would be warmer."

Cullin was having trouble with the corners of his mouth again. He put up his hand to smooth his beard. "Kian's right," he said. "We'd best go."

He kicked the stallion into a canter. Kerri gave me one last scowl, then urged the mare to follow. I said, "Tcha-a-a," again, and followed.

10

We showed our heels to Honandun. We didn't move with any particular alacrity, being fairly certain the city guard would not pursue us past the city gates, but we wasted no time, either. It had, after all, happened once or twice before when our welcome in the city had been temporarily withdrawn. Cullin's reputation being what it was, there was always someone who thought to challenge him, and his ability also being what it was, the challenger always ended up predictably embarrassed. Given time, bruised pride eventually settled down again. Cullin also being the best merchant train guard on the continent, the merchants of Honandun usually managed to sort things out before we returned to the city.

If I had been expecting Kerridwen al Jorddyn to complain about the abrupt exit, or about the relatively arduous pace Cullin set, I was again mistaken. She rode in pensive silence, keeping up as well as I did. She was as good a horsewoman as she was a swordswoman. But I kept glancing at her to find her gaze, speculative and thoughtful, on me. Or, mayhaps more correctly, on the sword I carried across my back.

It was nearly dusk when we left the track and found a small hollow among a copse of silverleaf and scrub oak by a thin thread of quiet water. I lit a small fire while Cullin unlimbered his bow and set out along the burn. Forty-five minutes later, a rabbit sputtered and crackled on a spit over the fire. When we finished eating, Cullin announced he would take the first watch. I told him to wake me at moonset, then wrapped myself in my plaid and curled up amid a heap of bracken, and was asleep in minutes.

Cullin woke me just as the moon touched the tops of the trees behind him. As he settled himself for sleep, I wrapped my plaid around my shoulders and moved to sit by the fire, my back to the fire, watching the moon slip down behind the trees.

Guard duty at night leaves a man alone with his thoughts. Even while my eyes and ears remained alert and watchful, I could let part of my mind drift. I drew the sword and held it across my knees, then got my sharpening stone and cleaning cloth from the wallet at my belt. The last light of the moon picked out the runes engraved on the blade, and I ran my fingers across them thoughtfully.

"Can you read them?"

Kerri's voice coming out of the darkness didn't startle me. The part of my mind still standing guard had heard her rise from her place by the fire behind me.

"No," I replied, not looking up. "Can you?"

She seated herself comfortably on the ground near me. I noted she, too, chose to sit with her back to the small fire so the light would not impair her night vision. She had, perhaps, done this sort of thing before.

"No, I can't," she said. "But then, it's not my sword."

"That makes a difference?" I bent over the blade, busy with the stone.

"It makes all the difference. No one can read the runes on another's blade." She watched me for a while as I ran the stone along the blade, honing it to a keener edge. We sat in silence for several minutes and she watched me care for the sword. Finally, she said, "Is it true, then? That story of how you came by the blade?"

I made an exasperated noise. It was all the answer the silly question deserved. I pulled an oiled cloth from the pouch on my belt and wiped the sword blade carefully before I thrust it home in the scabbard. Then, still ignoring her, I stood and stretched like a cat. She muttered something under her breath I didn't catch. I turned to see her looking up at me. There wasn't enough light to read her expression, but her taut posture spoke louder than words. I heard her take a deep breath, let it out in a gust.

"Kian, I have to know how you come to have that sword," she said, her voice under tight control. "I *have* to know."

"I told you how I came by it," I said. "If you choose to disbelieve me, there's not much I can do about it, is there now?"

"But it's a Celae Rune Blade—"

"For the last time, I took it from the man who owned it when he tried to take me back to a slave owner."

She shook her head. "You don't understand. A Rune Blade won't fight in a hand it wasn't made for. It won't accept the hand of a usurper."

I smiled wryly. "It accepted the hand of the man I took it from."

"No," she said. "It let you kill him. Unarmed as you were, it let you take it from him and kill him with it."

Exasperation welled up and exploded. "Swords don't do that, *sheyala*. A sword is just a sword. A length of tempered steel. It's not alive—"

"It's not? You felt nothing when Whisperer met your blade?"

I shivered. I couldn't forget that eerie thrumming singing through my body from the blade in my hands. "It's not alive—"

"No, not alive," she said softly. "But tuned like a harp to respond to a certain touch."

"Tcha." I turned away in disgust. No sense in arguing with her. She never listened.

"And there's another thing about a Celae Rune Blade," she said. "It finds the man it was made for. It may take a long time, but it will find the man who was born to wield it."

"Like that bounty hunter?" I asked.

"The bounty hunter brought it to you," she said. "And you can see the runes." She shook her head. "Can you read, Kian?"

"A little," I said. "A girl I once knew taught me how to read Falian." For the first time in years, I thought of Rossah. Again, I saw her crouching behind the stable, drawing letters in the dust with a twig. I hadn't thought of her for a long time. A house slave, she had been taught to read and write to assist Mendor's scribe. The pain of loss had faded over time to a dull ache when I called her to mind. "And my *ti'vata* taught me Tyran." I grinned. "She said a Clan Laird's grandson should not be thought of as being completely ignorant, in spite of what opinion a Celae swordswoman might have on the subject."

She leaped to her feet. "You certainly gave every indication of being stupid and ignorant," she snapped. "You've more than your share of arrogance, even for a Tyran clansman. I could have handled all three of those mercenaries."

I laughed. "You woke me up with all the racket you were making," I said. "I couldn't think of a faster way to quiet things down. Next time, pick a better place to prove how talented you are."

She ignored the gibe. "You call Cullin *ti'vati*," she said. "Father?"

I shrugged. "Foster father. He officially adopted me when I was eighteen."

She jerked as if I had hit her and stared at me. "Then you're not Tyran?"

"Yes, I am," I said. "Cullin is my uncle. My father was his older brother. Both my parents died when I was seven. I'm Tyran." And I was. Thoroughly Tyran.

"But the sword—"

I shrugged. "Mayhaps it's using me to take it to the proper hand," I said, and laughed. "If what you say about it is true. Now go and get some sleep, *sheyala*. It's late."

"What is that word you called me? *Sheyala*?"

"It's Falian. It means Outlander." I didn't tell her, since all Falians considered non-Falians coarse, uncouth and completely uncivilized, it also meant barbarian. Mayhaps she'd find out for herself. When she did, I'd have to be prepared to defend myself. Until then, it was a mild enough joke. "Go and get some rest."

In the morning, Cullin appeared in no hurry to continue our journey. There were no signs of pursuit behind us, and the road stretched long and empty ahead of us. We broke our fast on the leftovers from our meal of the previous evening.

"Before we continue this," he said to Kerri, "I wish to know what it is you expect from us for that generous purse you gave me yesterday."

Kerri looked at him. "To help me find Prince Kyffen's grandson," she said.

"A tall order, *sheyala*," I murmured. "Help you find a man you canna name, you canna describe, and might not recognize if you saw. It's like trying to find a single grain of wheat in a winter granary."

"I'll know him," she said with conviction. She gave me an unreadable glance. "I'm sure of it."

"How did it happen in the first place?" Cullin asked. "It's unlike the Prince of Skai to misplace a daughter and a grandson, I would think."

Kerri's mouth straightened and tightened at the amusement in Cullin's voice, but she made no comment on it. "A long story," she said.

Cullin smiled. "We have five days' journey to Trevellin," he said. "Time enough for the longest story."

She busied herself bundling her bedroll and tying it into a neat roll while she collected her thoughts. When she had it put together to her satisfaction, she made herself comfortable by the dying fire. "I'll try to start at the beginning," she said.

"A suitable place," I said, smiling politely.

She shot me a withering glance. I smiled again.

"Prince Kyffen had two children," she said, ignoring me now. "A son Llan, and a daughter Ytwydda, two years younger. Llan, of course, was the heir. Kyffen arranged with the Duke of Dorian for a marriage between Ytwydda and the Duke's son Tebor when Ytwydda became fifteen. Kyffen and Duke Balan were close friends, and they hoped the marriage would secure the relationship between their two provinces."

Cullin laughed. "Marriages arranged for political reasons sometimes dinna work out for the best," he said. "I take it this one didna, either."

"It never took place," she said. "Ytwydda and Tebor seemed to get on well enough the few times they saw each other before she came of age. Tebor was ten years older than she. It was likely they hadn't much in common when she was young. I'm told Tebor treated her as a little sister he was fond of."

"How did she feel?" I asked. I wondered if anyone had ever asked Cullin's wife Gwynna how she felt about being married off to someone when she had no say in the matter. I knew how a man felt about it. I was suddenly curious to know how a woman might feel. Again, I saw Nennia as I had seen her for the first time nearly four years ago, the day we were wed, shy and nervous as a fawn. We had no real chance to get to know one another before she died in childbed, giving birth to our son Keylan.

Kerri shrugged. "I don't know. My father was her second cousin, you know. They were together a lot as children, and great friends. She never said much about Tebor. But she was a quiet child, he says, and always kept her thoughts to herself for the most part. At least, she did about Tebor."

"What happened when she turned fifteen?" Cullin asked.

"Kyffen and Balan made all the arrangements for the wedding to take place a fortnight after Beltane," she said. "But on the morning Tebor's envoy came to take her to Dorian for the wedding, they discovered she was gone. One of her ladies was also gone."

"And neither has been seen since?" I asked.

Kerri shook her head. "That's the odd part. The lady—her name was Moriana—was found some years later, living in Gwachir on the south coast. In Mercia. She was married to a merchant there, and had been, apparently, for three years when they found her. She told Kyffen Ytwydda had run off with a young man she met at the Beltane Fire three days before they disappeared together. She said she had stayed with them until they got to Gwachir, then they got on a ship, and she met the merchant."

"Who was this mysterious young man?" Cullin asked.

"Nobody knew. Moriana couldn't even describe him. She said he had worn a cloak and hood all the time they were traveling. She never once saw his face clearly."

"Very astute of him," Cullin commented. He frowned thoughtfully. "It occurs to me that the present Duke of Dorian is not old enough to have a son of age to be the jilted bridegroom. Nor is his name Tebor."

"Tebor was killed," Kerri said shortly. "His younger brother Blais is Duke in Dorian now. Tebor wanted more than just Dorian. He made a pact with the Saesnesi to sell Ytwydda to them as a hostage if they would help him overthrow his father, and provide him with warriors so he could take over Mercia and Skai, too."

Cullin raised his eyebrows. "How did this come to light?"

"Prince Kyffen received a letter outlining the plot," she said. "It wasn't signed, but it contained too many correct details to be dismissed as the work of someone merely trying to discredit Tebor. Kyffen passed it on to Balan, and Balan investigated very quietly. It didn't take much to discover one of Tebor's conspirators and make him talk. Tebor tried to rise against his father, but without the Saesnesi, he failed. He was killed in the fighting."

"And nobody found out who wrote the letter?" I asked.

She shook her head.

"Might it have been the same mysterious stranger who made off with the Prince's daughter?" I asked.

"It might explain why the lady Ytwydda took herself out of Tebor's way," Cullin said thoughtfully. "The lady sounds no fool."

She glanced at Cullin, then at me. "That was considered," she said. "It might have been, but nobody knows for sure."

"If Llan was Kyffen's heir, why is the son of this princess so important?" I asked.

"Llan is dead," Kerri said, her expression bleak and an infinite sadness in her eyes. "He was killed nine years ago fighting the Saesnesi, who were raiding again. He left no children. Ytwydda's son is now the only blood heir to the throne of Skai." She looked down at her hands. "Llan was like an uncle to me, you understand. I loved him almost as much as I love my father. There was a special bond between us."

Cullin frowned. "And this grandson you seek," he said. "How does Kyffen know Ytwydda had a son?"

"You know about Tyadda Seers?" she asked.

Cullin nodded.

"Kyffen's seer is Liam ap Wendal," she said. "Shortly after Llan died, he saw Ytwydda in the glass. He said she was playing with a small boy, and the boy was her son by the man she had run off with. He—he said he saw her all dressed in black.

That meant she was dead. But the boy lived. He told my father the boy would probably be around eighteen, grown to a man. That was why we came to the continent back then. We had come looking for him."

"Why did you come alone this time?" I asked.

"My father is ill," she said. "We thought if I could find Cullin, he might be able to help. He had helped us before, when we were taken by those Maedun mercenaries, and my father liked him." She turned a steady gaze to Cullin. "He sent me to you because you know the whole of the continent well. If you were willing, you might even be able to say where the best place to begin looking might be."

"Is the search for this grandson so urgent now?" Cullin asked.

She nodded. "Kyffen is well over sixty, closer to seventy, now," she said. "He's still strong and active, but he knows he's aging. The only other heir is a distant cousin, and Kyffen says he'd not make a good prince. Aldan is a bard, and a very good one. He's a good man, but he's not a soldier, nor is he a leader of men. Kyffen's pinned all his hopes on finding his grandson. My father and I promised him we'd try to find him. Or I'd try."

I shook my head in exasperation. "You set a difficult task," I said. "There's precious little to base a search on there."

"Perhaps more than you might think," she said quietly. "Ytwydda was strong in Tyadda magic. Liam believes her son is, too. A man with strong magic couldn't be that difficult to find."

I shivered. "Magic," I muttered. "I want nothing to do with magic."

Cullin got up and went to the horses to begin saddling his bay. I followed. He glanced at me, raising one eyebrow.

"It's a chancy thing," I said. "Where do you start in a search like that?"

"I found you," he said, smiling.

"Aye, you did. But at least you had something to go on."

He shrugged. "She's sure she'll know the man if we find him," he said. "Is it worth our time?"

"It was a heavy purse she gave you," I said.

"Aye, it was. Well, we canna go back to Honandun for a while. I can think of worse ways to spend a season or two than looking for a lost heir."

"What about the others? They'll be going to Trevellin when Moigar finds them."

"They're all experienced guards," he said. "I can find them work. Thom can lead them almost as well as you or I could."

I glanced back over my shoulder at Kerri. She sat by the fire, studiously looking the other way, her face calm and composed. But her hands were knotted tightly together on her knees, and her shoulders looked tense. I looked back at Cullin. "You're the captain, *ti'vati*," I said. "I follow you."

"Aye, well," he said. He turned to Kerri and beckoned her over. "We'll see what's afoot when we get to Trevellin," he told her. "We can decide then what's best. It might be that someone there will be better able to help you."

"But I—"

"We'll decide in Trevellin," Cullin said firmly.

Kerri shot a glance at me, her eyes narrowed, but she said nothing. Instead, she merely walked away and saddled her mare.

11

Trevellin lay in a wide valley less than a league upstream from the sea on the Isgardian side of the River Shena. As a trading city, it was busier than Honandun, but had not the sprawl of buildings. Twice a year, the meadows around the city filled to overflowing with tents and stalls as merchants from all over the continent converged on the city for the trade fairs.

We stood on the hill overlooking the city, scanning the vast sea of colorful tents. Even from here, we clearly heard the tumult of voices crying the wares of merchants. Scattered phrases of music from pipes, harps, and tambours floated in the air as entertainers wove their way through the crowds, hoping for a few coppers.

I couldn't help it. My gaze was drawn from the bustle and confusion below us to the broad flatlands of Falinor across the river. It had been eight years since I had seen it. I found my hand clenching into a fist at my side as I stood there. Not very far from here, less than seven leagues south and east, I reckoned, was the inn where I had first met Cullin as a frightened, half-grown boy, a runaway slave. I had hardly thought about that boy in seven years. Until just now, he had been a blurred memory, less even than a recollection from a clouded dream.

Well, I was no slave now. Five silver and two ornate daggers had purchased my freedom. The sword I carried and Cullin's meticulous and exacting training had earned me the ability to keep it. I had a name now, and a family with it.

"We timed our arrival well," Cullin said. "Once the fair breaks up, there'll be merchant trains going in all directions. Thom and the men will have no trouble finding work." He mounted his horse and looked at Kerri. "And you, my lady, might well find someone willing and better able to help in your search for your lost prince."

Kerri slanted a glance across at me that I ignored, then made a "perhaps, perhaps not" gesture with her hand.

We rode down the track abreast. At the edge of the fair, we found a farrier's tent and left our horses to be penned in the enclosure he had roped off. The feed looked fresh and clean, and the other animals in the enclosure looked contented enough.

"I'm going to find a broker for Thom," Cullin said as we walked toward the thronged cluster of tents and stalls. "Kian, you had best see if you can buy us provisions. Keep Kerri with you until we see if there's anyone here we can trust to help her. We'll meet back here in two hours' time."

I had almost forgotten how a trade fair assaulted the senses. The air swirled with the thick smell of leather goods, wine, food of all descriptions, animal dung, human sweat, perfumes, and the smell of bodies left too long unwashed. It rang with the shouts of thousands of voices, crying wares, bargaining, and bickering, raised in song, laughter, or anger. It glittered with the colors of the tents, the gleam of metalwares and jewels, the shimmer of silks and satins, the sheen of furs, and the more prosaic glow of fruits and vegetables piled high on tables and nestled into baskets. It was impossible to move without being jostled on all sides by people wandering happily or hurrying through the mass of humanity crammed into the narrow aisles between the stalls and tents jammed cheek by jowl into every available space. Beneath our feet, the trampled grass lay dead and brown, choking in dust.

Kerri edged closer to me and I put my arm around her shoulders to prevent the crowd from separating us. She stiffened, glared at me, and muttered something under her breath, but didn't pull away. In that sea of moving bodies, it would be too easy to lose one another.

A display of weapons caught Kerri's eye, and she drew me toward it in order to take a closer look. She picked up a dagger that looked more like a piece of jewelry than a weapon. The merchant's eyes gleamed almost as brightly as the begemmed haft of the dagger as he volubly praised its workmanship, the keenness of its edge, its usefulness and suitability for so obviously a highborn lady such as herself.

Kerri laughed and replaced the dagger. "It's a pretty toy," she told the merchant. "But I have no use for it."

"Perhaps this, then?" the merchant said hopefully, picking up a more utilitarian dagger and displaying it with a flourish.

Kerri shook her head. "Thank you, no."

Disappointed, the merchant looked for the next prospective customer, and we moved away.

As we turned, we were nearly bowled over by two men shouldering roughly through the crowd. I looked up and stopped in mid-stride. One of the men was Drakon, son of Lord Mendor. Frozen, I stared at him. He had grown, of course, since the last time I had seen him, but I was incongruously pleased to note I was considerably taller and broader than he. The lank sandy hair was still the same, as were the pale blue eyes and the sulky and cruel droop to the corners of his mouth. A purple welt of burn scar tissue ran from the corner of his left eye, up across his temple, and back into his hair, which hung oddly over his ear. When the slight breeze lifted his hair a little, I saw that the ear itself was badly misshapen, the skin around it puckered and red. He was richly dressed in hunting leathers, with a silver-chased baldric across his chest, supporting a longsword at his hip. He looked at Kerri as a man looks at a tavern bawd, then glanced at me, contempt in his eyes, a sneer on his mouth, seeing only a Tyran clansman, dusty from travel. Then the disdainful expression in his eyes changed to shocked recognition and he stiffened.

"You!" he cried. His hand flew to the dagger at his hip. "I was told you were dead!"

My hand went to my own dagger. "You would do well to keep your blade sheathed, Drakon," I said softly.

He drew the hair back to display his disfigured ear. "You did this to me," he snarled. "I will reclaim you as my property, and I will see you hanged."

"If I were you, Drakon," I said softly, "I'd be verra careful how I spoke to the grandson of the Laird Broche Rhuidh of Tyra." I bared my teeth at him, a mocking imitation of a polite smile. "Ask Dergus how he sold me for a galley slave. Did he no tell ye? He'd no ken I purchased my freedom, would he, then? Nobody's property but my own now."

Drakon looked over his shoulder at the liveried houseguard who stood behind him. "This man is an escaped slave," he said loudly. "He's my property. Take him—"

He stepped aside as the houseguard leaped forward. I heard Kerri swear as I pivoted to meet the houseguard. Drakon went down as Kerri swept his feet out from under him. I hit the houseguard full in the face. He fell back, blood spurting from his ruined nose. There was no room to maneuver with the crowd jostling and swirling around us. The thirst for revenge was a sudden, hard need bursting through me, Rossah's blood crying out for vengeance, but I could not draw my sword and challenge Drakon right there. Too many people were in the way.

Even as I tried to fight my way through the crowd to him, Drakon scrambled to his feet and backed away. "I will kill you yet," he shouted. "You are a dead man, you slave bastard—"

I lunged after him, but he dodged away, then disappeared quickly into the throng. Kerri grabbed my arm as I tried to follow him.

"Don't be a fool," she snapped. "You'll never find him in this crowd. He won't fight you, anyway. I've seen that type before. He'll be more likely to wait in ambush for you, or send an assassin to put a dagger in your back."

She was right, and I knew it. But it still took all the self-control I had not to go charging blindly after him.

"I owe him a blood debt," I said, with more calm than the tension in my body laid claim to. "Both him and his father, Mendor."

She pulled me toward a large tent set with tables and benches, where ale and food were being served. "Let's get something to eat," she said. "I could use a glass of wine. If you like, you can tell me about it."

By the time I had told Kerri about the boy called Mouse, I had calmed down enough so that I no longer wanted to tear the fair apart to find Drakon. Rossah had waited these eight years with that infinite, sweet patience Mouse had always both envied and despised. She would wait a while longer. As I spoke, the urgency left me and a firm determination took its place. In the rash, fervent passion of youth, Mouse had made a vow for vengeance. Kian dav Leydon ti'Cullin was a man and, I hoped, more capable of rational thinking even when angered. Reason told me Mendor and Drakon could never think they had acted wrongly, ordering the death of one slave, the castration of another. They simply dealt with their property as they saw fit. But I was still in no mood to listen to cold reason. I was Tyran enough in my attitude toward slavery, perhaps even more so than Cullin. I had reason enough. There were, even in Falinor, slave owners who allowed their slaves the simple courtesy of the dignity of humanity. If nothing else, Mendor and Drakon deserved a hard lesson in the morality of slave owning. I was more than willing to serve as instructor in their learning.

Kerri listened without interruption as I spoke. When I finished, she remained quiet for a long time, her hands cupped around the crude earthenware goblet of wine. Finally, she looked up at me.

"You still don't remember your parents?" she asked.

I shook my head. "No. I don't really remember anything before I was seven. Just the occasional feeling I *should* remember something."

She made an odd little gesture with her eyebrows. "What a strange, lost feeling that must be," she said softly, displaying an insight not many people had. "But that might mean you're not really Cullin's nephew after all . . . "

Her line of thinking was almost visible. I laughed harshly. "If you're trying to fit me into the space left by your missing princeling, you can forget that idea right now. I'm no Celae."

"But the Rune Blade—"

I shook my head. "No, *sheyala*. By your own admission, only a Celae can read the runes on a sword, and I canna read them on my own."

"Who was your mother?" she asked, kiting off on a different tack.

"My mother was Saesnesi," I told her. "Saesnesi with a touch of Maedun blood. A far cry from a Celae. Besides, how old did you say your princeling was?"

"Liam said he'd be about twenty-seven."

I spread my hands. "I'm twenty-four, at least three years younger," I said, proving my point. "No, *sheyala*. I'm no Celae princeling. Get that out of your head."

"That blade tells me different."

I got abruptly to my feet. "It's time to meet Cullin," I said. "And it's time to find someone else to help you. If Cullin wants to do it, I'll go with Thom."

She stood up and glared at me. "You don't get shut of me that easily," she said. "If you aren't the prince's grandson, then you and that sword will lead me to him. Where you go, I go. Like it or not." She planted her fists on her hip and thrust out her jaw. Stubborn, she was. Like a rock. "If I don't go with you, I go after you. I stay close to that sword, like it or no. You're stuck with me, my friend."

12

Cullin was late. Nearly four hours had passed since we parted, and still no sign of him. It was unlike him not to be where he said he would be, when he said he'd be there. He had not even sent a messenger with word of why he was late.

I paced restlessly in front of the farrier's tent, unwilling to admit I was worried. The encounter with Drakon had unsettled me, and I didn't like the way Mouse's memories kept crowding into my mind, and one memory in particular. A small child screaming in helpless terror and pain, savaged by the dogs Drakon had set on her because the child's mother had accidentally spilled dirty wash water on Drakon's new boots. If I closed my eyes, I could still hear the child shrieking, and see the bloody foam around the mouths of the dogs. I clenched my fist angrily and tried to shake off the memories.

Could Cullin have run into Drakon? Drakon was never what even the most shameless sycophant would call a brilliant thinker. But even he was capable of connecting two Tyran clansmen. We are not all that common in southern Isgard. Drakon might realize Cullin was with me and think that he could get at me through him.

Kerri had been keeping herself busy packing the provisions we had purchased. She had them all neatly stowed in three sets of saddle packs by our saddles. Although she said nothing, I could tell that she, too, was worried. Finally, she came to stand beside me as I paused in my pacing to scan the raucous crowd again. But there was still no sign of Cullin's bright hair among the milling sea of people.

"He's perfectly capable of looking after himself, you know," she said quietly.

I didn't reply. In that massed throng, even Cullin might not notice a dagger in the hand of a passerby who jostled him. Not until it was too late, and the point of the blade had found his heart.

"Kian . . ."

"Stay here," I told her. "I'm going to look for him."

"You'll never find him in that," she said. "It will be dark in another hour, and you don't even know where he went."

All the hair on my arms and on the back of my neck suddenly prickled erect. Even as I turned, I caught the first whiff of the stench of magic. Behind us, a mounted troop of Maedun mercenaries filed down from the road toward the fair. There were at least forty of them, all wearing the blazon of an Isgardian lord's house on the left breast of their black tunics. I didn't recognize the crest. At the head of the column, next to the officer, rode a tall man in a gray, enveloping cloak. He sat his horse rigidly erect, looking neither right nor left, an expression of disdainful scorn on his sharp-featured face. The stench clearly emanated from him. It was so marked, I could almost see it hanging like tendrils of fog around him.

The officer rode more easily, casually glancing around, his mouth curled down arrogantly and contemptuously. As he passed the place where Kerri and I stood, the prickling sensation on the back of my neck intensified sharply. The officer looked straight at me, and our eyes met. I stiffened as I looked into those eyes, so dark they appeared all black. Startled recognition flashed through me, a brief impression of a sword spilling darkness all around the man. Then it was gone as quickly as it had come, and the officer's gaze slid indifferently past me, and the column moved away from us.

The encounter left me shaken. Surely I knew the officer from somewhere, I thought. But where? All my life, I had assiduously avoided even the most casual contact with Maedun. As the column disappeared, I shook off the odd feeling and turned back to scan the crowd around the tents and stalls.

"There are entirely too many of those arrogant lice around these days," Kerri muttered. Her mouth was drawn into a thin, grim line, and I remembered she had good reason to take an active dislike to Maedun mercenaries, too. "They were crawling thick as maggots on a week-old carcass through Honandun, and now here." She wiped her hands against the thighs of her breeks as if she had touched something foul and shuddered. "They had a warlock with them, too. Blood magic."

"Blood magic?" I repeated. "I didn't know there were different kinds. It all feels the same to me."

"Blood magic is the worst kind," she said. "The power comes from the shedding of blood. The more blood, the more powerful the magic. Wielded by an adept, it can kill."

I shuddered. Thinking about it gave me a blinding headache.

"Tyadda magic is air and earth magic," she continued, almost as if she were speaking to herself. She looked up at me. "You'd know the difference if you felt it."

I shook my head. "All magic gives me the shivers," I said. "I hate it. It sets my teeth on edge."

"Kian!"

The sudden shout snapped my attention instantly away from Kerri and the troop of Maedun mercenaries. Cullin wove his way deftly and adroitly through the crowd, nearly running in his hurry. He had changed out of his kilt and plaid into snug-fitting leather trews and jacket of dark-colored leather, a dark green cloak flung about his shoulders. He carried two bundles, one of which he flung to me as he came within range.

"Put those on while I get the horses," he said, his expression grim. I knew better than to argue with that tone in his voice, or that look in his eyes. I took the bundle and ducked into the shadow of the farrier's tent. The bundle contained leather trews and jacket and a dark blue cloak. As I got quickly into them, I heard Cullin say to Kerri, "You can come with us, my lady, but if you do, I think you owe us a few words of explanation." He did not sound pleased.

"I go with you and Kian," she said. "If you wouldn't mind." For the first time since I met her, there was an overtone of entreaty in her voice.

He had finished saddling the horses when I came running out from behind the tent. He tossed me the reins of the sorrel and vaulted up into his saddle. Kerri was already mounted and ready.

"Who did you kill?" I asked, mounting quickly.

"No one," he said. "Yet." He shot a significant glance at Kerri, then kicked the bay into a canter. "We've been too long out of touch," he shouted back at me over his shoulder as he guided the horse out onto the road. "All Hellas has broken loose around here."

The last of the light was fading from the sky when Cullin turned off the road onto a narrow, nearly invisible track leading down to a small stream meandering its way toward the River Shena. Thick clumps of tall aspen and alder lined the banks of the tiny burn, and bracken grew belly high to the horses, burgeoning green and fresh. The narrow track stopped in front of an abandoned stone cottage, the thatch of its roof falling away in places.

We took care of the horses, then Cullin and I set about gathering more wood while Kerri went into the derelict cottage to attend to preparing a meal. She was sitting quietly, legs folded under her, when we came in.

"What happened back there in Trevellin?" I asked, stretching to wring the knots out of my muscles.

Cullin wasn't looking at me. He leaned back against the moss-covered stone of the wall, arms folded across his chest, watching Kerri. She watched the fire, her face held coolly expressionless.

"I went to see Horak," Cullin said. "He was simply bubbling over with information."

I nodded. There was no mouse that crept or sparrow that cheeped between Saesnes in the north or Laringras in the south that did not come to Horak's attention. His network of informers was the envy of any royal house on the continent.

"What did he have to say?" I asked.

"It would seem that while we were in Laringras, there was a revolution of sorts in Falinor," Cullin said. "Several disgruntled lords, your friend Mendor among them, Kian, rose up against the king, backed by their armies of Maedun mercenaries. The king is dead, and a Maedun sorcerer sits on the throne. He calls himself the Lord Protector of Falinor. For all intents and purposes, Falinor is now a Maedun province."

I bit my lip thoughtfully. "And now Isgard is crawling with Maedun," I said. "It would appear that they want Isgard, too."

"And Laringras, and the rest of the continent," Cullin said.

"I don't see what that has to do with me," Kerri said primly, still watching the fire. "Anyone who was aware of the political situation on the continent knew Maedun has been plotting for nearly a century to create its own empire. Like the Borlani did before they fell."

"Aye, that's true," Cullin said. "But they've never had the leaders. It would appear now they've found one. But aside from that, my lady, Horak had more interesting information. He tells me the Maedun are searching every crack and cranny on the continent for a young Celae princeling."

Kerri looked at him for the first time. "Would you have agreed to help me if you knew the Maedun were also looking for Kyffen's grandson?"

Cullin said nothing. He merely met her gaze impassively. A slight flush crept up from her throat and suffused her cheeks.

"I didn't lie to you," she muttered.

Cullin inclined his head in acknowledgment. "No," he agreed. "But neither did you tell us the whole truth. Why is it so urgent to find this lost princeling?"

Kerri's jaw firmed. "I told you. Kyffen knows he's aging—"

Cullin raised one eyebrow. "My lady Kerridwen," he said softly, "the whole truth, please, or you go back to Trevellin or Honandun right now, and we go to Tyra."

Kerri clenched one fist and thumped her knee gently. "Very well," she said stiffly. "You know the Saesnesi are in Celi?"

Cullin nodded.

"They've established a firm foothold on the eastern coast of Celi," she said. "They use it for a base to raid the rest of the island. Every year the raids get worse. The Celae are a stubborn people." She slanted a glance up at him. "Much like the Tyr." That got a quick smile from him in acknowledgment. "They've spent centuries quarreling among themselves. None of them can get together long enough to meet the Saesnesi in force and drive them back into the sea. We need a strong leader, someone who can unite all the Celae."

"And this princeling is supposed to do that?" I asked.

She shook her head. "No, but his son will."

"This information comes from the same seer who told Kyffen about his grandson?" Cullin asked.

"Yes," she said. "You have to understand. Celi must be strong to meet her enemies, and we can't be strong unless we're united."

"The Maedun want Celi, too," I said.

She turned to look at me, then nodded. "Yes, they do. The Maedun have their seers, too."

Cullin waited for her to continue. When she didn't, he said, "All of it, my lady."

She made an irritated sound. "There are stories about an enchanter coming out of Celi who will destroy Maedun," she said. "The Maedun apparently think he'll come from Kyffen's line."

"And, incidentally, from this missing princeling," Cullin said.

"Exactly. Yes." She looked at me, then to him. "That's why it's so important we find Kyffen's grandson. Otherwise, Celi will go down like Falinor."

"And we're going to run into opposition from every Maedun we meet once it's known we're looking for this princeling," I said.

"Essentially, yes," she said. "I think so."

I shook my head in disgust. "How nice of you to let us know we might need to go around with drawn swords," I said sarcastically. "I would hate to die and not know the reason why the Maedun decided they wanted to collect my head."

A hint of a smile curled at the corner of Cullin's mouth. "Being prepared can go a long way in helping to preserve a head," he said. "Horak told me that there were a couple of Falian lords out after your head, too, Kian. But I think I know why they're anxious to add it to their collection."

I looked up at him, then laughed softly. "Mendor and Drakon," I said.

He nodded. "You, ah, left your mark on Drakon, I understand," he said. "And he heartily resents it. I take it you had a wee dustup with him at the fair."

"We ran across each other and had words," I said. "Yes."

Cullin grinned. "Aye, well," he said. "That certainly explains why there's suddenly a price in Falian gold on your head." He looked at Kerri again. "But why is there also Maedun gold posted on his head, my lady?" he asked mildly.

"Maedun gold?" I repeated blankly. "On my head?"

"I assume it's you," Cullin said. "Ten Maedun gold pieces for a young Tyr who carries a Celae Rune Blade."

Kerri's shoulders slumped and she closed her eyes, her face bleak. "Oh gods," she whispered. She looked up at me. "Kian, I'm truly sorry. I didn't realize they knew."

"Would you care to explain that?" I asked.

"They want you for the same reason I do," she said. "That sword. Kian, I've watched you use that sword. There are only two reasons why you use it so well. One is that you'll take it to the man it belongs to."

"The princeling," Cullin said.

"Yes," she said. "And the other reason is that you, yourself, might be Ytwydda's son."

I bit my lip. That would certainly explain the strange reaction of the bandit in the pass. He had recognized my sword, and therefore me. I was perhaps fortunate the archer's arrow had taken him before he could get away to pass along the information.

Cullin nodded thoughtfully. "So they want either to kill him, or follow him," he said slowly. "And in either case, by taking Kian, the Maedun will find the princeling."

Kerri nodded. "Yes."

"That's ridiculous," I exploded. "My mother was Saesnesi—"

Those golden brown eyes of hers stayed fixed on my face. "You need either royal Celae blood or Tyadda magic to use a Rune Blade as well as you do," she said quietly.

A shiver crawled down my back. "What do you have, Kerridwen al Jorddyn?" I asked.

She shook her head.

"What do you have?"

She sighed. "Both," she said. "You know my father is cousin to Prince Kyffen. And I have some Tyadda magic."

"You don't use it," Cullin said.

"No, I don't," she said. "Not very often, anyway, and certainly not here, where a Maedun might pick it up and track it."

I frowned as something suddenly occurred to me. "Wait a minute," I said. "If the Maedun are looking for me, why didn't that officer stop? He looked straight at me."

Kerri bit her lip. "He didn't stop because he didn't see a Tyr and a Celae woman," she said.

I stared at her. "What?"

She made an effort not to smile, but couldn't quite bring it off. "He saw an Isgardian farm woman and a dog," she said, and blushed.

Cullin burst into startled laughter. "A dog," he chortled. "A dog. That's magnificent! Superb!"

I boggled at her. "What?"

She held up her hands in a resigned gesture, and the smile twitched at the corners of her mouth again. "It was all I could think of on short notice," she said helplessly. "Forgive me, Kian. I used a small masking spell as they rode past. You probably didn't notice because the warlock's magic was so strong."

I remembered the sudden intensifying of the itch on the back of my neck. "I noticed," I said. "But you're right, I thought it was the warlock." I shivered, then became angry. "You used magic on me without asking me first?"

"There was no time—"

"And you called the Maedun arrogant," I said indignantly.

"So we've established that you do have magic," Cullin said quietly, giving me a look that shut me up quickly. "Tyadda magic and royal Celae blood."

"And I carry a Rune Blade," she said. "I was trained to use it starting at the age of five."

"What about me?" I demanded. "What do you think I have?"

She looked at me again. "Both, Kian," she said quietly. "I think you have both, too."

13

I was sitting guard duty, wrapped in my cloak for warmth. Within the ruins of the cottage, Cullin and Kerri slept. The fire on the hearth had burned down to embers and very little light glowed through the door, which hung askew on its hinges. Only part of my mind was alert and watchful as I sat huddled on a moss-covered stone, my back to the cottage wall, which still retained some small residual warmth from the heat of the daytime sun. Kerri had given me a lot to think about, and I was not having an easy time sorting it out.

The door opened behind me and Cullin stepped out into the wash of moonlight. He crouched down to sit on his heels, placing his back against the wall beside me.

"Could she have the right of it?" he asked, his voice troubled in the dark. "Could you be this lost prince of hers?"

I shook my head. "How could I be?" I asked. "She said the princeling would be twenty-six or twenty-seven. By your own reckoning, I'm twenty-three, almost twenty-four."

He smiled. "Being a long-lost prince could be troubling, I suppose," he said.

I gave a harsh grunt of laughter. "Being a long-lost nephew was hard enough to get used to," I said. "But it was enough for me. I've no ambition to be a prince."

He picked up a twig and made abstract little designs in the earth between his feet. "Twyla might have been Celae," he said. He looked up at me thoughtfully. "I never thought of it before, but she had the eyes. So do you."

"And the magic?" I asked and shivered. "Did she have the magic?"

He shook his head. "I never saw her use it. The Healing, aye. She used it several times, but no other magic. And Leydon never once said anything about journeying to Celi. He spoke of traveling the continent, but never of Celi."

"You told me you thought my mother was Saesnesi," I said.

"I did think so," he said. "Her hair was that pale, flaxen yellow you see in many Saesnesi, ye ken, not dark gold like Kerri's hair. Or her father's, either, for that matter. They look to be typical of the Celae who mixed with the Tyadda."

"Kerri says she thinks I have magic," I said. I shook my head. "But I've none. Only the Healing. And I *hate* magic."

"Then I think it more likely she may be right in thinking that you may be able to lead her to the princeling because of the sword." He shook his head again. "Who knows? I dinna ken what to think, to be truthful."

"I don't want to be a Celae prince," I said vehemently. "It's enough for me to be who I am. Just Kian dav Leydon ti'Cullin. It's enough to be your foster son."

He laughed and tossed away his twig, getting to his feet. "You may have a job convincing Kerri of that," he said. He put his hand on my shoulder. "I'll relieve you in two hours."

He went back into the cottage, and I sat there, remembering the night we met, and remembering the night two years later when he'd offered me the highest honor a Tyr could give any man. That night was much like this one. Mountains close. Stars in a clear sky overhead. But there was a fire burning on the ground and a merchant train camped nearby then.

I had been standing guard duty. When relieved, I went back to the fire. Cullin was wrapped in his plaid but awake and waiting for me.

"A messenger came from Tyra," he said quietly. "Gwynna has gifted me with another daughter."

I grinned. He loved his two elder daughters Elin and Wynn to distraction. There was more than enough love and pride to enfold another daughter. "*Ti'vati*, my congratulations," I said. "What will you call this one?"

"Gwynna says Maira." He shrugged, then smiled. "It's a good enough name."

"Let's hope this one looks like her mother, too, rather than her father."

Cullin laughed. "Oh, aye. A fearful fate indeed, being a

woman burdened with this face." He looked at me. "I had been hoping for a son," he said softly.

I said nothing. He didn't often speak of his family, and when he did, the pride he took in his daughters gleamed in his eyes and rang in his voice. I had never once before heard him wish one of the girls to be a son.

He was quiet for a long time. I thought he'd gone to sleep, but finally, he spoke again. "Kian, a man has need of a son." His voice sounded strained in the darkness. "I begin to doubt Gwynna will bear me one."

"Three daughters are enough to keep a man content in his old age," I said.

He chuckled. "Aye," he agreed. "I shall say, Elin, fetch my robe. Wynn, fetch me ale. Maira, fetch me bread and meat. And they'll scurry around more to keep me quiet than to serve me well." His tone changed again. "Kian . . . "

Cullin very seldom showed his serious side. I had only once heard that tone in his voice before, and that was when he spoke of the death of his grandfather. Sensing the importance of what he was about to say, I sat up and faced him. "Aye?"

"Kian, I've spent the last two years teaching you how to fight with that sword of yours, and you've learned well," he said. He looked at me, eyes narrowed in the flickering light. "You grew much as I predicted you would. You're no small man." He smiled. "You might just as easily be my son as Leydon's." He paused again. "Everything a man does for his son, I've done for you. I would take you as foster son, if you will. Make you my heir."

It left me speechless. It was a long time before I found my voice to accept the honor. So when we had delivered the pack train safely to Honandun, we made the trip back to Tyra, where I had undergone the adoption ceremony. Even Gwynna looked pleased, and made it clear she welcomed me as her son, and as a brother to the girls.

I looked up at the stars glittering in the dark sky above the ruined cottage. "I couldna be a Celae prince," I said aloud. "I do not *want* to be a Celae prince." And I couldn't have any magic. Save the Healing, which I had inherited from my mother, I couldn't have any magic. Not and feel the way I did about it. Surely Kerri was mistaken. She was allowing her need to find this princeling of hers to lead her to see him in me simply because I had accidentally come into possession of what she thought was a Celae Rune Blade.

Wasn't she?

The Watcher on the Hill stood quiet and still amid the circle of stones, looking down at me. The breeze that riffled my hair and stirred my plaid did not touch him. My feet planted wide in the white-starred velvet grass, I looked up at him, trying to see what lay under the shadows cloaking his face.

At the sound of a footstep behind me, I turned and drew my sword. The runes along the blade glittered and flashed, sending their own eerie light into the strange, distinctive glow of the sunless sky. A word sparked out at me. Strength. *It was just the one word out of many, but a deep satisfaction welled up in my chest, and I smiled as I raised my sword to confront him.*

"We meet again," my opponent said. He raised his dark sword in a mocking salute. "You can't defeat me, you know."

"Your magic has no life here," I said. "Not against the power of the Dance."

He laughed. "We shall see who is stronger," he said, then leapt forward, wrists snapping the sword into a swift, deadly stroke.

Again, I found myself fighting for my life against that sword. It sprayed its own darkness around itself as he swung it. Not only darkness, but cold, too—the deep, dank chill of the grave. He moved lightly, tirelessly, effortlessly, the muscles of his arms and shoulders rippling beneath the bronzed skin. And all the time, his lips drew up into a small, derisive smile that never faltered.

Back and forth across the small arena we fought each other, first one attacking, then the other. If he had weaknesses, I failed to find them, but he could not find mine, either. The air rang to the strident bell sound of steel against tempered steel. The clash and slither of thrust meeting parry echoed off the mountains behind us. Beneath our feet, the crushed grass bled its fresh perfume into the ringing air.

As it had happened before, I became aware that I was tiring faster than he. Time after time, I fell back before his attacks, forced to give ground. And again, there was no hidden well of vitality and stamina, no reserve resources I could find to draw the strength I needed. Remembering the last time we met, I lunged forward at him, stabbing out at him with the point of my sword. But he laughed and swayed gracefully away.

"It won't work twice, you know," he said. "You can't fool me like that again."

He spun away from my next thrust, then his sword came in under my guard, straight for my belly. I twisted desperately, barely managed to get my blade down to deflect his. It was almost enough. Instead of ripping through my belly, the tip of the blade sliced cleanly through the fabric of my sleeve and into the muscle of my right arm. My blood splashed to the ground, vivid red against the green of the crushed and trampled grass. The pain lanced like a blast of frigid cold up my arm, into my shoulder.

I stumbled under his renewed attack and fell to my knees. Shifting the hilt to my left hand, I swung backhanded at his ankles. He leapt nimbly up and out of the way, but the tip of my sword caught the heel of his boot. He lost his balance, fell, and came down heavily on hip and elbow. The sword went spinning from his loosened grip and sailed off, vanishing into its own darkness.

Instantly, my opponent was on his feet. He waited until I staggered erect, then gave me an ironic bow.

"For a big man, you are more agile than I gave you credit for," he said. "Next time, then." He stepped away and faded into the same darkness that took his sword.

Chest heaving with exertion, I turned to the Watcher on the Hill. Safe within the circle of the stone Dance, he looked down at me. Finally, he moved. He raised one hand, but whether it was in benediction or resignation, I couldn't tell. I put my hand to the wound on my arm and watched as the bleeding slowed, then stopped, watched as the skin drew closed until nothing was left but a thin, white scar.

Dawn streaked the sky with pink and yellow against pale azure. Carrying my sheathed sword, I left Cullin asleep by the fire and stepped out into the chill outside the ruined cottage. Kerri looked up at me from where she sat on the moss-covered rock by the wall as I came out, but said nothing. I walked past her down to the water, then followed the small burn upstream until I found a place where a gravel strand had made a clear crescent in the thicket of trees.

Echoes of the dream swirled through my head like wisps of mist. Pushing back the sleeve of my shirt, I looked at the thin, white scar on my arm for a long moment, then drew the sword and held it up to the first rays of the morning sun. The runes flashed and glittered, sparking and blazing in the light. I thought I could make out the word *Strength* on one side of the blade. The skin along my spine quivered slightly. What sort of dreams leave a man with a scar on his arm, and the ability to read something he never before could read?

"I dinna ken what kind of magic you have," I said, holding the sword up before my eyes. "But I want you to show me now. Now, while I can still fight you." The sword remained quiescent in my hands. I felt nothing. "If you're supposed to belong to this lost princeling of Kerri's, show me where he is. Start leading. By the seven gods and goddesses, start leading now, or I'll toss you into the burn and leave you there to rust."

Nothing happened. I had not really expected anything. It was the height of idiocy, standing in the light of the rising sun, speaking to a sword as if it understood, as if it were alive. But I shook the sword in anger and frustration. "I mean it. If you have magic of your own, show me now. Now, or Hellas take you . . . "

The sword began to resonate in my hands. Softly at first, then faster and faster until it felt alive. I became aware of a high, clear, sweet tone singing in the air around me, like a note plucked from a harp string in the highest register. At the same time, the blade began to shimmer, then to glow. At first, like the musical note, softly and gently. My hands on the hilt tingled and stung, and my whole body quivered like the air just before a lightning strike as the vibration traveled from the sword into me.

The musical note increased in pitch and volume, wild and keen, sharp, distinct, and crystalline around me, transmitting itself along the blade, through the hilt into my blood, my flesh, my sinews, until every nerve was alive to the music, thrumming in harmony with it. Overtones of triumphant jubilation sang in the note with shades and subtle nuances of burgeoning power. As the harmonic tone increased in pitch and intensity, so did the gleam of the blade. It moved swiftly through red to orange, then to yellow, until it was incandescent white, burning with a radiance to rival the rising sun, too painful to look at directly. The whole spectrum of the rainbow swirled and spun in wild patterns around me, edging the trees, the water, the gravel strand beneath my feet, with flashing patterns of coruscating color. The joyous chord rang wildly in the air. I had the distinct impression of something awakening and stretching after a long sleep.

The runes blazed brightly and clearly, flashing silver fire back to the rising sun. Words I could not read ran like liquid flame along the length of the blade with a life of their own, searing my eyes with their brilliance.

I yelled in terror. Sweat trickled coldly down my back, from beneath my arms, poured into my eyes, stinging. I tried to throw the sword down. But my hands felt welded to the leather of the hilt. I don't know if I could not let it go, or it would not let me go, but I could not hurl it from me. I had awakened it, and now it bound me to it. I could not loosen my grip. I could not drop the sword.

Slowly, inexorably, it began to pull, stretching my arms to their fullest extent. The tip quivered amid the brilliance, drawing me around with it to face northwest. The musical note moved into a minor key and a yearning that was not mine suffused my body. Home was in that direction. Home where I belonged.

The note changed. Something akin to firm resolution quivered through the bond connecting us, and the sword began to turn me, drawing me implacably around with it until we faced northeast. Determination and certainty filled me, a conviction of purpose. That way lay the goal. Northeast toward the far corner of Isgard, toward the border of Maedun.

The pull became stronger—irresistible, inexorable, overwhelming. My feet dragged in the gravel strand, but they moved. I had to move with the sword or have my arms pulled out of their sockets, torn from my body. I yelled again, but still could not loosen my grip on the sword.

Suddenly, Kerri was there, her sword drawn. She leaped in front of me and her blade came up to meet mine. I had the impression of a great explosion of heat and light and noise like a hundred crystal goblets shattering. Shards of luminescent brilliance fell like crystalline motes, flashing and sparking in the air around us. The bell and harp tone rose to a crescendo and splintered into fragments that glittered for an instant before vanishing. Then abrupt, ringing silence.

Kerri sheathed her sword and watched me anxiously, her eyes wide and startled. For a moment, I thought I could feel her fear, taste it as distinctly as I knew my own. I discovered I could pry my hands from the hilt of the sword. I rammed it home into the sheath and looked at the palms of my hands. They were reddened and blistered, dripping sweat. I rubbed them along the thighs of my breeks and slumped in combined relief and exhaustion.

"Gods," I muttered. "Gods, what in Hellas was that?"

"You awakened the sword," she said quietly. "You aroused it to its purpose."

I shuddered. But the magic the sword invoked was beautiful—the color and the wild, clear music. It left no taint in the air, no curl of nausea in my belly. It merely frightened me into cold, shivering immobility.

I looked at the sword, quiescent now in its scabbard, then turned and drew my hand back to hurl the Hellas-born thing into the water. But I couldn't. My arm froze, and something akin to pain slammed through me.

"You can't get rid of it now, Kian," Kerri said. "No more than you can get rid of your arm or your heart."

I turned on her furiously. "I don't want it," I shouted. "I don't want the accursed thing."

She smiled. "You're stuck with it," she said. "Just as surely as you're stuck with me."

I couldn't throw the sword away, so I slipped the harness around me and settled it onto my back. "Tcha," I said in disgust. Residual terror still caused tremors to quiver in my guts. "Tcha . . ."

"What did it show you?" she asked.

"Show me?" I repeated.

She smiled patiently, irritatingly.

I made an exasperated noise, then pointed northeast. "That way," I said. "It wanted to go that way. It pointed first northwest, then northeast."

"Toward Celi first," she said. She looked away, over the trees. "Home."

Home. I shivered again, remembering the longing and desire that swept through me as the sword drew me. Not my home. Never my home.

"What lies northeast then?" I asked.

She laughed softly. "Kyffen's grandson," she said. "You told it to lead. It's leading now, Kian, and we have to follow."

I stood there a moment, staring at her, aware my expression was anything but pleasant. It didn't make it any easier to realize that the whole debacle with the sword was my own fault. It was I, not Kerri, who had challenged the perverse thing to show me. I could hardly blame Kerri because it had. But that didn't prevent me being angry with her, as well as being annoyed with myself. It made for an unpleasant combination of emotions. When I tried to sort it out, I found frustration predominant. I couldn't decide whether I wanted to howl and snarl like a wolf, hit something, or simply stomp off in disgust. In the end, I did none of those things. I merely said, "Does that mean you're going to forget that ridiculous notion that I'm your lost prince?"

She turned away and walked upstream toward the ruined cottage. "Mayhaps," she called back over her shoulder. "We shall see what the sword tells us."

It took less effort than I anticipated for Kerri to persuade Cullin to go northeast toward Maedun. All he did was glance from her to me a few times, then smiled and shook his head like an indulgent father, amused by the antics of his offspring. I was about to snarl when I realized it would only heighten the image, so I wisely kept my mouth shut and went to saddle the horses.

PART

3

The Search

14

The countryside of Isgard was rife with rumor. Isgard had long stood uneasy with Maedun to its east, but reasonably secure with the sea to the west and Tyra to the north, neutral, but benevolently so. Falinor and Isgard had never been allies, but maintained warily peaceful relations because both were equally strong and war would have been mutually disastrous. Internal strife, coupled with a strong nudge from Maedun, had toppled Falinor. Faced suddenly with Maedun on two borders, Isgard hastily set about tidying its own backyard. It had always been easier for the noble houses of Isgard to hire mercenaries rather than take men from farms, or merchants from business, all of whom provided the houses with sufficient income to support extravagant lifestyles. Most of those mercenaries were Maedun, and the lords of the houses wasted little time in ridding themselves of what abruptly loomed large as a menace.

Every small village, every town, every roadside inn, was filled with men called to their lord's service. We heard stories of fighting between hastily trained local troops and mercenaries still in the service of lords who refused to relinquish them. There were more stories about the Ephir sending emissaries to Tyra and Saesnes to contract for an alliance in the event Maedun invaded Isgard. One innkeeper told us emphatically that Maedun had no wish to quarrel with Isgard mainly because Isgard was so much stronger than Maedun. An Isgardian officer who had been sitting quietly with his meal and his ale at a table in the corner of the inn laughed at him.

"Maedun will not invade Isgard," he agreed. "But not because we are the stronger. They will not invade because they yet lack the sorcerer to defeat us. Let that man appear, and we will see a Lord Protector on the throne of Isgard and the Ephir and his whole family put to the sword."

"Never," the innkeeper protested stoutly. "The men of Isgard will never let that happen."

"The men of Isgard will have little choice in the matter," the officer said, returning to his meal.

"The throne of Maedun must now be in strong hands as it never was before," I said to Cullin. The officer overheard me and laughed again.

"Not yet," he said. "But it soon will be, if that accursed General Hakkar has his way."

"Hakkar?" Cullin repeated. "I have never heard of him."

"Nor had anyone else until Falinor fell," the officer said grimly. "He is a brilliant general, I am told, and he is also something of a sorcerer. He is trouble no matter how you look at him. If the gods favor us, he will not be able to put his brother Vanizen on the throne." His eyes narrowed as he studied first Cullin, then me. "You have the look of Tyrs, for all you wear not the kilt. How stands Tyra in this?"

"Tyra is neutral," Cullin said. "We have learned how to treat with the Maedun. Their sorcery willna work in the high country, and Tyra has little else but mountains."

The officer grunted. "I've heard it said that the Maedun are hunting for a young Tyr," he said. "One who carries a Celae Rune Blade. The price in gold they offer might tempt an unscrupulous man. You might be wise to stay out of the way of any such man to prevent any mistakes in identity." He went back to his meal.

The advice was worth consideration. We took to the fields and forests after that as we rode northeast. The roads were inordinately full of patrols, and troops of Maedun riding east. Many of the departing mercenaries were accompanied by a man who exuded the harsh stench of magic. They gave no impression of searching for someone, but we thought it prudent and expedient to take ourselves well out of their way.

We were camped less than half a league from the city of Frendor under a gray, sullen sky, and I had lost another argument with Kerri. Our supplies were running low, and I suggested that I should go to the city market to replenish them. Kerri jumped up and insisted she should be the one to go, not I.

"The city is crawling with Maedun," I said. "You can't go alone."

She planted both fists on her hips and thrust out her jaw at me. "Are you implying I can't take care of myself?" she demanded. "Because if you are—"

"I'm implying that a woman alone is asking for trouble, *sheyala*," I said. "Especially a lone Celae woman."

"I'm not the one with ten Maedun gold pieces riding on my head," she retorted.

"I'm not the one three Maedun mercenaries tried to haul off into slavery," I snapped back. I lifted a hand to forestall her declaration she could have handled all three quite nicely, thank you, with no help from a half-naked barbarian. I had heard that refrain often enough to quote it chapter and verse from memory. "You can't go alone."

"Take you with me and have some Maedun try to collect those ten gold pieces? What makes you think I've got time to run around rescuing you if you're recognized?"

"You? Rescue me? Don't make me laugh. Besides, they probably won't recognize me dressed like this."

She snorted derisively. "Like that Isgardian officer didn't recognize you as a Tyr? Mayhaps if I cut off that braid and dyed your hair black for you, they wouldn't."

My hand went defensively to the braid at my left temple. "Now look—"

"No, you look." She took one hand off her hip and stabbed at my breastbone. "You are going to stop"—*Jab*—"treating me like some helpless female"—*Jab*—"and listen to reason"—*Jab*—"if I have to knock it down your throat"—*Jab*—"with my sword." *Jab*.

I took a couple of quick steps backward to avoid a collision with her chin, then slapped aside the stabbing finger. "By all the gods, *sheyala*, you'll stay here where it's safe," I roared, reverting to volume rather than reason. When had she ever listened to reason, anyway? "They'll recognize you—"

"Just like a man," she muttered in disgust. "When you

know you're losing an argument, you start yelling." The air around her shimmered very slightly, then I stood staring at an Isgardian farm woman, short, plump, and dark. Only the faintest ripple of a chill slid down my spine.

"Can you do this?" she asked sweetly. She reached up and patted my cheek with infuriating superiority. "See? I told you there was a difference with Tyadda magic."

I turned helplessly to Cullin for support. He shrugged, the corners of his mouth twitching. "I certainly wouldna recognize her that way," he murmured.

"I can hold this masking spell indefinitely and it's unlikely any Maedun warlock will detect the magic," she said. She shot me a look of triumphant, smug scorn. "Even you can't feel it, can you?"

I rubbed my arms, but the prickle along them was more because I knew what she was doing, rather than because I sensed it. "I can feel it," I muttered.

She caught the reins of her mare and mounted. "I'll be back by an hour before sunset," she said. She wheeled the mare and kicked it to a canter.

"Verra determined lass, that," Cullin said, watching her disappear down the dusty road. He grinned at me. "I'd say she won that argument fair and square."

"You were no help," I said.

He shrugged. "Aye, well," he said. "Mayhaps it's because I thought she might be right this time."

I made a disgusted noise and went to sit by the fire.

Kerri had been gone a little over two hours when I began to get twitchy. The nagging sense that something somewhere was seriously wrong drove me restlessly to my feet, forced me to pace fretfully back and forth across the small clearing around our campfire. Telling myself Kerri would be furious if I went into Frendor after her did not help. Neither did telling myself that, if she were in trouble, she had no one to blame but herself. If anything, it made the unsettled feeling in my belly worse.

Cullin sat by the fire, cleaning and honing his sword, and watched in amusement as I did a creditable imitation of a caged mountain cat. He said nothing when I walked over to the horses and stood with my hand on Rhuidh's withers, staring for several minutes down the road where Kerri had disappeared.

The fidgety unease increased, as did the feeling that something was drastically wrong. Kerri was in trouble, trouble she could not handle by herself. The second time my jittery pacing took me to where the horses were picketed, Cullin sheathed his sword and came across the clearing to join me.

"She's going to be furious with us," I said, picking up Rhuidh's saddle and settling it firmly onto his back.

"Aye, she will," he agreed, buckling the girth of his saddle around the bay.

"She's likely to see how close she can shave me with that greatsword of hers." I slipped the bridle over the sorrel's ears and fastened it. "Or she'll make a determined effort to shorten my height by a head."

"Most assuredly," he said, fitting the bit gently between the stallion's teeth. "One or the other. Or perhaps both concurrently and simultaneously if not consecutively."

I gathered Rhuidh's reins and mounted quickly. "I'm being foolish again, I expect."

"I expect so." He grinned and mounted.

"And you're humoring me," I said.

"No." He shook his head. "I've never seen you so agitated. I think you've cause."

"She's in trouble, *ti'vati*."

"She must be. Let's go, then, shall we?"

Frendor was less than a quarter the size of Honandun. Its only reason for existence was that it lay on the caravan route for trade goods going east from the coast, or west from the Great Salt Sea, and it was a convenient stopover for merchant trains to replenish their supplies. Its lord, the nephew of the Ephir in Honandun, had grown wealthy from the business of the merchant trains. His house, perched on a bluff overlooking the city, well away from the din and squalor of the marketplace, showed evidence of the wealth. The rest of the city did not. The taverns and inns that lined the streets displayed all the tawdry finery of a town dedicated to relieving a traveler of every last silver or copper coin it could squeeze out of him by catering to every common vice, and more than a few uncommon ones.

It started to drizzle as we reached the city, and we rode with the hoods of our cloaks drawn up over our heads to hide our hair and mask our faces. The rain served us well. No one would question the hoods in the rain.

We left the horses at the edge of the market square with a farrier who demanded three copper coins apiece to care for them, displaying a mouth full of gold teeth in a wolfish grin. Cullin handed the man the stallion's reins and returned the smile.

"If this horse is not here when I return for it," he said in High Isgardian, "I shall be pleased to extract its worth from your mouth, my friend. Directly after I cut out a slice of your liver to feed my dogs." He flashed a grin at me. "And my cousin here delights in carving his initials on the rear cheek of people who annoy him." He glanced at me again, then lowered his voice confidentially as he spoke to the farrier. "He tends to be a bit clumsy at times, especially if he's been drinking mead. He's been known to slip and remove some rather delicate portions of the anatomy."

The farrier displayed his dental wealth in a nervous smile. "No fear, my lords," he said hastily. "They be safe with me as in your own stable."

"I'm sure they are," Cullin said graciously.

I had not seen Kerri's black mare in the small pen. "We are looking for someone," I said. "A tall, blond woman or her servant, a small plump woman with dark hair dressed in brown." I took two coppers from my purse and tossed them casually from hand to hand. "They had a black mare with a white blaze down its face. The dark-haired woman might have been riding it."

The farrier's eyes never left the glinting coins. Reluctantly, he said, "I've not seen 'em, my lord. But if I do—"

I flipped him the coins. He snatched them deftly out of the air, and they vanished into a pouch around his neck almost too quickly for the eye to follow.

"You'll certainly tell us when we return for our horses, will you not?"

"Aye, my lord. I will, my lord."

We turned away and began walking toward the market square. The goods in the stalls of the market square were clearly second- or third-rate. The woolen yard goods were poorly dyed in dull and muddy colors, and if they felt as scratchy as they looked, would be highly uncomfortable to wear. The silver buckles and cloak pins looked flimsy, as if they contained a large percentage of tin. The fruits and vegetables, piled high on tottering tables, were spotty and withered, and thoroughly unappetizing.

In dismay, I surveyed the thronged square, wondering where to start looking. Frendor was not big, but it was more than large enough for one woman to lose herself completely within it. What had seemed so simple back at our campsite now loomed as an impossible task.

"This is going to be fun," I murmured. "We don't even know what we're looking for."

"I wondered when that might occur to you," Cullin said.

I glanced at him. "You didna have to come just to indulge me in this foolishness."

"No," he agreed. "But this is better than watching you wear a path in the ground."

Two women, dressed in bright diaphanous robes designed to display their charms rather than hide them, spilled out of an open tavern door and clutched at Cullin's arms.

"You look like a man who appreciates a good woman," one of them said. Her makeup was garish in the wan light.

Cullin smiled at them and gently detached their hands. "I am such a man," he said. "And that's why I'll decline your gracious offer." He glanced up the street, then suddenly put his arm around one of the women. "But on second thought—"

I followed the direction of his gaze and saw six Maedun soldiers shouldering their way down the rickety sidewalk toward us. I put my arm around the other woman, and we ducked into the tavern. The inside was lit to the brilliance of a Falian tin mine at midnight. The one window in the place was dirty and streaky. We stood huddled with the women close to it until the Maedun soldiers had passed. We extricated ourselves and went back out onto the sidewalk, followed by the hurled imprecations of the women, who thought themselves brutally and unjustly deprived of an hour's income.

"We surely canna just wander around these streets," Cullin said as we began walking briskly. "Is there no way you can find her? If you can tell she's in trouble, can you no use that same sense to tell us where she might be?"

I hadn't thought of that. And I wasn't sure it would work. I ducked into a dirty alleyway, drawing him with me, and drew my sword. I had invoked its magic once. I might be able to do it again. I only hoped I could control it if this worked.

The alleyway was filthy. It smelled of rotting food from a midden heap behind a tavern, stale urine, and excrement. But it was well shielded from the street. Ignoring the stench, I held up the sword and cleared my mind to ground and center myself. I became suddenly conscious of strange flows of energy, currents in the very earth beneath my feet, in the air around me, that I had never been aware of before. I tried to disregard the odd streams of energy swirling and eddying all around me and concentrated on the sword. I had worked its magic once before, but had no clear idea how to do it again. Cullin watched me skeptically as I frowned at the sword.

"Lead me," I said. "You did it before. Do it again."

The harsh glare of brilliance from the blade illuminated the dirty walls around us like a hundred torches flaring to life all at once. The sword tugged sharply in my hands, and the sudden wrench spun me around so abruptly, the blade clanged on the slimy stone of the wall behind me. I swore softly. Northeast. It had swung me northeast again.

"Not that way, you mindless piece of tin," I snarled. "We'll go there later. First, find Kerri."

The sword trembled in my hands. Almost like a question. Or puzzlement.

"Find Kerri," I told it.

Again, the only response was a quivering that itched and tingled against the palms of my hands.

"The woman, you ill-crafted, misbegotten excuse for a sword," I growled. Then, on sudden inspiration: "The bearer of the Rune Blade Whisperer. Find her."

The nature of the tremor changed and a sudden sense of purpose infused the sword. Slowly, it turned me to face the mouth of the alley. I sheathed the sword to quench the brilliant gleam, but it still quivered against my back, urging me back out onto the street. I turned to Cullin, who was pale beneath the shadow of the hood of his cloak.

"Are you all right?" I asked, startled. I had never seen him look completely undone like that before

"Aye, well," he said softly and shook his head. "I've naught against the idea of magic, ye ken. But I dinna like it performed right before me like that. I find it unnerving."

"*You* find it unnerving," I muttered. "Gods. I *hate* magic. And I hate this." I stepped out into the street. "The stupid sword says this way."

The sword on my back was like a phantom hand on my shoulder. Nudging this way and that, it led us through the confusing warren of streets. After a while, it became apparent it was leading us surely and unerringly toward the elegant houses belonging to rich merchants that nestled at the foot of the embankment below the lord's fortress manse. Twice, we had to duck into an alley to avoid Maedun mercenaries wearing Lord Balkan's blazon. Obviously, the Ephir's nephew was not one of the Isgardians who viewed the Maedun as a danger to the country.

The streets became marginally wider and cleaner as we approached the walled houses of the merchants. The guiding tugs of the sword on my back were more urgent now, and I began to feel a sense of foreboding. I was afraid it meant Kerri was not only in trouble, but in acute danger.

A man stepped out onto the street from behind a wall ahead

of us. Every hair on my body tried to rise up erect and sudden nausea churned in my belly. Even over the wet stench of the rain swirling in the garbage on the street, I smelled the gagging reek of magic surrounding the man. He was dressed as an affluent Isgardian merchant, but his hair and eyes were the black of a Maedun. As he closed the gate behind him and walked toward us, I swung Cullin into a narrow side street and hunched, shivering, into my cloak.

Gods, I had never felt magic that strong before, nor smelled so clearly the overlying stench of blood and death with it.

"Magic?" Cullin asked quietly.

Unable to speak, I stopped and nodded, weak and shaken by the nausea, my legs trembling with it. I could feel the man's eyes on my back as he walked past the entrance of the side street. Cullin pretended to consult a slip of parchment from his pocket and looked around as if checking an address, his face calm but his eyes gleaming brightly, alert and ready for any trouble.

"It's all right," he murmured a moment later. "He's gone past. I fancy we look well dressed enough to have business here."

My legs still trembled as we made our way back to the main thoroughfare. The Maedun merchant was nowhere in sight as we turned back on our original course. Cullin paused momentarily in front of the gate the merchant had come through and I saw him make a mental note of the name etched in the stone above the gate.

The sword tugged urgently. I stumbled forward a few paces, muttering a curse. The sword yanked at me again.

"All right," I mumbled. "I'm coming. I'm coming. Dinna get yourself in such a dither."

We were coming to the end of the street of houses, and still the sword led on, deviating neither right nor left. It began to rain harder as we passed the last walled house. The road before us turned sharply to lead up the back slope of the bluff toward Lord Balkan's manse.

"This could become verra interesting," Cullin murmured, wiping the rain from his face.

Tall trees lined the road up to the manse, their leaves gleaming wetly in the gray light. Lush grass interspersed with bushes grew thickly in the spaces between them. In the sun, it would be a pleasant park, but drenched and dripping with rain, it merely looked dreary and bleak.

A sudden flash of lightning bloomed in the west, followed by a growling peal of thunder. Cullin glanced up, then shook the water from the hood of his cloak.

"I would suggest we take to the trees if that sword insists on going up there," he said. "I wouldna want a reception committee awaiting our arrival."

"Aye, you're right," I said. The sword showed no sign of wanting me to turn from the road.

We crept up the hill cautiously. The walls of the fortress soared three man-heights into the air, topped by sharp, jagged stones. Turrets protected the corners and I saw the gleam of a guard's steel helmet in one of them. The massive wooden gates stood open outward, flat against the outer wall, but a shorter gate fashioned of iron bars closed off any entry to the courtyard. Two small sentry boxes flanked the gate inside the walls, built right into the stone of the wall itself. Cullin and I crouched in the soaked grass by some bushes and studied it carefully. It would be no easy task to get through that gate, even without the guards.

Some of the courtyard was clearly visible through the gates. As I watched, a man led a horse toward the stable. The sword on my back trembled violently as I recognized Kerri's mare.

15

Daylight faded quickly from the sullen black of the sky. Not the slightest gleam of color glowed in the west to mark the sunset. The rain let up a little, but lightning still flashed to the northwest, a little nearer now, judging by how close the crack of thunder followed the blaze of lightning.

The fortress manse was huge, so big it was impossible to estimate how many rooms it contained. Like Mendor's Landholding in Falinor, it probably had a series of cells deep under it, too, where prisoners who might never expect to see the light of day again could be kept. Kerri might be anywhere in that labyrinth, and Cullin and I could spend days looking for her.

But we did not have days. Unless we found some way through the gates or over the walls, we had nothing. We certainly could not expect Lord Balkan to invite us conveniently in, or obligingly deliver Kerri to us on demand.

"I'm open to suggestion," Cullin said softly. "Any ideas on how to get in there?" He paused thoughtfully. "And out again, of course. Preferably in one piece each."

"Aye, well, that's important," I agreed.

"It is. If the wee lassie is going to be annoyed wi' us, ye ken, far better it be because we rescued her rather than because we tried and failed."

I grinned. "Far better indeed. There may be another gate."

"Aye, there may. But locked just as securely as this." He let his gaze move along the high wall. "We might scale that. There's no place along it not in view of the turrets, but this rain might obscure a guard's vision enough. Those stones atop it look razor sharp, though. It would be tricky."

We heard the sound of a troop of horses approaching and ducked back deeper into the dripping shadows. The clatter of iron-shod hooves on the cobblestones was muffled by the steady downpour of rain, and we were barely able to flatten ourselves into the soaked shrubbery before the riders rounded the last bend before the straight stretch of road leading to the gates.

It was a troop of Maedun, their dark cloaks blending in with the swiftly approaching night. At the head of the troop rode the man we had last seen on the street in front of the walled houses of the merchants. Beside him rode a man cloaked in the gray of a warlock. I swore under my breath and tried to press myself right down into the spongy ground beneath my chest and belly. The sword trembled with urgency on my back, and I cursed it silently, terrified the warlock would sense its magic. It subsided sullenly, and I dared to hope neither the warlock nor the man masquerading as a merchant had noticed it.

They rode right past us. None of them so much as glanced our way. We climbed to our feet and peered through the screen of low bushes as the men and horses approached the gate. Two guards appeared out of the sentry boxes behind the grille of the gate.

"Tell the Lord Balkan the general has arrived," said the man in warlock's gray.

We could not hear the guards' reply, but the gates creaked open and the troop of Maedun filed through. As the last horse and rider went past, the gates clanged shut and one of the guards locked it. The riders wound their way toward the stables, and the guards retired to the dry comfort and warmth of the sentry boxes.

The idea bloomed nearly full-grown into my head as I studied the guards. "No exactly small men, those guards," I commented softly.

Cullin glanced at me, then grinned suddenly, his teeth flashing white in the gloom. "Aye," he agreed. "About our size, would ye say?"

"Nearabout," I said. I twisted around under my sodden cloak and detached my sword and scabbard from its harness. "Why, will ye look at this. My master the general has gone and forgotten his sword."

"Such a silly wee general," Cullin said. "And you being such a faithful servant and mindful of propriety, I ken ye're meaning to see he gets it."

"Oh, aye. I'd be remiss in my duty if I didna."

He unsheathed one of the daggers from his belt. "I'll give you a moment to distract the guards, then join you." He climbed to his feet and looked around. "I'll come up to the wall over there," he said, pointing to the shadows halfway between the gates and the corner turret. "There willna be enough torchlight to see farther than an armlength in this rain. We'll no be worrit overly much about the guards in the turrets if we go about this quietly and circumspectly."

I walked up to the gate as if I had a perfect right to be there, and banged on the gate with the scabbard. "Oy!" I called. "Be anyone in there?"

The two startled guards came tumbling out of the small shelters. "What be you wanting?" one of them demanded.

I held up the scabbard hopefully. "My master the general forgot his sword," I said. "He be in such a hurry to see the great Lord Balkan, he rushed off without it. I be bringing it to him."

The second guard thrust his hand through the bars. "Give it here," he commanded. "I be seeing he gets it."

I drew back, horrified. "By the gods, no," I cried. "He be a man of quick temper, the general. If I can get it to him without the great Lord Balkan noticing, I mayhaps be avoiding a flogging. You give it to him, and I be losing hide from my back for sure." I cowered down into my cloak, trying to look convincing as a frightened servant.

Apparently my description of the general's character was near enough the mark. One of the guards laughed and stepped up to unlock the gate. "You nip in and out right lively," he said. "Don't be getting us in trouble for letting you in."

"Oh, no, sir," I replied, slipping through the gate. Both guards had all their attention on me. Neither saw Cullin creep along the wall toward the open gate. "I be right quick." I smiled ingratiatingly at the first guard. "Right quick," I repeated and thrust my dagger up through his belly into his heart just as Cullin's dagger severed the spinal cord of the second guard. They went down without a sound.

I caught mine under the arms and dragged him into the sentry box, then darted out to close the gate, but didn't throw the lock. Cullin had already begun to strip the second guard in the other sentry box when I ducked back into the first. There was hardly room inside to turn around, but I managed to strip off the guard's uniform quickly enough, then peeled out of my wet leathers. The guard was almost as tall as I, but thicker through the middle. The breeks were baggy, but I cinched the belt tight enough to keep them up. The helmet was a bit loose, but stuffing my hair up under it prevented it from slipping down over my eyes. Clipping the scabbard back onto its harness on my back, I went out to meet Cullin. His uniform fitted a little better than mine.

I put my hand to the hilt of my sword. "Lead," I whispered fiercely to it. It quivered gently beneath my hand, then nudged me forward. Cullin fell into step with me, and we marched across the courtyard to the shelter of one of the outbuildings. If luck and the goddess were with us, we had a little over three hours until midnight, when the dead guards should be relieved, before anyone discovered we were in the manse. It might be enough time.

"Not through the main door, I'm thinking," Cullin said softly. "It's hardly for the likes of a pair of guards."

"A wee bit public," I agreed. "There's probably a kitchen door near the bake house around the side."

We met another pair of guards, arguing vociferously about something, as we rounded the corner of the house. I saw Cullin's hand go to his dagger, and mine was near the haft of my sword, but they did not so much as glance at us as we passed and went through the kitchen door, and didn't miss a beat in their argument. The cooks and kitchen staff looked up as we entered. One of the cooks waved us through a door to our left.

"Food in there for you," she called. "If there be any left. You be late."

"Cursed rain," Cullin called back cheerfully as I pulled open the door. It led to an empty mess hall. An archway at the opposite end opened onto a dimly lit corridor. We were obviously in the servants' wing. It was unlikely Lord Balkan had Kerri hidden here. We had to find our way to the family quarters. Or to the dungeons.

"Lead," I told the sword.

It led. It pulled us through twisting corridors, up and down curving staircases. In only a few minutes, I had lost all sense of direction. I couldn't tell whether we were heading deeper into the manse, or skirting the walls. We rounded a corner and suddenly found ourselves in the main wing. The floor beneath our boots changed from stone to warm, polished tile, and the walls of the corridors were paneled in rich, glowing wood. Carpet covered the floors of the rooms we passed, and I caught glimpses of tapestried wall hangings that would bring a fortune in Honandun.

Cullin heard the murmur of voices before I did. He held up his hand to stop me, his head cocked to one side, listening intently for a moment, then made a beckoning gesture as he turned down a fork in the corridor.

We stepped into a shadowed open space. Beyond us lay a large room, brightly lit by lamps and candles, a fire in the huge hearth taking the damp chill of the rain from the air. We stood in a serving alcove in the shadow of several huge pillars, each of them too big for two men to circle with their arms. Around us were tables holding spare candles, flasks of oil for lamps, trays of crystal and silver goblets, and decanters of spirits. Three large amphorae stood against the wall, giving off the rich, fruity scent of good wine.

I peered cautiously around one of the pillars. The room was lavishly furnished in opulently patterned, deep carpets, beautifully worked wall hangings, and thickly upholstered chairs and couches. Near the hearth stood a massive oaken chair, cushioned in red velvet, the coat of arms of the Royal House of Isgard, lacking only the Ephir's own triple plumes, engraved into the polished wood above the cushions on the back. Light gleamed on silver and crystal goblets and the ruby sparkle of wine on a low table next to a smaller chair. The man in the chair sat with one leg thrown casually over the arm of the chair as he toyed with a sword. My own sword thrummed on my back like a swarm of angry hornets as I recognized Kerri's Rune Blade.

"That is not for you," a voice said. A tall man dressed in ornate leathers and embroidered velvet entered the room and walked over to pour himself a glass of wine.

The man in the chair dropped the sword to the carpet. "Of course not, Lord Balkan," he murmured. "I was simply looking at it. I see no runes on the blade."

"You won't," Lord Balkan replied shortly. "But they are there, I assure you."

The man in the chair rose to his feet, reaching lazily for his wine on the table. With a startled shock, I recognized Drakon. I got another shock as the general entered, accompanied by the warlock, and closely followed by Mendor and Dergus Keepmaster.

"Ah, there you are, General Hakkar," Balkan said pleasantly. "I trust you approve of the offerings I have prepared for you. Fine gifts, both of them, I can assure you."

The general poured a glass of wine and critically studied its color and clarity against the light of the massed candles. Deciding it was worthy, he took a sip before speaking. "They both have a little magic," he said. "The woman more so than the man, but they will serve the purpose for now."

"You will gain more power from them, Lord Hakkar," rumbled the warlock.

Balkan raised his glass in salute to the general and smiled. "And when you are powerful enough, my friend, soon now, we will rid ourselves of my doddering old uncle."

The general returned the salute, his smile as cold as mountain glaciers. "And you will have the throne, Balkan," he replied. "And I shall have to call you my lord Ephir."

Balkan laughed. "Of course not," he said. "We are friends, are we not? There is no need of such formality between friends."

The general lifted his glass again. "As you say," he said graciously. He turned to Drakon, who stood leaning negligently against the fireplace wall, one elbow propped up on the marble mantelpiece. "What success have you in tracking down that young Tyr?" he asked.

Drakon shrugged. "We tracked them to an inn two days' ride from here. They'll be found shortly. They can't escape detection for long. Two men with red hair traveling with a Celae woman . . ." He smiled. "And we do, after all, have the woman, for all she says she left them at the inn."

"We will have the truth from her," Dergus said. "If the lord general would let me have a few moments alone with her . . . "

The general turned a mild gaze to him. "You will keep your hands off her, Dergus," he said softly. "Or you might find yourself giving up what little magic you have to me."

Dergus stepped back, his face going an unpleasant shade of pasty white. "Of course, lord General," he said hastily. "I was merely suggesting she could be persuaded into the truth."

"Of course," the general murmured. He looked at Drakon again. "Don't underestimate the men," he said coolly. "Tyran clansmen have a nasty habit of being far more clever than they look."

Drakon shrugged again. "The older one may need care in taking, but the young one is nothing but a runaway slave."

The general gave him a level look. "He carries a Celae Rune Blade, and by all accounts, it serves him well. You would be well advised to remember that, young cockerel."

"We will find him for you, Lord Hakkar," Mendor said smoothly. "Then the sword will be yours."

"But the slave is mine." Drakon's voice grew harsh. "For this, I kill him." He touched the scar at the side of his head. "For this, he surely dies."

"If he has power, he is mine," the general said. He smiled as Drakon started to protest. "He's mine, and his death is mine, but you may play with him to your heart's content before he dies. Will that serve?"

Drakon touched his deformed ear and laughed softly. "It will serve, my lord," he replied. "It will afford me great pleasure."

I didn't realize I was shuddering in the chill shadow of the pillar until my teeth began to chatter. I clamped my jaw as Cullin's hand came down on my shoulder. There was so much magic in the brightly lit room. It was almost overwhelming. A hard, black aura surrounded the general, blacker than a moonless night, black as the pits of Hellas. Not even all the light in the room could dispel the darkness around him. I was mildly amazed that neither he nor the warlock gave any indication of being aware of the quiet throbbing of the sword on my back.

But if the general could not detect that, how had they found out Kerri? Even I had not been able to sense the gentle masking spell she had used. And neither the general nor the warlock had perceived it at the market fair in Trevellin. I thought the stench of magic around the general was stronger now, but still, he showed no signs of curiosity about the alcove where Cullin and I stood hidden. Had Kerri made some mistake that gave her away?

The warlock raised his head suddenly and smiled. "They are ready for you now, Lord Hakkar," he said softly.

The general put down the half-finished glass of wine. "You wish to observe this?" he said to the others in the room.

"If we may, my lord," Mendor said, smiling.

"Then come." He left the room, and the rest fell in behind him.

They left Kerri's sword lying on the carpet where Drakon had dropped it. Cullin and I waited a moment or two to be sure they would not return, then stepped out into the room. Cullin went to the chair and stooped to pick up the Rune Blade.

"She's going to want this, I think," he said quietly. "Can we follow them?"

There was no sign of anyone in the corridor when we ventured out of the room, but the sword led us unerringly and certainly. I thought I detected an answering soft buzz from the Rune Blade Cullin had thrust through his belt, but I wasn't sure. It might only be my own taut nerves, stretched like harp strings, vibrating in my anxiety.

I had been expecting the sword to lead us downward, to the

dungeons. Instead, it guided us deeper toward the center of the building, toward the place the Keep would be if this house were built like a Falian manor house.

We passed other pairs of guards patrolling the corridors as we strode through the halls, our footsteps ringing confidently on the polished tile of the floor. None spared us more than a brief nod of greeting. Several times, servants stepped aside respectfully to let us pass. No one questioned our right to be in the corridor.

Quivering, the sword halted me abruptly at a heavy door. Cullin and I stood for a moment to either side of it, looking at each other, both of us wondering what we would do if the door were locked. Finally, Cullin shrugged and reached for the latch. It lifted, but the door remained firmly shut.

"Any ideas?" he asked, raising an eyebrow.

I shook my head helplessly. Behind my ear, the sword hummed a deep, low vibrato. I drew it and watched it for a moment, then experimentally placed the tip against the latch. The blade glowed with sudden, intense incandescence for a brief moment, then there was a soft click from the door. Cullin pushed gently against it, and it swung open noiselessly and smoothly on oiled hinges.

"Handy thing, that sword," he commented in a breathless whisper. "But it takes some getting used to."

I nodded in fervent agreement, then peered into the room. It was blacker than a well bottom inside. No light at all showed. I sheathed the sword and stepped into the room. Two paces brought me face first into thick, dusty-smelling black velvet draperies. I managed to stifle my sneeze and reached out to warn Cullin. I heard a faint, muffled thud as he closed the door.

There was not enough light to see each other as we edged along between the draperies and the wall. I got the impression of a circular room. The hangings, stretching from ceiling to floor, left a space not more than an armlength deep behind them. They muffled the sound in the room beyond them, but we heard something being dragged across the floor, then a moan. It sounded like a terrified animal.

We found a place where a faint gleam of light glimmered between two of the hangings that didn't quite meet properly, leaving a thumbbreadth of space between them. I reached out and carefully parted the curtains until we could see into the room.

Light came only from two guttering torches standing in brackets to either side of a raised dais in the center of the room. On the dais stood a small brazier, glowing sullen red against the dark, and a table holding a dagger with a wickedly curved blade. A man lay bound and gagged on the floor before the dais. The warlock knelt behind him, and the general sat on a low, carved stool in front of him. The whites of the bound man's eyes gleamed in the flickering light cast by the torches as his glance darted in mortal fear around the room, and he whimpered in terror through his gag. Balkan, Mendor, Drakon, and Dergus stood behind the dais, alertly interested, but out of the way.

But where was Kerri? I looked quickly around the room, and finally found her only by the gleam of dark gold hair spilling out from a crumpled heap of black velvet against the wall hanging. I touched Cullin's arm and pointed. He nodded. He had spotted her when I had.

The general reached for the curved dagger on the table above him. He tested the blade with his thumb and glanced at the warlock. "Remember," he said softly. "At the right moment. At exactly the right moment, or it will be no good."

"Yes, my lord," the warlock murmured. He put his hands to either side of the captive's head, and nodded at the general. The general plunged the dagger into the man's abdomen and ripped it viciously upward. As the steaming entrails tumbled and spilled out onto the floor, the general thrust his hands into the man's belly.

"Now!" he cried to the warlock.

The stench of magic clogged the air around me. Unable to move, unable to breathe, I stood frozen in horror, watching the scene in the room before me. The general, wrist deep in the entrails of the dying man, began to chant words I couldn't understand, couldn't quite hear. The voice of the warlock joined his as the warlock clamped his hands tighter around the man's head.

A black mist rose from the tangle of guts around the general's hands. Slowly, it circled his wrists, climbing inexorably along his blood-splashed arms. It began to shimmer, softly at first, with faint colors barely visible in the black vapor. As it reached his elbows, the colors became brighter—reds and oranges and yellows, swirling and pulsing with sullen light, like flames twisting through sooty smoke. The general cried out sharply as the mist enveloped his chest, reached higher for his head. His face stiffened and contorted into a mask of orgiastic ecstasy behind the mist.

My skin crawled and my very flesh crept, trying to retreat from the revulsion submerging me. Both chills and fever raged through my body, and I gagged and choked as the stench of the reeking mist reached me. I couldn't stop it. I turned away and spewed bitter bile all over the stones of the floor behind me.

Never had it been that bad. Never before had I experienced magic so vile, so incredibly evil. I knew now what Kerri meant when she spoke of blood magic. It was unspeakable terror, steeped in horror and pain, worse than any part of Hellas could possibly be, and, for a moment, I thought I might die simply through exposure to it. Weak and shaken, I pushed away from the wall and turned back to Cullin. He was not unaffected, but it was the sheer horror of the act itself that turned him pale, not the magic.

The light of anger flashed in his eyes. Slowly, he drew his sword. "Aye, well," he said quietly. "That's quite enough of that, I think." He stepped through the curtain.

16

For a long, stunned moment, no one in the room moved. Then the warlock jerked away from the disemboweled corpse on the floor and staggered to his feet. The general, still on his knees, glazed and frozen within the swiftly dissipating black mist, howled in agony, but didn't move. I saw the red globe of magical energy spring to life in the warlock's hands and stepped between him and Cullin just as he hurled it.

Hissing and sizzling, leaving a streak of burning air behind it, the ball flew straight at my head. Instinctively, I raised the sword to ward it off. I had meant only to try to knock it away. I certainly had not counted on the polished surface of the blade acting as a mirror.

The small globe hit the blade squarely, then bounced. It is the only word that fits. It bounced and flashed back through the fiery, smoking trail it had left in the air behind it, gathering the energy it lost in creating the trail. The warlock screamed like a woman as it hit him and erupted into flames that splashed like a fountain of liquid fire around him. The energy rebounded, spraying fire in a geyser of flames all around the room. Some of it caught the general and hurled him away from the body, sending him sprawling halfway across the room. The air around him sizzled and spit as the last remnants of the black mist quenched the flames.

The fire engulfed the body of the warlock and spread to the black carpet beneath him. Seconds later, the velvet wall hangings began to burn. Dergus was the first to come out of his shocked trance as the velvet hangings burst into flame behind him. He yelled in sheer panic and broke for the door, flailing blindly at the heavy draperies over it. He thrust his way through and disappeared. Balkan was not far behind him, both of them lost in terror and panic.

Cullin sheathed his sword and leapt across the room to

snatch up Kerri's limp body just as the draperies around her began to burn. I moved quickly to cover him, watching Drakon and Mendor. I saw Drakon reach for the dagger at his belt, hesitate, then turn away. Dragging Mendor with him, he stepped back, away from the raging wildfire.

Cullin had pulled Kerri away from the burning velvet. He beat out the flames in her clothing with his hands and I watched in horror as the skin and flesh of his hands appeared to catch fire, too. He slapped out the flames, then rose and slung Kerri unceremoniously across his shoulder.

Choking smoke filled the room. Everything around us burned at once, even the floor beneath my boots. Cullin's hand came down on my shoulder, and I realized I could not see Mendor or Drakon through the boiling smoke and flame. They were gone. Except for us and the charred bodies of the bound man and the warlock, the room was empty.

"Get us out of here," Cullin shouted in my ear over the roar of the fire. "Before the whole place burns down around our ears."

I grasped the sword firmly. "Lead!" I cried. It nearly pulled my arms out of their sockets as it complied.

The flames followed us out of the room. I thought the very stone and tile burned. I leaped over a smoldering chunk of white-hot, liquid stone and shuddered. Gods! Oh, gods! The rock *was* burning! It was wildfire born in Hellas the warlock had turned loose, and it gave no indication of stopping until it leveled the whole manse.

The sword led us at a dead run through the labyrinthine corridors. I recognized nothing as we ran. Surely we had not come this way. But the sword never faltered. I had to trust it. We would never find our own way out of this.

There were other people running in the halls now—servants, guards, members of the household. None of them paid any attention to us, all of them intent upon their own escape. One young girl dressed only in a bedgown ran screaming down the way we had come. I reached out to grab her arm and drag her back.

"Not that way, child," I shouted at her. "The fire's back there. Follow us."

For a moment, I was afraid she was too deep in panic to hear me. Then she gulped and reached up to push the mass of dark hair out of her eyes. She looked up at me and nodded. We began to run again, and she gathered up the skirts of her bed-gown and followed.

The obscene glare of the fire lit the whole house. Entire rooms exploded into flame to either side of us as we ran. In the passageway around us, molten rock dripped and flowed, its garish light flaring sullenly amid the smoke. I had never in my life seen anything like this, and I fervently hoped I never would again. Smoke thick as treacle swirled in the air, and the very air itself seemed afire. Blisters rose on the skin of my face and hands as I ran, following the sword. It was as if the flesh was stripping from my bones, like a fowl in an oven. I smelled the reek of my own singed hair and skin.

Blinded by the smoke, stumbling and staggering, we rounded a last corner and burst out into the Great Hall of the house. Ahead of us, people fled through open double doors into the refuge of a wet and rainy night. I stopped to catch my breath, panting, lungs burning from both the smoke and the exertion. The girl in the bedgown ran for the door without a backward glance. Beside me, Cullin leaned against the balustrade of a marble staircase, chest heaving. Kerri lay limply over his shoulder, arms and hair dangling. Her eyes were closed, and she was pale as chalk.

"Is she alive?" I asked.

"She's breathing," Cullin gasped. "Let's get out of here."

I nearly tripped over something soft as I began to run. I looked down to see a young boy, perhaps four years old, cling-ing mutely to the body of a woman. She had obviously fallen or been pushed down the stairs, and from the ugly, unnatural twist to her head, had broken her neck. The boy's black eyes were wide and staring in shock and terror above the round, childish cheeks. There was no color in his face, in stark con-trast to his midnight hair. He winced away from my boot, but otherwise didn't move.

Maedun. Even shocked immobile as he was, the air around him shimmered with the dark aura of latent magic. A hatchling sorcerer. Perhaps he would grow to be as powerful as the general, but he was yet only a child for all that, and frozen with fear. Left here, he would surely die, either trampled by people fleeing the upper levels in panic, or in the flames.

"Hellas-birthing," I muttered. He was only a year or two older than Keylan back at the Clanhold. I couldn't leave him here to die. I swore again, then sheathed the sword and bent to scoop the child off the stairs. "It's all right, laddie," I said. "You'll be all right. Come with me now." Small, chubby arms tightened convulsively around my neck, and he burrowed his face against my throat, his small body trembling violently. Cullin gave me a wry grin, and we ran for the door.

Nothing, *nothing*, will ever taste as good as that sweet, wet, fresh air I drew down into lungs burned raw from the smoke in the house. And nothing will ever again feel as good as the cool rain on my face as we ran down the steps into the courtyard. Behind us, every window in the house glowed with the demented glare of the fire. Even as I turned to look, a section of roof near the center collapsed, sending gouts of sparks exploding high into the air like lost stars.

"The stables," Cullin called. "We'll need Kerri's mare."

I nodded. It seemed unlikely that anyone would try to stop us. I swept the uncomfortable helmet from my head and discarded it as I ran, still holding the child.

"You there! Tyr! Stop!"

I swung around to see the Maedun general thrusting through the milling knots of people in the courtyard. The child in my arms gasped aloud and held out his arms. "Papa!" he whimpered.

Illuminated by the harsh, unholy glare of the burning house, the general was smudged and soot-blackened, his clothing singed and torn. He stopped suddenly when he saw the child in my arms, his face stark white under the dirt.

"Horbad," he cried. Slowly, he stiffened and looked at me. For that moment as our eyes met, the darkness around him faded and he looked no different from any other father concerned about the safety of the child he loved. In that brief instant, there was almost a sense of kinship between us.

"You have my son," he said, his voice quiet but carrying above the uproar behind him.

"I took him out because he was alone," I said. "I couldna let him die in there."

"He shares my magic. He will be powerful when he's a man."

"I know that, but he's only a child now."

"What will you do with him?"

"I intend to give him back to you."

The general did not move, nor did his steady gaze waver. "He will be your enemy when he's grown."

"I knew that when I picked him up." I brushed the wet, dark hair back from the child's forehead, thinking briefly of Keylan. The child rested quietly, exhausted but content, in my arms, his head laid trustingly against my shoulder. He smiled at me before turning his gaze back to his father. "Nevertheless, General," I said softly, "I dinna make war on children."

He took a deep breath. "I owe you a life, then," he said. He nodded toward Cullin, who still held Kerri over his shoulder. "Hers. I give you the woman's life in exchange for my son's. Take her and go. No one will try to stop you. Give me my son."

I laughed. "You'll pardon me if I don't quite trust you, General," I said. "You'll find the boy safe at the house of Grandal the Merchant." It was the name etched into the stone above the gate where we had seen him in the city.

He looked at the child, then at me. "Oddly enough, I trust you," he said. "I believe you're a man who keeps his word. You and I will meet again, Tyr."

"Aye, we will, General Hakkar," I agreed. "I have a name. I'm called Kian dav Leydon ti'Cullin. You would do well to remember it."

"I will remember," he said. His voice grew hoarse. "You've set me back half a lifetime, Kian dav Leydon ti'Cullin. And you very nearly killed me back there. By breaking the transfer spell, you've forced me to drain most of my energy just to recover. To survive the breaking. Half a lifetime." His voice rose. "All that time wasted. Wasted! How could an ignorant barbarian have so much magic and I not know it?"

I laughed. "I've been called a barbarian by better than you, General," I said. "And you're wrong. I have no magic. Just a sword."

"You should have killed me then."

"Aye, mayhaps I should. But you live yet. And so does your son."

"The next time we meet, we owe each other nothing."

"Only a death, General. Yours—or mine."

There was no need to wake anyone at the merchant's house to leave the boy there. The whole household, from master down to the lowliest scullery boy, was awake and staring at the spectacle of the conflagration on the bluff above. I placed the child safely into the arms of the housekeeper, telling her the boy's father would come for him soon, and Cullin and I hurried back out into the street.

I carried Kerri while Cullin led the mare back through streets crowded with people. An odd, carnival flavor pervaded the streets as the citizens of Frendor watched its lord's house burn. Around us, hawkers cried sweetmeats, ale, and wine, and the sound of voices raised in excited chatter and laughter filled the air. No one paid any attention to Cullin and me.

We found the farrier by his tent and reclaimed our horses. As we mounted to ride out of the city, Cullin cast a glance back over his shoulder at the fire, blazing like a beacon on the hill.

"You may have made a mistake letting that hatchling sorcerer live," he said.

I settled Kerri securely against me on the saddle and met his gaze. "Could you have killed him?" I asked.

He smiled ruefully and shook his head. "Of course not. But that only proves we're both of us fools." He kicked the bay stallion to a canter and we turned our backs on the city of Frendor and the fiercely burning manse of its lord.

It was two hours past dawn when we found a spot in the forest to make camp. Kerri breathed deeply and regularly, and her heartbeat was strong but slow in her chest. She had not regained consciousness. I laid her on her bedroll and turned to Cullin, who was tending the horses.

"Let me see your hands," I said.

"They're all right," he replied. "See to Kerri first."

He was going to be stubborn and noble about this. Well, I could be just as stubborn. I had already had a head start in obstinacy when I began learning from him, the master of intractability himself. "Cullin, your hands. Now."

He gave me an exasperated look, but he held out both hands. The blisters had broken and his palms were raw and bleeding, weeping clear fluid. The skin of his right wrist was red and blistered. It looked intensely painful. I took his hands in mine and drew in a deep breath. As I stared at his hands, healthy new skin began to appear over the worst areas. I had healed wounds for him before, and I knew his patterns now. Moments later when I let out the breath in an explosive gasp, his hands and wrist were pink with newly healed skin, and tender still, but whole. He stared at them and shook his head.

"It still takes a lot of getting used to," he muttered. "Better see to Kerri while I set up camp."

I knelt by Kerri and examined her carefully, but found no sign of injury save a small bruise along her jaw and a split lip. Nothing to explain the deep unconsciousness. I placed my hands to either side of her head, gently cupping her temples between my palms, fingers spread in the silken softness of her hair. I wondered if I could do this. An obvious injury, such as Cullin's hands, was not difficult to heal. All I had to do was concentrate on visualizing it whole and healthy. It took a lot of energy, but it was not particularly arduous. But what was I to do when I detected no injury? How could I see something as whole and healthy when I didn't know what was wrong? The general had given me her life, but would it be a life spent in a trance?

I stared at her blank, pale face for a long time. Then, suddenly, bright images swirled and darted through my mind. I knew them this time for what they were: Kerri's memories. I thrust myself deep into them, searching through them for some indication of what held her in the unnatural sleep. I walked through her memories as one would walk through a garden, the images like bright flowers or deep, cool shadows in green shade. I recognized her father in some of them, Cullin and myself in others. Surface things only. I had to go farther into her memories if I could.

I pushed deeper . . .

. . . And met blackness. The same hard, dark armor that surrounded the general. It surged outward, seized me, and tried to drown me, too, in its darkness. I fought it, like wrestling with the night itself. Smothering, hungry, clutching, it was all around me. I could not find anything to hold on to. It slipped through my fingers like quicksilver, only to wind tendrils of itself around my throat. I tore away wisps of it, but could not loosen its hold, neither on me, nor on Kerri. Choking and gagging on the foul stuff filling my nose and mouth, I struggled to breathe. I could not cry out, could not break away from the bond with Kerri that lashed me to the dark and formless enemy.

Then I thought I heard Kerri's voice, desperately faint, hopelessly distant. "The sword," she cried, the sound frail as a whisper on the wind. "Kian, the sword . . . "

But I could not tear my hands from her head to reach for the hilt at my left shoulder. My strength ebbed quickly. I would not be able to fight much longer. In despair, I felt the sense of triumph throbbing and pulsing through the black, formless entity invading Kerri.

Then, in a flash of lucid clarity, I knew what I had to do. As the last of my strength drained into the darkness, I formed an image of the sword. I saw its plain, leather-bound hilt fitted comfortably and snugly into my hands, saw the polished, graceful blade with its glittering runes spilling down the center. I made it glow with that radiant brilliance it had first showed me on the gravel strand of the small burn. I saw the light in a burst of color raying out to slice the darkness to shreds and tatters.

Terror and rage suffused me. Not mine. Not Kerri's. It emanated from the dark mist itself. In one last burst of passionate fury, the mist blew apart, fragments raining like splinters of rock around me. Then even the shreds were gone, and Kerri's eyes opened to stare wonderingly into mine.

"Kian?" she asked, puzzled.

I fell back, exhausted and drained. It startled me badly to see it was dark, and the moon rode among the dissipating clouds in the night sky. Cullin knelt on the other side of Kerri's bedroll, facing me, worry and relief warring for dominance on his face. Dizzy and weak, I put my hand to my forehead, unable to believe I had spent the whole day battling that black horror the general had set so deep into Kerri's mind.

"Are you all right?" I asked Kerri, my voice rusty and hoarse.

She nodded. "Yes," she said faintly. "Just very tired. What happened?"

I hadn't the strength to reply. "Later," I mumbled.

"I was afraid to touch you," Cullin said, his voice sounding as rough-edged as mine. "I thought you were both going to die on me, but I was afraid to touch you. Are you all right, *ti'rhonai?*"

He held out one hand. I reached across Kerri, caught it in both of mine. For a moment, we simply looked at each other, both of us grinning like idiots.

"I need sleep," I muttered, and crawled toward the pack I had left beside a thatch of willow scrub. I don't even remember wrapping my plaid around me before I was asleep.

17

I dreamed of the low hill crowned by the Dance of stones. *Again, I stood at the foot of the hill, my sword on my back, while the Watcher, still and erect as one of the menhirs, regarded me calmly from above. An odd sensation of peace permeated the eerie light. There was no disturbance to indicate the approaching presence of the opponent I expected to step forth at any moment from a darkness of his own making. But the pearlescent light remained tranquil and serene, and at last I knew he would not come this time.*

I turned to the Watcher and set my foot to the gentle slope of the hill. The Watcher remained unmoving as, one slow step after another, I climbed the hill. It took far longer than I thought it would to reach the outer ring of capped menhirs, and when I looked behind me at the way I had come, it looked a dizzying height above the small, circular patch of grass at the bottom of the hill. My breath caught in my throat, and I turned quickly back to the Watcher. But when I tried to step between two of the standing stones, I found I could not. I detected no physical restriction, yet something held me back, something intangible as air, but impenetrable for all that.

I wanted very badly to go to the polished altar stone at the heart of the Dance. There lay understanding and the answers to all the questions I had no idea how to ask. But I could not penetrate that barrier.

"You cannot enter here, my young friend," the Watcher said. "Not until you have defeated your enemy and fulfilled your purpose."

"My enemy is not here this time, as you see," I said.

"You have weakened him, but not destroyed him," said the Watcher.

"Where is this place?" I asked.

The barest suggestion of a smile touched his features. "It is a place men come to in dreams," he said.

I looked down at the scar on my arm. In this light, it was only faintly discernible. "What sort of dream will leave a scar on a man's arm?"

"A dream here. Should you fall to your enemy's sword here, you will never waken. Die here, and you die in the waking world."

"Do all men come here in dreams?"

"No, not all. I called you here."

"Did you also call my enemy?"

"No. He comes seeking you. He has his own magic."

"Who are you?" I asked. "Who are you that you can call me here against my waking will?"

"I am the one who sent the Swordmaster to you so that you might be prepared to take up the Kingmaker's Sword," he answered. "And I am the one who directed the sword to you so that you might complete your task."

"Kingmaker's Sword?" I repeated. I shook my head. "I am no king . . . "

"No," he agreed. "Nor will you ever be a king. But you will deliver the sword into the hand of the man who shall be. The sword will proclaim him, and you will know him."

Too many questions flooded through me. The one I chose to ask startled me.

"Who am I?"

His answer surprised me, too. "Who do you wish to be?"

"Just who I am," I said fervently. "Kian dav Leydon ti'Cullin. It's good name enough for any man."

"Then that is who you shall be," he replied. "Although men may call you otherwise for a time."

"How will they name me?" I asked.

"Who can say the future?"

I awoke lying curled in the shelter of a willow thicket, wrapped in both my plaid and Cullin's. I was warm and dry, and far too comfortable to feel like moving. But the sun was high in the sky, already past zenith, and we had to get as far away from the general, and Mendor and Drakon, as we could. I sat up reluctantly. My head was clear, and I was alert. My stomach thought it was pinned to my spine, though, and I was ravenously hungry. That might account for the slight residual weakness I felt.

Kerri sat by a small campfire, hunched over a cup of steaming herbal tea. She, too, looked as if she had just recently been dragged out of a comfortable bed. I dug out my own cup from my pack and went to join her. She hardly looked up as I reached for the kettle hanging above the fire.

"Where's Cullin?" I asked. The tea was strong and sweet, and sharply redolent of snowroot and kafe bean. It should revive me if anything could.

"Hunting," she said. "He should be back shortly."

"Good. I'm starving. How long have you been awake?"

"Not long. Only a few minutes." She looked up at me and smiled wryly. "Cullin tells me I slept for two days."

I smiled and took another sip of the steaming tea. "I slept for nearly three days the last time I Healed you," I said. "This is an improvement."

She made a sour face.

"What happened, *sheyala*?" I asked. "How did the general catch you?"

For a moment, I thought she wouldn't answer. Then she sighed. "I made a mistake," she said.

I raised an eyebrow. Only a fair imitation of Cullin's eloquent gesture.

"Don't you dare laugh," she said fiercely.

"I have no intention of laughing," I told her. And I hadn't. A mistake that nearly caused a death, perhaps even three deaths, was no cause for amusement. Not while the danger still hovered near. There would be time enough for amusement and teasing laughter when the tale could be told in the safety of home, after time had added enough distance to the raw edge of fear to soften it.

"And if you say I told you so, I'll have your ears." Her defensive ferocity hadn't abated.

"There's no much I could say to make you feel worse than you've made yourself feel, *sheyala*," I said gently enough. "What happened?"

"It was so stupid," she said in a dreary voice. "I ran into that general—Hakkar, he's called . . . "

"I know. Cullin and I met him, too, albeit rather informally. How did he find you out?"

"Remember when I used the masking spell in Trevellin?"

I nodded, then smiled ruefully. "The farm woman and her faithful dog."

"Yes. Well, I used the same semblance this time, too. Hakkar recognized me. It was incredible, but he did. He wanted to question me. When I tried to get away, he hit me. He knocked me out. I couldn't hold the spell unconscious. Next thing I knew, I was tied hand and foot in a horrid, black-draped room." She shuddered. "He came to talk to me. He asked about you and Cullin, and I told him I'd left you at that inn where the Isgardian officer told us about him. Then I remember looking into his eyes. It was like falling down a mine shaft. Deep and black and cold. So cold." She shivered again and drank more of her tea. "The next thing I remember is waking up and seeing you there. Gods, Kian. You looked like death itself."

"I felt like death." I hesitated, then told her about the black thing I had fought in her mind. She lost what little color she had, and the cup in her hands trembled violently enough to spill some of the tea.

She set the cup carefully aside, and clasped her hands between her knees. "Thank you," she whispered at last. She took a deep, steadying breath. "Cullin told me how you got me out of there. I owe you thanks for that, too."

"That's twice in the last moment you've thanked me," I said. "My heart canna take too many shocks like that."

One corner of her mouth tilted upward into a resigned little smile. "Well, don't become too used to it. It may never happen again." She picked up her cup and sipped the tea.

"I should hope not. It might lead me to think you're turning gentle and sweet."

That didn't get the reaction I had hoped for. She merely gave me that half smile again, her mind clearly on some other thing. Finally, she said, "Kian . . . "

"Aye?"

She looked up and met my eyes. "Cullin said you knew something was wrong. He said it was you who knew I was in trouble, and he simply came along with you."

"He was worrit, too," I said. "But mayhaps because I got so jittery."

She paused again, toying with her cup. "How did you know?"

I hesitated, unsure how to explain it. Hellas, I couldn't even explain it to myself.

"Please, Kian," she said. "Please. I have to know. It's very important."

I shrugged helplessly. "I don't know, *sheyala*," I said truthfully. "I just knew. I got all nervous and jumpy, and I just had to go after you. I still don't know why. I only know I was right."

"I was afraid of that." She looked away, then suddenly slammed her fist down onto her knee. "Damn!" she exploded. "Oh, damn, damn, damn!" She got abruptly to her feet and flung her cup at an elm tree. She missed. "Hellas-birthing," she muttered, and walked stiffly to retrieve the cup. Clutching it, she spun to face me, anger and something else sparking in her eyes. It might have been resentment. I didn't know her well enough to tell. "You know what that means, don't you?" she demanded harshly.

I was afraid I knew all too well. "The bond?" I asked.

"Yes," she muttered. "That accursed bond. We're bonded, you and I. And it's a true bond, damn all to Hellas. It wasn't supposed to happen with you. You're only a—a—"

"An uncouth barbarian?" I said helpfully. "An ignorant savage?"

She shot me a look so full of annoyance, it sizzled. She came back to the fire and sat down. "An Outlander," she said. "A non-Celae."

"Look, if it helps, I'm no exactly joyful about it, either," I said, becoming irritated myself.

"There's nothing we can do about it now," she said bleakly. "I think nothing short of death can break it." She looked up as Cullin appeared through the trees carrying a large goose. "There's no sense worrying about it now," she said. "We can't do anything about it. We'll see later."

We rode hard for what was left of the day. When we left Frendor, we had turned north toward the Tyran border and safety. Now we rode west. West toward Honandun.

"We must warn the Ephir," Cullin said as we packed up to leave the campsite. "He needs to know about Balkan and Hakkar."

"But the sword leads northeast," Kerri protested. "We have to follow it."

"We will," Cullin said. "After we've spoken to the Ephir."

She threw down her pack and stalked over to confront him, that look I was too familiar with in her eye. "No," she said firmly. "We go northeast, and we go now."

Cullin turned his head to meet her glare. "Isgardian silver has supported me and my family very well for nearly fifteen years," he said, tying off the last pack fastener on the saddle. "I'm not about to turn my back on that. We owe it to Isgard to warn them. West first, then northeast."

I stopped what I was doing and leaned my forearms on Rhuidh's withers to watch. This could become interesting. Kerri was beginning to resemble a small, one-woman thunderstorm about to erupt in a flurry of lightning bolts. In all the time I'd known him, I had seen Cullin really angry only twice. I doubted Kerri was able to rouse that anger, and I was fairly certain she had finally met her match when it came to being stubborn. Cullin hardly ever argued. He stated his intentions, then acted on them. I was fully prepared to be greatly entertained.

Kerri's fists went to her hips, her jaw thrust out aggressively. "I gave you gold to help me find my prince," she said. "You owe me service."

He dug into his pack, pulled out the small leather bag, and flipped it negligently to her. Her reflexes were excellent. She got her hands off her hips and up in plenty of time to catch the heavy bag before it hit her in the face.

"It's all there, my lady Kerridwen," he said. "But for expenses to date, of course."

Kerri flung the bag to the ground and snorted in derision. "Do you think they're likely to listen to a mercenary merchant train guard?" she asked scornfully. "Especially one wanted by the city guard for assaulting the cousin of the Ephir?"

Cullin smiled. "Mayhaps not," he said. He straightened, and by some unique alchemy, even in his stained, ragged, and singed stolen guard's uniform, attained a regal and dignified bearing any prince might envy. "But they will certainly believe Cullin dav Medroch dav Kian, the son of Medroch dav Kian dav Angrus, Eleventh Clan Laird of Broche Rhuidh of Tyra. Especially, I think, now that envoys have been sent to my father to contract for an alliance."

She glared at him. "But you simply can't do this," she cried furiously.

Cullin raised an eyebrow. "Can I not? I thought I just did." He looked at me. "Are you ready, *ti'rhonai*?"

"At your command, *ti'vati*," I replied.

Kerri turned to me. "You can't go with him," she cried. "You have to take me to the prince—"

I finished lashing my packs to the saddle. "Cullin is not only my *ti'vati*," I said, "he's my captain. He commands, I follow."

"But—"

"That's the way it is, *sheyala*," I told her.

Cullin mounted his stallion, then swung the horse around so he could look at Kerri. "You're welcome to accompany us, my lady," he said mildly. He kicked the stallion to an easy canter. I swung up onto Rhuidh and followed. We left her standing in the clearing. She was not a calm and content woman.

Cullin looked at me and allowed himself a smile. "She'll follow," he said confidently.

I thought of the stiffness of Kerri's shoulders and back. "I'm not so sure," I replied.

"She'll follow," he repeated. "She's stubborn and willful, but she knows we're right."

18

It took Kerri fifteen minutes to catch up to us. She drew up alongside Cullin and flung the leather bag at him. Cullin's reflexes were excellent, too. He snatched the bag out of the air and laughed as Kerri sizzled in silence. She glanced across at me. I didn't hide my smile quickly enough. A spark of pure fury kindled and blazed up in her eyes. The skin around her mouth paled and tightened, but she said nothing.

We made camp shortly after dark. Kerri's anger still flashed and flared around her, but she performed her share of the chores without protest. She did them in a cold, uncommunicative silence that I thought better than exercising the sharp side of her tongue. When the meal was ready, she took her portion and went to sit alone beyond the circle of light cast by the fire. Cullin said nothing, but I caught his eye across the flames, and I saw the distinct glitter of tolerant amusement in them.

We had finished our meal and cleaned up before Kerri came back to the fire. The food on her plate appeared untouched. She stood stiffly before Cullin, her mouth still pressed into a thin, bleak line. Cullin looked up at her but also remained silent. Finally, she let out a long breath and crouched down to sit on her heels before him.

"I apologize," she said quietly. "You were right. I was wrong. My prince would not thank me if Isgard fell and there was a chance I might have helped to prevent it but did not take it out of petulance."

Still, Cullin said nothing.

Kerri sighed again. "A stubborn race, the yrSkai of Celi," she said. "And I am the prime example."

Cullin laughed. "Near as stubborn as the Tyr," he said. "And both of us stiff-necked in our pride. Dinna worrit yourself, lass. I believe you'll always come about to do the right thing."

"I hope so," she said. She flashed a glance at me across the fire as if daring me to laugh or make a derisive comment. I raised both hands, palms out, in negation, and went back to the shirt I was mending.

Kerri took the first watch that night, claiming the need for quiet and time to think. Cullin told her to wake him at midnight, then wrapped himself into his plaid and curled down onto a pile of fresh bracken to sleep. I remained close to the fire with the shirt I was mending. It was nearly done, the rip under the arm almost closed. I am handy enough with a needle when the need arises, but the light was not good, and the work went slowly.

Kerri paid scant attention to me as I sat cross-legged, hunched over my work. She stood with her back toward me, the firelight glinting on the tawny spill of her hair down her back. Normally bound back into a thick braid, it was loosened now and tumbled across her shoulders in a wild fall of rippling waves. Her tunic and breeks emphasized the narrowness of her waist, the full promise of her hips. My memory supplied a picture of the curving swell of the breasts I could not see. It suddenly made me acutely and uncomfortably aware that there was a girl—no, a woman—under the tunic and breeks, behind that greatsword she called a Celae Rune Blade.

I glanced at the haft of the sword rising above her left shoulder. I had no wish to test the temper of that steel, nor the keenness of its cutting edge. It was more than enough to curb my natural erotic speculations in the interest of self-preservation. She had made her feelings about me clear enough before we left Honandun, and I had seen her handle that Rune Blade, and the dagger at her belt. I liked my hide the way it was right now, unpunctured and relatively intact.

She moved, turning to walk back to the fire. She crouched to sit on her heels, her expression remote and thoughtful as she poked at the coals with a stick, the amber-honey hair falling softly over her shoulders, shadowing her eyes. An unexpected and insidious tightness stirred in my groin that

took my interest abruptly out of the abstract and into the con-
crete, and I was suddenly glad I was sitting with the bulk of
the shirt in my lap. I bent my head to my task, concentrating
on the stitching in the poor light.

A few moments later, feeling myself being watched, I
looked up and found her face turned toward me. I could see
nothing of her eyes but deep shadows beneath the spill of hair
even though the firelight limned the soft, clean lines of her
cheek and jaw and showed me the full, unsmiling lips. She
flicked the hair from her face and turned back to watch the fire.

She said we were bonded—bonded by the link of our
swords. Both times I Healed her, I had shared her memories.
That never happened when I Healed anyone else, not even
Cullin, who was closer to me than anyone, except perhaps
Keylan. I remembered the strange thrumming sensation quivering up my arms when her sword crossed mine, the curious
way the air fizzed gently around us when I kissed her. I
remembered how the need to find her had driven me into
Frendor. I had known of the danger to her then. I wondered
about the nature of this bond. Had it anything to do with this
sudden awareness of her as a woman? She had been no hap-
pier about it than I, perhaps even less so, when we spoke upon
awakening this afternoon. And as I sat mending my shirt, I
could read nothing in her posture or her expression.

Watching her covertly as she stirred the glowing coals, I
had an almost-irresistible urge to get up and take her into my
arms. Almost irresistible. She still wore the sword, and the
dagger at her hip. And she certainly made it more than clear
that first day how she felt about any man laying a hand on her
without her express consent or invitation, both to me and to an
Isgardian seaman who would be a long time forgetting her.

But there was something about the way her face looked, lit
by the flickering light of the fire, shadowed by her tumbling
hair. She looked up and saw me watching her. For a moment,
her expression didn't change. Then there was a subtle shift in
the set of her mouth and the angle at which she held her head,
and I knew she was as aware of me as a man as I was of her as
a woman. She rose to her feet in one graceful, fluid movement,

and walked away into the darkness, back straight, denial in every line of her body.

I don't remember getting to my feet. I found her just outside the small circle of light, one hand braced lightly against the trunk of a silverleaf maple. She turned as she heard my footfall behind her.

"You said we were bonded," I said slowly, my voice sounding thick and blurred.

"We are." She met my eyes calmly. "It's not what either of us wanted, but it's there."

"How deep is the bond?" I wanted to reach out and touch the softness of her cheek, but I held my hand stiffly at my side.

"To the bone," she said. "To the heart and soul." She stepped away as if sensing my desire to touch her. "But not as man and woman." Her tone was flat and cold, and it stopped me dead. "Not unless you really are Kyffen's grandson."

"I'm not that man, *sheyala*," I said softly. "Honestly, I'm not. Even if I wanted to be, for you, I couldn't say I was."

"You carry a Celae Rune Blade—"

"Aye, but only because I took it from the man who owned it when he tried to take me back to Mendor. I carry it now only to give it to the man it belongs to."

She glanced up at me, an unreadable expression in her eyes. "You know this?" she asked.

"It was told to me in a dream," I said. "I—dream, *sheyala*. Sometimes I dream of a man on a hill standing in the midst of a Dance of stones." The soft shadows and the hushed serenity of the night made it easier to talk about the dreams I could just barely remember. "I used to dream of a Swordmaster, and dancing with the sword. Now I dream of a Dance of stones, and a Watcher on the Hill. And an opponent who comes out of darkness with a sword that spills night around it like a broken flask spills water."

"A Dance of stones?" she asked sharply. She stripped the hair from her face with one hand and reached out for my arm. "Tell me about the Dance, Kian."

I described it as best I could. She listened intently, a small, thoughtful frown drawing the golden brows together above the bridge of her nose, her lower lip caught between her teeth. When I had finished, she dropped her hand from my arm and turned away.

"In Celi, near the mountain we call Cloudbearer, there is such a Dance," she said. "But it lies on a plain, not on a hill. It's called the Dance of Nemeara, and it is as old as the island itself."

"Then I dream of a different Dance," I said. "One set on a hill. Not the same."

"This Watcher on the Hill said you carry the sword to give it to the man it belongs to?" she asked.

"He did. He told me its name. Kingmaker's Sword."

She turned back to me, her lower lip caught between her teeth again. "One of the swords of Wyfydd Smith," she murmured.

"Wyfydd Smith?"

"Come back to the fire, Kian," she said. "I will tell you about the Swords of Wyfydd."

The night had turned cool. I put more wood on the fire and we sat with our backs to the warmth. "Tell me about this smith," I said.

"He was the smith to the gods," she said. "They called him armorer to gods and kings. There's a song about him. I know part of it." She closed her eyes and began to sing very softly:

Armorer to gods and kings,
Wyfydd's magic hammer sings.
Music in its ringing tone,
Weaponry for kings alone.
He who forged the sword of Brand,
Myrddyn blessed it to his hand.
By iron, fire, wind, and word,
Wyfydd crafts the mystic sword.
Blades to fill a kingly need.
Royal blood and royal breed.
Wyfydd made and Myrddyn blessed,
Hilt and blade wrought for the best.

He alone its mettle test.
In but one hand each sword shall rest.

"A pretty song," I said, smiling. "But a legend."

"Not a legend," she said. "He was very real. He was in Celi when it was still Nemeara and belonged to the Tyadda. He crafted the first Rune Blades and filled them with both magic and music. Two of them he placed in hiding against the day they would be needed to free Celi of an oppressor. The rest went to men and women who had earned them." She reached up and touched the hilt of her own sword. "This one has been handed down for centuries. It was my father's, and his father's before him, and his father's mother's before that."

I glanced over to my sword that lay beside my bedroll. "And that one? How did it end up in the hands of a Maedun bounty hunter so that it fell into the hands of a runaway slave?"

"I had thought Kingmaker to be more ornate and jeweled," she said. A crooked smile twisted her mouth. "It was sent to Tebor of Dorian as a wedding gift by Kyffen. It was to be passed on to Ytwydda's son, and passed on to *his* son. Of course, at the time, everyone expected Tebor to be the father. But Tebor thought it confirmed that he was destined to be king of all Celi. After the battle in which Tebor died, it was gone. Everyone thought it had been taken by one of the Saesnesi who fought with Tebor."

"It may have been," I said. "And the Saesnesi who took it lost it to the bounty hunter."

"And now you carry it," she said. "A Rune Blade always finds its way to the hand born to wield it. I told you that before."

"Aye, you did," I said. "And now it seems I carry it to give to your long-lost prince."

"If you will let the sword lead you," she said. "I hope you will, Kian. It's important."

I looked at her. "Magic and music, you said the smith gave his blades," I said softly. "My sword has both. I've felt it and heard it." I smiled briefly. "Aye, and I've even used its magic." I looked at her and frowned. "How is it that the general or the warlock couldn't sense it? The general remarked upon it. He asked how it could be that I had used so much magic and he had not detected it."

"The swords can mask magic," she said. "A masking spell is all but undetectable because it directs the magic inward, toward what's being masked. You felt it in Trevellin because it was directed at you." She pointed at a rock. "Watch."

I looked. The air around the stone shimmered for an instant, then I saw a small, sleeping cat curled around itself. But I felt nothing. No prickling along my arms or the back of my neck, no nausea. And I smelled nothing but woodsmoke and the fresh scent of water and green, growing things nearby.

"My sword will do the same, under certain circumstances," she said and smiled. "Rune Blades don't have extremely strong magic, as a rule, but they have some."

"They have enough," I said. The cat turned back into a stone even as I watched. I rubbed my arms, then changed the subject. "Tell me how it fell to you to find this princeling."

She drew her knees up and wrapped her arms around her legs. "It's a long story," she said. "How much do you know about Celi?"

"Not much. Only what Cullin said—that centuries ago, a band of Tyran clansmen, warriors, went to the island after splitting off from their clan. A disagreement of some sort."

"When the Celae came to Celi, they found the Tyadda already there," she said. "My father is Tyadda. My mother was half-Celae. The Celae didn't conquer the Tyadda. They married them." She smiled. "It was a gentle conquest in that regard. But the Tyadda were already a dying race. They once had strong magic, but it was fading when the Celae came. Mixing the blood in some cases brought back the magic. My mother had magic."

"Still, why you?"

"I'm to be the prince's *bheancoran*."

"*Bheancoran?*"

"Warrior-maid. Each prince of Skai has one. It's like a personal guard, in a way, but it's more than that. I don't know if I can really explain it. Many of the women in my family were *bheancoran*. My cousin Eliene was to be Llan's, but he died before he became prince. The task of finding the lost prince is mine. He's sorely needed, Kian. I told you before, Celi has been invaded by Saesnesi, who plunder the land. They don't come to settle, only to steal and burn and pillage. They've established bases on the eastern shore now and raid from there. And there's no one to stop them."

I looked down at her. "You've been given a difficult task, *sheyala*," I said finally.

"That may be so," she said. "But I have to do my best." She looked into the fire, her expression remote again. "I had thought I would recognize him by the bond. Because I'm to be his *bheancoran*, I had thought we would bond when I saw him, and he would know me just as I knew him."

"Instead, you find yourself bonded to a savage and a barbarian," I said. I had been striving for levity, but it fell flat.

She looked up at me, her eyes shadowed, her lips soft and half-parted. She smiled. "I know what's happening to us," she said. "Do you remember what day this is?"

I had to think about it. It was the day after Vernal Equinox when Cullin and I brought the merchant train into Honandun. How many days, how many sennights since then? Enough had happened to fill a year's worth. When I counted the days, it startled me to discover it was only a season. One season.

"Beltane Eve," I said in surprise. "Tonight is Beltane Eve." Beltane Eve, the only night of the year when the Duality splits into its male and female aspects to couple by the fires as man and woman to bless the fertility of field and herd. The night when every woman represents the goddess and every man the god.

"Yes," she said. "I was thinking about what I would be doing if I were home tonight."

I knew what I would be doing. Dancing between the fires with an eye out for a light-footed and lighthearted lass wishing to offer me her heather-wine. The sudden warmth in my face was not from the heat of the fire.

"What would you be doing, *sheyala*?" I asked, knowing I

trod dangerous ground. "How do you celebrate Beltane in Celi?"

She set her chin on her drawn up knees, arms wrapped tightly around her legs. "There's a procession from the shrine to the oak grove where the fire is waiting to be lit," she said quietly. "Then we dance around it."

"Only one fire?" I asked.

She nodded. "Not so in Tyra?"

"No. We light two and dance between them. The women carry goblets of heather-wine to offer to the men they favor."

"Mead in Celi," she said. "One sip demands payment of a kiss."

"And if you offer the whole cup?"

She laughed softly. "The grass is always soft between the oak trees," she said. "I think it must be the same in Tyra."

"Aye, it is. And in the morning, the children drive the beasts between the fires, all the horses and cattle and sheep and goats, even the geese and chickens, to ensure an increase." I laughed. "And there are always a few Beltane babes born around Imbolc."

"We call them blessed," she said. "A child who can claim a god for a father and a goddess for a mother." She drew in a deep breath. "Liam believes Kyffen's grandson is a child of Beltane."

"*Sheyala*, do these princes marry their *bheancorans*?" My voice sounded unaccountably hoarse.

"Some do," she replied. "Kyffen married Demilor."

"As you might marry this prince."

She looked up at me gravely. "I might, Kian," she said. She turned again to watch the fire. "When we find him. If we find him . . ." Her voice trailed off into silence.

19

Traveling by merchant train, the journey from Frendor to Honandun takes a fortnight. We avoided the road as much as possible, but sunset of the eighth day found us on the outskirts of Honandun. Cullin led us through the streets away from the portside inns we normally used, toward the white stone elegance of the Ephir's palace. The streets here were lined by the sumptuous and expensive walled houses of the nobility and courtiers of Isgard. This was not a district normally frequented by merchant train guards. There was little chance we would be recognized.

Cullin finally stopped at an inn that would be vastly beyond the means of even a merchant train guard heavy with silver and a bonus in gold after a long and arduous trip south and back. I took the horses to the stable and flipped two ten-copper bits to the stablemaster, who eyed my clothing askance, but did not question my coin.

The inn stood three stories tall, built of stone and timber, its roof red tile instead of thatch. The windows were glazed casements with patterns of rose, blue, green, and yellow glass outlined by strips of lead, and flanked by neatly painted shutters. The sign above the door depicted the Ephir's crown pierced by the blade of an ornate sword, and the words "Sword and Crown" painted in flowing script beneath it.

I joined Cullin and Kerri, who were already inside. Men and women, richly dressed in velvets, silks, and glossy leathers, occupied most of the tables in the common room that boasted of a polished mosaic tile floor inlaid with copper and brass. Serving girls dressed in neat gray-and-white gowns, with spotless white aprons embroidered with the sword and crown motif, hurried back and forth between the tables and the kitchens or the bars, carrying trays laden with food or crystal decanters of wine or mead. There was nothing so prosaic as

mere ale in this room. A brightly clad minstrel strumming a
lute strolled among the tables and sang bawdily merry songs
for the entertainment of the inn's clientele. Few of them paid
him much attention.

The innkeeper wove his way deftly through the tables to
meet us. He gave us no welcoming smile as he shrewdly
assessed our clothing.

"How may I help you?" he asked in the carefully neutral
voice of a man ready to move to either welcome or rejection.
"Perhaps you'd be needing directions to more suitable accom-
modations?"

Kerri wore her trews and tunic, clean now, but rumpled.
Cullin and I wore traveling leathers we had purchased the
afternoon before from a merchant we found in a small town.
They fitted reasonably well, but were by no means up to the
standards of the clothing worn by the rest of the inn's patrons.
Compared to them, all three of us looked scruffy and unkempt.

Cullin drew himself up to his full height and positively
radiated his nobility like heat from a flame. "Is there better in
Honandun?" he asked, raising his eyebrow casually.

The innkeeper's smoothly affluent face grew red. "There is
not," he declared emphatically.

"Then we've come to the right place," Cullin said. "I am
Cullin dav Medroch, son of Medroch dav Kian dav Angrus,
Clan Laird of Broche Rhuidh of Tyra." His hand gestured
gracefully toward Kerri, then to me. "My lady Kerridwen al
Jorddyn, kinswoman to Prince Kyffen of Skai, and my son,
Kian. We are here to see the Ephir on a matter of some impor-
tance with a message from my father."

Instantly, the innkeeper's manner became deferentially
respectful. "You are welcome here, my lord," he said. "Only
tell me what you require, and it shall be provided."

Cullin looked distastefully down at his clothing. "First,
three rooms and a hot bath in each," he said. "Then, I think the
services of a fuller and a barber for my son and myself." He
smiled. "And I assume you have someone trained as a ladies'
maid for my lady Kerridwen?"

Kerri opened her mouth to protest she needed no such

thing, but subsided when I took her arm and squeezed none too gently.

"Of course, my lord," the innkeeper said smoothly. "I have the perfect girl for the lady, well trained and very discreet. And your meal? Would you prefer to take it down here, or shall I have something to your taste sent up?"

"Sent up, I think," Cullin said. "We have been traveling for almost a fortnight. It was tiring in the extreme."

"Of course, my lord," the innkeeper said. He snapped his fingers and two boys appeared to relieve us of our saddle packs. "I will have Lasa sent to the lady's room immediately. The boys will see you upstairs. You have but to call and I will have your meal sent up."

Kerri paused on the stairs and looked at Cullin, a hint of a smile on her mouth. "You do that very well," she murmured.

Cullin's smile was beatific. "It's an art," he said negligently. "And I was well schooled."

The next morning after we broke our fast, Cullin summoned a messenger and sent a note to the Ephir. By midmorning, a man wearing royal livery arrived at the inn bearing a formal invitation for the three of us to attend at the palace that evening. Cullin returned a gracious acceptance, then set the whole inn on its ear as he demanded—and got without question—all the services to see us properly ready and on time.

I have never in my life seen such dedicated, frantic scurrying around by so many people. Kerri disappeared into her room amid a bevy of ladies' maids and seamstresses. My dress kilt and plaid were snatched right out of my hands and spirited away to the fuller. A quietly dignified cobbler, old enough to be my grandfather, sat me down on a velvet upholstered chair in my room and called me "my lord" while he told me why this particular pair of boots and none other would suit my purpose.

He had no sooner left than a barber and his assistant descended upon me. They shaved me and washed my hair, then trimmed it, tasks I had been fully capable of performing for myself all my life, and I submitted with only a token protest. But when they brought out the tongs, I flatly refused to let them near me, despite their protestations of the dictates of fashion. My hair was perilously close to curling on its own after it was washed. It needed no extraneous attention from a pair of fashion-mad barbers. They finally left, bitterly disappointed, when I offered with heartfelt sincerity to throw the first man to touch my head with those godsforsaken tongs out of the window.

I had exactly ten minutes respite to replait the braid in my hair before a servant arrived with my neatly pressed, spotless kilt and plaid, carrying a snowy linen shirt across his arm. I looked with distaste at the fountains of frothy lace at throat and wrists. It looked like a year's worth of tatting, if what Gwynna produced was a good measure.

"Not really," I said in dismay.

"Yes, really," Cullin said, appearing at the door. He had not, I noticed, escaped the attention of the tongs. "If we are to be barbarians at Court, *ti'rhonai*, then we will be truly magnificent barbarians." He tossed me a clan badge, plaid brooch, and kilt pin, freshly polished to a soft, gleaming sheen. "Here. They left those with me. You'll need them."

"Barbarians," I repeated, eyeing the shirt. "Does that mean I can drink wine from the decanter and leer at the ladies?"

"I believe leering at the ladies comes under the heading of civilized behavior," he said gravely. "You'll have to content yourself with aloof disdain."

"I'm good at disdain," I said, considering. "But I'd rather leer."

"Of course," he said. "So would we all." He grinned and left me to my own devices and at the mercy of the servant.

"No swords, my lord," the servant said apologetically when I made to buckle mine on. "The Ephir allows no weapons in the palace."

"Wise of him," I muttered. I felt strangely naked and vulnerable without the sword, but I left it in the room.

The Ephir sent a carriage for us. The footman appeared at the door of the Sword and Crown just as Kerri swept down the stairs in a gown of something that shimmered like moonbeams on water, her hair pulled back off her face, dressed with pearls and bound by gold netting, a dark blue velvet cloak around her bare shoulders. Cullin bowed to her, then offered her his arm. She inclined her head graciously and placed her fingers delicately on his elbow. I trailed out to the carriage in their wake. Cullin and Kerri also looked odd without their swords. Perhaps we had been too long among bandits and potential enemies.

The reception room of the palace was full of people. The velvets, silks, laces, and glossy leathers they wore rivaled the priceless tapestry wall hangings in opulence, and their jewels glittered brightly as the crystal, gold, and silver under the massed light of hundreds of candles. I noted in passing there must be somewhere in Honandun some very rich chandlers. The ornate throne at the far end of the room near the marble hearth stood conspicuously empty as the heralds announced us. The ripple of conversation abated slightly as people turned their heads to look at us, assessing our importance to decide exactly how polite they needed to be.

With Kerri on his arm, Cullin advanced into the room, his grace and poise more than a match for any of his audience. A man separated himself from a knot of people and came to meet us, hand extended in greeting. He was clad in Isgardian trews and jacket in a soft gray, but wore a plaid in bright red, brown, and blue pinned over his shoulder. I noted reflectively that the foam of lace at his throat and wrists was even more elaborate than mine. Or Cullin's. His hair gleamed like polished oak and sprang from his head in tight, lustrous curls. Only the braid by his left temple and his neatly trimmed beard showed silver-gilt to betray any indication of age.

"Cullin, my dear boy," he called ebulliently. "How very good to see you again!"

"Sion, you old reprobate," Cullin replied, smiling. "It's been years." They embraced each other soundly, then Cullin drew Kerri forward. "Sion, I have the honor to present the lady Kerridwen al Jorddyn, kinswoman to Prince Kyffen of Skai.

My lady, Sion dav Turboch, Tyran ambassador to the Court of Isgard."

Sion dav Turboch took Kerri's hand and bowed over it, raising it briefly to his lips. "I've met your father, my lady," he said, his eyes twinkling merrily. "And I must say that he does not deserve a daughter so beautiful as you. You must favor your lady mother."

Kerri murmured something polite and smiled.

Cullin drew me forward. "Sion, this is—"

"Leydon's boy," Sion said, measuring me carefully with his eye. "I'd know you anywhere, lad. Last time I saw you, you could walk beneath a horse without bending your head. In fact, you were. Nearly frightened your mother's hair white."

"I've grown since then," I said, smiling. It was difficult not to smile in reply to the dazzle of his.

"Aye, well, I should hope so," he replied. "That must have been nigh twenty years ago."

Cullin looked around casually, smiling. "Have we established our credentials for all the watching eyes, Sion?" he asked.

Sion laughed. "Aye," he said. "I believe so. That's why I was sent to greet you. The Ephir trusts few people these days."

"As well he should," Cullin said. "And you're one of them."

"I have that honor," Sion said smoothly.

"Sion was one of the best swordmasters in Tyra before he turned his hand to diplomacy," Cullin said, still smiling. "His tongue was not always so polished."

"Because you were a stubborn and frustrating student," Sion replied. "But you were one of my best, much as I hate to admit it and give you reason to expand that pride of yours."

Cullin grinned at Kerri and me. "Sion also runs the best network of spies on the continent," he said. "Sometimes, he even tells my father what he knows."

"Only so much as is good for him," Sion said, comfortably complacent. He offered his arm to Kerri. "The Ephir has arranged a private audience before the meal, if you would be so good as to accompany me."

"You probably already know what news I bring," Cullin said as we fell into step with Sion and Kerri.

"No doubt," Sion said serenely. "No doubt, but it would be best coming firsthand from you, wouldn't it?" He smiled down at Kerri. "You make the other women in this room dim like candles before the sun, my dear." He patted her hand on his arm. "You shall have to let me take you around and introduce you so I may show you off."

"Go gently with the lady, Sion," Cullin said, amused. "She's *bheancoran* and very well trained."

Sion looked at Kerri with new interest. "Ah," he said. He smiled. "Then perhaps we will merely dine together and you will be so kind as to gaze besottedly at me to enhance an old man's reputation."

We had almost reached the door near the empty throne when a man wearing the dress uniform of an officer in the Honandun Guard intercepted us. The hand holding his silver-chased goblet flashed and glittered with rings, but the jewels could not disguise the whiteness of the knuckles. The set of his nose was badly off kilter, but all signs of swelling or bruising had faded. The nose did little now to enhance his good looks. He put me in mind of a meticulously bred but slightly stupid horse. Malevolence gleamed in his hooded dark eyes as he looked at Cullin.

"It would seem we meet again," he murmured. "I had thought you would not dare to return so quickly to Honandun."

"I take it you two have met already," Sion said.

"Not formally," Cullin replied politely.

"Ah," Sion said, nodding. "Tergal Milarson, Cullin dav Medroch of Broche Rhuidh. And the lady Kerridwen al Jorddyn of Skai, and Kian dav Leydon."

Kerri gave the guard officer a dazzling smile. "Why, Sion," she murmured prettily. "You had not told me that Honandun contained such handsome men!" She held her hand out to the guard officer and gave him the full effect of her brilliant smile. "Delighted to meet you, Captain Tergal." And she batted her eyelashes at him.

Tergal bent low over her hand, then straightened, smiling.

"It is a pity we could not have met before I had this unfortunate accident," he said, touching his nose briefly.

"Oh, but Captain," Kerri gushed. "It gives you such an interesting and *mysterious* appearance. This one—" She waved a dismissive hand in my direction. "This one has only looks but no substance. So very wearying, would you not agree?"

Heat climbed from my throat to suffuse my cheeks. I hoped Tergal would interpret it as cold dignity attempting to disguise wounded barbarian pride rather than near strangulation from the effort it took to repress the laugh bubbling up in my chest. Cullin put up his hand to stroke his beard and hide the corners of his mouth, but not a ripple disturbed the smooth, bland surface of Sion's face.

Tergal smiled again. "You are too kind, my lady," he said. "Perhaps you would do me the honor later of allowing me to present you to my cousin, the Ephir."

"That would please me immensely, Captain," she said, fluttering her eyelids again. "Once we have finished our business with my lord ambassador here, I would be delighted."

Tergal bowed. "Your servant, my lady," he said. "Until later then." He gave Cullin the smug, self-satisfied look of a mountain cat that has just successfully stolen a plump, juicy rabbit right out from between the teeth of a wolf. He made a stiff, abrupt bow to us and moved away. We had not seen the last of Tergal Milarson. He looked just intelligent enough to be sly, and certainly vindictive.

Sion offered Kerri his arm again. He bent over to place his mouth close to her ear. "Minx," he murmured just loud enough for me to overhear. "You drew his fangs very neatly, my girl." Kerri merely gave him a radiant, starry-eyed smile.

We left the reception room and passed into a brightly lit hall. Sion paused before a brass-bound door and knocked three times. From inside, a voice called: "Come."

The chamber Sion led us into was small and comfortably, if plainly, furnished. A wooden worktable stood facing the window. On the wall behind it hung a huge map of the continent, the countries all color washed in different hues: Tyra, a tapering green arrowhead running east from the coast; the block yellow shape of Isgard, and the sprawl of landlocked Maedun, blood red in the candle light. I had never seen a more finely detailed map, except perhaps for the one my grandfather owned, which hung in his own study at Broche Rhuidh. A sleek gray-striped cat lay curled in sleep on a wooden bench beneath the window. I had been expecting a demonstration of more opulent tastes, similar to the reception chamber, but this was a room in which Cullin's father, my grandfather, would have been at home. It sharply restructured my image of the man who ruled Isgard.

The man himself stood with his back to us, hands clasped loosely behind him, gazing out the window at the square below. He wore trews and jacket in simple, unadorned gray, and he was shorter than I expected—less than a handspan taller than Kerri. Narrow shoulders curved forward in an habitual slump, allowing the light to gleam on the pink scalp surrounded by thin, lank gray hair. Not a prepossessing figure at first sight, the Ephir.

Then he turned and the illusion shattered. The set of the Ephir's thin, nearly lipless mouth gave away nothing, nor did his pale gray eyes, small and closely set above the knife blade of his nose. They shone bright and gleaming as silver coins. They were as flat and impenetrable as coins, too, giving away nothing of what their owner thought. I thought perhaps they might allow a man to see whatever he wished mirrored there. The slouched posture, then, was a subtle subterfuge, an exercise in misdirection. The study in contrasts between the reception chamber and this room, between the slumped posture and the alert, watchful eyes, was meant to confuse and to keep both friends and enemies off-balance

Sion presented us, and the Ephir inclined his head in brusque acknowledgment as Cullin and I bowed, and Kerri curtsied.

"My lord Ephir," Cullin said, "I bring you greetings from Medroch dav Kian dav Angrus, Eleventh Clan Laird of Broche

Rhuidh of Tyra, First Laird of the Council of Clans, Protector of the Sunset Shore, Laird of the Misty Isles, Master of the Western Crags and Laird of Glenborden." The titles rolled effortlessly from his tongue. I always managed to trip over one or more of them when I tried it.

"Your father honors me," the Ephir murmured. "I had not expected him to send his son. But surely you are his younger son." He slanted a quick glance at me. "I was given to understand you had sired none but three daughters." In Isgard, a man's virility was measured by the number of sons he produced. In Tyra, a man's worth was measured otherwise.

"Kian is my foster son," Cullin said, undisturbed by the veiled insult. "The son of my brother, Leydon."

"So." The Ephir went to a chair behind the worktable. "Please, be seated," he said, gesturing toward wooden chairs before the table. The cat uncurled itself from the window bench and sauntered insolently across the carpet to leap into the Ephir's lap, confident of its welcome. The Ephir stroked the glossy fur and the cat's contented purring filled the room. "Perhaps you would be so kind as to tell me how thinks your father about the possibility of an alliance between Isgard and Tyra."

Cullin leaned back in his chair. "He would be amenable to hearing more of the details," he said. "Then perhaps would be willing to enter negotiations."

The Ephir put his hands on the table, palms flat, fingers splayed. "Negotiations will take time," he said. "Isgard already has enemies on two borders."

"She has enemies within, also," Cullin said. "When last did you speak with your nephew Balkan of Frendor?"

Something flickered in those flat, silver eyes. "I have not spoken with Balkan for nearly a season," he said. "Have you news of him?"

In terse, precise sentences, his voice flat and uninflected, Cullin told him what we had seen in Frendor, and what had transpired at Balkan's manse. When he finished, the Ephir remained silent for a long time, a faint frown drawing the gray eyebrows together over the silver eyes.

The Ephir looked at Sion. "Had you known of this?" he asked.

"One hears rumors, of course," Sion said. "Until Cullin confirmed it just now, I had no proof of anything happening in Frendor."

The Ephir's gaze remained on Sion, but didn't ruffle Sion's composure. I wondered if anything actually could. Finally, the Ephir looked back to Cullin. "I am in debt to you for that information," he said quietly. He touched one gnarled finger to his chin, the other hand dropping absently to stroke the cat again. "So my dear nephew thinks to depose me, does he? We shall have to do something about that." He got to his feet, sending the indignant cat scrambling to the floor. "Thank you," he said again, and gestured toward the door. "If you will excuse me, I have things I must do. We will speak again tomorrow, and perhaps begin working out a viable plan of mutual defense between Isgard and Tyra."

When we were once again in the hall and walking back toward the reception room, Sion said, "I shall advise your father to be circumspect in his negotiations with the Ephir."

Cullin grinned. "Very circumspect," he agreed. "I trust that man less far than I trust a Laringras whip snake."

Sion laughed. "He would fight the Maedun down to the last Tyr," he said. "Then he would negotiate a truce with Maedun that would no doubt be much to his own advantage. He's a wily old lizard, is the Ephir, and he's held Isgard strongly for most of his lifetime. No matter what he agrees to, he will move first to see Isgard with the advantage, whatever the cost to his allies." He shrugged. "But then, Medroch dav Kian, too, has always been as slippery as peeled willow and as hard to trap as a handful of quicksilver. I trust his judgment as much as I suspect the Ephir's principles."

Cullin paused at the door of the reception room. "You'll make our apologies to the Ephir when we don't come tomorrow, Sion?" he said. He glanced at Kerri and smiled. "We have pressing business in the northeast that needs to be attended to immediately."

"Of course," Sion said.

Kerri laughed. "And will you make my apologies to the good captain, my lord ambassador?" she said. She put her hand to her head and fluttered her eyelashes dramatically. "I think I've developed a terrible headache. I believe I must return to the inn."

"Kian will escort you back to the inn," Cullin said. "I want to stay for a while and test out the temper of this Court. I'll follow in an hour."

I offered my arm to Kerri. "I should be pleased to be your escort, my lady," I murmured politely. "If, of course, you don't mind being seen in the company of a man all looks and no substance."

"I didn't mean to imply you were only good-looking," Kerri said contritely. She smiled at me. "I meant you were all brawn and no brain. Brawn is *not* handsome." And she fluttered her eyelashes at me as she took my arm.

They came at us from the shadows as we stepped down from the carriage. I had just turned to extend my hand to Kerri when I saw the quick, furtive movement off to one side. I spun to meet them, already reaching behind my left shoulder for my sword before I remembered in despair that it was still in my room at the inn. I had no weapons but my hands.

I counted four of them as I turned quickly, pushed Kerri unceremoniously back into the carriage before she could protest, and slammed the door. "Get her out of here," I shouted to the startled driver. He gave me one terror-filled glance, then shouted to his horses, slapping the traces hard onto their backs. They lurched into an uncoordinated canter and the coach whirled away, leaving me alone with the four attackers.

I had only time enough to drive my shoulder into the belly of the man who leaped after the carriage and knock him to the cobbles before something bashed into my head. It turned me off as effectively as pinching out a candle.

20

Sick. I was sick.

Sick and dizzy.

I was hurt. Dimly, I remembered I could Heal it if I wanted. I could make it stop hurting. Ground and center. Ground and center. But there was no ground. No center. Just dizziness and pain.

The world spun too fast and my head whirled with it. Spinning too fast and in too many directions at once. I was caught in the middle and it was tearing my head apart.

Spinning and dizzy and sick.

The plane of the world began to tip, slowly at first, then more rapidly, until it was a sheet of glass tilted at a crazy, impossible angle, and I felt myself sliding toward the edge. Desperately, I tried to flatten myself against it. There was nothing to hold on to.

I fell off.

I lay facedown across something that lurched and jolted, driving flashes of pain like shards of glass through my head. The taste of blood filled my mouth, thick and sharply copper-metallic against my teeth. I could not move to ease the thumping pulses of agony jarring through my head. I realized vaguely that my wrists and ankles were lashed to something, forcing me to maintain the folded position. The crushing, throbbing pain drove out coherent thought. Consciousness rode the crest of the pain like a dolphin rides a wave. I slipped into a dull stupor, enduring only from moment to moment, waiting with torpid patience for the jolting to stop. After an eternity, it did stop, and I hung there in a red haze that felt like peace by contrast.

I thought I saw Dergus Keepmaster with the shadowy,

nearly transparent figure of the general behind him. Dergus pointed a bony finger at me, and a thin thread of black mist poured out of him and wound itself around my head. It poured into my nose and mouth, and slithered down my throat, into my chest, tangling itself around my heart and lungs.

A hand grasped my hair and yanked my head up. I stared foggily at a face, blurred and disembodied, that floated in the haze before mine—a face bearing a terrible, purple burn scar along the left side, the ear deformed and ugly with it. The mouth moved and made sounds, but I could extract no sense from them. Just meaningless noises. I closed my eyes.

It was quiet and dark, and there was no place on my body that did not hurt. Head most of all. Every time I drew in a breath, my ribs protested violently to the abuse. My hipbones felt as if they had been pummeled by Gerieg's Hammer. Hands and feet throbbed painfully with each pulsebeat. But my head. . . Oh, gods, my head had been torn in two and clumsily fastened back together by half a hundred horseshoe nails.

Dizzy and sick, I lay on my side and tried to sort out what had happened to me. The pounding headache scrambled my brain and banished all coherency. All I knew was I hurt, and I must be still alive because not even Hellas could hurt like this.

How long I lay there, I could not begin to guess. Gradually, recollection trickled in thin, tangled threads into my memory. Sequence was hopelessly shuffled. Nothing made a lot of sense.

. . . *Kerri in a shimmery gown, her hair done with pearls and gold.*

. . . *Cullin, lace at his throat and wrists, sitting before a polished worktable, leaning forward, his face serious in the light of banked candles, while a small man with narrow shoulders listened with a frown on his face.*

. . . *Turning, reaching for a sword that was not there.*

. . . *Drakon's face grinning at me in malice and anticipation, his scars livid in the sunlight.*

. . . *Men running, taut with purpose, out of shadows, noiseless, like wolves rushing a stag.*

. . . The Ephir of Isgard turning from a window to display silver-coin eyes, flat and watchful as a lizard's reptilian gaze.

. . . A carriage clattering madly down a cobblestone street.

Pieces of a jumble puzzle for a child's amusement. Where did each piece fit? And if I could fit them together, how did the picture they made explain why I hurt so much?

The only useful conclusion I came to was I had been betrayed, either for the Maedun gold on my head, or the Falian gold placed by Mendor and Drakon. And since it was Drakon's face that persisted in sliding through the tangle in my mind, it was reasonable to assume it was also his gold that had been paid to send those four thugs tumbling out of the shadows. Sorting that out left me inordinately pleased with my reasoning. Torn in two my head might have been, and lurching along like a wagon with one square wheel, but at least it was working again, after a fashion.

Now that I had a plausible explanation of what had happened, the next question I needed answered was, where was I? That I was lying on the ground under a shaw of holly was partial answer. But was I still in Honandun? And if I wasn't in Honandun, where was I, and where were they taking me?

I had missed something important in my slow limp through logic. Patiently, doggedly, I went back over the jumble pieces, like a priest telling over his prayer beads, looking for the thread in the tangled skein I had missed the first time. But nothing new presented itself. Another sorting through produced the same result. But I knew I had missed something. Something important.

Mayhap Kerri was right when she called me dull-witted—
Kerri!

The realization jolted me like a burst of lightning. My head thumped and pounded with the startled shock.

Hellas-birthing. Kerri was with me when the thugs attacked. I remembered throwing her back into the carriage and sending it careening down the street. Had the driver succeeded in taking her out of danger? Had she been able to find Cullin to tell him what happened?

Gods, but my head hurt!

Why was I lying here, suffering the agony of the damned, when I could Heal myself? That thump on the skull the thugs had dealt me must have truly scrambled my brain.

I concentrated.

Nothing came.

I met only emptiness, a void where the quiet place should be. My heart lurched in terror, and I recalled a nightmare. No ground. No center. Only an insanely tilted world too smooth to hang on to. My head throbbed and clanged, shattering coherent thought.

It's because your head is addled by the blow they gave you, I told myself firmly, reaching desperately for calm amid the storm of fear and pain that threatened to swallow me whole. I tried again. Then again. But there was nothing there. Nothing but an impenetrable blackness, cold and empty and deep. The harder I struggled, the more the emptiness grew until the edges of it were sharp as honed blades to flay the flesh from my bones.

Finally, exhausted, I gave up. It was useless now. Perhaps later when I had more strength.

As I lay there, I became aware of a different strangeness. A hollowness . . . No, a silence. A silence that had not been there before. The absence of a subaural sound, so familiar and intrinsic, I had not noticed it until it was gone.

The link with the sword—and with Kerri—was gone.

Pain knifing through my hip woke me. My body spasmed like a gaffed salmon trying to escape. The movement reactivated the pain in my head and I tried to bring my hands up to cradle the pounding ache. The sight of my hands, swollen to twice their normal size and dark with trapped blood, wrists bound tightly by thick leather thongs, startled me into full alertness. Warily, I looked up to discover the cause of the new pain in my hip.

Drakon of Glaecyn Landhold stood over me, lips skinned back from his teeth in a feral grin. In the morning sun, the scars on his head showed livid purple, hideously puckered and shiny. Behind him, four men sat around a small fire, huddled over handfuls of bread and cheese. Several horses grazed, picketed securely, nearby.

"Awake at last, are you?" he said softly.

I lowered my hands to my thighs. My ankles were also bound. I sat there, watching him, but said nothing.

The smile stretched wider. "I trust you spent a pleasant night."

"I've been more comfortable," I said.

"You'll be less so shortly, I imagine," he said. "I shan't kill you. You need have no fear on that account."

I met his gaze squarely. "I know you won't," I said. I managed a smile. I think. From the stiffness in my face as I bent my lips, it might have been more of a rictus. "You dare not kill me."

He lost his smile. "I merely promised your death to another," he said. "However, there are certain matters still outstanding from before you left us so abruptly at Glaecyn. According to law, the sentence may be carried out at any time."

A cold chill rippled through my belly, and my testicles tried to shrink right up into my body. I smiled at him again. "*Qu'resh zith masht'n*," I said clearly. It was the worst insult one could offer a Falian, to call him a fornicator of hounds, a sire of mongrels. On far less provocation, duels had been fought to the death.

His face turned an unpleasant, pasty white, and his mouth tightened. I could not get out of the way of his hand, but I managed to turn my head enough so that the blow merely cracked against my cheek and jaw rather than my eyes. It was more than enough, though, to explode pain like long splinters of oak through my skull.

Breathing hard, Drakon drew back. "At least I will still be able to fornicate when this is done," he snarled. "I almost regret that I will not have sons or daughters of yours to house in my slave quarters."

I spit out a mouthful of blood, but he moved his boot and I missed. "Any son or daughter of mine would do for the right side of your head what I did to the left."

"Lord Drakon?"

Drakon turned quickly, stepping back. A man stood at the edge of the holly bushes. A Maedun soldier, wearing the flash of the House of Balkan on the left breast of his black tunic.

"What do you want?" Drakon demanded.

"We are ready to leave, my lord," the Maedun said. He gestured to me. "Did you want him tied to the packhorse again?"

Drakon looked down at me, then shook his head. "He can ride," he said. "We'll make better time that way. Tie his ankles to the stirrup straps. And loosen the bonds on his wrists so he can hold on to the saddle. I don't want him falling off and killing himself before we can deliver him to the general."

Sitting the horse was an agony, but nowhere near as bad as being carried slung like a sack of meal across a packsaddle. My feet were numb, and I had no control over the horse with my hands bound and the reins knotted across the pommel of the saddle. Dergus Keepmaster held the lead rope with obvious pleasure. With the pain running rampant through my whole body, it was not difficult to ignore the smug, malicious glances he kept shooting back at me over his shoulder.

Each breath sent knives of pain lancing through my bruised and battered chest. Every jolting step caused flashes of pain to explode behind my eyes. My hipbones ached dully, making any effort to move with the horse next to impossible. By midday, I had drifted off in a haze of misery and merely tried to endure.

One of the soldiers gave me a cup of water when we stopped for the midday meal, but it was obvious they didn't think it worth wasting food on a man under sentence of death. When they finished their meal, they tied me to the horse again, and we continued the journey eastward.

Late evening found us near a river I recognized as the River Shena, which curved sharply south a little more than twenty leagues east of Honandun to flow into the sea at Trevellin. It startled me to discover we had traveled so far. I must have been unconscious for a night and a day and most of a second night, rather than just the one night I had reckoned on.

Shortly before dusk, Drakon led our small party away from the track. A fire glowed near the bank of the river. As we pushed through the screen of bushes, Mendor rose from his place by the fire to meet his son. Five or six more Maedun soldiers watched as Drakon and Mendor greeted each other, but they did not move.

One of the soldiers freed my ankles from the stirrup straps and dragged me off the horse. I barely felt my feet under me, large, clumsy, unresponsive lumps of clay in my boots. He led me, stumbling and wobbling, down to the water and indicated I could drink and relieve myself if I needed to. The current was strong near the center of the river, rushing in oily smooth ripples and swells, but near the bank it eddied gently enough.

I fell to my knees and plunged my bound hands into the cold water. It tasted of mud and waterweed, but my throat was parched and dry. I gulped down several handfuls, then had to fight to keep the water in my belly. I knelt there, breathing deeply for a moment until the cramp of nausea abated.

The riverbank rose more than a meter on both sides of me, overhanging the water, trailing threads of grass and willow branches into the river. Where I knelt, the bank had crumbled to form a small half circle of sandy beach, like a bite taken out of the fabric of the bank. Above grew a thick copse of elm and alder, ringed by low bushes. The campfire burned near the edge of the bank, hidden from the track by the shrubbery and a small fold in the land itself.

My guard yanked me to my feet. They were a little steadier beneath me now, but the rush of returning circulation was painful. I could feel my toes flexing within my boots as the Maedun prodded me back up the gentle slope to the fire. He bound my ankles again and left me sitting with my back against the slender trunk of an elm while he went to claim his meal.

Sometime later, another soldier brought me a heel of dark bread and a strip of leathered venison. He dropped both into my lap and returned to the fire without speaking. I looked down at the bread and meat in my lap. Slave rations. Half a loaf of dark bread and a strip of dried meat a day. In disgust, I pushed the food away. I doubt my belly would have accepted it anyway.

Closing my eyes, I leaned back, tilting my head until it rested against the bole of the elm. Two days since I had been taken? Surely Cullin was now following the trail. He would set all Honandun on its ear in searching for me, as efficiently and easily as he had set the inn of the Sword and Crown on its ear. Even the Ephir could not simply ignore the kidnapping of the grandson of Medroch dav Kian of Broche Rhuidh, a man near as powerful in his own country as the Ephir was in his.

A shadow fell across my face. I opened my eyes to see Drakon standing over me, silhouetted against the light of the fire behind him.

"Have you grown too proud to eat my bread?" he asked.

I closed my eyes again.

"Your arrogance will not last long once we get across the Maedun border," Drakon said. I heard his feet rustle in the grass as he moved. A glance through slitted lashes showed him just out of kicking distance, his shoulder propped against a tree. "If you're waiting for your friends to come for you," he went on, "you'll be waiting for eternity."

I looked up at him. He bared his teeth in a cruel parody of a smile.

"Eight years ago, you took a woman from me," he said. "A woman I genuinely looked forward to having. That debt is repaid now." The smile widened, turning down at the corners. "We caught the carriage before it got too far away. A most spirited woman, your Celae sword-wielder. She provided me and my men much entertainment before I cut her throat. Rather a waste, but she was not worth the trouble of bringing along."

My hands spasmed on my knees. Something squeezed my heart in my chest, and the breath clogged in my throat. I tried to tell myself he was lying, but I knew. The link with the sword, the link with Kerri, was no longer there. It had been gone since I had regained consciousness. She had said the bonding was breakable only by death. If the bond was gone, there could be only one reason for it.

"You needn't think to wait for your friend to rescue you, either," he said bluntly. "Your big Tyr is dead, too. Tergal ordered him killed as he left the Ephir's palace. An easy bow-shot from a second story window. I'm told your friend took the arrow in the spine just below his neck. He's quite dead, I assure you."

I looked up at him. "I owe you blood debt for three deaths, then, Drakon," I said hoarsely.

He sneered. "You are in no position to claim blood debt," he said. He laughed, a low, nasty sound in the stillness of the night. "Tomorrow evening, perhaps, when I am less fatigued, I think I will see how well that hair of yours burns. Will the flame be the same color as the hair?" He touched his damaged ear and smiled. "It will be pleasant to hear you scream as I did." He paused to consider his next remark. "I remember it being so very painful. I wonder if I remember aright. Ah well, you shall soon be able to tell me."

I searched fruitlessly through my dreams for the hill crowned by the Dance of stones, for any sign of the Watcher on the Hill. I found nothing but a cold, dead, blighted land, the grass burnt and flaked to ash beneath my feet. Skeletons of blasted trees raised branches, wasted and withered by the desolation, in supplication to a pitiless, ash-clogged sky, colorless and bleak as banished hope. I walked the salt-strewn ground endlessly, the only thing moving in all that vast, devastated landscape. Ash stirred up by my feet rose to hang in a dry, choking haze around me. There was no help here, no hope of aid. My soul shriveled within me until it was as lifeless and arid as the land.

I awoke with moonlight spilling through the trees, my vision blurred by tears. Bright sparkles radiated out from the edges of the moon through the prism of moisture in my eyes. I had not shed tears since the day so long ago when I had wept for Rossah. My grief for Cullin demanded more than mere weeping. It raged for vengeance, as did Kerri's humiliation and death at the hands of Drakon's Maedun mercenaries. I lay curled around my raw, aching misery, feverish and ill, and wept until there were no more tears within me. There was no solace in knowing Sion dav Turboch was there to see Cullin properly home even if there was no one who would ever see me home to Tyra; there was no one to perform the final ritual for me.

The moon stood directly overhead when I levered myself to a sitting position beneath the elm tree. Only dim embers glowed in the fire pit. Lumpy figures wrapped in cloaks and blankets lay randomly placed around the fire, unmoving. Occasionally, the low snoring of deep sleep carried on the still air.

A sentry sat against a tree several meters from me, head down, chin against his chest, hands slack on his knees. I watched him for a few moments, but he did not move.

As I lay there, listening to the night sounds of sleeping men and moving water, a plan born of fever and desperation formed slowly. Images of the general kneeling before the disemboweled corpse in Frendor danced vividly in my head. Other pictures flashed through the memory—the agonized screaming of men shrieking and tortured as Mendor's stock tenders left them eunuchs, writhing in the filth of the sheep pen.

I will not let them do that to me. By all the seven gods and goddesses, they will not do that to me. Ill and hurt I might be, but they had not taken away my obdurate stubbornness.

Slowly, carefully, I tested my feet. I felt them move in my boots. My hands were numb, the fingers too thick and clumsy to untie the knots in the thongs around my ankles. I could not walk, and I could not ride, but if I had the courage for it, there might be one means of escape, dare I try it. It was dangerous. I might not survive, but if I died this way, I would at least accomplish half of my purpose. I would cheat Drakon out of the pleasure of torturing me, and I would deprive the general of any benefit he might gain in my death.

I turned onto my belly and glanced at the sentry. Still, he had not moved. Slowly, painfully, I crept forward on knees and elbows, hunching and straightening like a measuring worm.

Something rustled in the grass behind me. "Crawling suits you," Drakon's voice said, full of malevolent amusement. "I have been patient enough with you. My patience is now at an end."

I eeled around to see him silhouetted against the moonlight behind me. The pale light gleamed softly on the dagger he carried in his right hand. He took a step toward me. All the anger, all the pain, all the grief swirling through me suddenly coalesced into cold, white rage. My body tensed like a leaf spring, waiting for him to take that last step which would place him close enough to me.

He shifted his grip on the haft of the dagger and lunged at me. I drew my feet back, then lashed out. One of my feet caught him on the hipbone and the jarring shock of it traveled clear up to my spine. The other foot sank into the softness of the pit of his belly. He screamed shrilly, and I heard an answering shout from the suddenly awakened men by the fire.

I rolled desperately, closer to the bank of the river. A sudden, crushing sensation caught me and pinned me to the ground as securely as if I had been arrow-shot. I was less than an armlength from the lip of the riverbank, but I could not move. Breathing hurt, and my heart felt squeezed between the jaws of a vise. Dergus moved out of the trees and stood over me, grinning wolfishly, as Mendor stooped to help Drakon to his feet.

"He's still bespelled," Dergus said casually. "I've deepened it. He won't move."

Leaning most of his weight on his father, Drakon limped closer. He drew back his foot and kicked me above the hipbone. I had not even the breath left to cry out in pain.

"I'll kill him," Drakon shouted. "I will kill the bastard—"

"You will not," Mendor said, pulling him back. "Not yet."

"Look what he did to me," Drakon raged, spittle flying from his lips in a fine spray. "I will kill him—"

"You will have your time with him," Mendor said. "Come."

Dergus stooped and put his hand to my head. "He'll cause no more trouble now," he said.

Nausea gripped my belly and I felt as if I moved far away from myself. From a great distance, I watched Mendor lead Drakon back to the fire. The weight released me, and I drew in a great, rasping breath. When I tried to move, I found I could not.

I felt detached and separated from my body. I knew what Dergus had done to me, but was unable to care. When two of the guards dragged me back under the copse of elms, all I could do was close my eyes and sleep.

For five days we rode eastward across land flat as a plate. The horizon stretched interminably like a fine wire ahead, unbroken by hills or even trees. The grass, already turning brown under the heat of the sun, rustled dryly beneath the hooves of the horses, and clouds of insects rose from it like drifts of smoke to mark our passage. Occasionally, I saw a small farmstead huddled in the shelter of the trees along the river, the only water on this vast plain.

As the days passed, the feeling that my head was wrapped in wool did not decrease, nor did the strange, floating sensation of detachment. The bruises on my chest and hips gradually healed, turning from the color of ripe eggplant to ugly saffron and green, then fading entirely. Riding became easier as the pain diminished, and I was able to move with the rhythm of the horse with a little less difficulty. They had loosened the bonds at my wrists enough so that the swelling in my hands had gradually disappeared. I rode between two Maedun guards, one of them with the lead rope of my horse tied to his saddle, the other, behind me, holding a rope tied in a noose around my neck. The message was more than clear. If I tried to escape, my neck would be snapped as easily as the neck of a felon on a gibbet, but I was no more danger to them than one of the rabbits that fled the hooves of the horses in the thick grass.

At the head of the small column, Mendor, Drakon, and

Dergus set a harsh pace. We traveled from dawn to after sunset, making up to ten leagues a day.

About midmorning of the sixth day, I saw the first faint outline of mountains to the north on the horizon. They looked like little more than a low bank of cloud that faded to nothing as it stretched eastward, but they marked the southern border of Tyra. We were not more than fifteen leagues from the northeast border of Isgard, where Tyra, Maedun, and Isgard come together, and not more than three or four leagues from Maedun. Something tugged at my heart, a ghost of longing, but it was gone before I could grasp on to it.

Shortly after midday, Mendor and Drakon swung sharply south. An hour later, we began to follow a rutted track along the river. It was a little cooler with the water close and the thick stands of trees lining the bank.

We rounded a bend in the road to find the walls of an isolated landholding directly ahead of us. As we approached, the gates swung open, and shut with a clang behind us as we passed through.

Mendor, Drakon, and Dergus dismounted and tossed the reins of their horses to servants who came running to catch them. With bemused indifference, I recognize Lord Balkan descending the wide steps to the courtyard to meet them. I suppose it was too much to hope he had not survived the conflagration in Frendor if the others had escaped.

One of the Maedun soldiers cut the bonds that lashed my ankles to the stirrups and hauled me down from the horse. I stumbled as I hit the ground, and the soldier jerked me back roughly by the rope around my neck. Docile and passive as a lapdog, I let him lead me away.

My head felt clear for the first time since Dergus had touched me at the riverbank. The apathetic detachment had faded gradually since I had been thrown into the small, dank cell. I had no way of telling how much time had gone by. A narrow slit of a window, barely wider than the breadth of my hand, let in a dim glimmer of light and the faint sound of moving water.

The scraping of a key turning in the lock of the door sounded overly loud in the quiet. I looked up from the corner where I sat huddled against the damp stone walls of the cell. The heavy door opened ponderously and showed the silhouette of a man framed against the dazzle of the evening sun. It took me several moments to recognize Drakon. Behind him stood two guards.

I struggled to my feet, my back pressed against the damp stone wall behind me. I couldn't remember the last time they had given me food or water, and I was dizzy and weak, unsteady on my feet as a newborn colt. Drakon took two steps into the cell and it gave me no little satisfaction to note that he limped slightly.

"They have an interesting custom in Maedun," he said, his voice slurred as if he were partly drunk. "They brand their slaves on the cheek and breast. We've never done that in Falinor. We think it lowers the value of a slave to disfigure him. Balkan has an excellent blacksmith here. He's made me a very nice branding iron with my House crest on it."

I said nothing. I needed my breath and my strength to remain erect.

"I can't decide whether I should have you branded before or after I put you into the hands of the Herdmaster." The tone of his voice was both falsely musing and mocking at the same time.

A wracking cough bent me over when I tried to reply. I straightened slowly, catching my breath, and looked at him. "I willna care much after, I expect," I said with false calm, determined he would not goad me into the outburst he obviously wanted from me.

"I would think you're right. It will be interesting to find out." He laughed softly. "They're waiting for you in the sheep pens," he said. "And I'm ready to be entertained."

"Hellas take your black soul, Drakon," I whispered hoarsely. The rock of the wall felt cold and slimy beneath my fingers, like the skin of a fish. Cold rage burned quivering in my belly. "I will lay a curse on you with my dying breath before the general kills me. I have magic. Magic the general wants. You can't escape the curse. Have you ever watched a man die of a curse, Drakon?"

Drakon stepped back quickly, his face paling. He gestured to the guards behind him. "Bind his hands," he told them. "Then bring him along."

The last glow of sunset dazzled my eyes after so long in the dark cell, but the fresh air revived me, and I felt a little stronger. I allowed myself to stumble and stagger as the guards pulled me along, each with a hand on one of my arms.

They led me out through a small gate in the wall past two sentries armed with bows held ready. Ahead, near the bank of the river, stood a long, low open shed facing onto a pen ringed around with a rail fence. The pen was empty save for one man dressed only in a pair of trews and a leather apron that covered most of his chest and hung to his knees. He barely glanced our way as we came out through the gate into the meadow.

The only entrance to the sheep pen was on the side nearest the shed, close to the bank. The path was narrow and my guards had to walk in the grass alongside it to maintain their grip on my arms. We were nearly to the pen when the guard nearest the bank tripped on something hidden by the grass and went sprawling onto his face. He lost his grip on my arm as he fell swearing, but pulled me away from the other guard before he let go. The second guard made a startled exclamation and instinctively turned toward the fallen guard.

I remained standing on the path, confused for only the instant it took for my brain to realize I was free. Instinct took over. I was less than five strides from the riverbank. I whirled and began running clumsily. I heard a whirring rush of air, like the slither of an animal in dry grass, then something struck me a hard blow on the shoulder. The point of the arrow penetrated deep enough to protrude through my shirt just below my collarbone.

Even as I began to fall, I flung myself desperately toward the bank. Then, muttering a prayer to all the seven gods and goddesses, I dived forward and gave myself to the river. The last thing I heard before I hit the water was Drakon shouting incoherently at the guards in rage and frustration, demanding they plunge into the river after me.

The shock of the cold water closing over me made me gasp.
I swallowed half a liter of the muddy water, coughed and
choked, then rolled onto my back in an effort to keep my face
above the water. Air trapped in my filthy shirt and plaid
helped, but it would not remain there for long.

Tentatively, hesitantly, I reached for the healing power,
afraid of what I would find—or not find. At the first touch of
that vast, chilling void, I drew back, shuddering.

The current swept me quickly past the tree-lined bank, west-
ward to the sea. I fought only to keep my face above the bubbling surface. I lay on my back in the water, watching the stars
slowly appear one by one against the black curtain of the sky.
The trees along the riverbank became only darker black shadows against the faint glow of the sky, moving with incredible
speed. I had not realized the current was so swift.

Then, caught in a wide sweep of a bend, the river spun me
like a fallen autumn leaf. Even as I struggled to right myself,
my body slammed into something hard and unyielding. A dead
tree, half-submerged, stripped of all but a few sharp stumps of
branches. One of the stubs stabbed painfully into my chest and
caught me there. Even as I struggled to free myself, the force
of the current slammed my shoulder against the solid wood of
the trunk and the arrow shaft broke. Pain tore through my
shoulder, blinding in its intensity, and I lost consciousness.

21

I stared directly into the face of the oddest apparition I ever remembered seeing. Grizzled, unkempt hair spiked out in all directions around the sharp-featured face. He looked like a silver northland owl, bushed out in its winter plumage. Black eyes, deep-set beneath shaggy white eyebrows, yet bright and inquisitive as a wren's, held cheerful amusement and avid interest. The skin around his eyes and covering the wide brow was curiously unlined and smooth, making a startling contrast of youth and age between it and the flaring halo of wild, gray hair. A wide, gap-toothed grin beamed from behind the bush of frizzy beard. The toothy skull of a tiny rodent dangled from one ear, half-hidden by the untamed thatch of hair. I gaped in startled amazement for a moment, then shuddered and closed my eyes, hoping that, if this were another nightmare, it would go away quietly and leave me to die in peace. Or if I were dead and this was Hellas, that it would let me be and allow me to suffer my due torments in solitude.

The apparition cackled merrily. "Ye can open yer eyes, lad," it said. "I be no wraith from Hellas come to carry ye off. Just old Jeriad, I be. Old mad Jeriad, they calls me. Mostly harmless, they says."

I opened my eyes again. With something close to bemused detachment, I saw that the face had not gone away, nor had it changed. Only vaguely curious, I looked around. I lay on a pile of bracken between two layers of furs and skins, none of them too clean, in a semicircular room walled in undressed stone. Dim natural light filtered in from somewhere, and a single torch, guttering and giving off more smoke than light, cast writhing shadows across the room.

The strange man crouched on the packed earth floor, sitting on his bare heels beside my pallet. He wore a one-piece garment of tanned and stitched deerhide that covered him from throat to ankles but left his arms bare. Those arms looked like they were made of skin, bone, and gristle, thin as birch twigs. They looked withered and wasted with age and went with the wild, gray hair only thinly streaked with black, but contrasted starkly with the oddly youthful face.

He thrust a crudely made earthenware cup at me, its contents steaming gently.

"Drink this, boy," he said and cackled again. "It be bitter as sin and death, but it be making you feel alive again." He pushed the cup with surprising strength into my hands and nodded eagerly as I lifted it to my mouth. "Drink up. Drink up. It be naught but snowberry root, willow bark, and chalery leaf."

I took an experimental sip. He was right. Vile-tasting as swampwater. I made a wry face and tried to give back the cup.

"Nae, nae," he insisted, pushing it back. "Drink. Ye've lost blood from the shoulder. That be helping to build more."

I held my breath and gulped it down in one long swallow, trying to get it through my mouth fast enough to avoid tasting it. My stomach contracted sharply as the drink arrived all of a piece with a hard splash, but I held the revolting stuff down and lay back against the furs, gasping.

The old man clapped his hands in glee, then took the cup. "Good lad. Good lad. If ye can keep it down, it be working quick and lively for ye. Feel better soon, ye will." He set the cup aside and squatted there, his head cocked to one side like a bird, studying me with unabashed curiosity. "Quite a size, ye be," he said in delight. "Quite a size, indeed. It be a good time I had to drag ye up from the river, boy. The river, it be sending me gifts now and then, but never something like yerself. Ye be ill-used, lad. Ill-used. Be ye on the run from the Ephir's guardsmen, then? Hounds from Hellas, they be, for sure, and the old Ephir be the chiefest hound."

Keeping up with his jackrabbit conversation was making me dizzy. The old man grinned and reached out to pat my shoulder. As the gnarled hand touched me, I noticed for the first time that my shoulder was wrapped in a poultice made of leaves and grass, secured by a strip torn from the hem of my shirt. It didn't hurt at all. And neither did my chest. Or my head. Whatever else he was, he was knowledgeable in the arts of healing.

"There be'd poppy in the drink, too, lad," he said. "It takes away pain and gives sleep. Ye be needing sleep to heal yerself. Go off wi' ye now. Ye be safe wi' old mad Jeriad. Ye be safe."

I believed him. My eyelids sagged on their own accord, and I gave in to sleep without a struggle.

I knelt, head bowed, in the midst of the featureless, blighted landscape, ash caked around my nose and mouth. Beneath my knees, the gritty cinders bit deeply into my skin. My blood, lurid red against the colorless ground, made small lumps of clotted grit that crumbled to dust at a touch. A wind I did not feel moaned and howled, sifting clouds of ash like drifting rain from the gray of the sky.

This was a dreamscape of my enemy's making. His hand, the darkness he carried with him, had sculpted these dunes of ash and cinder. He drew me here against my waking will just as surely as the Watcher on the Hill drew me into his own dreamscape. I had neither the strength nor the skill to resist either of them.

Pain rasped through my chest with each choking breath I drew. Hollow urgency pounded in my blood with every hammering beat of my heart. My enemy was near. I had to get away. Every heartbeat brought him closer and I could not let him find me. I had no sword, no weapon of any kind. Here in this dead, burnt land, he could kill me as easily as he breathed, and there was no way I could oppose him.

I staggered to my feet. The effort made me dizzy, but I forced myself to stumble forward. The ash dragged at my boots as I sank to the ankles in the fine, powdery stuff. Pain wracked my whole body. I had to drag each foot free of the clinging grit, willing the muscles of my leg to swing the foot forward. One foot after the other in slow, aching progression. Too slow. Too slow. The struggle left me exhausted after only a few dozen steps. But I had to go on. I had to. He was behind me, and his sinister laughter, ringing with triumph, carried on the wind. Sobbing in frustration and defeat, I fell again to my knees.

Another sound rode the wind, thin and sweet as a cool trickle of clear water after a drought. A woman's voice? In my delirium of exhaustion and pain, I thought it called my name. I listened, not breathing, concentrating on the sound.

Yes! A woman's voice. Kerri's voice! And she called to me. Called my name.

I rubbed the grit from my crusted, reddened eyes. I saw nothing but the bleak, gray land. Ash clogged my throat when I tried to call out to her, and I could not manage even a hoarse croak.

"I'm here," I thought desperately. "I'm here, sheyala!*" But the link between us was barren and empty.*

And my enemy was nearly upon me.

I threw back my head and opened my mouth to shout defiance at him. No sound came out. Ashes filled my throat, strangling my voice, choking me, and I could not breathe.

The knowledge that Cullin was dead swept over me as soon as I opened my eyes, and submerged me in a wave of grief and loss. Cullin and Kerri. Both gone. This business with Mendor and Drakon was none of their fight, but they were dead because of it, and I was alive. Through some quirk of the gods' humor, I was alive, dragged out of the river by a half-mad bird of a man. I could not remember freeing myself from the dead tree. It seemed unlikely the old man could have extricated me from that himself. But surely I would have drowned had I not been impaled upon the sharp stub of branch that kept my head out of the water. Mayhaps old mad Jeriad was stronger and more spry than he looked.

I owed him my life. For whatever reason he had been down searching along the riverbank, I owed him thanks and I owed him my life.

And I owed Drakon and Mendor a death—three times over. The debt would be paid. And soon.

Old Jeriad scuttled into the half-circular room, carrying a brace of skinned rabbits in one hand. "Ah, look at ye," he cried happily. "Look at ye, boy. Ye be awake and color be in yer face. Ye be not the half-drowned near corpse I dragged from the river. The drink always works. Always. Be ye hungry now?"

"Aye, verra hungry," I admitted.

He chuckled. "Young men be naught but walking appetites," he said. "I remember. I remember well." He brandished the rabbits. "These be sizzling quick now, and there be fresh greens and bread. Good for you. Be making you strong. Healthy again. Wait you here. Dinner be soon. Wait you here." He vanished through the hide that served as a door. Moments later, he was back, carrying a cup which he thrust at me. When I drew back in distaste, remembering the foul taste of the last concoction, he cackled in amusement. "It be only water, boy," he said. "Just sweet water from my own spring behind the dun. Drink it. Ye be needing it. Drink up. Drink up."

I thanked him and took the cup. He sat on his heels beside me, knuckles of one hand on the earthen floor between callused feet for balance, and watched me closely. "Ye lost people," he said suddenly. He put one gnarled finger on my chest just below my breastbone. "There be a darkness in ye, boy. A darkness. Not of yer own making, but it be there nonetheless. Have ye run afoul of them, then? The black sorcerers?" He shook his head. "Bitter bad, they be, lad. Bitter bad." A troubled expression flitted across his face. "They be out there now. Searching all up and down the river and along the water meadow. Searching well. They not be seeing old mad Jeriad, but I watched them. They be gone now. Gone upriver." He cocked his head to one side and fixed me with that raptor's sharp gaze. "Be it you they search for, boy?"

"I think so," I said. I described Mendor and Drakon to him, and he nodded eagerly.

"Aye, lad," he said. "Those two be'd with the black sorcerer's men. Bitter bad, they be. After ye, be they?"

"They killed the man who was the only father I knew," I said. "My friend and my kinsman. And they killed a young woman who had asked me for help."

"Wicked bad," he mourned. "Wicked, they be. I know them. Wicked men, all."

I looked at him. The black eyes, strands of midnight black among the yellowish gray hair. "You're Maedun yourself," I blurted in sudden recognition.

He held up a hand, waving it in negation and shaking his head vigorously. "Nae, nae," he sputtered. "I be nothing. Just old mad Jeriad. Once, I be Maedun. Mongrel, they called me. None of their own. None of their own." The black eyes glinted. "Mother be Celae. You know Celi, boy? Nemeara it be once. Celi now. You know the Fair Island?"

"I've heard of it," I said hoarsely.

"My mam had magic," he said confidentially. "Celae magic. Some came to me. Not enough. Nae, not enough. Be taking a lot of Celae magic to beat back the black sorcerer."

I looked at him in shock, a sudden, cold sensation in my gut. I saw the smooth, unwrinkled skin around his eyes and covering his forehead and the high cheekbones. Not an old man, after all? But gods, surely not only twenty-seven. Surely not only three years older than I.

He dragged a hand through his hair, sensing my discovery. He cackled in delight. "Magic," he told me. "Magic did this, boy. Magic be hard to control. He tried to take my magic, the black sorcerer. He tried, but I tricked him. Burn me, it did. Burned him, too. They say it addled my wits. But I be alive and others be dead, and he can't find me now. No, he be thinking old Jeriad be dead." He winked and chortled again. "We won't be disabusing him of that notion, will we?"

I shook my head. "Of course not," I said. "Tell me about your mother, Jeriad."

"She be'd Celae," he said and laughed. "She be dead, too. Dead these fifteen years past. Escaped him that way, she did." He sprang up suddenly. "Rabbits be cooked," he announced. "Be ye hungry?" And he skipped away.

I tried to organize my spinning thoughts. Jeriad a prince? Gods, he appeared no more capable of being a prince than a fox is capable of flying. But twenty-seven? He could not be that young. Surely he could not be Kerri's lost princeling. But his mother was Celae, and he had magic. I had lost the sword, but was it still leading me? Leading me to this? To Jeriad?

Oh, Kerri, I thought bleakly. *Kerri, I think I've found your lost princeling, and he's a travesty. I'm so sorry,* sheyala. *But what will I do with him? And what do I do now?*

He brought the meal to the small room in shallow baskets, together with an ewer of fresh water. He ate with all the fierce concentration of a wild animal, discouraging all conversation. My own concentration was hardly less intense. The simple food was good and I was more than hungry enough to do it justice.

Halfway through the meal, I heard the faint but unmistakable sound of metal clinking against stone and the soft whicker of a horse. I froze, and Jeriad grinned widely around the rabbit haunch as he continued, unconcerned, to gnaw at it. He glanced up through the fringe of his hair, black eyes glinting, reminding me sharply of a hawk peering through a thicket.

The horse's foot clanked against a stone again. I sat, unmoving, hardly daring to breathe as I waited for the shout of discovery outside the stone walls. But it did not come, and Jeriad grinned wider than ever.

Presently, Jeriad cocked his head to one side and listened intently. "They be gone," he announced calmly. "They be wanting you bad, boy. But they be gone now."

"Why did they not look in here?" I asked, curious and puzzled, as well as vastly relieved. Then I shivered. "Did you use magic?"

"Magic?" He hooted with delighted laughter. Even his beard seemed to curl upward with mirth. "Nae, nae. No be magic, boy. Show you in the morrow, I will. In the morrow after noontide when you be feeling better." He fixed me with that shrewd, bright raptor's gaze. "And mayhaps you be telling me why the black sorcerer's men be looking for a young Tyr nobleman, will ye not?"

"I'll tell you now," I said. "I'm called Kian dav Leydon ti'Cullin." My name obviously meant nothing to him. I had not expected it would, but I owed it to him. "Two of the men out there are Falian nobles, my enemies. The others are Maedun mercenaries. They're General Hakkar's men."

He nodded. "Aye, the black sorcerer. I had dealings with him. A wicked man. Heart be black as his name. He tried to take my magic." He frowned, then grinned slyly. "But he failed. He failed. Old Jeriad tricked him. Why they be hunting you?"

I told him the story, including how Drakon had gleefully informed me of Cullin's death, and how Kerri died. Jeriad listened carefully without interrupting, nodding now and then. His intense, watchful gaze never left my face. When I finished, I found my hands clenched so tightly, my fingernails had dug bloody half-moons into my palm.

"These be wicked times," he said, shaking his head. "Be sad and terrible times." He gestured to the food in my lap. "Eat, boy. Be good food there. Don't be wasting it."

I looked down at the half-eaten meal. I had lost my appetite. "I'm not very hungry," I said apologetically. "I'm sorry. It's good, but . . . "

He snorted in derision. "How ye be expecting to heal if ye no be eating?" he demanded.

"I'm sorry," I said again.

He bounced up and took the small basket. "Be good for breaking yer fast, then," he said cheerfully. He put his hand on my forehead. "Sleep then," he said quietly. "Sleep be good, too."

My eyelids suddenly felt too heavy to hold open. In spite of myself, I began to drift off into sleep. I heard his voice as if from an incredible distance.

"Others be searching for you, lad. Not the black sorcerer's men. Others be coming to look for you."

The next afternoon, Jeriad changed the dressing on my shoulder and pronounced me fit enough to get out of bed for a short while. The wound had already begun to close and appeared to be healing well enough. I saw no signs of wound fever, and the skin felt cool and healthy when I placed the inside of my wrist against it.

When he had finished with my shoulder, he brought me my clothing. The boots were dry, but stiff as jerked venison. The

shirt, wrinkled but clean and neatly mended, was ragged at the
bottom where he had torn the strip to bandage my shoulder
and patch the corresponding rip in the shirt. It still boasted its
cascade of lace at throat and wrists, but the lace was tattered
and frayed as a wind-flayed leaf. The kilt and plaid were in little better shape. He had mended the rents as best he could with
threads drawn from the fringed end of the plaid, and the regular pattern of the tartan was skewed over the mends. I was not
about to complain, though.

I dressed quickly, and tried to thank him, but he merely
cackled with glee and waved away my fervent expressions of
gratitude. When I tried to give him my plaid brooch, he looked
first at it, then at me, exasperation plain in his eyes.

"Now what would old mad Jeriad be wanting with the likes
of that?" he demanded. "I be having no need of pretties." He
beckoned. "Come. Come. I be showing you why those
accursed riders never be finding old mad Jeriad. Come."

He ducked through the skin door covering, then held it
open for me, beckoning again. I followed him through into
another semicircular room, this one half-full of jumbled rock.
A few feet from the opening, a curving stone staircase, the ris-
ers broken and cracked, hugged the gentle arc of the wall.
Halfway around the curve under the stairway, a rough arch
opened. I had to stoop to see into the opening.

The chamber appeared natural, the walls made of rough,
raw stone. Sand white as snow covered the floor. I heard the
hollow, musical sound of water dripping slowly far back
within the cave. A fire blazed a few meters from the entrance,
and the smoke wafted gently toward the back of the cave. It
explained part of my question of the night before. Drakon and
Mendor's men had not been able to smell the fire because the
smoke had dissipated long before it reached the open air. It
was a very clever arrangement for a man who did not wish to
be found.

Jeriad tugged at my arm to urge me out of the underground
chamber. He scampered up the steps and stood waiting for me at
the top. I followed cautiously, a little more unsteady on my feet
than I would have liked to be, and mindful of the broken steps.

When I reached the top of the stairs, I looked around in astonishment. I stood against the crumbled remnants of the walls of what had once been a tower. Behind me, the undressed stone rose twice the height of my head, a tall triangle of rock, thrusting out of the ground like a broken tooth. Ahead of me was another tumbled pile of stones. Jeriad scrambled over them, waving me forward, a wide grin splitting his face.

A little less agile than he, I climbed the pile of rock and found myself standing in the ruins of what had been the main room of the tower. It was hardly recognizable as such now, though. Except for the one section of wall by the steps, the whole tower lay in a scattered heap, covered by thick growths of bracken, moss, and wildflowers. When I turned around, even though I knew the entrance to the lower floor was there, I could not see it. All that was visible was a pile of rocks. The pattern of light and shadow hid all signs of it.

"You see?" Jeriad chortled. "You see? Old mad Jeriad be more clever than they think."

I grinned. "Not so mad," I said. Somewhere in the distance, water flowed noisily between narrowed banks. There was only one place I knew of on the Shena where the water boiled and seethed over rock-strewn rapids—Pagliol's Needle. I was back in Isgard. The river had carried me a good five leagues from the Maedun border. It had served me well. I turned back to Jeriad. "I will have to leave soon," I told him.

"Not yet," he said, shaking his head. "No, not yet. Ye be needing more healing first. Two days. Mayhap three. Then go. Not yet."

I nodded. "No, not yet," I agreed. "But soon. I have to think where I'll go and what I'm going to do."

"Two days," he said, holding up the corresponding number of fingers. "Three." Another finger came up. He shrugged. "Then you think. Now you rest and heal."

I nodded again. "Now I rest and heal. And I thank you." *Rest and heal,* I thought. Just this short excursion out into the open air had tired me. I didn't want to admit it, but I needed the time to grow stronger before I set out after Mendor and Drakon. And to think about what I was going to do if this strange, birdlike creature really was the lost princeling Kerri sought. "Mayhaps you'll tell me about your mother."

He grinned at me. "Mayhaps," he agreed. "You go and rest now."

Even as he spoke, weariness spread through me. I was weaker than I had thought.

Gray sky, drifts of gray ash.

I threw back my head and shouted until my throat was hoarse. "No! No, you cannot make me come here. Your magic cannot hold me." Rigid with effort, I fought against the ensnarement.

Then I saw it. A dark haze on the far horizon. Panic leapt in my belly. He was coming, spreading darkness before him as a cloud spreads shadow. I heard his laughter even as I turned to run.

"You cannot avoid me." His voice boomed like thunder all around me. "I am stronger than you are now."

"No!" I shouted, struggling through the treacle-thick layers of ash. "I weakened you. You have no power."

His laugh echoed through my skull. "Then stay and face me, Tyr. Stay and test my power."

My limbs were made of wood, clumsy and unresponsive. When I shot a glance over my shoulder, my heart surged in terror. The darkness claimed fully half of the land behind me. Searching tendrils snaked out, reaching for my legs, which creaked and groaned like a reef-wrecked ship as I floundered through the ash.

"You are weaker than I, Tyr," his voice thundered. Black, glowing eyes glittered in the midst of the darkness. "Turn. Turn and meet your death."

I brought both my fists up to my head. "No!" I shouted. "You cannot take me. I will not let you—"

"You have no choice . . . "

A tendril of the thick, sticky fog reached out and wrapped itself about my throat. Pain and fever flared up like a pine torch.

22

I came thrashing and gasping out of sleep to find Jeriad kneeling beside the pallet, his hand resting gently on my forehead. My breathing came in great, labored shudders, and my heart knocked against my chest like a blacksmith's hammer. Sweat rolled in thick, viscous streams down my forehead into my eyes, across my cheeks and throat, and the furs beneath me were disagreeably slippery and wet with it.

"It be the darkness they put in ye, boy," Jeriad was saying, his voice soft and gentle. "It be only the darkness. Ye be safe now. Safe here with old Jeriad. Rest ye. Rest ye now."

I fell back against the sweat-slick furs, my breathing easier now as my heart rate slowed to a pace nearer normal. Jeriad let his hand slip from my forehead.

"It be the darkness takes ye to evil places when ye sleep," he said quietly. "It be the darkness, boy. I be not a good enough healer to banish it."

"Darkness?" I repeated blearily. He had mentioned it before, I remembered, shortly after I awoke the first time. Or was it the second? It was too difficult to think properly. My head felt thick, as if it were stuffed with wool. Then I remembered how I had found only a bleak and empty void, a black abyss, when I had tried to reach out for the quiet, healing place within me. Was that what he meant? "What darkness?"

"Sorcery," he said. "The black sorcery. They put it there, deep within you, boy. Old Jeriad be not good enough to cut it out of ye. It be taking stronger than my poor magic to defeat it."

"Dergus," I muttered. "Dergus put it there. And I haven't got the sword to help me now." Where was my sword now? Did the general have it? And Kerri's? I shuddered. Two Celae Rune Blades in the hands of a man like the general. Could he pervert their magic to act for him?

Jeriad rooted around behind him, then turned back to me

holding a steaming cup. "Drink this, lad," he said. He grinned. "Nae, it be not the vile one. This be sweet and soothing. Takes the ache out." He pushed the cup into my hands. "Drink now. This be helping to keep the darkness at bay. Drink ye, and I be guarding yer sleep for ye."

"Is he out there?" I asked. "The black sorcerer? The general? Is he out there now?"

"Nae, lad. Nae. But he be sitting in the middle of the darkness like a spider in its web, waiting to draw you in. Like a spider. Every time ye fight him, it weakens ye. But it weakens him, too. It weakens him, too. Pray the Duality ye be stronger." He patted my shoulder. "I be watching. He'll not be taking your magic."

"I don't have magic," I mumbled. "No magic."

"Sleep, lad. Sleep now. . . "

"Why are you doing this for me, Jeriad?" I asked, fighting to keep my eyes open. "Why?"

He chuckled. "A Tyr once fought for me," he said. "I be paying a debt I be glad to pay."

Heavy lassitude spread slowly through my limbs. Jeriad snatched the cup from my hands as my slack fingers let it fall. I was afraid to go back to sleep. My enemy awaited me in sleep, and the Watcher on the Hill had told me if I died in that dreamscape, I died in the waking world. I could not keep my eyes open. Whether it was Jeriad's potion, or the darkness within me calling me back to the dreamscape, I did not know. But I slept again.

Three times during the night, my enemy drew me into the desolate waste of his dreamscape. And three times Jeriad's gnarled hand on my brow called me back to wakefulness and escape. The last time that he pulled me away from the dreadful gray place, and I awoke staring and gasping, it was dawn. He knelt by the pallet, worn and gray as his hair and beard, his eyes sunk farther into his head, shining feverishly bright.

"It be growing," he muttered irritably. "The darkness be growing in ye. The black one be growing weaker, but so be you. Soon the darkness be too strong. I be unable to call you back."

Fever raged through me. My lips were dry and cracked, and my hands shook so badly, I could not hold the cup of water he gave me. He held the cup to my mouth and I drank gratefully. I hardly noticed the taste when he fed me another portion of his vile decoction of snowberry root, willow bark, and chalery leaf.

I fell into a restless sleep. With the coming of dawn, it seemed my enemy lost his power to drag me into his dreamscape. But other fragmented dreams troubled my sleep. Disturbing images of Kerri's sword glittering bright as she fought by my side and at Cullin's back in Honandun. Cullin's face, lit with joy, as he held his youngest daughter for the first time. Kerri with the silver gleam of moonlight glowing in her hair. Cullin patiently teaching a gawky, adolescent boy the intricacies of sword work. Cullin laughing, with the sunlight in his hair turning it to molten copper. Dreams of the halls of Broche Rhuidh hung with the dark fir boughs of mourning.

I awoke once to find Jeriad's face close to mine, his hands gripping my hair. I stared at him stupidly for a moment, not knowing who he was or why he knelt there, eyes like a raptor's glaring into mine. Scalding pain bathed my shoulder and the foul stench of wound fever filled my nose. My head throbbed and pounded hard enough to blur my vision. Every muscle, every joint hurt with a deep, gnawing ache. I had no strength. There was no inner sanctuary, no safe grounded place, no center. Lost in a haze of pain and utter, abject weakness, I turned my head away from that fierce, piercing stare. In a startlingly clear moment of lucidity, I suddenly realized I was dying. I accepted the knowledge with relief. The concept held no fear, only the promise of serenity and the loss of pain.

"Leave me to die in peace," I mumbled, and my lips cracked and bled with the movement.

"Nae, lad," he said fervently, grasping my head between his hands and turning my face back toward him. "Nae. Ye be healing, lad. Healing, I tell ye. It be the dark spell makes ye think different. Ye must fight it. Fight the darkness."

His voice echoed hollowly in my ears. So far away. So very far away. Meaningless noises. I made an irritated sound and tried fretfully to push him away.

He grabbed my shoulders and shook me so hard, my eyes crossed and my hair flopped, stinging and smarting, into my eyes. It snapped me wide-awake, and I stared into his face. His eyes glinted furiously under the shaggy mane of gray hair, his mouth set in a savage snarl.

"You won't be dying on me, you lout of a Tyr," he shouted. "Pass this night in safety, and you will win this time. You will fight, Kian dav Leydon ti'Cullin. You *will* fight."

I closed my eyes until the room stopped spinning, then I looked at him again. "Fight," I muttered. "Aye. Fight . . . "

Dream. Hallucination. Reality. Madness. All was madness. I was adrift on a sea of insanity where everything boiled and bubbled together with no demarcation between what was real and what was not. It battered me against treacherous shoals that might be rock sharp as daggers, or cloudy drifts of snow.

Jeriad unwound the bandage from my shoulder and I stared in horror at the open, suppurating wound. Even as I watched, it turned black at the edges and the corruption and putrefaction crept down my arm and across my chest to eat into my heart. I screamed while Jeriad chuckled merrily.

The muscles of the Stablemaster's arm flexed and rippled beneath the sheen of sweaty skin as he brought the willow switch down again and again across the back of the boy who knelt in the straw before him, wrists lashed to the hitching ring on the side of the stall. With every blow, the Stablemaster muttered, "Stubborn. Willful. Obstinate . . . " The boy's hands made white-knuckled fists and the muscles of his jaw bulged with the effort to keep his teeth clenched to prevent any sound from escaping his lips. He was determined not to give the

Stablemaster, or the young lord who watched avidly, the satisfaction of hearing him cry out.

The general knelt with his hands plunged deep into the entrails of a man who lay, bound and writhing in agony, on the floor before him. Dark mist throbbing with dull, sullen color twined around the general's wrists and arms. The face of the man on the floor was Cullin's.

Jeriad knelt beside me and placed a cold, wet cloth on my forehead. He bent and held a cup to my lips to let the cool, sweet water trickle into my dry throat. "Tyrs be a stubborn people," he murmured. "Fight . . ."

Kerri stood with her fists planted firmly on her hips, jaw thrust out, her nose inches from mine. "You are the stubbornest mule ever they hung two legs on to walk like a man," she shouted.

I grinned at her. "Why, thank you, *sheyala*," I said.

I lay spread-eagled and bound, naked in the filthy mud of a sheep pen and Drakon stood over me with dirt-encrusted pincers clutched in his hands. The expression on his face was one of unholy ecstasy as he leaned forward and raised the pincers.

Cullin crouched sitting on his heels in the straw of a stable and grinned at me. "Men with red hair like ours are sometimes obstinate," he said. "We do as we will."

A woman with hair like sunshine and moonlight mixed together plucked a small boy out of the dust beside the pony. "You have to set your will against the pony's, my wee horseman," she said, laughing, as she brushed him off. "If you're determined enough, you will win."

The light of one torch, guttering fitfully in the night, cast deep, flickering shadows across Jeriad's face as he sat cross-legged beside me, his eyes bright points beneath the shaggy gray eyebrows. Slowly, he climbed to his feet. "I be fetching them, boy," he said. "You'll see. I'll be fetching them for ye."

"Don't leave me alone with him," I muttered.

"It be too strong for me, boy," he said. "My magic be too poor to help." He slipped through the hide curtain over the door. He was gone and I was alone.

With each plodding footstep, ash rose in a fine haze and drifted up to clog my nose and mouth, caking in my throat. The unchanging, sunless sky hung low above my head. The dull light cast no shadows, neither mine nor that of the occasional twisted skeleton of a tree I passed in my aimless walking.

His sudden laughter rolled like a peal of thunder across the desiccated wilderness. Hopeless despair settled like a leaden cloak on my shoulders, and my knees sagged as I began to sink to the ash and cinder of the ground. But I held myself to my feet and turned. He stood at the crest of a small rise far behind me, a blacker shadow within a dark mist. His sword, held high before him, devoured the wan light and radiated its own darkness. His eyes glittered brightly, the only spark of light in the darkness around him.

A wave of weakness swept over me. I reached out a hand for balance and found a tree beneath my fingers. I looked at it in surprise. It was only a slender sapling, not much more than a stripped, charred trunk, splintered at the root, and certainly nothing to rely on for support. But it felt solid and firm beneath my hand.

Then, as I turned back to look at my enemy, a tiny spark of anger kindled somewhere deep within me. Its meager light glowed, feeble and faint, nearly overwhelmed by the darkness, but it lived. I clenched my hand around the charred trunk.

By the gods, no, I thought. I will not give up this easily. Even the Mouse would not give up against worse odds.

I wrenched at the slender tree trunk. It came away easily enough from its shattered and splintered base. I broke the branching tip under my foot and was left with a staff half again as long as my outstretched arms. When I tested its strength, the charred bark crumbled against my palms, but the staff did not break.

My enemy approached slowly. He did not move cautiously, but as a man might who wished to prolong a long-anticipated and enjoyable event. He laughed again.

"A flimsy weapon," he said. "Do you think that twig will stop this?" He brandished his sword. A spurt of thick, black shadow erupted from the tip and eddied around his arm.

The spark of anger found more fuel. It cut a tiny crack into the heavy darkness Dergus had woven in me, and let a small trickle of strength ooze out.

"If I'm to die, I'll die fighting you," I said quietly. "I'll not kneel meekly to your sword."

He was now close enough for me to see his features clearly through the swirling darkness around him. "Look at your shoulder," he said, smiling confidently.

Even as he spoke, I felt the pain and smelled the putrefaction. The little spark wavered and flickered. I tightened my grip on the staff, concentrating on the spark. I fed the pain to it to fuel it.

The staff twisted suddenly in my hands, snaking and writhing to wrap itself about my arms. I held a serpent that wound its coils around my wrists. Flat, lifeless yellow eyes, slitted with black, glared above a wide, red mouth holding dripping fangs. Fear bloomed in my belly for an instant. My heart hammered wildly against my ribs. I took a quick, unsteady breath, then fed the fear to the spark, too.

Quickly, I slipped my hand along the cold loops of sinuous muscle to grip just under the flat, triangular head. Venom dripped from the needlelike fangs, but I held the head harm-

lessly away from my flesh as I looked back to my grinning enemy.

"Can you not win against me, even in a place of your own making, unless I am crippled and weaponless?" I asked softly.

"You are powerless against me," he cried.

I looked at the sleek, evil head of the snake in my hands, then down at the suppurating wound in my shoulder. "By all the gods," I muttered. "I will not let you win so easily. In the name of the Duality, I won't." The spark became a small ember, burning brighter and stronger. The serpent stiffened in my grip, straightened slowly, became a charred staff again. The wound in my shoulder closed to the half-healed state I knew it to be back in Jeriad's hidden chamber. And carried on the breeze, faintly from somewhere, came the barely perceptible scent of something green and growing. I looked back at my enemy, saw lines of strain in his face, and I laughed.

"The Tyr have always been a stubborn race," I told him. "And I as much as any of them."

He grinned, a ghastly stretching of lips away from teeth. "Then you will die stubborn," he said. "But die you will."

He closed the distance between us in one lithe bound, his sword moving across his body in a wide sweep. I swung the staff around and caught the blade near the hilt. The blade narrowly missed taking my fingers off as it slid along the wood, spraying chunks of blackened bark as it went.

He pulled the sword free and I leaped back, holding the staff level in front of me, watching his hands. They would tell me which way he planned to come at me next.

The overhand blow aimed at my head nearly caught me by surprise. I lifted the staff, angled sharply, and the blade chopped into it a handbreadth beyond where I gripped it. A chunk of the wood spun off into the ash.

I smelled it again. Only the barest trace of something green and growing wafted on the breeze; something alive in the midst of this wasteland. I snatched a quick glance around and saw a patch of grass, not much bigger than my own footprint, five or six paces behind me.

Hope flared, and a tiny curl of flame wavered up from the

ember within me. I ducked under my enemy's next swing and
rammed the truncated end of the staff against his knees. He
staggered back, and I spun to run for the small patch of green.
Even as I reached it, it widened to give me room to place both
my feet on it.

He sprang after me, sword raised. The thrust tore through
the fabric of my shirt. The cold steel sliced along my ribs and I
saw the bright blood well up. It splashed to the ground, and
the few blades of grass beneath my feet curled and crisped,
turning brown and lifeless as they flaked into ash. I barely had
the strength to slam the staff against the hilt of his sword to
deflect the next blow. We stood, chest to chest, separated only
by the flimsy staff and the chill, dark metal of his sword blade.
He struggled for a moment, then suddenly pushed hard, and I
fell away from him. He caught the staff with the tip of his
sword. The force of his blow tore it out of my hands, shattered
into three pieces as it fell uselessly to the ground.

His next swing would kill me. I grabbed at his sword hand,
gripping his wrist tightly between my two hands, and lashed
out at his legs, hooking my foot around his ankles. We fell
together. I swung my elbow and caught him on the jaw.

While he lay, half-stunned, I staggered to my feet and
reached for his sword. But as I touched it, the icy cold of the
hilt seared my hand like fire. I cried out and dropped it.

He laughed unsteadily, his breath coming in short gasps.
"You cannot take it from me," he said. "The sword of a
Somber Rider is quenched in blood." He grinned. "This one
was quenched in Celae blood. It burns any hand but my own."

I stumbled away from him, the wound in my side staining
my shirt and kilt scarlet. Even as I staggered back, he got to
his knees, then to his feet. I turned to run, looking around frantically for another tree, for anything I could use as a weapon. I
heard his laughter behind me as I ran, but his footsteps were
nearly as slow and heavy as mine.

Even as I ran, the small spark of hope and anger began to
die and despairing futility took its place. I could not win
against him, not here in this bleak and lifeless place. The thick
ash dragged at my boots, and the wound in my side drained

my life into the cinders. With every step I took, I knew he was gaining on me. Black tendrils of the darkness he carried with him reached out to drag me back, insinuating themselves around my arms, around my legs, my throat.

The air ahead of me began to shimmer. For an instant, it effervesced slightly, like dust motes sparking in the sun. I heard a voice. Cullin's voice, faint and remote, but completely recognizable, speaking from an unthinkable distance. "Give it to him. Quickly."

Then Kerri stood there in the midst of the sparking air, and she carried my sword. "I cannot enter farther," she whispered, her voice as thin and attenuated as fine gold wire. "I bring you this." She jammed the sword, point first, into the ash so that it quivered there, gleaming and bright. She stepped back, nearly transparent in the wan light, but the sword stood solid and gleaming in the ash. Even as Kerri began to fade and disappear, green spread around the tip of the sword, eating away at the colorless ash in a growing circle.

My heart leaped in my chest. "Don't go, sheyala," I shouted. "Don't go."

"I could not find you until you began to break the spell." Her voice was no more than a rustle of sound on the breeze. "But I cannot stay . . . "

The tip of my enemy's blade tangled in the hair at the back of my neck. I surged forward, my hands stretched before me, reaching for the sword planted in the middle of the circle of green. The ash and cinder sucked at my boots, and I fell, but my hands found the cool, fresh grass. I rolled desperately as the black sword slashed down into the ash where my hips had been only an instant before.

I came to my knees, and my hands closed around the hilt of the Rune Blade. The darkness within me shattered and spun away in crumbling fragments as I lifted the blade. It was as if the sun had come out after a storm, and massive shackles fell from my arms and legs. The sword felt light and alive in my hands, singing with power. The runes along the blade glowed and sparked, and the words they formed leaped out at me. **Take up the Strength of Celi.**

I shouted in triumph as the words burned in the feeble light of the sunless sky. The wound in my side still leaked blood as I spun to face my enemy, but strength flowed into me from the sword in my hands. The blade radiated brilliant light in coruscating colors as I raised it to meet the black, light-absorbing blade of my enemy. Weakened I might yet be, but now that I held the sword, we two were evenly matched again.

Back and forth across that small area of life in the dead land we battled each other, neither of us able to gain advantage over the other. But this time, I was not always on the defensive as I had been in our last two encounters.

My breath came in painful rasps and the sword cut in my side spread icy cold through my chest. The face of my enemy paled until it was puckered with lines of strain, and his breathing became as uneven as mine. He lifted his sword as if it were made of lead, and his arms had wasted to threads, but my own blade was no less heavy, my arms no stronger.

Then I lunged at him, using the last dregs of strength. The tip of my sword went deep into the muscle of his right arm. His sword fell from nerveless fingers as his blood, black-red and viscous, flowed down his arm in thick ropes and clotted against his wrist and hand. The sword vanished as it hit the ground, once again swallowed up in its own darkness.

I had no strength left. I could not raise the sword for the last, killing blow. The sword lowered of its own accord, point going deep into the soft, living turf. Gasping for breath, my enemy stepped back toward the rim of the trampled grass.

"Next time we meet, you will die," he panted. "Next time we meet, I shall be stronger." He faded into the blackness that swirled up swiftly around him to claim him.

I fell to my knees, clutching the sword for support. When I found the strength to lift my head, I saw the gently rounded hill before me, its summit crowned by the stone Dance. The Watcher on the Hill stood in the opening of the inner horseshoe of menhirs, but he did not look at me.

The runes on the blade blazed up brightly in front of my eyes. **Take up the Strength of Celi.** My head sagged forward. I leaned my forehead against my wrists as I held on to the

familiar worn leather hilt, and I closed my eyes in relief and
thankfulness, muttering my gratitude to the Duality, the seven
gods and goddesses, and even to the Watcher on the Hill.

When I opened my eyes again, I still held the sword, but I lay
on my back, one hand clutching the hilt to my breast, the fingers of the other spread along the deeply engraved runes above
my belly. I looked up and saw Kerri kneeling on the hard-
packed earthen floor, her face drawn and worried. Cullin hovered behind her, looking no less distressed. I smiled. "Hellas is
not so bad," I murmured, and drifted back into sleep.

23

I lay bemused on the pallet of bracken and furs in the semicircular room, watching a splash of sunlight creep slowly across the beaten earth of the floor. Dust motes danced lazily in the sunbeam—pure, golden sparks of light in the cool dimness of the room. From the angle at which the narrow ray of light arrowed through the chink in the wall, I knew it to be midmorning. I lay quietly, content and relaxed, knowing myself to be healing quickly now. My beard, growing in after—how many?—days of illness, itched fiercely, and I badly needed a bath to sluice away the sweat-stink of fever and fear, but it would wait quite safely. There was no hurry.

I had awakened some time ago to find myself alone in the chamber, but I heard Jeriad muttering to himself on the other side of the hide curtain. For now, I was not unhappy to be by myself. I touched the narrow ridge of scar tissue along my ribs, thinking of the dream. I had not killed my enemy this time, but I had fought him to a draw and beaten him back once more. If we met again—when we met again—I thought, I might be strong enough to defeat him once and for all. In the dream, I had regained my sword, and I had read the runes spilling along the blade.

I remembered dreaming of Cullin and Kerri, too. They had looked not like shades, but warm and alive, as real as I. If they were in that strange land by the towering Dance of stones, I was more than willing to return as many times as I was able, if it meant I could speak with them again. Small comfort, perhaps, but I'd had little enough of comforting things for the last while.

Jeriad came through the hide curtain, humming and chuckling merrily to himself. He carried a wooden bowl between his gnarled hands. The scent of venison and vegetable stew came into the room with him, and my stomach awoke abruptly, complaining violently of hunger and clamoring for food. I sat up as Jeriad crouched by the pallet, grinning widely as the little rodent skull dangling from his earlobe.

"That smells suspiciously like food," I said, smiling as I gestured toward the bowl.

"Look at ye," he chortled. "Look at ye, now. Bright-eyed and chipper as a squirrel, ye be. Ye be healing well now. I knew it would work. I knew it."

He thrust the bowl into my hands. I was right. Venison stew. I wasted little time in diligently and earnestly employing the horn spoon to transfer the stew from the bowl to my demanding belly. It was unutterably delicious, the plentiful chunks of meat tender and perfectly seasoned, the gravy rich and thick. Jeriad sat there pleased with himself, and watched me eat, still grinning, and bouncing like an excited child.

"The darkness be gone, boy," he said happily. He placed one finger on my breastbone and chuckled. "See? The darkness be gone from ye. It be gone. Ye be fresh new and clean. I knew it would work. I fetched them for ye, I did. Fetched them, and they came right off."

I looked up at him, but didn't stop eating. "You brought my friends into the dream?" I asked around a mouthful of stew.

"I fetched them I did," he said, nodding and grinning. "Be not so mad, old Jeriad. Be not so mad."

"But how—?"

"They be searching for ye," he continued, paying no more attention to the last question than to the one before it. "I found them and fetched them back for ye." He gave an odd little skip of glee, still crouched. "They bringed the sword for ye. Did ye see it, boy? They bringed the greatsword for ye." He gestured over his shoulder, chuckling again.

I glanced up, then almost dropped the bowl of stew. My sword in its battered leather scabbard hung on a stout wooden peg pounded into the undressed stone of the wall on the opposite side of the room, behind the pallet. It *was* my sword. Unmistakably my sword. The worn, leather-bound hilt carried the stains my hands had placed there. I knew it as well as I knew Cullin's face.

"Where did you get that?" I demanded, my voice sounding

rusty and rasping, all thoughts of food banished. "Where did that sword come from?"

Jeriad laughed. "I told ye, boy. I fetched them for ye, and they bringed the sword. Didn't I tell ye so?"

An arm swept aside the hide curtain across the door. Cullin stepped aside to let Kerri enter the room first, then followed her in. They stood there, side by side, faces grave and solemn. The shaft of sunlight slanted down across their heads and their hair blazed molten gold and copper flame in the dim light. The blood drained from my head, leaving me dizzy and giddy. The room spun dangerously for an instant. Jeriad snatched the half-empty bowl from my suddenly nerveless fingers as I sat there and simply stared for a long, timeless moment.

"He told me you were dead," I said hoarsely. "Drakon told me you were both dead."

Neither of them spoke, but Kerri crossed the small room slowly and went to her knees on the edge of the pallet. She reached out a hand and put gentle fingers to the side of my face, running them delicately down my cheek and jaw. I couldn't tell if she were trying to assure me she was alive, or satisfy herself that I was still alive. Cullin walked across the room behind her and sank to a cross-legged position by my shoulder. His eyes were peculiarly bright, and my own eyes stung suspiciously.

"We thought you were dead, too," he said quietly. "We could hardly believe Jeriad when he came bounding out of the reeds along the riverbank like a wild man and insisted we go with him because you needed us." He reached out a hand, and I gripped it in mine. It felt warm and solid and comforting, and too real to be another dream. "When we got here, you looked like you were dying. I didn't think you were breathing until Kerri put the sword in your hands. Even then, it was half a day before you began to look even halfway alive."

Questions welled up and overflowed, but I had not the voice to ask them. All I could do was look from one to the other in wonder. I was foolishly close to tears. I turned to see Jeriad nearly dancing with delight, still crouched and holding the wooden bowl.

"Thank you," I said to him.

Everything about him curled upward in mirth—mouth, hair, beard, the sun-creases at the corners of his eyes. "Ye beat the darkness," he sang. "I be fetching your people, but ye beat the darkness, boy. Ye beat the black sorcerers." He leaped to his feet, frowning suddenly. "But ye need rest, boy. Rest."

"In a moment," I said to him, then turned back to Cullin and Kerri. "But how did you find me?"

Cullin laughed. "A long story, *ti'rhonai*," he said. "And time enough for the telling later."

We sat together, Cullin and Kerri and I, in the small half circle of the underground chamber. Jeriad flittered and fussed about for all the world as if he'd hatched us himself, until Cullin's big hand on his arm brought him down to a dubious perch next to him.

"Roost there a wee while," Cullin said firmly, "and I'll no be worrit about you stepping in the wine."

Jeriad settled, thin arms wrapped tightly around his upraised knees, watching Cullin through the fringe of hair across his forehead.

"How did you find me?" I asked. I looked at Kerri. "What happened after you got back into the carriage?"

Kerri had reverted to normal since Jeriad had shooed her out of the chamber earlier in the day. She glared at me. "Got back into the carriage," she repeated. "Listen to the man! You *threw* me back, you imbecile. By the time I got the driver to stop the stupid horses, I was ready to strangle you, even if I had to go through all four of those thugs to do it."

I had more than enough strength to glare back. "What exactly was I supposed to do?" I demanded. "What could you have done in that fancy gown? Walloped them with one of those ridiculous satin slippers?"

"The carriage whip was weapon enough to stop the only thug who tried to get into that carriage," she said with smug satisfaction. "I took one of his eyes out, and he won't be seeing too clearly out of the other for a good, long time, if ever."

Cullin held up both hands, one palm facing each of us, and cut off my retort before I could take the breath to begin. "Enough," he said quietly. I knew that tone in his voice. He doesn't use it often, and he seldom has to use it more than once on each occasion. Kerri recognized it, too. She transferred her glare to him, then subsided into grudging silence like a cat stroked tail to ears. "If you two canna refrain from going for each other's throats, this telling will take most of the night, and Jeriad will likely thump the both of you on the head with a large stone to get some peace and quiet." He paused significantly. "If I dinna do it first, ye ken."

Jeriad chuckled. "See?" he said knowingly to Cullin. "I be telling ye he be better."

Cullin looked at me, looked at Kerri, then nodded. "Right," he said. "Now, if you'll hold your peace, I'll get on with this."

"Please," I said.

"When Kerri got back to the palace, I was in with the Ephir again," Cullin said. "That weasel Tergal had set a man on the second floor to skewer me with an arrow as I left. Fortunately, Sion foresaw the distinct possibility Tergal would do exactly that. He grabbed the archer by the scruff of the neck and the poor wee fellow couldn't blame Tergal fast enough. We took him to the Ephir, and the Ephir called Tergal. When I accused him of ordering his man to kill me, Tergal went into a towering snit and tried to say I deserved the arrow because of what I'd done to his nose." He looked at me and grinned. "Actually, I believe it was your fist he encountered so abruptly, *ti'rhonai*."

"It very well may have been at that," I said. "The tavern was not what might be described as very well lit."

He laughed. "Tergal is not, I understand, one of the Ephir's favorite kinsmen, but kinsman he is, and the Ephir was caught between loyalty to his youngest cousin and a possible alliance with Tyra."

"He chose the alliance," Kerri said dryly. "That was about when I came storming into the Council Room and demanded something be done immediately about those four thugs."

Cullin reached for the wineskin that lay in front of his knees. "The lady Kerridwen can throw a fairly impressive royal rage herself," he said. "Within half an hour, the Ephir had guardsmen scouring every inch of Honandun, and they were quite prepared to take the city apart, brick by stone by board, to find you." He took a sip of the wine and offered it to me. I shook my head. I didn't feel quite ready to test the staying power of my belly just yet.

"It was Cullin who thought of the sword," Kerri said. "We left Sion calmly suggesting to the Ephir that Tergal's head on a pole would perhaps be minimal retribution for his dishonorable act of attempting to kill the son of the Clan Laird of Broche Rhuidh. I swear I saw Tergal's knees trembling, and the Ephir was certainly not a happy man."

"We had a wild ride in that carriage going back to the inn," Cullin said. "We had surmised by then that it was Mendor and Drakon who had taken you. Tergal swore innocence to that, and it sounded like the ring of truth to me."

"You were right about Mendor and Drakon," I said. "They were taking me to the general. And Drakon had scheduled some entertainment for himself." I grinned wryly at Kerri. "It would have spoiled me for next Beltane Eve."

My attempt at humor fell remarkably flat. Kerri shuddered, and Cullin's mouth lengthened to a grim line. "One more thing to add to their account then," Kerri muttered.

I reached out and touched her hand. "That fight is mine," I told her. "There's no need for you to risk your life and the search for your lost princeling over that."

She snatched her hand away and glared at me. "Don't you go telling me which fights I can't choose to take up," she said coldly. "The experience with Mendor and Drakon certainly hasn't made you any more brilliant. Your head is just as thick as ever." She snorted. "Solid bone. Or rock."

"If you two are finished, mayhaps I can continue?" Cullin said. He waited, but neither Kerri nor I had much more to add. Cullin nodded and went on. "We went back to the inn to get the swords and our horses. Kerri changed out of her ball gown while I got my sword, then got yours, too. I couldna do anything with it, of course, and for a while, we thought that Kerri might not be able to, either."

"Cullin suggested helpfully that it seemed to work better for you when you swore at it," she said, and glowered at me again. "You show no respect, Kian dav Leydon. I'm surprised the sword didn't slice off your hand for you after that."

I grinned. "I was in no mood for its nonsense when I invoked its magic," I said. "I take it you managed, though."

"Finally, I had to go through my sword to yours," she said, nodding. "But, yes. I made it work. And it led us straight out of the city." She dropped her gaze to her hands in her lap. I noticed her knuckles whiten as she knotted her fists together. "Then, the next morning," she continued in a softer voice, "the sword just went still." She looked at me. "Before that, I could almost sense your presence. I believe I could have even without the sword. I think it had to be the bond—"

"I know. I felt it, too," I said.

"Then the link just seemed to fade out and die away," she said. She glanced at Cullin, then back to me. "We thought you were dead then," she said. "The sword could tell us nothing, either."

"Dergus and his spell," I said. "It was the next day Drakon told me you were both dead, and I believed him only because I couldn't feel the link with the sword, or with Kerri, anymore. It was not"—I paused, searching for the right words—"one of my better nights," I finished inadequately.

"I can vouch for that," Cullin said fervently. "We had been following the sword's lead until then. After that, we had to track by sight. Not the easiest country on the continent to track across. We had to take it verra slowly." He looked at me, his mouth set into a grim line. "At the very least, *ti'rhonai*," he said, "we were going to exact vengeance for you, and I vowed I would see you home."

I looked at Jeriad, who had been sitting quietly, like a fascinated child listening to a bard's tale. "You told me they were searching for me," I said, only now realizing what he had meant. "I thought you were telling me it was the general out there, too, as well as Mendor and Drakon."

Jeriad looked affronted. "I be telling you others be searching for ye," he said indignantly. "Not the black sorcerer or his men. Others." He nodded toward Kerri, then Cullin. "Others, lad. Others."

"And he found us," Cullin said, smiling. "We encountered a troop of three or four Maedun mercenaries—"

"Four," Kerri interrupted. "There were four of them." She gave me her smug smile. "Two each."

Cullin laughed. "We were, fortunately, less startled upon meeting them than they were at meeting us."

"What happened?" I asked.

Kerri smiled, mildly complacent. "Their bodies might wash up somewhere around Trevellin," she said negligently. "Or there may possibly be some well-fed fish in the Shena for the next while."

"That was when Jeriad came bounding out of the reeds," Cullin said. He grinned. "Like to stop my heart right there and then. Neither of us had heard him approaching."

"I told them ye needed them, boy," Jeriad said with quiet dignity. "I knew both greatswords had power. I told them ye be in mighty need of them."

"I heard your voice," I said to Cullin. "In the dream. I heard your voice telling Kerri to give something to me. The sword?"

He nodded. "We couldna even tell if you were breathing when she put it into your hands." He cocked an eyebrow at me. "It must have been a terrible dream."

"It was." I told them about the gray and lifeless wilderness, and about the enemy who stalked me through it.

Kerri shuddered when I had finished. "I think I saw part of it," she murmured. "When I put the sword into your hands. All dead and gray and bleak as lost hope."

"Aye," I said. "And when you gave me the sword, it began to change back to a living place."

"Was it the general in the dreams, Kian?" Cullin asked. "Was it the general you fought?"

I tried to recall the face of the man I had seen both in Trevellin and in Frendor. "No," I said slowly. "Not the general. Someone else, I think, but Maedun, too. Like the general. He was somehow familiar, but I can't recall ever seeing the face waking." I looked at Jeriad and remembered something else. I took a deep breath. "Jeriad, would you please fetch my sword for me? Take it out of the scabbard and bring it to me. I have to see something."

Kerri started to rise. "I'll get it," she said.

I caught her arm and shook my head slightly. Puzzled, she settled back and watched as Jeriad bounced up and scuttled across the room to where the sword hung on the wall. He pulled it free using both hands, and, holding it like a banner pole before him, brought it back to me.

"What's on the blade, Jeriad?" I asked quietly.

He frowned and leaned back to see better. "Be markings," he muttered. Then he grinned widely and let go of the hilt with one hand so he could reach out and touch the runes. The sword was too heavy and he nearly dropped it. Cullin reached out a quick hand and caught it deftly by the hilt before it hit the floor. Jeriad dropped into a crouch and ran one finger along the blade, tracing the markings. He chuckled. "Be a Celae Rune Blade," he exclaimed. "Ye carry a Celae Rune Blade, boy, and ye be a Tyr. This be passing strange."

I took the sword from Cullin, wrapping my hand around the plain leather of the hilt. I turned to look straight at Kerri. "His mother was Celae, *sheyala*," I said. "He has some magic, and I believe he's much younger than he looks."

Kerri paled. Her hair, bound in a long braid that fell across her shoulder, snapped as she turned to stare at Jeriad. "Him?" she asked faintly.

"He sees the runes," Cullin said softly. He raised his eyebrow at me. "Are ye sure, *ti'rhonai*?"

"No," I replied. "I'm not sure at all. But I think there's a possibility." Jeriad still crouched on the floor beside me, his hand slowly stroking the blade, a distant expression on his oddly youthful face. "Jeriad?"

He looked up.

"Jeriad, will you tell us about your mother?"

His eyes narrowed as he looked back and forth between Kerri and me. Finally, he shook his head. "Tell her," he said, pointing his chin at Kerri. "Be Celae, her. Tell her, I will."

24

Cullin sat cross-legged, elbows on his knees and fingers tented beneath his chin. We heard the quiet murmur of voices through the hide curtain across the chamber door as Kerri and Jeriad spoke together in the cave where the fire burned. Occasionally, Jeriad's chortling laughter rose above the soft whisper of sound. I wished I could hear what they were saying.

Cullin stretched to ease the cramps of sitting motionless for a long time. "He seems a most unlikely candidate for a prince," he said, voicing my own thoughts.

"Aye," I said. "Most unlikely indeed."

He grinned. "Even more unlikely than you."

I made a sour face. "Mayhaps," I agreed reluctantly. "But I canna help feeling the sword drew me here." I glanced toward the hide curtain. "And he knew the sword for what it was, *ti'vati*. That's more than I did for all the years I carried it."

He picked up the sword and pulled it partway out of the scabbard to examine the blade, then turned it over to look at the other side. Finally, he shook his head. "I see no runes on this blade, *ti'rhonai*," he said. "I never have."

I reached out and traced the engraved figures with my finger. "There," I said. "It reads, *Take up the Strength of Celi*."

One red-gold eyebrow rose ironically. "Celi, is it?" he said. "And you a Tyr." He turned the sword. "And what of this side?"

Again, I traced the runes. "Here," I said.

"And they say?"

I shook my head. "I dinna ken," I said. "I can't read that side."

He glanced at me quizzically. "Yet you can read the other."

"From the dream."

"It's strange dreams you have, *ti'rhonai*." He thrust the blade home in the scabbard and got to his feet to hang it back on its peg.

I was about to reply when Kerri and Jeriad came back into the chamber together. Jeriad glanced at me, his expression troubled, then turned to Kerri, watching her worriedly through the shaggy fringe of unkempt hair.

"May I tell them, Jeriad?" Kerri asked, her voice more gentle than I'd ever heard it. "Would you allow me to tell Kian and Cullin what you told me?"

"Be making us enemies, the lad and I," Jeriad muttered.

"No," she said. "You saved his life. He won't be your enemy." She looked at me. "Kian?"

I'm quick enough when I have to be. I met Jeriad's anxious eyes. "Nothing you could say can make me your enemy," I told him. "Even if you wished to be an enemy, I could not consider you one after what you've done for me."

"Be truth?" Jeriad asked.

"Be truth," I replied. "I swear by the Duality, and by all the seven gods and goddesses."

"Be swearing by that sword, too?" He gestured toward the sword hanging on the wall behind me.

"By the sword, too," I said. "What is it you didn't want Kerri to tell us?"

Jeriad dropped his gaze and knotted his hands together. I could have sworn he looked ashamed of something. "She be telling," he muttered. "If ye be needing me, I be out there. I be needing more snowberry root." He ducked quickly through the hide curtain.

Kerri sighed and shook her head. "Poor, sad little man," she said softly. "He's quite fond of you, Kian. Like one of the sick or injured animals he treats, only more so."

"He told me the river often brings him gifts," I said. I smiled. "He said it had never brought him anything quite like me before, though."

"What is it he didna want to tell us?" Cullin asked.

Kerri sank down onto the floor beside him and crossed her legs beneath her. She raised one shoulder in an oddly resigned gesture. "He didn't want you to know that he's General Hakkar's brother," she said quietly.

"Brother?" I repeated blankly. "Hellas-birthing. Brother?"

"Half brother, actually." She scrubbed her hands across her cheeks and eyes wearily. "You were right, Kian," she said. "His mother was Celae, he does have some magic, and that poor, troubled man is only thirty years old. He looks older than my father."

"Thirty years old," I repeated. "Not your prince, then?"

She shook her head. "No, not the prince. It would seem my search won't end quite this easily."

"You said he was the general's half brother," Cullin said.

She nodded. "Yes. His mother's name was Amalida. She was taken in a Saesnesi raid and sold to a Maedun lord. General Hakkar's father, he says. Jeriad calls him Hakkar, too. He says the father traditionally passes on his name and power to his eldest son. The general's name was Horbad then."

"The child Kian carried from Balkan's manse," Cullin said thoughtfully. He glanced at me. "His name was also Horbad."

Kerri nodded again. "Tradition in Maedun families if they have some magic," she said. "Apparently they have some way of passing the magic on and each generation becomes stronger than the last. Part of the father's magic stems from the bond he forms with his eldest son. Jeriad wasn't very clear on how that happens, but he thinks without the son, the father's magic is not so potent. There are very few of them, though. Jeriad says not more than ten families in all Maedun. One such now sits on the throne in Falinor as Lord Protector."

"And Jeriad?" I asked. "Where does he fit?"

"Hakkar the elder took Amalida to his bed," she said. "Jeriad was born a year later. He inherited some of her magic. She had a little, Healing for instance. Jeriad has some of it. But he inherited some of his father's magic, too. The two were thoroughly incompatible. Once both of them began to manifest themselves, it nearly drove him mad, he says."

"What happened to his mother?" I asked. "Jeriad says she died to escape the black sorcerer."

Kerri made a distasteful face. "This part is rather horrid," she said. "The general was always looking for ways to make his magic stronger, Jeriad says. Then about fifteen years ago, he apparently stumbled on a way. It—it involved a lot of blood."

"We've seen examples of the method," Cullin said grimly.

I shuddered, remembering the small, black-draped chamber, the blood pouring from the disemboweled man, and the dark mist winding around the general's arms. He had wanted to do that to Kerri.

"Yes, well," Kerri said, "apparently it took a fair amount of experimentation and practice before he perfected it. His first few victims were only stray hedge wizards. Not a lot of power, but a little. Then he thought to see if he could seize Celae magic and make it work for him. Jeriad's mother threw herself out of a tower window when the general tried to take hers."

"Gods," Cullin said, appalled.

Kerri had gone pale. She looked ill, but she continued. "When he lost Amalida, the general went after Jeriad."

"His own brother?" Cullin asked, straightening up in genuine shock. "He would become a kinslayer?"

"Jeriad's mother wasn't Maedun," Kerri reminded him.

"Oh, aye," Cullin said, and shook his head. "A mongrel then. Kin to no man. The Maedun have always been incredibly stupid in that way. I suppose he thought that made Jeriad fair game for him."

"Did he say how he managed to escape?" I asked. "He told me only that he tricked the general."

"It wasn't very clear," Kerri said. "He said the general—he calls him the black sorcerer—took him to a small room and cut his throat." She had to swallow hard before she could continue. "In a panic, Jeriad found his Healing in time to save himself. When the two magics met, there was a tremendous explosion, he says. He regained consciousness first and ran. He told me he doesn't remember much about anything for a long time, but when his wits returned, he was here and looked as he does now."

"He told me the magic burned him," I said.

"It did more than that," Cullin said softly. "It stole his youth from him."

"But he's alive," I said. "He tells me he's grateful for that. In fact, he seemed quite gleeful about it."

"The general obviously has perfected his technique over the years," Cullin said. "He must have found a way to take Celae magic after all." He gave Kerri a bleak smile. "He wanted yours, too, my lady. Not a pleasant prospect."

Kerri shuddered and nodded. "And I have you and Kian to thank that he did not get it," she said. "Jeriad says the Maedun believe they have a destiny to rule the world. And the general believes it's his destiny to rule Maedun through his brother."

Cullin tapped his chin thoughtfully. "Remember that guard officer we met who told us Hakkar wanted to put his brother on the throne? What was his name, the brother?"

"Vanizen," I said absently, thinking about something else. "The general told us we set him back half a lifetime. Remember? When we met him in the courtyard of Balkan's manse?"

Cullin nodded slowly. "So he did," he said. "Then mayhaps we've been given some time to prepare for the war coming."

Kerri's eyes blazed with intensity. "This makes my search all the more urgent," she said. "Celi must be strong and united to fight the Maedun."

"Can you not use your magic?" I asked.

She shook her head. "You don't understand Celae magic," she said. "Tyadda magic, actually. It can't be used as a weapon. It's a gentle magic, Kian. Like Healing. It won't let you use it to kill."

"Not even for defense?" I asked.

She shook her head again. "No. Don't you think if it could be, we would use it against the Saesnesi?"

"Aye," I said. "Ye would at that, I suppose."

"So we have to find Kyffen's grandson," she said, pounding her fist gently onto her knee. "We simply have to." She looked up, an odd expression in her eyes. "Kian, Jeriad told me that the man in the Dance told him to go down to the river the night he found you. He said he was asleep when the man in the Dance told him to wake up and go to the river because there was a task there for him to do."

"The man in the Dance?" Cullin repeated. "Who—?"

"The Watcher on the Hill," I said slowly, comprehension dawning. "The man in my dreams. Who is he, *sheyala*?"

"Truly, Kian, I don't know. But I wonder if he might be Myrddyn. The enchanter who worked with Wyfydd Smith."

I stood on the green velvet of the grass, my sword sheathed across my back. It vibrated gently against my flesh, and its melodic murmur whispered in my mind's ear. Before me rose the familiar gently rounded hill with its crown of stones. A soft breeze ruffled my hair, spilling a few stray strands into my eyes; I lifted a hand to brush them away. The air was soft and refreshingly cool, and suffused with serenity and peace. I raised my eyes and found the Watcher on the Hill standing amid the horseshoe of polished stones.

I began to climb the hill, once again surprised by how long it took me to reach the summit. As it happened before, I could not pass beyond the first ring of menhirs. That invisible barrier held me back. I stepped back away from it and waited patiently for the Watcher on the Hill to acknowledge my presence.

He came forward slowly. Beneath the shadow of his brows, his eyes glowed with a soft, lambent gleam. He paused between two of the standing stones and smiled.

"Your wound pains you," he said, his voice only barely more than a whisper.

"It heals," I said.

He reached out, his arm penetrating the barrier as easily as penetrating mere air, and touched my shoulder. All the residual ache drained away instantly. I did not have to look at it to know it was completely healed. Nothing was left but the scars, front and back. He smiled again and retreated behind the barrier.

"Why am I here?" I asked.

"I called you," he said. "I would remind you your task is yet to be completed."

"You have not told me what the task is."

"Oh, but I have."

"I must give this sword to the man who would be King of Celi," I said. *"Is that it?"*

He smiled. *"Yes."*

"Who are you?" I asked. *"Are you Myrddyn?"*

"That is one of the names they call me," he said. He made a broad gesture to include all of the Dance of stones. *"This was always my place, even before those who named me came here."*

"My enemy," I said. *"Who is he?"*

"He is the enemy of all," he said. *"You will meet him again."*

"And will I defeat him?"

"I told you before, I cannot read the future. I can only see the shapes of what might become. You have weakened your enemy. You have been given time. I cannot say if it will be enough time to avert what might be."

"That is no answer, old man."

"It is the only answer I can give."

"You speak in riddles," I said, frustration knotting in my chest. *"Can you tell me if Kerri will find her princeling?"*

"Yes, I believe so," he said. *"But I cannot tell you if the princeling will find himself."* He smiled gently. *"Go now, my son. You have a long journey before you."*

"Where is this place?" I asked. *"Is this the Dance of stones Kerri speaks about? The Dance in Celi?"*

"This place is where it is." He turned to walk back to the central horseshoe, then paused and looked back over his shoulder. *"Do not forget the lessons the Swordmaster taught you. You will be needing that skill."*

"Wait," I called. I pushed against the invisible barrier, but could not break through. *"You have to tell me what I must do."*

But he did not reply. Finally, I turned and began the long trek to the foot of the hill.

Dawn was barely more than a faintly perceptible fading of the black of the sky in the east when I left the ruined tower carrying my sword. My shoulder was a little stiff, but the soreness was gone. I wore only my kilt in the predawn chill and the dew-wet grass was cold beneath my bare feet.

I found a flat, open spot and unsheathed the sword. It settled into my hands like an old friend as I wrapped my fingers around the worn leather of the hilt, perfectly balanced and harmonious. I held it up to the achingly pure first light of morning and watched the runes flash and spark in the clear air.

"Which way?" I asked quietly.

The soft thrumming began in the blade and gradually spread through the hilt into my hands, then up my arms into my chest. The sweet, melodic tone sang all around me. Gently as a persuasive lover, implacable as fate, the sword turned me to face east, into the brightening sky. Whatever it sought, it still lay east of north.

"Very well," I said. "Northeast it shall be. But now, dance with me again."

Then, slowly at first, I began the stylized movements, the kata the Swordmaster of my dreams first taught me and Cullin later reinforced. I went through all the routines, moving slowly as a Laringras *bhak* dancer who always seemed to be dancing underwater. My shoulder and arm had lost much strength while I was ill. I had Healed it the evening before, finding with relief the centered space and feeling the gentle eddies of force connecting me to the ground. It was like returning to the home place after an absence far too long.

So now, as the sky paled to dawn, I danced the sword on the wet grass, gradually increasing the tempo of the stylized steps and movements. But I could not reach my normal speed. I had lost much since I was taken from Honandun. It would come back, though. With practice and perseverance, it would come back. It would be there when I needed it.

Sweat rolled freely down my face and my chest, my arms and belly when I finally sheathed the sword again, and I was blowing like a wind-broken horse. But I was smiling as I made my way back to the ruined tower. It stood sharp and jagged against the brilliance of the new sun, its long shadow stretching across the grass toward me. Watching it, I found myself grinning widely with the sheer, sensuous pleasure of merely being alive on a summer morning.

A slender shadow detached itself from the deeper shade cupped in the ruin of the tower. Jeriad skipped lightly over the tumbled piles of fallen rock, humming to himself. He stopped dead when he saw me with the sword. He had been avoiding me since he had given Kerri leave to tell Cullin and me his story. Standing there, half in and half out of the shadow, he reminded me of a startled wild animal, poised for flight.

"Jeriad?"

He leaped lightly to the ground at the base of the fallen tower. "Ye be up early," he said.

"I was practicing with the sword," I said. "I'm a bit rusty after being ill for so long."

He grinned with a hint of his former ebullience. "Ye be young," he said. "The skill be returning soon."

"I hope so." I paused, then: "Jeriad, we're going to leave today. The lady Kerridwen has an urgent task to perform, and Cullin and I are sworn to help her. You wouldn't take my plaid brooch in payment for what you've done for me, but will you take the hand of a friend given in gratitude?" I held out my hand to him.

He stared first at my hand, then into my eyes, his eyes again like a raptor's, fierce and bright. "A friend?" he repeated.

"Aye. A good friend, Jeriad."

"It be my own brother's men tried to kill you," he said warily.

"Aye, it was. But it was you who saved my life. I judge a man by his own actions, not the actions of his kin. Friend?"

He chortled happily and skipped forward to take my hand in both of his. "Friend," he said. "Good journey to ye, friend."

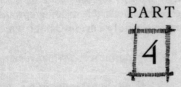

PART

4

The Prince

25

Kerri spotted the ravens first. We were not gone more than an hour from the ruined tower when I noticed her staring upward and behind us, and glanced up, idly curious about what seemed so fascinating.

"Look at those birds," Kerri murmured. "Whatever are they doing?"

Hundreds of the huge, black birds circled lazily in the sky behind us. Cullin caught my eye, his expression grim. We had both seen ravens circle like that before. Carrion eaters, they often flocked to the scene of a bandit massacre of a merchant train or travelers. These birds were not in any hurry, nor were they jostling each other for best advantage. They merely circled with endless, hideous patience. That likely meant there was enough cooling flesh to go around.

"We have to go back," I said, thinking suddenly of Jeriad.

Cullin glanced at me, then at the ravens. "Aye," he agreed. "I think we must."

Kerri looked at us in shock. "Go back?" she repeated. "Whyever for?"

I didn't bother to answer her. I turned Rhuidh and dug my heels into his flanks. He leapt forward and settled into an easy canter as I leaned forward across his shoulders. Moments later, I heard the sound of two more sets of hooves pounding behind me.

Three or four furlongs from the river valley, we began to hear the faint sounds of men shouting and the clangor of weapon on weapon riding the breeze. The clamor of the ravens all but drowned it out. We slowed our horses to a cautious walk.

"Not over yet," Cullin said softly.

Kerri looked at him, puzzled. Sudden comprehension widened her eyes. "A battle?" she asked. "Fighting?"

"Aye," Cullin said. "And a lot of it, at that, from the sound of it." He listened for a moment, his head cocked to one side. "And bitterly fought."

Kerri started to spur her mare forward, but Cullin leaned casually sideways in his saddle and grasped the mare's bridle, arresting the movement before it began.

"Where in the name of the seven gods and goddesses do you think you're going?" he asked mildly.

"We have to help them," Kerri said.

"Help who?" I asked, my tone more sarcastic than I had intended it to be.

She glanced from Cullin to me, startled, then back to Cullin. For a moment, anger flashed in her eyes, and I thought she was about to perform her thunderstorm imitation again. But she subsided and nodded. "Of course," she said finally. "We don't know yet who's fighting whom."

"A wise person doesna charge headlong into a bear's mouth," Cullin agreed. He gave Kerri a tight-lipped smile. "Mayhaps it's Maedun slaughtering each other. In that case, we would do well to leave them merrily to it."

Kerri managed a return smile. "Mayhaps even encourage them in it," she said. "I see what you mean."

Cullin beamed at her like a proud father whose offspring has just done something particularly clever. "See, *ti'rhonai*?" he said to me. "I told you she was a highly intelligent young woman."

Kerri glared at me, and Cullin laughed. "We'll go to see what's going on," he said. "But carefully."

As we neared the brow of the low hill, the hair on the back of my neck suddenly prickled erect. The characteristic stench of magic came to me, but faint and nearly spent. Whoever else was on the other side of the rise, some of them were Maedun and they had warlocks with them.

We left the horses in a small hollow, tethered to scrub thornbushes, and crept to the crest of the hill. We lay hidden by the tall, dry brown grass. Below us lay the shallow bowl of the valley. To the right was the winding glimmer of the river, flanked by broken, sedgy ground. Beyond this, the field rose gently, covered thickly with grass and scrub bushes. The broken tower stood far to our left, alone and dark, standing amid the puddle of its own shadow. There was no sign of Jeriad. I hoped he was safe, hiding in the cave beneath the tower. I thought he had enough good sense to stay well out of the way of any fighting, especially when there were Maedun and warlocks involved.

The bottom of the bowl seemed filled with a seething mass of men, struggling together. The air rang with the clash and clangor of weapon meeting weapon. I had been in the midst of more than a few minor skirmishes with bandits. From within, it was impossible to tell exactly what was happening when groups of men came together in battle. I discovered it was nearly as difficult to figure out what was going on when one was merely an observer. It took a while to sort it out, but there was no doubt the dark-clad men were Maedun, and they fought under Balkan's banner.

It was obvious we had arrived in time to watch the end of the battle. There were far more black-clad Maedun bodies trampled into the sodden grass than Isgardians.

The fighting was fiercest near the center of the valley. I recognized the Ephir's banner in the middle, carried by a standard bearer hard-pressed to keep up with his lord. The banner bore the blazon of the eldest son of the Ephir, Glaval. Glaval himself, tightly surrounded by a band of personal guards, fought a man I thought might be Balkan. It was difficult to tell from this distance.

The battle was all but over. There were few of the Maedun left standing. The Maedun, breaking from stand to fighting stand, were pressed gradually backward toward the small stream. The Isgardians followed them with steadily growing ferocity and triumph. Men began to run in behind the fighting troops to bring out the wounded and dying. Glaval's banner forged steadily ahead.

Then, Balkan fell to Glaval's sword and disappeared beneath the hooves of the horses. With Balkan dead, the Maedun lost their enthusiasm for the battle. Quite suddenly, they broke and ran. Glaval led a mopping-up action as we watched. Those

Maedun still mounted, spurred their horses in a disorganized retreat, and fled the valley to the east. The few Maedun afoot who could find a horse followed them moments later.

That quickly, it was over, and a ghastly silence, broken only by the harsh cries of the ravens, descended onto the valley.

"Verra interesting," Cullin murmured. "Was there magic there, *ti'rhonai?*"

I nodded. "Aye, there was," I said. "But only faintly now. Most of it is gone." Maedun warlocks were reputed to be able to turn weapons back on the user. What had happened to that ability down in the bowl of the valley was not immediately clear. But it was obvious, at least to me, that the general was not with Balkan's Maedun mercenaries. The unique stench of his personal blood sorcery was missing.

"No General Hakkar then," Cullin said.

I shook my head.

"Aye, well, perhaps you really did set him back."

"Look. There's someone coming this way," Kerri said quietly, pointing downhill.

Below us, a troop of five or six mounted men broke away from the main body of Glaval's men and began moving up the hill toward us. As they approached, we got to our feet to meet them. There was little to be gained by getting caught hiding in the grass and mistaken for spies. The leader reined in sharply, startled by our sudden appearance.

"What be you doing here?" he demanded, one hand going to the hilt of his sword.

"Merely passersby," Cullin said. "We heard the fighting and stopped to investigate."

"You be a Tyr by your dress," the leader said. "What interest does Tyra have in Isgardian affairs?"

"None at all, I assure you, until an agreement is reached between the Ephir and the First Laird of the Council of Clans of Tyra," Cullin said, smiling.

"Mayhaps you might explain that to my lord Glaval," said the leader, a captain of the guard. He glanced at the place we had left our horses. "Those be your mounts?"

"Aye, they are," Cullin said. "We thought it best to leave them out of sight of the fleeing Maedun."

The leader grunted, then motioned two men to retrieve our horses. We mounted without protest and followed the captain down the hill. We dismounted at the periphery of the battle-field and handed the horses over to a foot soldier. The captain led us around the worst of the carnage. Even so, the ground underfoot was sodden with blood.

Beside me, Kerri made a strangled sound. I turned and saw what she was looking at. The burial detail had pulled away the last body from a small mound of dead, revealing something straight out of a nightmare. It had been a man, once. Now, it looked like nothing more than an empty husk, something a snake might leave behind after shedding its skin. Still vaguely man-shaped, it was white and bloodless as snow, the skin stretched over the bones, dry and severely withered, with a bizarre, papery texture. The skin had caved in over the chest and belly as if there were nothing beneath, not even muscle, and the arms and fingers were nothing but sticks beneath the transparent, flaking skin. The faint stench of magic, with a peculiar overlay of a scorched scent, emanated from the husk.

Kerri stared for a moment at the mummified corpse in hor-rified fascination before she turned away, mouth drawn down in revulsion. "Like it had been sucked dry," she murmured. "It's horrible."

"A warlock," the captain said, negligently. He gestured to the pile of bodies the burial detail was removing. Most of the corpses were roughly dressed and pierced with spears and pikestaffs. Common foot soldiers. "Throw enough men at them, and they burn themselves out," the captain continued. "They had four with them. Once they were dead, the battle was ours."

"How many men died to get them?" Cullin asked.

The captain shrugged. "They were only peasants," he said.

Kerri shuddered again. "So much blood," she said. "So very much blood."

Cullin looked down at the desiccated husk, then around at the scattered dead. "With this much blood, I would think their magic might be very strong."

Kerri shook her head. "No," she said. "Maedun magic feeds on blood, but it needs suffering, too. Torture to death. This—" She gestured around her. "This is a clean death." She made a wry face. "Relatively clean, anyway."

The captain frowned at her, then shrugged and beckoned us to follow him. He led us across the field to the small pavilion that had been set up for Glaval. His banner fluttered briskly on its standard above it. The entrance faced the side of the hill, away from the scene of the carnage. He looked up as the captain entered with us in tow.

"I found these people on the hill, my lord Glaval," the captain said. "They claim they are not spies, but I thought you might want to question them yourself."

Unlike his father, Glaval was tall and heavily built, but he had inherited the flat, gray eyes that resembled silver coins. His hair and beard were nondescript brown, and even on the battlefield, he wore them curled and dressed to the height of fashion. He studied us for a moment, his eyes and face expressionless. Finally, he allowed a hint of a smile to play around his mouth.

"Ah," he said softly. "The man who gave my father the information. You are Cullin dav Medroch of Tyra, I expect."

"I am he," Cullin said, graciously inclining his head in acknowledgment.

"My father was somewhat annoyed when you refused his kind offer of hospitality," Glaval said. "You left the city rather abruptly, I understand."

Cullin smiled. He held his body relaxed, but alert and ready. "Aye, well," he said apologetically, "the Ephir's offer was most generous, but I had urgent business elsewhere that needed attending to. Regretfully, I had to refuse."

"He mentioned that the offer might be reiterated," Glaval said. "He does not offer hospitality often." He smiled thinly. "And he is not a man to trifle with."

One of Cullin's eyebrows rose fractionally. "Nor am I, my lord," he said. "Or my father, either, for that matter."

"The Ephir thought you might be of great assistance in the negotiations between himself and your father." Glaval said.

Cullin smiled again. "I doubt that. My father often employs me to deliver messages, but I fear he has little faith in my ability as a negotiator." He made a deprecating gesture. "I'm no much of a diplomat, ye ken."

"On the contrary," Glaval said, matching Cullin's smile. "I believe you might make a very good negotiator."

"Or perhaps a hostage to guarantee negotiations in good faith?" Cullin asked. He shook his head. "I fear you place too much value on me in my father's estimation. I am, after all, only a younger son, with an older brother who has three sons."

"You devalue yourself too much," Glaval said. "I will be moving on to the late Lord Balkan's country estate as soon as we're finished here. It would please me if you would join me there." He made a small gesture with his left hand.

Even as the guard behind us began to draw his sword, Cullin had his own out. Mine came out nearly as quickly. Glaval stepped back, his eyes going wide in shock for an instant, as the point of Cullin's sword rested gently against the hollow of his throat. I turned to face the guard behind us, my sword pointed loosely at his belly.

I smiled politely. "'Twould be a foolish thing to do, drawing that blade," I told him. "The gesture might be completely misunderstood. We wouldna want that, now, would we?"

He swallowed hard and shook his head, glancing nervously at Glaval.

Cullin smiled. Glaval stepped back from the point of the sword, his eyes narrowed. Cullin swung the sword so that the flat of the blade slapped into the palm of his left hand. "You were admiring the workmanship, my lord? They say that Tyran weaponsmiths turn out the finest blades on the continent."

"Very fine, indeed," Glaval said warily.

Cullin grinned. "Aye, one of the finest, this." He made no move to sheathe it. "My father carries one much finer."

"As befits a powerful man."

"Unfortunately, like many Tyrs, he might be a bit rash in the use of it on occasion."

"It would be a fine thing if he and my father come to an

agreement whereby that fine sword might be used against the Maedun."

"That would be good," Cullin agreed gravely.

"When next you see your father, pass on my greeting," Glaval said.

"I'll be sure to do that."

"Mayhaps one day you might avail yourself of our hospitality," Glaval said smoothly.

"Mayhaps," Cullin agreed. "You will, of course, convey our apologies to the Ephir."

"Naturally," Glaval said. "I regret that my previous offer might have been misconstrued."

"A most courteous offer," Cullin said. He glanced at me. "Are we ready to go, *ti'rhonai*?"

"I believe so, *ti'vati*." I sheathed my sword.

Glaval escorted us out of the tent. Kerri gave him her dazzling smile as we moved out into the strong sunlight. "You certainly are different from your father, my lord Glaval," she said. "Might I be correct in assuming you resemble your lady mother?" She fluttered her eyelashes at him. "She must be an extremely handsome woman."

Glaval looked down at her, his expression shuttered and unreadable. "And you are a most devious and clever woman, my lady Kerridwen," he murmured.

Kerri laughed for the benefit of the watching soldiers, a silvery tinkle of sound, and playfully slapped his arm. "Why, my lord Glaval, what pretty compliments you pay," she simpered. "Thank you very much."

We left him just outside the pavilion. Kerri was wrong. He very much resembled his father.

I turned toward the tower, Cullin and Kerri close on my heels. Kerri glanced back over her shoulder as we walked away, but there was no sign of pursuit. "You've made a bad enemy there, Cullin," she said.

"Aye, perhaps," Cullin replied. "He didna look too happy when we left. I expect he's rather cross with us."

I looked back. Glaval had gone back inside his pavilion. A guard stood stiffly on either side of the entrance. Neither of them were looking at us. "I wonder if that was his own idea, or whether he had his orders from the Ephir?"

One corner of Cullin's mouth lifted slightly. "If it was the Ephir's orders, then the Ephir will be cross with him." He laughed outright. "And my father is going to be cross with them both when Sion's spies tell him about this. The Ephir might discover how difficult it is to deal with an irritated Tyr. As I told Glaval in such a roundabout manner, my father does not take kindly to threats of blackmail, no matter how good the cause seems to be to the other side."

Kerri smiled. "You mean negotiations might become bogged down?"

I grinned. "Indeed. But only if my grandfather is in a good mood when he hears the news. If he's a tad out of sorts, the Ephir might find an army of very annoyed Tyrs on his north border." I glanced at her. "What would Kyffen's reaction be to a threat like that?"

Kerri laughed. "You mean before or after he burned down the Ephir's palace?" She paused, considering. "Preferably while the Ephir was within it, and in an awkward position." Then she became serious. "We had better hope neither Glaval nor that guard fancies himself in need of Falian or Maedun gold pieces. I wouldn't trust either of them not to seek that sort of revenge."

"Nor I," Cullin said. "You'll want to speak with Jeriad, Kian. I'll fetch the horses and join you shortly."

Kerri and I came to the first tumbled stones around the broken tower. I scrambled up over the jumble into the ruins of the main room. There was no sign of Jeriad. I called his name, but there was no reply from within the tower.

"Kian?"

I turned. Kerri stood with one hand to her mouth, staring down at something in the tangle of grass and bracken near the foot of the tower. Her attitude told me everything. Reluctantly, hopeless resignation lumping hard in my belly, I made my way slowly back across the weed-choked rocks to her side. As I reached her, she turned mutely to me and pressed her face into the hollow of my shoulder. My arms went instinctively around her as I looked down.

They had caught him running, from the position of the body in the grass. One blow from the sword of a horseman sweeping past had caught him across the throat. Most likely, he was dead before he fell to the ground. Whether it had been a Maedun sword, or an Isgardian blade, was impossible to tell.

"Hellas-birthing," I muttered. I closed my eyes and lowered my head so that my cheek rested against soft hair on the crown of Kerri's head.

"Kian, he looks so—so uncomfortable there," she said, her voice choked with grief. "Can we do anything for him?"

"We'll bury him as befits a friend," Cullin said. I hadn't heard him come up. He had tethered the horses a short distance away.

Kerri stepped away from me. "We'll give him a Celae burial," she said softly. "Tonight, shortly after moonrise. That's the way we do it at home."

Cullin stooped and picked up the broken body, cradling it in his arms as he might a child. "He'd like that," he said. He turned and made his way over the jumble of broken rock to the tower.

Kerri and I followed. Cullin laid Jeriad carefully in the ruined main room and straightened his limbs. Kerri darted down the hidden steps and returned moments later with one of Jeriad's fur robes. She covered him gently, then scrambled over the broken stones and began gathering strands of ivy and wildflowers. When she had enough, she sat cross-legged at the foot of the tower, weaving the greenery into a hoop to grace Jeriad's cairn.

Toward evening, Glaval's troops moved on. They took their wounded with them in large, clumsy wagons. Their dead they left behind in neat rows of graves. They had not been so careful with the Maedun dead, nor with the late Lord Balkan. The Maedun dead lay tumbled all anyhow into a pit and covered with raw earth. Balkan's body lay with them. His head went with Glaval in a leather sack to decorate a pole over the gate of what had been his country estate as a warning to discourage any other minor Isgardian lords who might think to aid the Maedun. With the dead safely buried, the ravens dispersed, too.

I watched them go, resting for a moment as Cullin and I dug a grave for Jeriad. Once the last wagon had rumbled over the crest of the hill, and the last horseman disappeared, the quiet peace of a summer early evening descended once more over the valley.

A random thought occurred to me. "I wonder if Mendor and Drakon fought under Balkan's banner here," I said, more or less thinking out loud.

"I would doubt it," Cullin said, turning back to the grim task of digging.

"We would never be so lucky," I agreed, and picked up my shovel again.

We buried Jeriad just as the moon rose above the horizon, huge and yellow as a pumpkin. When we had placed the last stone on the cairn, Kerri brought the hoop of ivy and laid it carefully on top.

"May your soul be brightly shining so the Duality find you quickly, Jeriad, son of Amalida," she said softly. "Your days are counted and totaled, and the Counter at the Scroll will know you. Find peace, my friend."

26

They came on us in the half-light just before dawn, that hour when sleep is deepest and the spark of life is at its lowest ebb. They came on foot, silently, so they would not warn us by the clatter of iron-shod hooves on stone, or the rattle of bridle metal, so no nervous whicker from their horses would elicit a startled response from ours. By the time Cullin's shout roused me from the depths of a dream, they were upon us.

Instantly awake, I leapt to my feet, sword in hands. Cullin already stood, blade flashing quick and deadly about him, sur-rounded by a knot of a half dozen of Mendor's mercenaries. I had time only to see a flash of movement from the opposite side of the fire—Kerri plunging forward—before three of them converged on me, faces intent in the feeble glow of the fire. And hovering on the fringe of the fight, Drakon and Mendor, Dergus between them, stood shouting orders to the mercenar-ies. Then I lost myself in the frenzy of the sword in my hands.

Lost in the clash and slither of steel meeting gleaming steel. Unlike the fight in Honandun, where I merely sought to disarm, here I coldly raged to kill. All the lust and thirst for revenge for Rossah's death buried deep in my soul erupted and screamed for fulfillment. My body moved automatically, schooled through the years by Cullin's patient teaching. Arms, wrists, and hands became extensions of the sword, all parts moving as one in thrust and parry and slice. Blood ran red on the blade, filling the runes carved deeply into it.

The three Maedun mercenaries fell, but I hardly noticed. I was peripherally conscious of Cullin wading through the knot of mercenaries around him to engage Mendor, and Kerri inexorably beating back two mercenaries near the ruined tower. I turned to meet another foe and found myself face-to-face with Drakon himself. His lips drawn back in a snarl, he lunged forward, swinging his sword in a two-handed slice at my belly. I got my blade up in time to parry the stroke, then reversed my sweep to slash at his throat. He leapt back out of the way, feinted toward my head, then deftly changed the direction of his thrust to stab at my belly again. His rapid movements swung his hair away from his deformed ear, exposing the ugly, puckered scar.

"I damaged you, didn't I?" I taunted, then lunged at him, and laughed as he leapt back. "You'll carry that scar to your grave, Drakon. No matter whether I live or die, you'll carry my mark to your grave."

He made an inarticulate sound, and attacked furiously. I ducked away from him and laughed again, infuriating him even more. He sprang at me, missed, and stumbled past.

"Kian! Your back!"

Cullin's voice sounded clear over the clash and clatter of steel meeting steel. The stench of magic thickened the air and the hair on my arms and neck prickled as it rose like the hackles of a wolf. Too late, I spun to see Dergus, still hovering near the edge of the fight, gathering his magic, his dark eyes smoldering as he watched me.

Cullin spun away from Mendor and leaped toward me. The dull red bolt of searing light lanced from Dergus's hand, meant for me. But Cullin had thrown himself between us. The flash exploded against his back and I saw his eyes widen with the sudden shock of pain. Writhing in agony, he staggered, half–bent over, toward me, and Mendor lunged forward to plunge his sword into Cullin's belly.

As Mendor stepped back, yanking his sword free, Cullin fell to his knees, then slowly bent forward, both hands pressed against his belly. He looked up at me as he knelt there, an odd, listening expression on his face. Then he closed his eyes and fell onto his side.

"No-o-o-o!" I shouted. "No!" Not so soon after believing him dead and finding him still living. Not now. Gods, not now. Not like this.

Grief tore through me like the god's wildfire. Throat raw with my incoherent bellowing, I turned my back on Drakon, my left hand groping frantically for the hilt of the dagger at my belt, my right still clutching the sword. There was little time to aim, but the dagger left my hand to fly straight and true. The blade bit deep into Dergus's chest. He clutched at it with both hands, then toppled to the ground.

Kerri shouted a warning. I spun back to face Drakon. Even as his sword sliced deep into my side and caught on my ribs, I swung the Rune Blade. It resonated with a life of its own, a strength of its own, as it sliced into the side of Drakon's neck and cleaved down through his body, to separate both head and shoulder, together with the arm, from his torso. The two pieces fell together, and I staggered around in time to see Kerri, her face contorted with rage and grief, duck under Mendor's swing and thrust her blade up through his belly, deep into his heart.

There were only a few mercenaries still on their feet. With Mendor, Drakon, and Dergus now dead, they had little stomach for continuing the fight. Within moments, they were gone, melting away like spring snow into the strengthening dawn light.

I could no longer stand. Blood poured from the wound in my side, but strangely, there was no pain, just a cold numbness that encompassed the whole left side of my body. Still clutching my sword, I fell to my knees and crawled to where Cullin lay crumpled in the grass. I laid the sword carefully on the ground, then gently turned Cullin to lift him, holding his shoulders in my arm, cradling his head against my breast. Even as I started to gather my will to send it into him, he opened his eyes and looked up at me.

"No, lad," he whispered. "'Tis a mortal wound. Save your strength for yourself . . . "

I put my hand to his belly, then gasped as I felt the empty numbness there. I was unable to reach into the wound with the Healing force. Even as I tried, I felt him slipping farther from me.

Kerri dropped to her knees beside us. Her hand went to Cullin's forehead. "I have some skill as a Healer," she said. "Please, Cullin. Let us try. We have to try—"

"No," Cullin murmured, his voice barely a whisper. "It will do me no good." His right hand came up, and I grasped it with my left. "Am I avenged now, Kian?"

"Aye," I replied hoarsely. "Twice over. I accounted for Dergus, and Kerri's thrust took out Mendor."

He laughed softly, then coughed. A trickle of blood ran out of the corner of his mouth, and Kerri gently wiped it away. "I don't know if that will make this business of dying any easier or not," he said. "You'll see me home, then, Kian?"

"Aye," I said. "Aye, that I will, *ti'vati*. . . ."

He smiled. "You've been a good son to me," he whispered. "You've been such a son as any man could wish, son to me as much as the girls are my daughters, for all you sprang not from my seed." He groped for the pouch at his waist. "The parchment. . ."

"I'll see to it," I said.

"It's uncommon cold for summer," he murmured. "I can barely see you, Kian. It's so dark here . . ." He closed his eyes and I felt his spirit gently part with his body, painlessly at the end, and in peace.

I laid him back against the grass and bent to touch my lips to his forehead. It was the last thing I remember before darkness closed in around me.

Pain was everywhere around me, a solid presence in the dark. I couldn't breathe for the agony ripping through my chest. I tried to reach for that centered well of quiet deep within me, but the torment was too much. I couldn't find it, couldn't grasp it with the pain slashing and tearing at me like the teeth of a northern silver wolf.

Kerri was there beside me in the flickering darkness. Her voice came to me faintly through the haze of agony. "Work with me, Kian. I can't do this alone." Her hands were cool on my fevered forehead and cheeks. "Please, Kian. You have to work with me . . . "

Gradually, after a lifetime—a hundred lifetimes—the pain diminished. Breathing still hurt, but no longer felt like monstrous jaws crushing my chest. Kerri faded from the darkness and receded until I could no longer sense her presence.

Then there was an old man. No, not old. Young-seeming, but with hair and beard silvered and patriarchal. Behind him, faint and indistinct, rose the columns of a temple. Not a temple. Rock. Living rock, in a circle . . . The Watcher on the Hill. I recognized him and despair washed through me as I waited for the appearance of the opponent who had met me twice before in the dream. I was unarmed now, weakened and hurt. I could not defend myself against anyone. But my opponent did not appear, and when I turned as stiffly and painfully as an old man, I saw why.

Cullin stood there behind me, dressed in his plaid and kilt, his sword held ready in his hands, guarding my back as I had guarded his so many times. His white teeth flashed in the grin I remembered so well. Then, when I knew finally my opponent would not come this time, I turned to see Cullin watching me, his eyes sorrowful and grave. When I reached out to take his hand, he shook his head and faded into the darkness. "Not yet, Kian." His voice came from a terrible distance, so faint, I hardly heard it. "Not yet . . ."

I awoke on the pallet in the ruined tower. Kerri knelt beside me, her attention on a cloth she was dipping into a bowl of water. She wrung it out and placed it on my forehead. My side was stiff and sore and each breath hurt enough to make me dizzy. I groped with my right hand and found a thick padding of bandage. Kerri gently pulled my hand away and laid it back on the pallet.

"Lie still," she said quietly. "You're healing now. For a while, I was afraid you were lost, too."

Very slowly, moving myself piece by piece, I managed to sit up. The pain in my side was like a knife blade going in again. Kerri put her hands to my shoulders and tried to force me back down onto the pallet.

"Kian, no," she said in alarm. "Lie down. You must rest."

"No." I warded her off and fought my way to my feet, swaying as dizziness and pain swept through me.

"What are you doing?" she cried. "You're gravely wounded. You have to rest—"

"I live," I said shortly, pushing her aside. "And while I live, I have a duty to perform. Where is he?"

She gestured to the doorway. "Out there."

Something akin to fear clutched at my belly. "You haven't buried him already, have you?"

She shook her head. "No. I thought to wait until you were out of danger."

I let out a quick breath of relief. "I have to go to him," I muttered. I tried to take a step. To my dismay, my knees buckled, and I would have fallen if Kerri had not clasped her arm around my waist and propped her shoulder beneath my arm.

"Kian—"

"Please," I said, steadying myself against her. "I have to go to him."

Raw, intense need rasped in my voice. Kerri sighed, then acquiesced. "Very well," she said, taking most of my weight on her shoulder as she helped me to the door. "You should be dead, too," she muttered. "The wound is a bad one. I'm not much of a Healer—"

"I'm all right," I insisted.

"Can't you Heal yourself first?" she asked. "You're in too much pain now—"

"I'll sleep too long afterward if I do," I muttered "And I won't have enough strength. I have to do this now. Before it's too late."

Cullin lay under the open sky in the broken shell of the upper room, cushioned by the cloak of one of the dead mercenaries. Kerri had laid him out with his arms crossed, and covered him with his plaid. I stumbled to my knees beside him and reached out to touch the forehead that had the color and chill of pale marble. I took the plaid, folded it carefully and laid it to one side.

I had seen this ritual performed only once, years ago. Cullin himself had done it for a clansman killed by a bandit. Now I had to do it for him. "*You'll see me home, then,*" he had said as I cradled his head against me, and I promised him.

Every clansman carries a square of oiled parchment in his wallet just for this purpose. Cullin's was carefully rolled and tied with three cords, two silver and one black. I took it from the wallet and unrolled it before I set it atop the folded plaid.

The two daggers, hilts inlaid with silver and gold wire, were still sheathed at his belt. I took one of them and placed it to the left of the parchment. The second one I drew and touched the hilt first to my own forehead, then to his.

I gripped his braid carefully, then slid the dagger between my hand and his temple and sliced it cleanly from his head. I placed it meticulously at the top of the parchment, then turned back to remove the earring and laid it at the bottom edge. I clenched my hands for a moment to steady their trembling, then gently unfastened his shirt to expose his breast. My breath caught in my throat and I tried not to look at the terrible wound in his belly.

The next part was the hardest. I had no stomach for this. But I had promised him, and there was no one else to do it.

"I'll see you home, *ti'vati*," I whispered, then took a deep breath, placed the point of the dagger under his breastbone and opened him. Behind me, Kerri made a soft, horrified sound, but she said nothing, and she made no attempt to interfere.

There was no blood, of course, but my stomach contracted sharply, and I had to fight the nausea that threatened to choke me. I found his heart and freed it from the large vessels holding it in his chest. I was shivering uncontrollably as I drew it out and placed it gently in the center of the square of parchment. I wrapped the braid around the heart, placed the emerald earring on top, then carefully folded the parchment into an envelope and tied it with the black cord.

Tears blurred my vision and I could hardly see what I was doing as I rolled the parchment packet in the plaid. I placed his sword on top of the roll, then cleaned the dagger on my own kilt and crossed both daggers on the blade of the sword. I tied the bundle in the middle with his belt and each end with the silver cords, then sat back on my heels, still trembling.

"I'll see you home, Cullin dav Medroch dav Kian of Clan Broche Rhuidh," I said distinctly. "In this task I am both your son and your liegeman. I will see you safely home." I had to sit there for a long time before I could turn and look up at Kerri, who stood behind me. She hadn't moved.

"We can bury the body now," I said. "I'll see him home tomorrow."

"Perhaps not tomorrow," she said gently. "But as soon as you're well enough to travel. We'll see him home together, Kian."

Drakon was dead. Dead by my own hand, as was Dergus. Mendor was dead, felled by Kerri's sword. Cullin was avenged. But it wasn't enough. By all the seven gods and goddesses, it wasn't enough. Nothing would ever be enough, because nothing could bring him back. Grief and loss were tangible presences in my restless sleep. Troubled dreams I could not remember kept me tossing fretfully on the thin pallet, shivering with the cold, hollow ache in my heart.

Then suddenly, in the dream, another's grief merged with mine. Along the faintly throbbing tendrils that bound me to the sword—and to Kerri—came the awareness of a deep and infinite sadness.

The shared need to comfort and take comfort pulsated quietly between us in the night. I turned and found solace and understanding in the form of a slim, warm body next to mine, and gentle hands brushing my hair back from my forehead. Smooth, silken skin felt gloriously alive under my stroking hands. I found her mouth in the darkness, and it was sweet as springwater, soft as rose petals, beneath mine. My readiness was a sudden hard urgency, and hers a welcoming openness.

The bond between us merged us into one entity, a wondrous *we* far more than merely the sum of *her* and *me*. She filled all the hollow, empty spaces within me, completing all my patterns perfectly. Sensation crackled back and forth between us along the threads of the bond until I could not tell where I left off and she began. Slowly, we moved through all the stylized rituals until all the gifts that were there to be given and taken were presented and received, and we subsided together into the sweetness of shared sleep.

In the morning, I awoke to see Kerri wrapped in her cloak, fully dressed and fast asleep, curled on a pile of furs near the wall by the door, and I wasn't sure if I had dreamed our coming together, or if it had been real.

27

We made ready to start north shortly after dawn two days later.
I strapped the heart bundle securely behind my saddle. My
hand lingered on it for a moment before I mounted. For the
first time in eight years, Cullin would not be riding beside me.
He would not be there to help and guide me. From now on,
for the rest of my life, I had only myself to rely on.

Kerri's mare stood saddled and ready. Kerri knelt in front
of the two cairns, hands resting on her knees, head bowed.
She had fashioned a hoop of ivy to place on Cullin's grave,
decorating it with a narrow braid cut from her own hair. She
didn't bother explaining it to me, but I recognized the gesture
as one of respect and honor and was grateful for it. Cullin had
deserved her regard and had more than earned it. I had already
paid my final respects to Jeriad, and taken my leave of him. I
would say my farewells to Cullin at Broche Rhuidh.

I mounted and caught up the lead rope of the stallion. Kerri
looked up, then got to her feet and mounted her mare. She
glanced at the heart bundle behind my saddle, then at me, but
said nothing. We rode out of the river valley in silence.

Patrols of Isgardian soldiers watched the roadways, question-
ing travelers moving both eastward to Maedun and west toward
the coast. We were accosted several times in the first day and
questioned closely. Since I was obviously a Tyr and we were
moving north rather than east or west, we were not detained long.

We saw unmistakable signs of a country preparing for war.
Many of the small villages we passed through were bereft of
all men of fighting age. The fortified landholdings bulged with
soldiers, who spilled out into clusters of tents pitched around
guarded walls. Everywhere, the banner of the Ephir fluttered
above the standard of the local landholder. Strangers, once
welcomed in the small inns and taverns, now met hostility and
suspicion.

"They're frightened," Kerri said quietly as we left the tavern where we had stopped for the midday meal.

"Aye, but they've reason," I replied. The sword on my back shivered as we turned north again. It had been troubling me all morning. It wanted to go east, not north. A sensation much like an aching tooth shot through my spine. I reached behind me to put a hand on the heart bundle and ignored the sword. The ache subsided.

For the rest of the day, the sword kicked up a minor fuss, but I managed to ignore it. Dark found us well into the foothills, a long way from any villages or towns. We found a sheltered space by a small stream and made camp for the night. While Kerri saw to the horses, I prepared a sketchy evening meal.

I watched her as she sat by the fire, still unsure whether I had dreamed about her the other night, or if it had really happened. We spoke very little, each of us immersed in our own thoughts.

I awoke in the night with the note of the sword singing loudly in my head. I sat up and groped around until I found the scabbard and picked it up. Even shrouded by the stiff leather, the blade gleamed brightly.

"I can see you and I are going to have to have this out," I said grimly. Kerri slept curled down into her cloak on the other side of the fire. I got up carefully so I wouldn't waken her, and took the sword deeper into the trees.

I took it out of the scabbard and held it up before me. The blade glowed incandescent white and the harmonic note it made as it vibrated rapidly screeched all around me, painful to the ears as the rasp of a file on metal. I gritted my teeth and shook the sword.

"Listen, you misbegotten lump of tin," I snarled, "if you can't understand duty when you see it, you're no use to me." I stabbed the point of the blade down into the ground and pried my fingers off the hilt, one by one. It didn't want to let me go. It was like peeling the skin off my palms to wrest my hands from the hilt.

The sword quivered and howled, the light emanating from it

surging back and forth between angry red and incandescent white. Hellas-birthing. All I needed was a sword that threw a towering temper tantrum when it didn't get its own way. I stood before it until it finally settled to a churning orange brilliance.

"I have a duty to perform," I told it calmly. "If you can't understand that, you can bloody well stand there until you rust. I can do without your magic, my friend. But you can't do without me right now."

The sword seethed and fizzed, its light bright enough to sear my eyes. The pitch of the harmonic rose furiously. I folded my arms across my chest and watched it, trying not to think about how ridiculous this really was. No man should have to argue with his sword.

"Rust," I repeated. "Right there."

Finally the sword subsided. I sensed acquiescence in the tone of the harp and bell tone. I let it stand there for a moment before I put my hand to the plain leather-bound hilt.

"Once I've seen him home," I said. "When I've seen him home, we'll follow."

The hilt settled into my hand, comfortable and familiar, fitting into my palm as if it had been crafted for it. I sheathed it and made my way back to the glowing embers of the fire.

Kerri sat up as I wrapped myself in my plaid again. Her tousled hair fell forward over her forehead and she raised a hand to brush it back. "Quite a performance," she murmured. I thought she might be smiling.

I just looked at her for a moment in exasperation. "I *hate* magic," I said with heartfelt fervency, and placed the sword on the ground by my head. "I really hate it."

Late afternoon the next day gave us a glimpse of towering, snowcapped peaks as we rode side by side in silence on the narrow track. The day had been hot, the smell of dust hanging thickly in the air, but as the sun sank toward the mountains, a welcome cool descended. It was the first real summer day of the season. Midsummer could not be far off now. It startled me to realize I had completely lost track of time. Always before, seasons were counted by places. Midsummer usually found us descending the eastern slopes of the Laringras Alps.

It came crashing down on me again that Cullin was dead. There were to be no more companionable evenings by a campfire with a merchant train nearby. No more joyous brawling in taverns. No more testing each other's skill with the sword. No more laughing together. That was gone with Cullin. Gone forever.

Kerri turned in her saddle to look at me, her eyes wide and sad. "I keep forgetting he's gone," she said, something akin to surprise and wonder in her voice. "It's silly, but I keep expecting to see him come riding back down the road any instant."

It was so close to my own musings, it startled me, and for one wild moment, I wondered if this bond between us allowed us to share each other's thoughts. I met her eyes, then looked away toward the mountains. "I know," I said. "So do I."

We lapsed back into silence. After a while, I said, "I had a very strange dream two nights before we left Jeriad's tower."

For a long time, there was no sound but the slow clopping of the horses' hooves against the hard-packed surface of the track. Finally, she said, "A dream?"

"About you, *sheyala*." I glanced at her. She appeared absorbed in the small task of picking a burr from the mare's glossy black mane. The heightened color in her face might have been from the blaze of the sun all day. But it might not.

Again, there was a long pause before she replied. The burr was well tangled in the mare's mane and required some time to remove properly. She looked up at me at last. "A pleasant dream?"

"Aye. Verra pleasant."

"Oh?"

I smiled. "Not one I'm likely to dream again, I expect."

"You wouldn't want to?"

Rhuidh shied as a pheasant broke cover and flapped madly into the air beneath his feet. When I had him settled down again, I looked at Kerri. She had recovered her composure and met my eyes coolly.

"It's not that I wouldn't want to, ye ken," I said. "I wouldn't refuse it if it was offered. But I learned a long time ago it's not something one can expect or demand just because it came one's way once. Dreams are peculiar that way."

"I see." She put her heels to the mare and cantered ahead. I lost sight of her as the mare rounded a bend in the track.

But Kerri was waiting as I came around the bend leading the stallion, still at a sedate walk. She glared at me. "That was certainly a lot of bush-beating, Kian dav Leydon," she said severely. "Let me just say this, then the subject is closed. It wasn't a dream, and I seldom make the same mistake twice." She paused, marshaling her thoughts. "And one more thing. Stop calling me *sheyala*. I'm not a barbarian." She paused again, then sighed. "No more than you are."

As we approached the mountains, the road wound west of north, skirting the southern ranges of the Tyran Crags. The high passes, still choked deep in snow, would not be open until more than a fortnight past Midsummer. The track we followed intercepted the road north from Honandun that wound through the low, wide valley of the River Lauchruch, making an easily traveled road.

The days were hot now, almost uncomfortably so. But the gradually thickening forest as we left behind the Isgardian plain provided welcome shade, and the nights were still cool.

We rode through the gold-dappled shade provided by oak and silverleaf maple. Here and there among the hardwood trees, tall, straight pines and firs made patches of darker green. To our right, rocky outcroppings thrust up through the loamy soil, reflecting the heat of the sun back down onto the track. Ahead, a thin, white thread of water cascaded off one of the small bluffs in its hurry to join the stream paralleling the track, a veil of spume making rainbows around the rock.

Just as we reached the ford, my stomach suddenly knotted in a spasm of nausea and the hair on the nape of my neck and my arms rose as I shuddered. I recognized the now-familiar stench. Only the black general exuded that particular reek. I reined Rhuidh to a quick stop, holding up my left hand to Kerri. She drew the mare up beside Rhuidh and looked around quickly.

"What is it?" she asked, barely loud enough to be heard above the song of the waterfall.

"Magic," I said. "Blood magic. Very close."

"Maedun?" She reached up to make sure of the sword on her back.

I nodded. "Aye, Maedun. I think it's the general. It has his signature."

"Hellas-birthing," she muttered. "An ambush ahead then."

"Aye. Just around the bend on the other side of that small crag."

She glanced around, standing in the stirrups. To our right, the cliff rose sheerly three man-heights. To the left, the stream tumbled and churned across its rocky bed, making impossible footing for horses, doubtful and dangerous for people. There was nowhere to go but forward, or back the way we came.

"He picked his spot well," Kerri said bitterly. "How many of them are there?"

I shook my head. "I can't tell. I can just smell the magic. I recognize the stink of that accursed general."

She relaxed back into her saddle, wrists crossed on the pommel, and looked at me. "What now?"

I hesitated. I couldn't help thinking that Cullin would know exactly what to do. He always did. There might be half an army of Maedun around that bend, or as few as half a dozen. This far into Isgard, the latter possibility seemed more likely. Either way, Kerri and I were outnumbered, even if the presence of the general were discounted. I wondered exactly how seriously Cullin and I had weakened him.

I scrubbed my hand across my cheek and jaw. "We have two choices," I said. "We can go back . . . "

"Or?"

I grinned suddenly, knowing what Cullin would do. "Or we can go charging around that bend at full gallop and hope to startle them right out of their boots."

She stared at me. "That's the craziest idea I've ever heard," she said. Then she grinned. "It's so crazy, it might just work. They certainly won't expect us to do anything that insane."

I gestured toward the waterfall. "They wanted the falls to

mask any noise they might make so it wouldn't warn us," I said. "We can play the same game. They probably won't hear us coming until we're nearly on top of them."

Kerri dismounted to check the girth of her saddle. It was a good idea, so I slid off Rhuidh to check his girth. The last thing we needed was a loose strap dumping us onto the ground in the middle of a troop of hostile Maedun.

Kerri settled herself back into the saddle and drew her sword. "Ready?" she asked.

"In a moment." I slipped the halter off the stallion and stuffed it into my saddle pack. The stallion would follow us. I needed both hands free, and Rhuidh didn't need another horse tethered to him to hamper his movements. I made doubly sure the heart bundle was securely fastened behind my saddle, then mounted. "Ready," I said.

The horses picked their way carefully across the stream. It was only a few paces wide, and barely deep enough to cover their hocks, but the stones were round and smooth, and none too firmly rooted in the streambed.

On the other side, Kerri gave me a tight, fierce grin and flexed the wrist of her sword hand before raising the blade to the ready position. I drew my own sword and nodded to her.

Rhuidh leaped forward eagerly as I put my heels to his flanks and leaned forward across the pommel of the saddle. The black mare, fleet as a hawk, surefooted as a dancer, was half a length ahead as we rounded the bend, Kerri bent low across her neck. Rhuidh, neck stretched into the gallop, tail streaming, flew close behind.

The cliff curved away from the track and the trees closed in on the right. A mounted Maedun soldier, little more than a black shadow detaching itself from the shade of the trees, sprang onto the track long seconds too late to intercept the mare, but in plenty of time to meet the sweep of my sword as Rhuidh thundered past. The startled horse, suddenly riderless, shied violently and blundered into another horse, dumping the second rider onto the road.

Ahead, a third Maedun, overconfident when he saw that Kerri was a woman, urged his horse into the middle of the track, a grin of anticipation stretching his lips back across his teeth. The mare, neatfooted and deft, swerved to the Maedun's left, opposite his sword hand. Opposite Kerri's sword hand, too. Leaning sideways in her saddle, Kerri flipped the hilt of her sword into her left hand and swept it out in a vicious back-handed arc. The blade sliced through the Maedun's throat, half-severing his head.

Another rider leaped out of the trees, sword raised, riding straight at me. There was no time to swing my sword. I lowered it and used it like a lance. The point went into the Maedun's belly. I nearly lost my seat and my grip on the hilt as he went down. I was off-balance as I jerked the blade free, but Rhuidh never missed a step, dancing sideways to place himself firmly beneath me. He kept his pace smooth and steady as I pulled myself back into the saddle.

Then we were through the ambush and running free down the track. Kerri turned to take a quick glance over her shoulder, her hair flying wildly around her face. She held up four fingers, and I nodded. Only four of them in pursuit behind us. But one of them was the general. I smelled the characteristic reek of his own unique magic, strong and nauseating.

I bent lower, murmured encouragement to Rhuidh. His ears twitched and his stride lengthened.

The stench of magic suddenly thickened and intensified. I snatched a look over my shoulder and saw the general gather his magic. Nausea churned sharply in my belly, and I wondered if I might be quick enough this time, and lucky enough, to catch it on the blade of the sword and reflect it back at him.

But the magic wasn't aimed at me. The dull red bolt sailed over my head, well above me. Perhaps the general wasn't strong enough to use it against a man. But he was certainly strong enough to use it against rock and earth. Only a few lengths ahead of Kerri, a great fissure opened across the track, at least two man-lengths wide, perhaps three.

Kerri had no time to prepare the mare properly. I saw her bend farther forward and touch the mare's neck. The mare's nostrils flared, displaying the red interior, and she gathered herself, muscles bunching and flexing in her hindquarters. She launched herself across the void, Kerri clinging to her back. For a moment, horse and rider appeared to hang suspended in midair, the horse stretched gracefully, the rider hugging tight to the extended neck. One forefoot, then the other, landed on firm ground on the far side of the chasm, hind feet following easily, and Kerri was safely across.

I bent closer to Rhuidh's neck, whispering to him. We would not cross so easily or effortlessly. I was at least five stone heavier than Kerri, and Rhuidh had never liked jumping anything, let alone a gulf like the one ahead. But neither he nor I had any choice. I doubted I could have stopped him in time to prevent us from tumbling into the abyss. As we approached, I saw the dizzying depth to the chasm. I leaned forward, flat against Rhuidh's mane, praising his competence, his strength, his fine courage. His muscles bunched under my thighs as he gathered himself. He launched himself into the air, and I closed my eyes, not daring to look, hardly daring to breathe. Then, because I couldn't stand not knowing, I opened my eyes again. We were not going to make it. Rhuidh simply didn't have the strength to bridge a gap that wide.

The jar as his forefeet hit the ground nearly unseated me. They scrabbled on the very edge of the lip of the gulf, then his back feet landed half a pace ahead of his forefeet. He lunged forward desperately, found purchase, and surged onto firm ground. We were across and safe. An instant later, the bay stallion landed gracefully behind us.

Kerri had reined in a short distance down the track, her face white and drawn, and turned the mare to watch me. Relief wiped her face clean of all expression for a moment before it widened into a broad grin. Rhuidh pulled up beside the mare, panting and blowing, but dancing with the pride of his breathtaking accomplishment. I slid to the ground to see the general sitting his horse on the far side of the chasm.

"Next time, Tyr," he shouted. "Next time, you will be mine."

I sheathed the sword that was still clutched tight in my hand. "Or you will be mine, General," I called back.

He turned his horse and rode back down the track.

28

We came at last to the Clanhold. Its forbidding gray granite walls rose from the top of the steep rise like another of the rugged crags that surrounded it. News of our coming had preceded us. By the time we rode into the courtyard, they were waiting for us on the broad stone steps leading up to the entrance of the Great Hall—Rhodri, Cullin's brother, and his wife Linnet and their three sons, Brychan, Landen, and Tavis, now grown to men; Gwynna, straight and slim as a lance, with Elin, Wynn, and Maira at her side; Medroch, the Clan Laird, standing straight as a sword blade a little apart from the rest. None of them moved, none of them said a word as someone took the reins of my horse and I dismounted, the heart bundle held cradled in my arms.

I stood for a moment at the foot of the broad steps. My eyes met Gwynna's. I saw pain and grief there behind the stoic mask she had impressed upon her features. I could not bear to look at my foster sisters. They were not so well schooled as their mother in shielding their emotions. Elin, taller than her mother, and graceful as a young willow tree, held young Keylan securely in her arms. At only three, he had no concept of what was happening. He looked at me, laughing, and reached out to me. Elin quieted him gently. I turned away and mounted the steps to stand before Medroch. Silently, he held out his arms, and I placed the heart bundle into them.

"I have seen your son home, Medroch dav Kian dav Angrus," I told him, keeping my voice steady only with an effort. "I have seen my foster father home to his Clanhold, as I so swore to him when he died in my arms. I wish it duly noted that I have discharged my obligation as his liegeman in this duty."

Medroch's eyes flicked to the bundle he held, and for the briefest fraction of a heartbeat of time, his pain flared in the gray depths. Then he looked back at me. "It is so noted," he said, his voice clear in the silence. "You have my acknowledgment of my debt to you in this matter." He paused. When he spoke again, his voice contained the barest suggestion of a tremor. "Will you further serve my son by keeping vigil with him on this night of his homecoming? You were unable to stand vigil with your father. Will you stand it with your foster father?"

I barely managed to hide my startled surprise. The keeping of the vigil was for a man's nearest relative—father, brother, or true-son. Not foster son. It was Medroch's right, his privilege, or Rhodri's. Offering it to me was an honor I had not expected. I went to one knee on the worn granite.

"I gladly accept this duty and this honor," I said, my voice sounding hoarse and raw in my own ears.

Rhodri stepped forward and held out his hands. I placed mine in his and let him raise me to my feet. "You are well come home, Kian dav Leydon ti'Cullin," he said.

Turning his hands in mine, I bent and touched my forehead to them, then stepped back and went to Gwynna. She held out her hand. I took it and raised it to my lips. It trembled in mine.

"*Ti'vata*," I said, straightening up again. "I am sorry to bring you such evil tidings."

"Kian, my son," she said and smiled. It cost her an effort. "I am only happy that he had you to perform this service for him." She looked over to where Kerri stood alone at the foot of the steps. "Will you present your companion to us?"

Kerri came forward, and I presented her to my grandfather. Medroch extended his hands to her and smiled.

"You are doubly welcome here, Kerridwen al Jorddyn," he said quietly. "Both as friend to my son and grandson, and as kinswoman to my friend, Kyffen of Skai." He presented her to Rhodri and Linnet, then to Gwynna.

I turned to Elin and held out my arms for Keylan. She handed him over, then smiled at Kerri and murmured a polite greeting before following Medroch and the rest of the family back into the Great Hall. Keylan came to me with a bubble of delighted laughter, his small, chubby arms tight around my neck, warm against my skin. I shushed his laughter gently, then brushed a few copper gold curls out of his eyes. Brown-gold eyes, like mine. I saw Kerri notice those eyes, then glance quickly from me to Elin. At fifteen, she was as beautiful as her mother, with Cullin's green eyes, her hair her own shade of rose-gold, ruddy and gleaming as it rippled down her back.

"Yours?" Kerri asked softly.

"Mine," I confirmed. "Elin is his aunt. She's my sister."

Kerri reached out to stroke a gentle finger down the child's cheek. Keylan regarded her for a moment with that frighteningly grave solemnity of the very young, then turned his head and rested his cheek on my shoulder.

"I didn't realize you were wed," Kerri said. "Or that you had a family."

"Nennia died birthing Keylan," I said. "We had only one season together."

"I'm sorry. Did you love her?"

"No," I said, remembering a slender and timid girl. She was as elusive and gentle as a springtide fawn and as trusting as any young thing never exposed to hurt or betrayal. I had made a special effort to treat her tenderly, and she had responded shyly to that tenderness. The day Cullin and I left to meet another merchant train, she had demurely told me she thought she might be with child. Before I came home again, she was dead, and Keylan was nearly a season old. "In time I might have," I said, cupping Keylan's head in my hand. "But we met for the first time the day we were wed. I was fond of her. I believe she was fond of me."

"You never once mentioned her. Or the child."

"Aye, well. Cullin didna speak much of Gwynna and his girls, either," I said. "It's a private thing, ye ken. For home only."

"In," Keylan said imperiously, pointing toward the door. "In." So we turned and went into the Great Hall.

I dressed that evening in a new kilt and plaid, one containing the narrow golden yellow stripe of a younger son of the house of the Clan Laird. Servants hovered in the chamber, but I shooed them out and replaited the braid by my left temple myself. For Cullin,

I twisted a thong of black-dyed leather into it. I was just fastening it with a ring of hammered copper that nearly matched the color of the braid itself when someone knocked on the chamber door, and Rhodri came in. He, too, wore kilt and plaid, but with the wide gold stripe of the eldest son in it. The ruby in his ear flashed and sparked in the torchlight.

"Are you ready?" he asked.

I nodded.

He held open the door and inclined his head, waiting for me to proceed him into the corridor. We walked together along the flagstone hall to the steps leading down to the Great Hall, where the rest of the family waited. Just before we started down the steps, Rhodri put his hand on my arm.

"Kian," he said quietly, "I want you to know that I think my father's choice was wise. You are the one to hold vigil."

All I could do was thank him.

They were all there as we descended the steps and came out into the Great Hall. Medroch stood by the hearth, the heart bundle on an ornately carved table at his elbow. Gwynna and the girls stood to one side with Linnet and her three sons. Kerri was there, dressed in a simple but elegant green gown, a plaid pinned across her shoulders by a plain silver brooch. I glanced at Gwynna, who was pale and expressionless, and wondered if she had given Kerri the plaid to wear. It was an odd gesture. The tartan was only for kin, and I wondered briefly if Gwynna was expecting Kerri to come into the family as a prospective kin-daughter.

Medroch waited for me to approach him. Slowly, with infinite care, he turned to the heart bundle on the table. He unbuckled the wide leather belt and untied the two cords that held it together, then slid the great two-handed sword out from beneath the bindings. Holding it balanced across the palms of his hands, he moved to face me, straightening his arms to offer me the sword.

"This is the sword of Cullin dav Medroch dav Kian," he said quietly. "To you, Kian dav Leydon ti'Cullin, is the keeping of this weapon now entrusted. It is yours to offer in service to Clan Broche Rhuidh."

I held out my hands and Medroch placed the sword across them. I walked slowly across the Great Hall to face Gwynna. She held out her hands.

"I charge you with the care and keeping of this sword until I have need of it and come to claim it," I said.

"I accept the charge," she replied.

I placed the sword into her hands. It was heavy, but Gwynna bore its weight with the same quiet strength she bore her grief.

When I returned to face Medroch again, he had unwrapped the plaid, exposing the folded parchment. I watched as he placed it into a carved marble box. He secured the box with wax, then drew the signet ring from his finger and sealed the box, pressing the signet into the hot wax. He stepped back.

"See him home, Kian," he said. "And see him safe through the night."

As I picked up the box, a piper began to play, so softly at first it was little more than a whisper of sound through the Great Hall. I turned away from Medroch to see that Rhodri was the piper. He wheeled slowly and led me out of the Great Hall, the eerily melancholy wail of the pipes becoming sweet and poignant in the dark of the night.

Each phrase Rhodri played had meaning. As a weaver gathers the threads of a tapestry to weave an image, so Rhodri plaited the musical phrases together to tell those who knew how to speak the language of the music the story of Cullin's life. Medroch was in the music, as was Rhodri himself and my father Leydon, and Gwynna, and Elin, Wynn, and Maira. I was there, too. The sum of his life was a unique melody, hauntingly beautiful and powerful.

We came to the small circle of stones tucked into a fold of the side of the mountain. Seven columns of smooth-hewn stone rose to half again the height of a man. In the center stood a pillar set on a plinth, chest high, flat and polished on the top. Beyond lay the crypts, where generations of the people of Broche Rhuidh lay in niches carved into the mountain to receive them.

The wail of the pipes faded behind me, then ceased as I walked slowly between two of the standing stones and placed the box on top of the pedestal. As I stepped back, Rhodri came forward and placed his hand on the box.

"Be welcome at the end of your journey, Cullin dav Medroch dav Kian," he said softly. "I leave you with your *ti'rhonai* to stand vigil and to see you safely home."

"I will guard his journey," I said quietly.

Rhodri nodded, then walked quickly away. I didn't watch him go. Instead, I knelt in front of the pedestal, then sat back on my heels and drew my sword, holding it across my lap. The naked blade gleamed softly in the faint light of the stars, the runes deeply etched and prominent against the bright metal. I reached for the deep well of quiet within myself and emptied my mind as I raised my eyes to the small box above me.

I loved him. I knelt and let that love settle around me like a warming cloak in the chill of the night.

I do not know what I expected to happen as I knelt there, eyes fixed unwaveringly on that polished and carved marble box. Memories of Cullin filled me. I saw him again as I had seen him that first night at the squalid inn near the Isgardian border in Falinor. His laughter rang softly in the air around me. Images of his face, illuminated by hundreds of campfires in places all over the continent, swirled through the night. I saw him again as he drilled me in swordplay, demanding my best and receiving it because he expected nothing less. I saw him with Gwynna and his daughters, love and pride glowing in his eyes and softening his features. And I saw him, cloaked in sorrow, as he told me of the birth of my son and the death of the young wife I hardly knew.

Time passed. It may have been one hour, or ten, or a hundred. Gradually, I became aware of a heightened sense of hushed silence in the night. All senses suddenly cracklingly alert, I straightened, still on my knees, but no longer relaxed. My hand slid slowly up the blade of my sword, the etched runes distinct and defined beneath the pads of my fingers, until I grasped the hilt firmly.

The air by the pillar began to effervesce gently, like the

water of a mineral hot spring, sparking with thousands of tiny points of light. It swirled, still fizzing softly, then suddenly coalesced, and Cullin stood there, whole and complete, and looking no older than I. Hand resting on the marble box, his face lit with laughter, he looked down at me as I gaped in astonishment. It was his shade I stared at, I knew, but he appeared solid enough to reach out and touch.

"Ye've seen me home," he said quietly. "Ye've served me well, and I thank you."

"It was an obligation I owed," I said.

"There are no debts between us, *ti'rhonai*," he said. He glanced out beyond the standing stones, where the darkness gathered thick as pitch. There was a strangeness to him I couldn't place until I realized he wore no sword, no weapons of any kind. Then I remembered that Gwynna now held his sword. He had no need of it here. Not now. He looked back at me. "No, I need no sword," he said. "But you will. There are enemies out there you will have to face."

"You've taught me well enough, *ti'vati*," I replied.

"Aye, and ye've learned well."

The texture of the darkness between the two westernmost stones changed subtly. A man stepped into the circle and Cullin turned to meet him, smiling. I had seen his portrait hanging in the Great Hall. It was my namesake, my great-grandfather. Another man followed him, then a woman. My father Leydon dav Medroch, and his mother, the lady Brynda. I knelt there, staring, as one after the other, they appeared out of the dark, a line of men and women, his people stretching back generations into the past, all come to guide him home.

Cullin's grandfather spoke, his voice soft and vibrant in the night. "It's time to come home, Cullin dav Medroch, beloved grandson."

Cullin started to leave, then turned suddenly back to me. He held out both hands. I gave him mine and he raised me, then kissed both my cheeks. "We'll meet again when it's time," he promised. "Your son will see you home, just as you saw me home."

The assembled company of men and women shimmered

before my eyes. One by one, as they had come, they winked out. Cullin was the last to go. He did not look back.

I didn't realize I had been holding my breath until my chest began to ache. Slowly, I sank down to my knees and closed my eyes, then jerked stiffly erect again as a gentle touch of moving air brushed past my cheek.

A woman stood before me, smiling. She had a beautiful smile. She seemed little more than a girl. Her hair was silver-gilt, curling around the perfect oval of her face. Eyes as golden brown as shaded brook water looked into my own, and I knew her.

"Mother?" I asked, wonderingly.

She bent and brushed the fingers of her hand gently along my cheek, then stepped back. She held out her open hands without speaking. For a moment, I didn't know what she wanted. She smiled again, and I picked up the sword and gave it to her. She held it before her, gripping the blade, then let it rest, point down, on the ground. One hand went to the hilt and gently caressed the rounded knob of the pommel. It began to glow softly, no longer a small globe of leather-bound metal, but a faceted gem, flashing color in brilliant rays into the darkness. She stepped away, leaving the sword balanced in the earth. She glanced up, as if listening to a voice I could not hear, then nodded acquiescence.

The scintillating light of the sword's pommel illuminated her face. I took a step toward her, then another. She reached up and touched my face again, her fingers light and gentle as the brush of a moth's wing. Love and pride glowed in her eyes, and my throat constricted painfully.

I reached out to take her in my arms, but even as I did so, she began to shimmer. My arms closed on empty air, and she was gone.

When the first light of dawn finally stained the sky behind the crags, I looked up. The box stood cracked and shattered on the plinth. Except for a faint, powdery residue of fine, gray ash, it was empty.

29

I took the sword and climbed the path to the high crag overlooking
the sea. Memories crashed and broke in my mind like breakers against the rocks of the shore. I let them ebb and flow aim-
lessly, not making any attempt to render sense out of them.
Time enough for that later.

The sun was not high enough yet to reach into the small,
sheltered enclave. I sat on one of the moss-cushioned rocks
and stood the sword before me, holding it balanced with my
left hand, my right hand resting on my thigh. Very slowly, I
reached up and placed my right hand on the leather-bound orb
of the pommel. It felt warm, as if it still retained the heat of
my mother's touch.

She had given me a gift, but I was not sure I wanted to
accept it. With the gift came an obligation I did not want. But
it was the only gift my mother had ever given me. How could
I refuse it?

Quickly, before I could think too much about it and change
my mind, I took the small black knife from my boot and
slashed the leather bindings on the pommel. The leather peeled
away in two neat pieces, the rind coming off an orange.

The faceted gem beneath, big as a plover's egg, clear as
still water, glittered brightly as a single ray of sunlight spilled
over the edge of the rock around the enclave and touched it.
As I watched, the light filled the gem until it overflowed and
washed down across my hands like warm honey. I looked
down into the gem, down into a vast depth, a globe of crystal
light and dancing shadows. In the center, a point of light
glowed brighter than the splinters of color the sun shining
through the gem scattered around me.

I closed my eyes for a moment against the glare and
rubbed them. When I looked again, the brilliant point of light
was still there, flickering like a fire seen at night on a distant

hillside. Then I realized it was a fire—a huge fire flashing and flaming in a clearing amid a grove of tall oaks. I saw the figures of men and women, all dressed alike in simple white tunics dancing and leaping around the flames.

The fires of Beltane Night. The night—the only night—when the Duality split to become god and goddess to join the celebration and couple as man and woman to assure the fertility of field and forest, river and sea. The night when every woman represented the goddess and every man the god. On this night, a princess might offer mead to a shepherd, or a chambermaid to a prince. No class distinction existed between gods and goddesses. Children born of Beltane Night were lucky and blessed, able to claim a god as a father, and a goddess as mother.

Men and women danced joyously to the haunting melody skirled out by the pipes. The women carried goblets of golden mead, dancing carefully so as not to spill the liquid. Blessed and lucky for the coming year was the woman who spilled no mead on this night.

Gradually I became aware that I could see only two dancers clearly, a man and a woman. All the others faded into the background and became mere shadows around the fire.

The woman, little more than a girl, really, was in the first bloom of womanhood. Silver-gilt hair like moonbeams and sunlight plaited together, tumbled down her back, rippling to the swaying movements of her dancing. She was not tall, nor was she pretty, but she possessed a lithe grace and an animation in her face that made her powerfully attractive. Her smile lit her face and eyes from within like the Beltane Fire lit them from without.

The man was also very young, not more than eighteen or nineteen, his eyes gray as the smoke rising from the fire. He moved with the supple symmetry of a natural dancer, or a born swordsman, the muscles set neat and tight against his frame beneath the taut skin. His hair, glinting copper gold in the firelight, was bound back from his forehead with a plain leather thong. The single braid falling from his left temple blended in with the rest of his hair beneath the thong.

They danced on opposite sides of the fire, but each was searching for the other amid the throng of dancers. The man adroitly turned away when it appeared that any other woman was about to offer her goblet, and he moved swiftly partway around the fire.

The woman paused momentarily in her search to offer a sip of mead to a man, who accepted, laughing, and gave her the expected kiss in return for the gift. The woman smiled at him, and danced away, goblet held carefully in both hands.

They both saw each other at the same instant. The man's face, which had been gravely serious, broke into a smile as he whirled through the throng of dancers toward her. She remained where she was, waiting for him, dancing alone amid the surging crowd.

He reached her, and, for a moment, they simply danced facing each other, each looking deep into the eyes of the other. Finally, the woman held up her goblet.

"Mead, my lord?" she asked breathlessly.

He smiled and took the goblet. "Your gift brings me great pleasure, my lady," he said. He drained the mead from the goblet and flung the empty cup into the firelit darkness, heedless of where it landed. Wordlessly, she held out her hands to him. He took them and spoke a word quietly.

"What was that you called me?" she asked.

"Twyla," he said, smiling. "In my country, the *twylitha* is the breeze that comes off the mountains in the heat of summer. Clean and cool and refreshing. Something wonderful. Almost miraculous."

"Then I shall allow you to call me Twyla."

As they began to sway together to the lilt of the pipes, he bent forward to place his lips near her ear. "Ytwydda—Twyla, my soul lies cupped in the palm of your hand," he murmured.

She froze for an instant, drawing back so she could look up into his face, her eyes wide and startled, lips parted. Then she smiled and the sun rose in her eyes. "Leydon, your soul is sheltered safe within my hands and my heart," she replied clearly.

He laughed in sheer delight and swept her up into his arms.

She clung to him, laughing, too, as he ran through the dancers, carrying her toward the soft spring grass waiting for them in the shelter of the oak trees.

The light in the gem fractured into a thousand shards, scattering like drops of water in a cataract. I drew back, blinking in the strong sunlight, my eyes still adjusted for the flickering darkness around the Beltane Fire. My head ached as if the fragments splintered from the gem had embedded themselves like slivers of glass into my skull. I sat shivering in the hot sun, my arms wrapped around my chest, trying to warm myself. The sword stood balanced before me, the gem still gathering the light.

"No more," I whispered, but I reached out to cup the gem between the palms of my hands, and bent forward to look into it again.

There were four of them this time. Leydon dav Medroch, Twyla al Kyffen, a very young Cullin, who strongly resembled his older brother, and a small boy of six or seven. The men stood back to back, the woman and the boy between them, their swords flashing in the late afternoon sun, as they fought a horde of bandits. Cullin fell, his sword dropping from his hand. The boy tried to pick it up, but it was too heavy, and he himself was cut down moments later by a savage blow to the side of the head. Twyla reached down to snatch up the fallen sword, standing over the boy's body, and turned to swing it at the man who had felled the boy.

A man dressed in black sat a horse on the periphery of the fight. He smiled as the sheer press of numbers overwhelmed Leydon and Twyla. He gestured to the man standing on the ground beside him and bent down to speak with him.

"Make sure they're all dead," he said. "The boy especially. Your men may do what they will with the woman, but she must be dead when they finish. Do you understand?"

"Of course, General," the other man said. "Leave it to me."

The general nodded in acknowledgment, then turned his horse and left, still smiling.

A shadow fell across me as I sat, both hands gripping the hilt of the sword, forehead pressed to my wrists. I looked up, my vision blurred and watery.

Medroch stood before me, gentle gravity marking the lines of his face. I saw him for a moment through the eyes of a young child looking at the grandfather he adored, tall and straight and strong, the gray gone from his hair and beard, the lines less deeply etched into the skin around his eyes. For a long moment, I simply stared up at him until, finally, he became again the grandfather I was familiar with. The amethyst in his ear flashed violet sparks against the silvered copper of his braid.

"They came for him," he said at last.

"Aye, they did."

"As they came for your father the night I stood vigil for him." His hands clenched into fists at his side, and he looked away for a moment. "Two sons," he said softly. "Two sons, I've lost." His gray eyes turned again to me. "And you've lost two fathers, lad."

"Where was my mother buried?" I asked.

"In the crypts. Cullin brought her home, too, when he saw your father home."

"And they came for her, too?"

"Brynda stood vigil with her," he said. "They came for her." I nodded.

"It's not an easy thing," he said. "To stand vigil."

"No." I looked up at him again. "You knew, didn't you? You knew who my mother was." There was a simple sense of inevitability about it that was inescapable.

For a moment, I thought he might not answer. Then he nodded. "Aye," he said. "I knew. Kyffen was my friend. I sent Leydon to him as an emissary to warn him of Tebor's treachery."

"Sion's spies?" I asked.

"Aye. A good man, Sion dav Turboch. He suggested sending Leydon. He showed a certain talent for the work. I told Leydon to deliver the message anonymously, if possible." He smiled briefly. "I didna tell him to run off with Kyffen's daughter, though. Nor did I tell him to go bounding around the continent with her for three years before he brought her home."

I glanced up at him. He had unwittingly answered a question that had puzzled me. A simple explanation of why I was three years younger than Kerri thought her prince to be. "You said nothing. You never said anything to me."

"No." He sat on the stone beside me, resting his back against the sun-warmed rock of the cliff, and closed his eyes.

"Did Kyffen know? Did he know where his daughter went?"

Medroch shook his head. "No. Twyla made us swear we would never tell anyone. She feared for your safety."

"But after?" I asked. "After she and my father were dead. You didn't tell him then, either."

"A vow of never means never, Kian."

"Aye. I suppose it does."

"We thought you were dead, too. Then when Cullin brought you home, it wasna my place to speak with Kyffen. You made no vows, but you remembered nothing. You had to discover the truth for yourself, and take it to him."

I nodded. "A hard thing," I said, "discovering the truth."

"The truth sometimes is, lad. A hard thing, indeed." He glanced at me, a hint of a smile playing at the corners of his mouth. "Perhaps ye'd best tell the lass her quest is over."

I made a wry face. "That willna be easy, either."

He made an eloquent gesture, and I got reluctantly to my feet. My head ached, and I felt drained and empty as a licked pot. I picked up the sword and sheathed it carefully, then bent to pick up the husk of leather that had enshrouded the gem. I walked to the edge of the cliff and hurled it as far as I could toward the sea below. I lost sight of it long before it hit the water.

"Aye, well," I said. "If it must be done, sooner is best."

Medroch got to his feet and came to the edge of the cliff.

He put his hand to my shoulder. "I'll walk back wi' you, lad,"
he said. "Ye can tell the lass after you've eaten and taken some
rest."

Kerri was in the courtyard with Keylan when Medroch and I
walked through the open gates. I stopped to watch them. My
son held a wooden practice sword, his sturdy young body faith-
fully copying Kerri's posture as she demonstrated a high block
moving to a backhand sweep. Only three, but already, he
showed promise of the same mastery his foster grandfather had.

"A fine son, Kian," Medroch said quietly, watching them,
too. "Ye can be proud of the lad."

"Aye," I said, smiling. "Verra proud."

Medroch watched Kerri critically for a moment. "The lass
moves well, too," he said. "For all that gown is hardly the garb
for sword work."

"Dinna let her hear you say that. She'll tear strips from
your hide. She's a tongue like a rusty razor when she wants
it." Kerri showed Keylan another move, and then crouched to
hold his arms to guide him through it. "You go ahead," I told
Medroch. "I'll be along in a moment."

"Ye dinna have to tell her now, ye ken," he said.

"I know. This is something different."

Keylan saw me then, and a delighted grin wreathed his
small face. "Look, *vati*," he called, waving the wooden sword.
"Look. Look at my sword." He came running across the courtyard, short, sunburned legs churning, and flung himself into
my arms, sword and all, as I stooped to catch him and pick
him up. The sword fetched me a good clout on the side of the
head as he swung it around to show me.

Kerri turned, smoothing her skirts with the back of her
hands, and met my gaze above Keylan's bright head. She smiled
briefly as I gently pushed the wooden blade to a safe distance
beyond my ear. The child babbled on about the sword for a
moment, then wriggled with impatience to be set down again.

"Show *Vati-mor*," he said.

"It's truly a wondrous sword," I said gravely, crouching

down in front of him and running a finger along the wooden blade. "And you will be truly a fine swordsman when you grow up. Run along now and show Medroch."

Kerri hadn't moved. She waited as I crossed the courtyard. "You look tired," she said.

"Aye, well, it was a long night. I need to speak with you, *sheyala.*"

"Right now? Shouldn't you rest first?"

"This won't wait." I took her arm and led her to a stone bench beneath an apple tree. The small, hard green fruit clustered thickly on the branches, nearly hidden by the leaves. Somewhere in the highest branches, a thrush poured out its ardent little heart in sweet song to the morning.

Kerri sat on the bench and looked up at me. "What is it you need to speak with me about?"

I reached up and plucked a leaf from a heavily laden branch. The pale underside had a vaguely furry texture against the pads of my fingers. "I'm going away for a while after I rest," I said. "I want you to stay here until I get back."

Her eyes narrowed. "You want me to—" She bounced to her feet, fists landing on her hips. "Now you wait one moment there, Kian dav Leydon. You want me to stay here while you go haring off somewhere taking that sword with you?"

"I'm going after the general," I said.

She rolled her eyes and raised both hands, fingers spread, in exasperated supplication to the gods. "He's going after the general," she said to no one in particular. "All the seven gods and goddesses save me from imbecilic Tyrs." One finger came out to jab me in the chest. "If you think for one moment you're going off on a ridiculous crusade like that, and leaving me here, you've certainly managed to addle your brain completely, my friend."

"Kerri—"

The fists were back firmly on her hips, her jaw thrust out aggressively. "Don't you *Kerri* me, you overgrown lout," she cried. "You are not going off without me, and that's flat."

"*Sheyala*, this could be dangerous."

"Dangerous?" she repeated. She laughed incredulously and rolled her eyes again. "Dangerous? Now what in the world would possibly make you think going after the general could be dangerous? Kian dav Leydon ti'Cullin, you are an idiot! A complete and utter fool. A dim-witted—"

"Hellas-birthing," I muttered. I wanted to grab her by the arms and shake her until her teeth rattled and her eyes crossed, and I shook some sense into her. Instead, I planted my hands on my own hips and leaned forward, placing my face inches from hers. "Kerridwen al Jorddyn," I shouted, "for once in your life, will you shut up and listen for a change?"

She stepped back, stiff with indignation and outrage. "Don't you *dare* shout at me," she cried. "And what about the prince? What about Kyffen's grandson?"

"When I get back, you'll have your prince," I told her.

"And what if you managed to get yourself killed?" she cried. "What then, you barbaric moron?"

"Then Medroch will show—"

"Medroch? Medroch?" She waved her hands furiously. "I need you and that sword to show me."

"Tcha-a-a-a." I turned away. I wanted to strangle her. Well, no, not exactly. Spank her, mayhaps. Tie her up and deliver her to Gwynna for safekeeping. She would most certainly meet her match in my foster mother.

Kerri grabbed my arm and spun me back to face her. "Give me one good reason why I should stay here," she shouted. "One good reason why I shouldn't go with you. And don't tell me because it's dangerous. I said a *good* reason, not some stupid male idea of protecting a helpless female."

I did grab her this time, my hands gripping her shoulders. I very nearly lifted her off her feet as I dragged her closer to me. "I'll give you a reason," I roared. "Because my soul lies cupped in the palm of your hand, Kerridwen al Jorddyn."

It was a ridiculously drastic measure, but it shut her up instantly. It was not what I had meant to say, but once said, I couldn't unsay it. And besides, I realized it was true. Kerri blinked once, then her eyes grew wide and startled. "What?"

I took a deep breath. "Kerridwen al Jorddyn, my soul lies cupped within the palm of your hand," I told her, much more quietly and calmly this time.

She stared at me. "This is absurd," she said faintly.

"It is," I agreed. "Highly absurd, but true."

I watched in fascination as a faint flush of pink began to rise in her, first in the part of her chest exposed by the low neck of her gown, then up along her slender throat, then finally, into her cheeks. She blinked again, and took a deep breath.

"Kian dav Leydon ti'Cullin," she said softly, "your soul is sheltered safe within my hands and my heart."

My hands still gripped tightly to her shoulders. She was going to have a fine set of ten small matched bruises there soon. I let go of her shoulders and caught her around the waist instead, pulling her against me as I bent my head to kiss her. We were both breathless when I finally let her go and stepped away.

"I'm going to rest now," I said. "We'll talk later." I began to walk to the house.

"Kian?" she called. "Kian, why does the general want you dead? He can't take your magic if he kills you without all that horrid ceremony."

I turned. "We'll talk later," I said again.

"Yes," she agreed. "We will most certainly talk later."

We said our betrothal vows and became duly handfasted in the Great Hall that afternoon in the presence of Medroch and the rest of the family. We would wed in Skai next Beltane, an auspicious time to begin a marriage.

The next morning, demure as a new bride, Kerri kissed me good-bye at the head of the broad steps leading from the Great Hall to the courtyard. But it didn't surprise me in the least when the black mare came tearing up behind me half an hour later and fell into step with the sorrel. Kerri gave me one sharp, fierce, challenging look, daring me to try to send her back. I merely smiled and shook my head in resignation.

"What about your prince?" I asked.

She smiled. "Not every *bheancoran* marries her prince," she said.

"This one won't," I said firmly.

30

I awoke just as the moon rose above the crags. Kerri slept with her forehead nestled into the hollow of my throat, her breath stirring warmly against my skin. Gently, careful not to waken her, I slipped out of the bedroll and went quietly to the far side of our small fire, the polished disk of silver I used as a shaving mirror in my hand. I sat on a fallen log, thinking hard.

Magic. Celae magic. Tyadda magic. Gentle magic. How does one go about invoking it? The masking spell Kerri had shown me, giving a rock the semblance of a sleeping cat, had looked simple enough. It hadn't looked as if it cost her a great deal of effort. We were going to need foolproof disguises if we were going to enter Maedun and track down the general. The masking spell seemed a plausible answer.

Ground and center. As I settled myself, I again became aware of the lines of power in the ground beneath me, in the air around me. Like the silver threads of rivers in a valley seen from the peak of a crag. I reached out, found I could trail my fingers through them the same way I could trail them in the water of a stream. I drew on the power and envisioned myself with hair black as midnight, eyes only a shade or two paler.

I felt nothing. No shiver of rising hair on the nape of my neck or arms. Not even the slightest ripple of nausea. I lifted the polished disk and peered into it. I still looked like me. It hadn't worked.

How difficult can this be? I vaguely remembered working small magics under my mother's tutelage when I was very young. If I remembered it aright, I had simply grasped the power in the eddies around me, and done it then. This spell should be child's play. Why was it not working?

I reached out into the stream of power again, and concentrated. When I lifted the mirror to look, nothing had changed. It was not a Maedun face I stared at. Merely my own.

Disappointed, I got to my feet to return to the bed . . .

. . . And found Kerri standing by the pile of bracken, sword in hand, ready to take off my head.

I barely managed to duck under the savage curve of her swing, flinging myself to the ground and rolling desperately away. I sprang to my feet, ready to dodge again as she spun, sword ready for another swipe.

"*Sheyala*," I cried. "Don't. It's me." I let go of the thread of power I still held. Kerri staggered with the effort of stopping the swing of the sword in mid-motion. She let her arms fall limply to her side, sword still grasped in both hands, and stared at me.

"Kian?"

I stepped forward and took the sword gently from her. "I didn't think it had worked," I said. "I'm sorry."

"I saw a Maedun," she said blankly. "I swear I saw a Maedun soldier. That was you?"

"I tried to work a masking spell," I said. "I thought it hadn't worked. I saw no change when I looked in the mirror."

I had frightened her badly. Twice. Her reaction was to ignite like a pine torch. "You imbecile," she cried. "Don't you know anything? Of course you didn't see any change. You were inside the stupid spell. What did you think—" She broke off abruptly. She shot a glance at my sword that still lay on the ground beside the bedroll, then looked at me again, her eyes narrowed suspiciously. "You were trying a masking spell?"

"Well, we need some disguise if we're going to go bounding around Maedun tracking down the general," I said.

She brought up her finger and shook it under my nose. "Don't you go trying to sidetrack me that way, you asinine barbarian," she said in a dangerous voice. "*You* were working magic? You?"

I sighed. "Aye," I said. "Me."

"Celae magic?"

"Ye might say so."

She stood there for a moment, seething and fizzing with barely suppressed fury. I expected her to explode about my ears like a batch of chestnuts in a fire. Instead, she made a visible effort to take herself in hand, and looked up at me, eyes narrowed.

"You had best explain yourself, Kian dav Leydon," she said quietly. "And quickly."

"I expect I'd best had," I agreed.

I led her back to the bedroll and sat down. She hesitated for a moment, then sat beside me. It took a while, but I told her what had happened a fortnight ago when I stood vigil with Cullin, and what I had seen in the crystal the next morning. She listened without interrupting. When I finished, she said nothing. For a moment, she just sat there, staring at the fire. Finally, still without a word, she got up and walked into the shadows of the trees around us.

She was gone a long time. When she finally came back, I was sitting cross-legged on the bedroll with a warmed-up cup of tea. She sat beside me, drew her knees up, and wrapped her arms around them.

"You didn't know until then?" she said softly.

"No."

She glanced at me. "Do you remember her at all now?"

"A little. More every day, it seems. And him, too."

"Why didn't you tell me before this?"

"I was going to, *sheyala*. But somehow, the time never seemed right."

"I should box your ears," she said with patient resignation.

"Quite probably."

Unexpectedly, she laughed. "This *bheancoran* looks likely to end up marrying her prince after all," she said.

"No, *sheyala*," I said. "Not if you plan on marrying me."

She jerked as if I had hit her. "You won't come to Celi?" she asked, dismay and shock clear in her voice. "But—"

I shook my head. "I didna say I would not go to Celi," I said. "I merely said I would not be a prince."

She eeled around so that she knelt in front of me. "But you're Kyffen's grandson," she said, her face troubled. "You *have* to be his heir."

I shook my head again. "No, I don't have to be his heir," I said. "Kerri, I've no training to be a prince. At the time when princes are learning the art of governing men, I was cleaning out stables. While a prince's heir is learning diplomacy and proper manners, I was living half-wild in slave quarters. I've no talent for it, nor do I have the inclination."

"But—"

"*Sheyala*, Skai isn't my country. Celi isn't my country. They aren't home. Tyra is home. I can't think of myself as being Celae, or even yrSkai. I'm a Tyr. I'll always be a Tyr. You can't have a Tyr as prince of Skai. It wouldna be right."

"But you are Celae, though," she said. "Through your mother."

"But I've never known Celi, nor Skai either." I looked away for a moment. "Cullin could have done it," I said. "All that flaming nobility of his was ingrained so deeply into him, it was more than just a part of him. He could have been a prince. I can't."

"I've seen you act like that, too, Kian. It's part of you, too."

I shook my head. "No, *sheyala*. With me, it was always just an act. A part I played. Like a cloak I put on when I needed it."

"But—"

I reached out and put a finger over her lips to silence her. "If I have to, I'll stand regent for the heir," I said. "I think I can do that much. There is another heir, remember."

She settled back onto her heels, biting her lip thoughtfully. "Keylan," she said at last.

"Keylan," I agreed. "And he's young enough to be properly trained in all he has to know." I grinned at her. "That's why I wanted you to stay at the Clanhold while I tracked down the general. Even if I didn't come back, you'd have your princeling. Medroch would have told you."

She glared at me. "You idiot," she said. "Do you think I would have let you go alone anyway? Kian dav Leydon, you have a skull thicker than two short planks, and you're only slightly brighter . . . "

I hooked my hand behind her head and pulled her forward to kiss her. It shut her up immediately. It was a technique I would have to remember for future use.

Kerri drew back after a moment and smiled sweetly at me.

"And don't start thinking this is changing my mind," she said softly. "You are still a thickheaded dolt at times, and I consider it my bound duty to inform you of that fact as needed."

I met her gaze levelly. "This bond," I said at last. "Does it allow you to read my mind, too?"

"Men are not difficult to read," she said. "And you especially." She put her hand behind my head. "Now. Where were we?"

Three days later, we stood on the high flank of a mountain, looking out over the vast plain of Maedun. Below us, the mountains ended as suddenly as if a blow from Gerieg's Hammer had fractured the bones of the range of crags and spread them flat like bacon drippings on bread. I had only twice been in Maedun, and neither journey had been pleasant. A suspicious and unfriendly lot, the Maedun, when it came to strangers.

Kerri raised a hand to brush back a stray wisp of hair from her eyes. "It even looks darker out there," she said quietly. "Jeriad told me there were no more than ten families in all Maedun who had sorcerous ability. Not really that many."

"More than enough," I said, "if they're all like the general."

She shuddered. "I wonder if they all know how to steal another's magic."

"I would think not," I said. "I can't see the general sharing that secret with anyone else. He wants all the power for himself."

"He must be quite mad," she said slowly. "He frightens me, Kian. He frightens me more than anything else I've ever encountered in my life."

Rhuidh nudged me in the back and I reached behind me to shove his nose away, then realized he was nowhere near me. He stood beside Kerri's mare, contentedly cropping grass several meters upslope. Another distinct nudge, pushing me a step or two south. I put my hand up to the hilt of the sword.

"Now what do you want?" I muttered irritably.

Kerri looked at me, surprised. "What?"

"Not you," I said. "This stupid sword."

"The sword?"

I drew the sword and held it in front of me. An aura of volatile color flashed and flared around the blade and the distinct harp and bell notes sang in the air around me, nearly visible in their crystal clarity. The vibration traveled quickly into my hands, up my arms into my chest. Slowly, gently, the sword drew me around.

Southwest. It pulled me southwest.

I made an irritated noise and tried to turn east again. But the sword was implacable. It wanted to go southwest.

"Confound you," I muttered. "You ridiculous, ill-crafted, miserable chunk of tin. Why can't you make up your mind?"

"What is it?" Kerri watched the sword in fascination. "What does it want?"

"It wants to go southwest now," I said, exasperated. "It kicked up such a fuss about going east, and now that we're going east, this ridiculous, misbegotten slice of misery wants to go southwest. Southwest!"

"Kian—"

"Tcha-a-a-a." I slammed the sword back into its sheath.

"Kian, perhaps the sword knows where the general is better than we do. Perhaps it's showing us where to find him."

I looked at her blankly.

"It led us northeast before," she said. "Maybe it knows we have to eliminate the threat he poses before we can go home."

I thought about it for a moment, then nodded. "It could be," I said slowly. "Northeast toward the general before. It certainly wasn't trying to tell us Kyffen's grandson was that way. It knew, even if I didn't, who I was."

"He told you Cullin and you set him back half a lifetime," she said. "Perhaps we have to set him back a full lifetime in order to give Celi time to prepare, to settle the Saesnesi problem and become strong enough to resist a Maedun invasion."

The sword kicked again, strongly enough to make me stumble forward a few paces. Southwest again.

I reached up and gripped the hilt. "Stop it," I snarled. Then to Kerri: "We go southwest then." I grinned. "That way, I might not have to frighten you by turning into a Maedun soldier again."

She glared at me. "You made a terrible Maedun soldier," she said disdainfully. "You're far too clumsy."

I smiled beatifically at her. We had argued long and loud before I managed to convince her she had to put on the semblance of a man if the disguise were to work at all. Women in Maedun never carry swords. Any woman caught carrying a man's weapon was immediately executed. The Maedun regard their women as being good for only two things—bedding and breeding. I cited the example of how little the death of his wife had affected the general, who was, in essence, the quintessential Maedun soldier. Kerri finally agreed reluctantly with me. It was the first argument I had ever won against her.

"Not nearly so terrible as you," I said mildly. "You walked funny."

"I walked funny," she repeated indignantly.

"Aye. You walked funny. If you want to masquerade believably as a man, you have to walk like you're carrying something valuable between your legs." She opened her mouth to make a suitably caustic retort, but I cut her off. "Like a Maedun soldier would believe in his crass arrogance." I turned to gather in the horses. "The sword leads southwest. Shall we follow?"

31

We descended into the foothills, then moved out onto the rolling grasslands of the Isgardian central plain. Patrols of Isgardian soldiers swarmed everywhere along the roads. This close to the Maedun border, they were hostile and belligerently suspicious of all travelers. Kerri and I lost a lot of time being stopped constantly, and thoroughly questioned, before we stumbled onto the ideal disguise. We traveled under the semblance of couriers, bearing the blazon of the Ephir himself. It not only prevented our being taken aside at every turn for interrogation, it earned us the unquestioned right to deference and every assistance to speed us on our way. In only a day or two, my ability to cast and hold a masking spell was, by sheer force of necessity, almost as good as Kerri's.

We rode hard from dawn to dusk, then commanded the best accommodation available for the night. The horses received preferential care, too. They needed it more than Kerri or I.

Straight as the flight of an arrow, the sword led us southwest. It hummed and vibrated on my back like an anxious shepherd, pushing us to the limits of the horses' endurance. The landscape around us became only an unchanging blur of endless seas of prairie grass and gentle hills.

The farther southwest we progressed, the more urgent the sword's insistence on haste became. We came to the River Shena and commandeered a ferry to take us to the south bank. Once we had crossed the river, I realized the sword was leading us straight to Frendor, where the charred and gutted remains of Balkan's manse stood on the bluff overlooking the city.

By the time we reached the locked and guarded gates to the city late in the afternoon on the eve of Lammas, the sword fairly danced with excitement and tension on my back. It wasn't until we were inside the city, and safely settled for the night, that the sword finally subsided a little.

We stood by the narrow window in the tiny sleeping room of the inn looking out at the nearly deserted streets of the city. Only the occasional person moved out there. Those who weren't soldiers slipped furtively from shadow to shadow, spending the least time possible on the street if their business took them there for any reason.

"What now?" Kerri asked wearily.

"A good night's sleep first, I think," I said. "The sword isn't kicking up such a fuss now. I'm fairly sure this is where it wants us to be."

She stepped back from the window so there was no chance she might be seen from the street. "The general is out there somewhere," she said. "That man gives me chills down my spine."

I smiled ruefully. "He has that happy faculty, does he no?" I stretched to ease the kinks out of my back. "The streets should be thronging with people for tomorrow's celebration. Two strangers won't be so conspicuous then. We'll let the sword show us where he is and spy out the lay of the land."

"And come up with a plan?"

"One of us is bound to, don't you think?"

The celebrations began shortly after dawn. The sun was barely above the horizon when the streets began to fill with people. Women dressed in flowing robes of gold, red, orange, and russet, their hair twined with garlands of grain, flowers, small fruits, and vegetables, trailing bright ribbons, wound their way through circle dances, catching up men in the center until a small forfeit was paid. The men, even more brightly dressed than the women, carried staves decorated with garlands and ribbons, representing the sickles and scythes of the harvest. Harpers and pipers strolled among the crowds while hawkers cried sweetmeats, ale, meat pastries, and fruit. Children darted everywhere, laughing and screeching with excitement. Most of them already appeared to have sticky hands and faces from the sweetmeats.

Kerri and I ventured out after breaking our fast. My sword wore the semblance of a harvest staff. Kerri's hair, trailing ribbons and garlands, completely hid the slight shimmer in the air above her left shoulder masking the hilt of her sword.

We drifted with the crowds, but always following the gentle guidance of the sword. We didn't hurry. That would have made us stand out in the festive throng like wolves in a sheep pen. But in only a short time, it became apparent the sword led straight to the section of the city where the houses of the wealthier merchants stood surrounded by their formal gardens and high walls. With sudden certainty, I thought I even knew which house.

A man spun out of the swirl of celebrants and caught Kerri, his arms to either side of her, his staff clasped behind her back. "Forfeit for the harvest," he cried, pulling on the staff that was hard against the small of her back. For a moment, Kerri resisted, startled. Then she laughed and put her hands to the man's cheeks and gave him his ransom. He obviously wanted more from the kiss than she gave, but he released her and danced off to find a more willing hostage. A few moments later, we were caught in the center of a winding circle of men and women who wouldn't let us go until each of us had paid forfeit to everyone else.

"They celebrate enthusiastically here, don't they," Kerri said breathlessly as we made our escape.

The house we sought no longer bore the name of Grandal the Merchant above its gate. The house, similar to the other houses on the street, sat in the center of its broad gardens. In the front, formal plantings of hedges, shrubs, and flowers. In the back, the kitchen gardens of herbs and vegetables. The back of the house contained the kitchens, the laundry shed, and the servant quarters; a separate bake house was set behind the kitchens. The family quarters were in the front.

The crowd was a little less thick in this district, and better dressed. We moved from group to group, always keeping the house in sight. The gates were closed tight and locked, but no guards stood behind them. We saw no movement at all from inside the house. Except for the thin thread of smoke coming from the kitchen chimney, it looked deserted.

A little before midday two servants left the house, dressed

in their carnival finery. They were swirled up into the crowd and disappeared in moments.

As midday approached, Kerri circulated among the groups of dancers, exchanging forfeits for snippets of gossip. She came back to me, hands laden with a thick meat pie, fruit, sweetmeats, and a flask of pale wine. We settled into the shade of a topiary hedge to eat. The merchant's house was just across the street and down two houses. We had a good view of the front gate and the top half of the house above the walls.

"The merchant is gone," Kerri said. "In fact, everybody could hardly wait to tell me gleefully that he had chosen the wrong side in a disagreement between Lord Balkan and the Ephir. For a while, his head graced a pole near the south gate to the city."

"Not a well-liked man, then," I said, reaching for another slice of the meat pie. It was stuffed full of tender chunks of meat, seasoned vegetables, and herbs, all swimming in rich gravy. Definitely better fare than we would have found in the commercial section of the city.

"Not well liked at all," Kerri agreed. "I was told he dabbled in everything from light magic to the sacrifice of children. At any rate, nobody misses him."

"Who lives there now?"

She smiled and licked her fingers. "A cousin of the merchant, they said. One man, his son, and two servants."

"No guards?"

Kerri shook her head. "The new tenant is not well liked, either, it seems," she said. She picked up a pear and rubbed it on the sleeve of her robe. "I was told he was of the same ilk as his ill-fortuned cousin. There are a lot of stories about terrible things happening in that house. Screams in the night. That sort of thing."

I looked at the house. "That sounds like the general," I said. "But I can't believe there are no guards."

"The general has a dog," she said. She made a wry face. "The woman who told me said it frightened the children half to death. They're terrified of it. They won't go near the place."

"A dog? We should be able to handle a dog."

"I should have found some goblets or cups for this wine," she said, unstoppering the flask and taking a sip. "Do you want to go in there? Or do you want to try to lure him out?"

"I think I should go in," I said. I reached for the flask, still watching the house, then looked at her when she didn't release her grip on the flask.

"What do you mean, you should go in?" she said. She had that look in her eye again. "*We* are going in, or nobody is going in."

This was neither the time nor the place for an argument. "We'll go in, then," I said.

She smiled and handed me the flask. "Look at the house next door," she said. "Fruit trees all along the wall between the two houses, and they didn't lock the gate when they left the house. How long is it since you fell out of an apple tree?"

"Too many years," I said. The trees looked close enough to the wall. Some of the limbs overhung the general's yard, but they were flimsy branches. I didn't think they would take my weight. But I might manage the leap from the tree to the wall without killing myself. Once on the wall, it was only a drop of three meters to the ground on the other side. Not a difficult drop. It had the advantage of putting us into the rear garden, where there was less chance of the general seeing us.

Getting out again might be a little more difficult, but we would have less need for stealth then. We should be able to walk out the front gate.

"When it gets dark?" Kerri asked.

I nodded. "They'll light the bonfire in the square at sunset. Most of these people will be gone by dark."

She rubbed her arms, watching the general's house. "I wish there was another way," she said softly. "I don't like this." She looked at me, her eyes troubled. "He knows who you are, doesn't he?"

"He commanded the bandits who killed my parents," I said. "He knows. But I don't think he realizes I know, too."

Evening came slowly. Light faded gradually, bleaching the sky to pale turquoise in the west. As the twilight deepened, the glow of the bonfire in the main square lit the sky. The crowd began to thin as one by one, or in couples or small groups, people slipped away to the fire. They carried with them the first fruits of the harvest to offer in thanks. Before long, the street of merchants' houses was deserted. The only people not at the fire were the ill and the infirm. Everyone else, from infants to the eldest, was now at the bonfire.

Kerri slipped out of the brightly colored robe and stripped the garland from her hair while I freed my sword of its decoration and fastened it to the harness on my back. We kept to the shadows as much as possible as we made our way to the house next to the general's. Kerri was right. The gate was unlocked.

It was a simple matter to climb one of the fruit trees against the wall. The leap to the top of the wall wasn't as far as I thought. Quickly, I slid over the edge, hung by my hands for a moment, then dropped to the grass on the other side. An instant later, Kerri landed beside me with a muffled thud.

"All right?" I whispered.

"Yes."

We crouched in the shelter afforded by the wall, watching the house for signs of movement. The sudden stench of blood magic close by caught me by surprise. Not the general. A different magic. Fetid and evil. Not human.

Claws scrabbling madly on the grass, the dog appeared out of the shadows. Blacker than the shadows. Blacker than the night itself. Eyes glowing sullen red in its midnight face. Fangs gleaming phosphorescent green, long and deadly as knives. It came in a lethal rush. In an eerie and appalling silence, purposeful as a slung spear, huge as a half-grown pony.

Before I could move, before I could even speak to warn Kerri, the dog leaped. Sensing the movement, Kerri reacted instinctively, throwing up her left arm to protect her throat. The dreadful jaws clamped down on her arm. Woman and dog tumbled backward into a heap against the stone wall. The fabric of Kerri's sleeve shredded and tore in the terrible jaws, then the skin and flesh of her arm. The dog shook her like a terrier shakes a rat, still in that ghastly, unnatural silence.

For half a heartbeat, I crouched in the grass, frozen and

stunned, staring blankly. Then I held my dagger in my fist
without any recollection of drawing it. I flung myself on the
monster, encircled its throat with one arm. Again and again, I
plunged the blade into its flanks until I lost count of how many
times I stabbed it. Stinking blood poured out over my hands
and arms. Scalding blood like molten lead.

Kerri had gone limp, her lacerated arm still in the grip of
those terrible jaws. The dog let go of her arm and snapped at
my leg, its eyes glittering madly, bloody foam dripping from
its jaws.

Sobbing with effort, I rolled clear and scrambled to my
feet. The dog lunged for Kerri's vulnerable throat. The jaws
snapped shut a fingerbreadth short of the rapidly pulsing hollow of her throat. The dog struggled forward, snarling, intent.

The stench of putrefaction rising from my bloody hands
nearly made me gag. My gorge rose even as I pulled my
sword, then desperately swung it at the dog's head. The blow
had to be exact, perfectly timed. If I miscalculated by even a
fraction, I would kill Kerri, too.

The blade began to glow as I swung it. It sliced cleanly into
the stiff fur behind the abomination's ears with a sound like an
ax biting into a tree trunk. The force of the blow sent the head
spinning off into the dark. It hit the wall behind Kerri with a
wet splat, and the body collapsed into a tangled heap, the legs
still twitching wildly. The body began to sizzle and spit,
steaming and bubbling like a roasting pig.

I dragged Kerri away from the seething carcass, my breath
coming in harsh, gasping sobs. She rolled into a huddle,
cradling her ruined arm against her belly, a dark trickle of
blood spilling from her lip where she had bitten through it in
the effort not to cry out.

"Give me your arm." My whisper sounded as loud as a
shriek in the stillness.

She looked up at me blankly, eyes wide with shock in her
chalk-pale face. She either didn't hear me, or didn't understand in her shock. She trembled like a woman dying of exposure and cold. I reached out and took hold of her arm. She
whimpered faintly and huddled closer around it.

"Please, love," I said gently. "I have to see it."

The tension drained suddenly from her body. She extended the arm, still shuddering violently. My belly contracted in a spasm of nausea as I looked at the torn and shredded flesh exposing the stark white of the bone beneath. But I placed my hands over the tattered skin and muscle and closed my eyes.

I knew her patterns now. Carefully, meticulously, I gathered together the rags of tissue and set them in their proper place. It took a long time. The damage was so great, I feared I might not be able to repair it. But gradually, the flesh grew together, then the skin drew closed over it. Then, before I released her, I went deep, deep into the fabric of her patterns and calmed the quivering terror. I saw her relax as first the pain left her, then the shock. Lastly, I reached up and drew my finger across the bitten lip and watched as the injury vanished.

"What was it?" Kerri asked, still pale and shaken, but no longer gripped by the mindless shock. "What in the name of the seven gods and goddesses was it?"

I looked behind her. The dog was gone. In its place lay a putrefying, gelatinous mass, still bubbling occasionally and releasing the stench of a charnel house. I shuddered and looked away, back at Kerri.

"Some magical construct the general put together to welcome guests," I said. My head ached abominably and I had barely enough strength to stand. "Are you all right?"

"I feel a bit like I might want to start screaming any second," she said breathlessly, a slight tremor still in her voice. "But yes. I'm all right. But you look terrible."

I managed a smile. "Thank you, my lady," I said. "It's compliments like that which makes you such a pleasure to be with. I think it's time to make our valiant assault on the house."

She got to her feet. She was a little steadier than I, but not much. "Let's hope there are no more reception committees like that accursed dog," she muttered. "That was enough to last me a lifetime."

32

From the corner of the house where we crouched against the timber
and plaster wall, we could see light gleaming in the windows
of one of the front rooms, throwing shadows of plantings
toward the street. We made a quick circuit around the house.
The rest of it was dark.

"Kitchen entrance?" I asked softly.

Kerri nodded. "I think so."

The servants had left the door unlocked. I lifted the latch
carefully and nudged the door open a few inches. Only darkness and silence inside. I slipped through the door, beckoning
for Kerri to follow. We waited for a moment or two while our
eyes adjusted to the complete blackness inside the room. The
characteristic stench of the general's blood magic was faint
but unmistakable in the house.

After a minute or two, vague shapes appeared out of the
gloom—blocky worktables, low benches, cupboards. I
stepped carefully around a worktable laden with pots and
pans, groping in front of me for the door leading to the rest of
the house. I found it, but only because it was made of dark
wood and showed up faintly against the whitewashed wall.

Someone had paid meticulous attention to the hinges of the
door, and kept them well oiled. The door opened smoothly
and soundlessly. I started to step out into the hall, then
stopped so suddenly that Kerri trod on my heel.

A huge, manlike shape crouched in the hall some three
meters from the kitchen, its back to us. Its misshapen head
nearly scraped the lofty ceiling, and its shoulders nudged the
walls on either side of the hall. Greenish, scaly skin radiated
the same pallid glow as fungus in thick, dank forest. Even
crouched, the monster was twice my height and three times
my width. Scythelike claws hung from the ends of massive
fingers longer than my hand.

I pushed Kerri back into the kitchen, gently closed the door, then leaned on the wall and blew a long breath up past my eyebrows. Kerri and I both spoke at once.

"Mother of all," she said in awe.

"Hellas-birthing," I muttered.

"No wonder he needs no guards," she said. "How are we going to get past *that*?" Before I could stop her, she opened the door a crack and peered out at the monster.

Startled shock kicked in my chest, then I dragged her back and shut the door again. "By all the seven gods and goddesses, are you looking to get killed, woman?" I demanded.

"It never moved," she said thoughtfully.

"It's jammed into that hall rather tightly," I said dryly. "It doesn't have to move much. One swipe with those claws would reduce both of us to stewing meat."

"But it didn't move when we went into the hall. It must have heard us open the door. Do you smell anything?"

Something was percolating through her mind, but I couldn't quite see what she was getting at. "Just the general," I said. "Not very strong in here. But he probably doesn't spend much time in the kitchens."

"But you smelled the dog." She bit her lip, not looking at me, eyes narrowed in concentration.

I waited.

"The dog," she went on, frowning. "It was real. He corrupted the form of a real dog to make it. What could he corrupt to form that thing in the hall?"

"A man?"

"Mayhaps," she said doubtfully. "A travesty of a man." She opened the door again and stepped out into the hall. I made a soundless yelp of exasperation and hastily drew my sword, then launched myself after her. Confounded, foolhardy, stubborn woman! She would be the death of both of us yet.

When I caught up to her, she stood well within reach of those long arms and terrible claws. Swearing under my breath, sword gripped tightly in both hands, I pulled up short in surprise. The creature still had not moved.

"Look at your sword," she whispered.

I looked. It appeared normal to me.

"Look again," she said. "It's not glowing. It glowed when you used it against the dog."

She was right. The sword wasn't glowing. It was merely a honed metal blade, quiescent and waiting in my hands.

"An illusion," she said. She stepped forward before I could stop her and put her hand against the monster's back. It went right through. She turned back to me, teeth gleaming in the faint light as she grinned. "Illusion," she confirmed. "It's not real."

I lowered the sword, then put my own hand to the green, scaly skin. My hand went through, too, with only a faint, tingling sensation of cold. I shivered. Gods, I really *hate* magic.

"Let's go call on the general then," she said. She drew her sword and walked right through the man-thing in the hall.

We passed quietly into the passageway leading to the family quarters without meeting any more unpleasant surprises. The reek of the general's magic was strong enough in the long corridor to raise the hair on the nape of my neck. Halfway down the hall, a sliver of light spilled onto the thick carpeting through a partly open door. But for a faint, arrhythmic clicking noise coming from the room, there was no sound at all in the house. The walls were more than thick enough to block the distant music and laughter of the Lammas celebration outside.

Swords drawn and ready, Kerri and I crept down the hall, the carpet muffling our footsteps. We paused outside the door. The clicking sound was louder now. It reminded me of something, but I couldn't remember what it might be.

I leaned against the wall beside the door, listening intently. Kerri still looked pale, and her tattered and bloody sleeve hung in shreds and ribbons down her arm and across her wrist. I don't imagine I looked much better. The encounter with the dog and the monstrous illusion outside the kitchen had left me shaken, and Healing Kerri had used up more strength than I wanted to admit.

Finally, I looked at her, raising one eyebrow. She nodded. I reached out and pushed the door open. The room was a small one. Inside, light came from only three candles, one of them near the empty hearth where the boy Horbad sat playing knucklebones—the clicking sound I had heard. He paid no attention to me, intent upon the game. The other two candles were in sconces on the wall behind a chair near the window. The general sat in the chair in three-quarter profile to the door, his face masked by shadow, his feet resting comfortably on a low hassock. He held another child on his lap, wrapped in a soft, blue blanket and sleeping. One small, bare foot pushed out from beneath the blanket.

"Come in, Kian," the general said quietly, without rising. "I've been expecting you. Ah, the lady Kerridwen, too. Welcome, my lady. You got here faster than I thought you would."

The sword glowed softly in my hands as I stepped into the room. Behind me, Kerri moved quickly sideways along the wall, covering my left.

"You knew I'd come after you sooner or later, General," I said. "There are some long-outstanding debts between us to be settled."

He turned in the chair so his face was no longer in shadow. The child in his lap slept on, undisturbed. "You might be interested in knowing that the men who sold you to Mendor's stablemaster died for it shortly after."

"For disobeying your orders," I said.

"Exactly. Yes. But now I have you again, and Kyffen's line will end here."

"You take a lot for granted, General Hakkar."

"Do I?"

I smiled. "I don't intend to let you kill me without a fight. You may find that I'm stronger than you."

"You won't fight me," he said. "My magic is stronger now."

"So is mine."

He smiled and I shivered in spite of myself. The stench of his magic filled the air between us, a visible miasma rippling in waves. "You won't fight," he repeated. The dark haze between us shimmered and wavered. He smiled again and slowly turned back the blanket covering the face of the child he held. "Look here."

The room became suddenly darker. My heart kicked in my chest and breath left me as if I had taken a mortal blow to the belly.

The child was Keylan.

There wasn't enough air in the room to fill my lungs properly. I made a choked sound and lurched forward a pace or two. My son didn't move. He lay in the general's arms, eyes closed, one small fist curled near his cheek.

"How did you get my son?" I demanded, my voice hoarse and raw. *Maedun soldiers loose at Broche Rhuidh?* I shivered, seeing visions of Cullin's daughters and Gwynna lying in their own blood. Medroch's people would die to the last man to protect any child of the Clanhold, and Keylan was Medroch's great-grandchild.

"I sent men to fetch him," the general said pleasantly. "The child was playing in the orchard. They simply picked him up and brought him to me."

"The rest of my family?"

The general laughed. "The rest of your family is safe," he said. "My men did not wish to cause an annoying disturbance and be delayed. It's only you and the boy I want." He drew his finger hard down the side of the child's cheek. A red welt rose quickly on the fair skin, but still Keylan didn't move.

The room felt cold. I was cold. My belly knotted with a tremor I couldn't control. My throat and mouth rasped dry as desert sand, but the hilt of the sword in my hands was slick and slippery with sweat.

"You returned my son to me," the general went on. "Shall I return your son to you?"

I said nothing, waiting.

"After I've taken his magic, of course."

I thought my grip on the hilt of the sword might bend it. "He has no magic," I said hoarsely.

"But you do."

"Yes."

"Would you trade your magic for his life?"

The tremor in my belly became a hard, juddering shiver. "Yes," I said. I drew in a painful breath. "Give the child to the woman and let them go first."

He looked up, surprised. "Why should I let the woman go? She, too, has magic I need."

"You once gave me her life in exchange for your son's," I said. "Give her my son's life in exchange for mine."

The boy Horbad sprang to his feet, scattering his knuckle-bones, and ran to his father. He put his hand possessively to Keylan's head, his fingers clutching tightly in the copper gold curls.

"He's mine," he cried. "You promised him to me."

"There will be others, Horbad," the general said soothingly. The boy went sullenly back to the hearth and resumed his game.

The general got to his feet. "Place your sword on the floor," he told me. Slowly, I bent and laid the sword on the carpet. I straightened and stepped back.

The general turned to Kerri. "My lady, if you will be so kind," he said.

Kerri glanced at me. I nodded and she came forward to take Keylan from the general, cuddling him into her arms. "He's so cold," she murmured, her cheek against the child's forehead.

The general stepped back and reached behind the chair. When he straightened again, he held a sword in his hands, a sword blacker than the night.

"Take Keylan home, *sheyala*," I said quietly.

"It's too late, Tyr," the general said. "Your son has already given up his magic to my son." He reached with the tip of his sword and flipped aside the blanket covering Keylan.

Kerri made a choked, horrified sound and fell to her knees. The front of Keylan's shirt clung, tattered and bloody, to the gaping wound in his belly.

I stared, unable to think, unable to move. Frozen and turned to stone, all I could see was that terrible, yawning rip in my son's tiny body. Grief squeezed my chest until every beat of my heart hurt like a knife thrust, and my breath rasped like a file against my throat.

Slowly, I turned back to face the general, my mouth filled with the taste of blood where my teeth had pierced my lip. I was aware of every muscle in my body, every sinew. Cold, alert and ready.

"You bastard," I said softly. "Mongrel whelp of a bitch hound . . ." I dived forward, snatching up the sword, and rolled to my feet, crouched and eager.

Beneath the palms of my hands, every ridge of the leather binding of the sword hilt felt clear and distinct. The sword in my hands blazed up into flaring, incandescent white, and the screaming, discordant note of its vibrato filled the room.

"I will kill you, General," I said softly. "I will kill you, then I will follow you to Hellas and destroy your soul."

Even as I sprang forward, the stench of magic intensified in the room until the air was almost too thick to breathe. A globe of dull, red light appeared in his hand. But he threw it at Kerri, who still held the unmoving body of my son cradled in her arms. The air around her shimmered for an instant as she tried to meet his magic with her own. The fireball splashed against her, spraying liquid fire around her, wrapping her in glaring flame. It sizzled and spit, then vanished. The force of the magic threw Kerri, Keylan clutched tight against her, back hard against the far wall. Her head slammed into the plaster. She slumped forward and didn't move. The bond between us flickered along the threads of the link.

"Forgive me, *sheyala*," I murmured. "This is more important than what's between us."

A sheet of intense, blinding flame leaped up in front of the general. Instinctively, I flinched back, then plunged forward, uncaring, into the fire, intent only on killing the general. But even as I touched the fire, it wavered, then vanished.

Illusion. It was another of the general's illusions.

He raised his sword to meet mine, dodging back behind the heavy chair. I couldn't reach him. There wasn't enough space to maneuver in the room. Too many obstacles between us.

Another huge, scaly man-thing appeared in the room, towering over Kerri. It reached out knifelike claws toward her. I didn't turn, didn't take my eyes off the general.

"Another illusion?" I asked softly. "Surely you can do better than that. Where's your real magic?"

He kicked the hassock, sending it spinning toward my feet. I jumped over it easily, but I couldn't get close enough to him with the chair between us.

"Did we hurt you that badly, Cullin and I?" I said. "You have nothing left, General Hakkar. You're a dried husk. You're nothing but an illusion yourself."

"I have enough magic, Tyr," the general snarled.

The air between us thickened with foul, black mist. It wrapped itself in snaking tendrils around my throat, suffocating and strangling. Cold as lost hope, it fastened itself to my soul, draining my strength and will, sucking the spirit from me, replacing my lifeblood with its own chilling void. I coughed, choking and gagging on the loathsome stuff, tasting death against the back of my tongue. Fingers of the mist closed about my heart, squeezing until each labored beat was agony.

The general laughed. "Can your magic defeat that?"

Celae magic. Tyadda magic. Gentle magic. It would not allow itself be used as a weapon. But I could use it in a different way. With the last of my strength, I reached out, grasped one of the threads of power surging through the ground beneath my feet. The darkness of blood magic within me burst and shattered as it met the clean earth and air magic. I wove the Celae magic like strands of spiderweb into a noose, threw it, and snared it around the general. I *yanked*.

33

We stood facing each other at the foot of the hill crowned by the stone Dance. The sky glowed in twilight colors, neither dawn nor dusk, but a time removed. At the top of the hill, the menhirs rose starkly silhouetted in black against the sky. Beneath my feet, the grass released its fresh perfume into the air, rising about me in a soft cloud. This wasn't my place, but it was a neutral place. The general faced me, wearing the face of the opponent who had called me to battle in this place so often before.

"Now we see, General," I said. "My magic won't work here, but neither will yours."

"Your son is dead," he said. "Your woman is dead. What do you have left?"

"The pleasure of killing you, General."

We circled each other warily. I watched him, picking out small details of stance and pose. He balanced easily on the balls of his feet, sword held in both hands. Dark eyes narrowed to slits, he studied me as carefully as I studied him. He was as accomplished with the sword as I, perhaps more. But neither of us was at the peak of strength; his weakened yet by the effort to recover from the shock of being torn from the magic transfer; mine by the effort to Heal Kerri. Which of us was stronger now?

"I admit there is a small possibility you might succeed in killing me," he said, his lips stretched back over his teeth in a dreadful parody of a smile. "But Kyffen's line is dead. You will sire no sons on the Celae wench, even if you survive this meeting."

"I will have more sons by her." I sidestepped quickly to my right, searching for an opening. He countered, his sword making small, purposeful sweeps before him.

"She's dead."

"Not a good wager, General." I stepped to my left, took a quick, experimental swing at his legs to test the balance of my sword and his alertness. He parried the blow and our blades met with a quick, whispering slither.

He disengaged and stepped back. "You will die here, and Maedun is safe," he said.

"Maedun is not safe," I said. I'd finally realized the significance of what I'd seen back in his parlor. "My son is not dead."

"You saw his belly opened like a gutted fish. He is dead."

I laughed at him. "Just another of your flimsy illusions," I said. "You scraped your fingernail along his cheek, General. I saw the welt it raised. Dead flesh will not show a welt. You did not kill him."

"But I will," he said. "Horbad will have his magic yet. When my warlock arrives—"

Circling, circling, each of us looking for an opening to attack. Sudden spurt of black-red blood as my sword flashed past his guard and thrust into the muscle of his arm. Spray of darkness from the black sword as he leapt back and away from the next attack.

He lunged at me, his sword making a wide, sweeping arc toward my head. I blocked it, then cut at his belly. He parried the blow deftly, and jumped back out of reach.

"My son," he panted. "Horbad will kill your son. The day will come, Tyr . . . "

I flexed my wrists. The sword felt light in my hands, eager as a leashed hound for the hunt. "My son will be able to fight his own battles," I said.

"Horbad will have my name and my power," he said. "He will add his own power to mine. Your son cannot stand against him."

"The boy may gain your name," I said grimly. "But he won't have your power. You can't give it to him if you die here."

He feinted to his right, came at me with a slicing cut from the left. I swung my sword down, blocked his with a ringing clang, then carved a blow at his belly. He leapt back, brought his blade up to parry mine.

"And I intend to see that you die here," I said, disengaging quickly and dodging back.

Again, we circled. He attacked and I lunged forward to meet him. Back and forth across the trampled grass, each straining and striving to tear the guts from the other. Blind to everything but the swing and slice of the other sword. Breath rasping in great gulps, his face pale, sweating. My own cold, as the wind of my own movement dried the moisture on my brow and cheeks.

Whirl and thrust and sway. Feet moving in elaborate patterns on the level grass. A spasm of pain in my shoulder, my own blood vivid red spilling down my arm. My arm trembled from the chill of the black blade.

Circle and circle. Warily watching each other. His eyes black as night, black as the pits of Hellas. Soft brush of the topaz in my ear against my cheek as I swayed to my right. The blade of his sword sucking in light, spitting out darkness and cold. Brilliant luminescence of my own blade, glittering in its aura of color.

I gripped tighter to the plain, leather-bound hilt nestled into my hands. "Dance with me," I whispered to the sword, a lover to a lover. "Dance for me. *Now!*" I sprang forward, the sword in my hands singing fiercely and sweetly in the eerie light.

Light and shadow, day and night. My sword and his. Flashing, flaring, and I was lost in the intricacies of the dance. Clash and clangor of steel against tempered steel. Fire and heat from my blade; darkness and dank chill of the grave from his.

How we danced, the blade and I. Lost in the complex movements, the precise rituals of the dance. Back and forth under the glowing sky. Thrusting, parrying. Slash and riposte. Cut and slice. Whistling blades flashing—mine singing, his howling and screaming.

We danced, the general and I. Death in his face. Murder in my heart. Back and forth, we battled each other. Muscles shrieking in protest, weariness building inexorably, the sword heavy in my hands. His face drawn into lines of strain.

I saw the opening I sought so desperately. A sudden, slight uncertainty in his stance, a hesitancy in his guard. I leaped forward, taut with purpose.

I swung the sword in a short, backhand sweep. The glowing blade flicked under his guard and into the muscle of his belly. The black sword spun off into the dark at the edge our circle. Shock and astonishment widened his eyes as he dropped to his knees.

"My son—will kill—your son," he gasped, then fell to his side, glazed and empty eyes looking through me, beyond me to eternity.

I stood leaning on my sword, gasping for breath, sweat running in streams down my face, my shirt soaked, the waistband of my breeks sodden with it. I reached up with a hand that might have been made of lead and wiped the stinging moisture from my eyes.

The general lay crumpled on the grass. As I watched, a dark mist rose from him and slowly dissipated in the clean air of the circle. His body withered and shriveled until it was little more than a husk, frail enough for the gentle breeze to shred and fray.

Something moved beyond the circle. I straightened slowly to meet the opponent who stood just outside the circle, cloaked in shadow, a darkness of his own making swirling around him. He was younger than the general, his features less firmly shaped. The dark aura of power that surrounded him was thinner, more tenuous.

"That is mine," he said, his voice a rustling whisper in the mist surrounding him. He pointed at the black sword resting in the grass an armspan beyond the general's clawed fingers.

Still breathing unevenly, I raised my sword and moved to stand between him and the black sword.

"Then come and claim it. But you'll have to go through me." I stepped back, inviting him into the circle with me.

He stepped forward, barely onto the grass. The mist parted around his face, revealing features familiar, yet foreign. He glanced at the black sword, then back at me.

"You cannot touch it," he said. "Remember how it burned you when you tried to take it from my father?"

"I don't want it," I said.

"Then you have no objection if I take it?"

I grinned, baring my teeth at him. "Come and try."

He held up both empty hands. "I have no weapon."

"But I do."

I sensed rather than saw him tense himself to dive for the sword. I lifted my sword and slammed the brightly glowing blade down on the obsidian sword. The glaring explosion nearly blinded and deafened me. The black sword shattered under my blade. Numbing shock traveled up my arms and into my chest, smashing the breath out of me.

My opponent howled with rage and scrambled away from the dark splinters on the grass, a long fragment embedded in the flesh of his palm. He rolled back to the edge of the circle and staggered to his feet, cradling his injured hand to his chest.

"It was mine," he shouted. "It was mine."

I lowered my sword and rubbed my tingling arms. My sword still sang a high, clear note of triumph. I had no breath to reply. I merely watched him as I stood, sucking in deep, gasping gulps of air.

The dark mist swirled around him again, and I thought it might be thinner, more tenuous, now. He looked at me, black eyes glittering with rage.

"You have won for now," he said quietly.

"I have gained time," I said.

He gave me a small, mocking bow. "Put it to good use," he said. "You should have killed me, too, when you could." He stepped back out of the circle and vanished into the whorling mist.

I came back to myself, panting and gasping for breath, standing in the parlor of the merchant's house. The body of the general lay at my feet, his blood staining the carpet in a wide, black pool. Fingers like talons reached for the hilt of a sword that was not there.

I lowered my sword, and fell to my knees, exhausted. The boy Horbad came slowly from the hearth to stand before me. The hard, dark aura of latent power shimmered around his head. He stood before me, trembling, cradling an injured hand to his chest.

"My father is dead," he cried, his voice shrill and piercing. "You killed my father."

I looked at him. He would grow to be the mortal enemy of my son. He was a child. A five-year-old boy. The sword in my hands twitched, but I could not bring myself to lift it and remove that childish head from the small shoulders. Keylan would have to learn to deal with him, for I could not.

I looked into the small, immature Maedun face. It wavered, began to change, until another face lay superimposed above it. An adult face. The face he would wear when he was grown. He laughed as he saw my recognition.

"You killed my father," he said. "But you didn't kill me." He turned and ran, stumbling across the carpet and out into the passageway.

Chest heaving, breath still rasping in my throat, I crawled across the carpet to Kerri. She lay slumped against the wall, Keylan cradled in her arms. Groggily, she looked up at me.

"You disappeared," she muttered. "You and the general. What happened?"

"We went somewhere else," I said. "It's all right, *sheyala*." Keylan moved sluggishly in her arms, whole and unharmed. "Are you all right?"

She nodded. "You used magic?"

I nodded. "I used the sword's magic."

She looked up at me, then smiled and shook her head. "You used your own magic," she said. "The sword always responded to you." Keylan stirred again, and she stroked his forehead soothingly. He reached up and put his arms around her neck, burrowing his face into the hollow of her throat.

"Is he all right?"

"I think so," she said. "It must have been a holding spell. As soon as you and the general vanished, it broke the spell."

I gathered them both into my arms, my cheek tight against Kerri's hair. "It's time to go home," I said.

Epilogue

Dun Eidon, ancestral home of the prince of Skai, sat like a jewel at the head of the deep inlet where the River Eidon emptied into the sea. Built of white stone, its graceful colonnades and soaring towers glistened against the background of winter-bare trees and mountains, secure behind its tall, crenellated walls of granite. A small village nestled close to the walls, the neatly thatched roofs of the buildings golden in the sun against the layer of snow still lying thick on the ground. At the foot of the road leading down from the west gate of the palace, a stone jetty thrust out into the clear, blue water of the Ceg. Two tall-masted ships rocked gently at anchor at the end of the pier amid a cluster of small fishing boats like two swans among a flock of ducks.

On the side of the mountain rising above the palace, surrounded by twelve oaks hung with leafless strands of ivy, the shrine of the Duality serenely overlooked the village and the harbor. Beyond the shrine stood a small stone circle, a Dance of seven menhirs, each three times the height of a man, one for each of the gods and goddesses.

Below the palace between the village and the pier, men and boys trained with swords, spears, and bows, some of them bare to the waist and sweating despite the late winter chill. The voices of the weaponsmasters rang clearly in the still air. Among the dozen or so small boys training with the Swordmaster, the bright red-gold hair of Keylan, Prince of Skai, stood out vividly in contrast with the dark gold or black hair of the others. At five, and tall and sturdy for his age, the young prince demonstrated a marked aptitude, a grace and skill more common in older, more experienced boys.

Two men stood at the edge of the trampled snow defining the practice field, watching the boys practice. Red Kian of Skai, father and Regent to the young prince, stood taller and broader than the man beside him, his red hair glowing in the early afternoon sun. Jorddyn ap Tiernyn, captain of the company and Kian's father-in-law, watched the boy thoughtfully, critically appraising the prince's skill.

"One day soon, he'll be as proficient as you," he said, relaxing and smiling as he watched his foster grandson.

"As good as my uncle Cullin was," Kian replied.

A horse and rider hurled themselves down the track from the palace, heedless of the slushy surface in their haste. Kian frowned at the recklessness, then stiffened as the rider brought the horse to a skidding halt only a bare meter away from the two men. The rider slid from the saddle in one smooth, skillful motion, and dropped to one knee in the snow.

"My lord Regent," the boy said breathlessly, "I am sent to tell you the lady Kerridwen has been brought to bed early with the child and has need of you."

Kian paled and glanced up at the palace behind him. "It's still a fortnight 'til Imbolc," he said. "It's too early . . . "

Jorddyn put his hand to Kian's shoulder. "Go to her," he said. "She'll be all right, but best you go now."

"I lost one wife to early childbed . . . "

Jorddyn smiled. "A fortnight early is not unusual for a first birth," he said reassuringly. "Kerri herself was earlier than that, and both she and her mother came through it splendidly. Go now. I'll bring Keylan and follow shortly."

Kian ran for the horses tethered behind him and sprang to the saddle of his stallion. He put heels to the horse's flanks and bent low over the saddle as the horse leapt to a gallop.

People thronged the outer chamber of the apartment the Regent and his wife shared. Women hurried back and forth purposefully, faces set into harried and intent expressions. Kian shouldered his way through to the inner door. The midwife met him as he stepped through into the bedchamber.

"The lady Kerridwen does well," she said briskly, anticipating his question. "And you have two fine sons."

Kian glanced over her shoulder at the bed. Kerridwen lay

with her eyes closed, a small weary smile turning up the corners of her mouth. Her hands lay folded peacefully across her flat belly. Kian looked back to the midwife.

"Two sons?" he asked, eyes widening in shock and surprise. "Two?"

The midwife laughed. "Twins, my lord Regent. Both healthy and strong. Beautiful children."

But Kian wasn't listening to her. He went quickly to the bed and fell to his knees, taking Kerri's hand in his and pressing it to his lips. She opened her eyes and smiled at him. They had no need of words with each other.

The midwife placed the babies on the bed within the circle of Kerri's arms. Kian looked down at them in awed silence. Finally, he said, "They have no hair."

Kerri glared at him, then laughed and shook her head in fond resignation. "Of course they do," she said softly. She reached out and stroked first one small head, then the other. "It's so fine you can hardly see it, that's all. In a fortnight or two, it will thicken."

Kian looked doubtful, but he nodded. "What will you name them?" he asked.

"I thought we might call the eldest Tiernyn, for my grandfather," she said. "And I'd like to call the younger Donaugh."

He smiled. "It's a good name," he said. "They're both good names."

A silver crescent of moon tossed among the clouds above the crest of the mountains as Kian stood over the cradle where his newborn sons lay sleeping. He held his sword in both hands, one hand grasping the hilt, the flat of the blade against the palm of his other hand. Kingmaker, the sword was named. He had carried it for eleven years—eight years not knowing its purpose, and for the balance of that time, waiting for it to declare its true owner.

The sword glowed with a soft, lambent gleam, and a low musical note, like bell and harp together, sang quietly in the room. Slowly he knelt and held the blade above the tiny, sleeping form of first one child, then the other. As he held it over

Tiernyn, the eldest, the glow brightened and the musical note became a joyous chord.

He climbed to his feet and took the sword to the window. Slowly, he traced the line of runes on one side of the blade. *Take up the Strength of Celi.* He looked at the words for a long time, then turned the blade over. The runes engraved into the blade on the other side glittered in the combined light of the moon and the glow of the blade. He reached out one finger and thoughtfully traced the words—the words he had never before been able to read.

Now lay me aside.